BACKHANDED COMPLIMENTS

BACKHANDED COMPLIMENTS

A Novel

KATIE CHANDLER

ATRIA PAPERBACK

New York Amsterdam/Antwerp London
Toronto Sydney/Melbourne New Delhi

ATRIA
PAPERBACK

An Imprint of Simon & Schuster, LLC
1230 Avenue of the Americas
New York, NY 10020

This book is a work of fiction. Any references to historical events, real people, or real places are used fictitiously. Other names, characters, places, and events are products of the author's imagination, and any resemblance to actual events or places or persons, living or dead, is entirely coincidental.

First Atria Paperback edition June 2025

ATRIA PAPERBACK and colophon are trademarks of Simon & Schuster, LLC

Simon & Schuster strongly believes in freedom of expression and stands against censorship in all its forms. For more information, visit BooksBelong.com.

For information about special discounts for bulk purchases, please contact Simon & Schuster Special Sales at 1-866-506-1949 or business@simonandschuster.com.

The Simon & Schuster Speakers Bureau can bring authors to your live event. For more information or to book an event, contact the Simon & Schuster Speakers Bureau at 1-866-248-3049 or visit our website at www.simonspeakers.com.

Interior design by Davina Mock-Maniscalco

Manufactured in the United States of America

1   3   5   7   9   10   8   6   4   2

Library of Congress Cataloging-in-Publication Data has been applied for.

ISBN 978-1-6680-8678-0
ISBN 978-1-6680-8679-7 (ebook)

For Miranda, the compliment to my backhand

AUTHOR'S NOTE

The professional tennis season is always shifting and changing for one reason or another. For all die-hard tennis fans, I have taken certain liberties with it and moved tournaments to different parts of the schedule to better suit the narrative. My sincerest apologies to The Canadian Open for cutting you out of this novel entirely.

Content warnings: mentions of emotional child abuse (pages 244–46), depictions of anxiety disorders, panic attacks (pages 256–60), and explicit consensual sex.

BACKHANDED COMPLIMENTS

ONE

JULIETTE

It starts as all vile things do.

On Twitter.

"One more question," the media officer says, and Juliette Ricci smiles, hoping it comes off as sweet and placating. A camera flashes and she struggles to maintain the smile, her eyes stinging. All she wants to do is to dunk into an ice bath until the heat bubbling under her skin abates. At least all the questions have been softballs about her last match, the semifinal. All about her strengths, her weaknesses, her condition after a grueling three sets in the Melbourne sun.

A disheveled reporter clears his throat and corrects his askew glasses. "You will be playing Luca Kacic in the final." Juliette clenches her teeth. She thought she'd wriggled out of having to say a single word about Kacic, but reporters will never miss a chance to pit two women against each other for the sake of article clicks. "Tennis fans online are already frothing at the mouth for this burgeoning rivalry. Lucky Luca versus the Bridesmaid. Given this is your first time playing Kacic, do you have any idea how you'll combat her good fortune and finally snag a big title for yourself?"

It takes every ounce of self-control to keep her thin smile plastered on her face. Juliette knows she should be better at this. She has been playing this media game since she was fifteen, when the majority of the questions centered around living up to her potential as the younger sister of two tennis stars. But she doesn't know how to keep her cool and tiptoe around the snarky questions about being the *bridesmaid* and never the *bride* of the Women's Tennis Asssociation.

Until this Australian Open, she's never made it past the quarterfinals in any Slam. She has hardly any big titles to her name, only a single WTA 1000 last year.

And even Luca Kacic had commented in her earlier press conference about this being Juliette's first *real test* on a big stage.

"*Such a shame she only won because her opponent sprained her ankle in the third game,*" Kacic had said with a subtle, scathing judgment that had made Juliette's skin flush. Still, a win is a win to Juliette.

"Well," Juliette drawls, aware of every eye locked on her. She preens, exhilarated at being the center of attention. "I've watched a couple of her matches." An oily feeling expands in her gut, and she takes a deep breath. She could be neutral and professional . . . or she could do anything to achieve the mental edge over Kacic and win. "To be honest, I find her game wholly unoriginal, and her serve is over-hyped." She shrugs, as if she doesn't care about Kacic. "I guess she really has been skating by on *luck*," Juliette says, resisting the urge to roll her eyes at how stupid the nickname is. "Twitter is right about that."

"So, would you say you're looking forward to tomorrow's match?" the reporter asks, leaning forward with a hungry gleam in his eyes like a shark.

Juliette knows it's a long shot that Kacic will even see this press conference, but she can already see her own words splashed all over her feed. She knows her younger sister, Livia, is most likely screaming into her pillow about damage control.

At this moment, Juliette doesn't care.

She doesn't even have to fake her smile. "Of course. I always look forward to winning."

LUCA

Luca Kacic watches Juliette Ricci's press conference four times in a row. She shouldn't have clicked on it. Tomorrow is the biggest match of her life; if anything, she should be analyzing Ricci's past matches to learn how to beat her. Although, she knows if she turns on an old match, all she'll focus on is the fluid grace of Ricci's movements, the way the sun adores her high cheekbones, the glistening sweat in the dip between her collarbones. Nerves twist in her stomach again, nausea at the thought that she's never been in a Grand Slam final before. The furthest Luca has gotten before was the quarterfinal at last year's US Open, which ended in a thorough loss. Anxiety had made her rigid and tight, barely able to move to hit the ball.

Even though Juliette's scathing words ring through her headphones, she can't help but keep watching. Luca hates how drawn she is to Juliette already, and they haven't even met on court yet. For months, she's been distracted by a curiosity she can't squash, no matter how many times she tries.

Luca traces her fingers along the familiar curve of each letter of her soulmark, slightly raised like a scar. The twisting loops that slide into each other, the sharp slash connecting the double letters; they weave together to tell her who was made to love her. It appeared when she was a toddler, when her soulmate was born, the name drawn in barely visible silver. Now, it tells everyone she hasn't touched her soulmate yet. Not that she ever lets anyone see the mark. Soulmarks are secretive, intimate; no one likes speculation about their mark. Luca is as careful as she can be, covering it with a wristband when she plays. Still, nearly universal secrecy is what makes the headlines so splashy when a celebrity does accidentally reveal their mark.

As she replays the conference, Luca can't exactly parse what she's watching for. Maybe a crack in Juliette's media armor; a flicker of nervousness or a flash of excitement. Maybe a sign that Juliette is looking forward to this or that her words are just a facade. That maybe Juliette feels the same tug in her stomach, the same giddy excitement that Luca could be the one made for her. That's why she clicked on Juliette's press conference; there is a nonzero chance Juliette Ricci is *her* Juliette. It would make sense to Luca if they were. Juliette Ricci would understand what it means to be a top player—the pressures, the scrutiny, the travel—and they could work through that together.

But instead of feeling her stomach fill with giddy butterflies about the possibility that this woman could be her soulmate, her stomach twists with disappointment at Juliette's calculated and cruel words.

Juliette is the youngest of the tennis-playing Ricci sisters, only a year and a half younger than Luca, but she turned pro young, while Luca played in college first. Touted to be better than both of her elder sisters, she shot up the rankings with consistent results but has yet to win a big title.

Well, Guadalajara counts points-wise, but she didn't win the tournament outright. It was a tragedy that Chen Xinya rolled her ankle. Luca had been looking forward to that matchup and had said as much in her press conference yesterday.

Luca has watched over the years as Juliette stalled around the seventh or eighth place in the rankings, intrigued both by Juliette's attitude on the court and at the possibility that this was *her* Juliette. Despite how she sometimes acts on court when she's losing, Luca can't deny that Juliette Ricci is as vibrant as a sunbeam, especially when she's playing her best tennis. She's had a few good wins over several top players, like her sisters and American Remi Rowland, but never at crucial points. Clearly, Juliette sees this as her opportunity to establish herself, like Luca, and unfortunately, she's not above trash talk.

On-screen, Juliette is still flushed from her win, her big, doe-brown eyes soft and almost innocent. Her lion's mane of brown curls float around her shoulders, untamed and gilded from the sun. Her smile widens, her cheeks crinkling as she says her final statement.

"*I always look forward to winning.*"

Luca scoffs. As innocent as a snake in the grass.

She's halfway through a fifth watch when a key card clicks in her door. She scrambles to shut her laptop, getting tangled in her headphones in the process.

"Luca?"

"Yeah?" Luca manages to close her laptop and drops her headphones onto it. "What's up?"

Her coach, Vladimir Orlic, stands with one hand on the doorknob.

Her best friend and sunshine incarnate, Nicholas Andrews, slides in behind him, carrying a plastic bag full of food. He lost earlier in the day. Luca is always impressed by how he's able to keep smiling; after she loses, she mopes facedown in bed with a trashy reality show on the TV to chase away her thoughts.

"What were you watching? Porn?" Nicky asks with a waggle of his brows.

"Of course not," Luca snaps, although heat burns across her cheeks, and she knows it makes her look guilty. "Just a press conference." Luca waves them in and swivels in the desk chair, twisting her long legs beneath her.

Nicky rips open the plastic bag, the scent of fresh herbs filling the small room. Pesto, her favorite. "Oh, Juliette Ricci?" He frowns. "She is a piece of work."

Luca can't deny that. "Toss me silverware," she says, not wanting to talk about it.

Nicky shakes his fluffy ginger waves off his face. "Hope she's not *your* Juliette." He tosses her a plastic fork.

Luca nearly drops the utensil and carefully avoids Vladimir's gaze from where he sits on the couch. She shovels a forkful of pesto spaghetti into her mouth, swallowing it and her anxiety down.

"You're gonna crush her tomorrow, Lou," Nicky says, flashing her a smile. "I'll be watching from an airplane, unfortunately, but I know you're gonna win."

Luca's stomach sinks. She'd hoped that Nicky would stick around and be in her player's box for the final, but she hadn't asked. Maybe it's for the best. Nicky is only a friend—her only friend—but if he were to suddenly appear in her box, it would raise questions about the nature of their relationship. Luca doesn't want or need that kind of distraction or speculation.

Luca shrugs. "We'll see. I'll do my best."

"Do you want to talk about the final now or after a sleep?" Vladimir asks, breaking her out of her thought spiral. It's his usual question whenever Luca is overthinking something. He gives Luca a choice about *when* Luca talks about it, but she always has to talk about it.

When Luca first met Vladimir, on her fifteenth birthday, she thought he was the boogeyman coming to eat her for talking back to her father. Well over six and a half feet tall, with piercing blue eyes, sleeves of tattoos scrawling across his arms, and long ink-black hair framing his hollow cheeks, Vladimir Orlic is absolutely terrifying.

Over time, Luca has come to appreciate the dichotomy between Vladimir's appearance and his personality as a gentle giant, a vegetarian, and the owner of three cats. There's no one Luca trusts more.

"After a sleep," Luca decides, twirling her fork through her pasta. She wants more time to process everything. Vladimir would probably recommend that she focus on her tennis, not on Juliette Ricci's mind games. Easier said than done.

JULIETTE

Juliette lounges in her ice bath and stares at her wrist. Her skin is numb, but her chest is throbbing with untamed nerves. She's already starting to regret what she said in the press conference.

Even though Juliette claims not to have seen many of Kacic's matches, she's done her research. Her father and coach, Antony, has even sent her a six-page document on every aspect of Kacic's game. "Lucky Luca" Kacic is the tour's newest sensation, a college star recruited from Croatia to play at Florida. She graduated from college to the tour and, at twenty-four, has already captured dozens of titles and points, catapulting her into the Top Ten. One more win and she'll have a Grand Slam trophy in her hands and the number one ranking spot wrangled from the current holder, Zoe Almasi.

Juliette rubs her thumb across her soulmark. Silvery like starlight, barely there, raised like a tattoo and proclaiming Juliette's soulmate to be a *LUCA*.

Juliette tips her head back against the metal lip of the bath and stares at the ceiling. Could she be *that* Luca? Her sisters certainly think so. Although they've been setting her up with Lucas of all genders for years, they love to tease her about Luca Kacic whenever they get the chance.

Last spring, after Luca won three straight tournaments and officially caught the eye of the media, she posed for a tennis magazine. The photos were the usual staged ridiculousness, with Luca Kacic gazing off into the distance, racket over her shoulder and light brown hair whipping in the breeze. Her sisters had made her a poster with the final picture from the photoshoot. They hadn't even been able to give her the present without dissolving into giggles.

The photo showed Kacic in all her gangly glory, all broad shoulders and pointy elbows, her mile-long legs and slender waist. Juliette had grumbled about it, but she had to admit that there is something undeniably alluring about Kacic. She was sweaty in the photo, as if she had been practicing for hours under a burning hot sun. Her cheeks were flushed, and there was the slightest curl of her lip in a near smirk. But it was her eyes that made Juliette's mouth go dry. She was looking up from under her lashes, as if, with one glance, she knew every secret. Even shaded by her visor, her eyes burned with intensity.

Juliette is still grateful her sisters didn't choose the picture of Kacic rubbing the sweat off her face with the hem of her tank top, exposing her expanse of pale skin and mouth-watering abs. She didn't throw out the poster either. It's rolled up tight and slightly crumpled in her apartment closet in Monte Carlo.

The alarm on her phone blares, and Juliette jerks upright. With shaky arms, she pushes herself out of the ice bath and shivers. By this time tomorrow, she will know once and for all if *this* Luca is her soulmate.

Her stomach lurches, bile in the back of her throat. She hopes Luca Kacic isn't *her* Luca. It would be the biggest cosmic joke, one she would find decidedly unfunny. And even if she is, it doesn't matter. Juliette doesn't want or need her soulmate. She never has and never will. She needs to win. Romance will only distract her from her goals. She is committed to tennis, through and through. She's spent so many years dreaming of winning a Grand Slam title, and so Juliette narrows her focus to what that moment will feel like. Lifting the trophy, seeing her family's smiling faces, finally shedding the media's idea that she isn't good enough.

She ducks into the shower to scrub the ice-cold water from her skin and lets all thoughts of Kacic swirl down the drain.

TWO

JULIETTE

Luca Kacic starts the Australian Open final with a double fault. Juliette bounces on her toes as Kacic's first serve sails out. Her second serve snaps into the net. First point to Juliette.

Juliette knows this won't be that easy, but as she walks to the opposite side of the court, she hopes maybe it will be. The crowd murmurs, perhaps about the perceived nerves, perhaps about the press conference comments. Juliette tries to ignore the hushed chattering, but it echoes in her head anyway.

She crouches, watching Kacic twist the racket in her hand and breathe out. Despite how even-keeled Kacic seems, it's clear she's not immune to nerves. Still, Kacic settles easily and wins her first service game.

Juliette tightens her ponytail as they switch sides, annoyed at herself for not getting more returns in the court. She pauses at her bench to sip her electrolyte mix, and her eyes fall onto Kacic. It's a mistake.

So far, Juliette's been ignoring her opponent. She can't let her focus slip for a moment. Kacic is all elegant lines and hard edges, her long limbs gleaming with sweat already. The muscles beneath her skin shift, power in her shoulders and lean forearms. Her hair is tied into a high ponytail, braided down so it isn't flying all over her shoulders. A black visor obscures her face as she looks at the ground, but Juliette's mouth goes dry anyway.

Then Kacic looks up. Juliette jolts as Kacic's eyes skate over her. Juliette clenches her jaw and refuses to look away. Kacic is impassive, but her chin tilts up, as if challenging her. Heat coils in Juliette's stomach, a corrosive tincture of anger and defensiveness as she stares back.

It lasts only a fraction of a second. Kacic blinks first and stalks away from her bench. Juliette strides to the other side, and they pass each other with a wide breadth. Kacic wants this as much as she does, and that desperate energy crackles on Juliette's skin, in tune with the frantic want swirling in her chest. Tennis may be a sport without physical contact, but a match is about a connection between players. A conversation where every serve is a statement and every backhand a question. But this match already feels like an argument, one that Juliette intends to win.

She holds out her racket to the ball kid, who diligently puts four balls onto the strings. She plucks at them, twisting them in her fingers as she selects the two she wants.

She looks up at her box and sees her family all clustered together. Her three sisters. The elder two, Octavia and Claudia, flank the youngest, Livia. But her focus lands on Antony. He's nodding slowly at her, but something about it is less encouraging and more threatening.

Don't fuck this up.

Juliette turns back to the baseline and knocks two of the balls back, stuffing one up into the compression shorts beneath her skirt. The fuzz is soft against her skin, comforting and familiar.

As she goes to serve, her fingers lock too tightly around the handle of her racket. She glances up at Kacic before she rocks back. Kacic is crouched, swaying at the ready, a panther in her pure black dress and Adidas shoes.

With two more bounces for luck, Juliette spins her first serve in, her arm stiff through the motion. As soon as it bounces, Kacic pounces, crushing the ball down the line.

The crowd roars but Kacic doesn't even pump her fist. She simply moves to the other side as if this is just another day at the office. Juliette grits her teeth, annoyed.

Quiet falls as Juliette bounces the ball. She hits a sharper, faster ball and Kacic responds with a deep, spinning shot into Juliette's backhand. Juliette stays her ground on the baseline and crouches, angling the shot back. Kacic lunges and slices it back, but it drifts wide. Juliette pumps her fist at her box, and her sisters clap encouragingly.

With a few good serves, Juliette settles the vibrating nerves that threaten to overwhelm her and manages to win her service game. It's now Kacic's turn for a rebuttal.

In the next game, Juliette puts more balls in the court, but Kacic is ruthless with her shots. She clips lines, maneuvering Juliette out of position and striking winners from the middle of the court. It's a master class in how to hold serve, and Juliette would be impressed if it wasn't being carried out against her.

Back and forth they spar until Juliette holds for the final time to reach an even six games. Tiebreaker.

Kacic will serve first, and then they'll take turns serving until one of them earns seven points and is ahead by two, winning the set. All Juliette has to do is win two sets, and the match will be hers.

She can hear her sisters yelling her name and clapping. Antony shouts something in Italian, but Juliette is locked in. She doesn't need his help.

"Quiet, please," the umpire says as the crowd continues to roil with noise, excited that the final has been so close. "Players are ready."

Juliette closes her eyes and breathes, dancing on her toes. These are the kind of matches that make or break a player. This is the final of a Grand Slam, and while Juliette has been shaky on keeping her nerve, this is what she has trained for.

As the crowd finally quiets and Juliette crouches into her ready position, she watches Kacic step up to the baseline. She flicks her braid over her shoulder, almost impatient with the movement. The humidity presses down on them, damp and heavy, and Juliette wipes the sweat from her upper lip with her wristband. Desire burns against her skin. She *needs* this.

Is Luca feeling the nerves too? The excitement? Does the need to win also course through her veins, hot as white flame? Does that override any aches and pains from an hour's worth of brutal tennis in the Australian heat?

Juliette's heart thunders against her chest. A familiar ache throbs in her forearm, the back of her bicep, because damn, Kacic hits hard. But this is the culmination of all they've worked for in this set, their closing arguments. She won't give in, she won't give up. Kacic has been fighting her just as hard, so she doesn't have an advantage over Juliette. This is Kacic's first Grand Slam final too, and she won't let Kacic have any mental edge over her.

Juliette stares across the net and a jolt races through her as Kacic meets her gaze, a fraction of a second before she eases into her elegant service motion. Time shivers to a stop and the tightness in her chest snaps, a reverberating vibration like a string breaking after an off-kilter shot. Juliette's knuckles blanch around her racket. Kacic launches into her service motion, but the tension doesn't break. It prickles along the back of Juliette's neck. The ball flies, lifting out of Kacic's open fingers as her racket arcs through the air, cutting across the fuzz of the ball. Juliette blocks the ball back, muscle memory saving her the point. Juliette's legs move anyway, dragging her to the center of the baseline. The shot is weak and Juliette watches Kacic hesitate. She eases off her forehand, and Juliette's body makes the decision to move before her mind does. She sidesteps to her backhand and the ball connects beautifully, lancing down the line with precise power. Kacic lunges for it, but it tips off the end of her racket.

Juliette clenches her fist and lets herself smile, all thoughts of her aches and pains dissipating. Whatever this energy is that courses between them, Juliette will take advantage. She only needs to hold her serve for six more points, and the set will be hers. Another set after that, and she'll be lifting the Australian Open trophy.

Juliette wins the next two points fairly easily, one with a forehand winner and the other with Kacic missing a backhand by a larger margin than she probably should have. Maybe she's getting tired and her muscles are tightening up. She won the first point, and Kacic is faltering under this contest of wills. Confidence floods her until Kacic takes her next two points with twin aces, but she's able to scrape a win in the next rally, putting the score at 4–2 in Juliette's favor. The points are flying by and then they switch sides. Juliette gulps down a few mouthfuls of water. She watches Kacic walk around the net, her fingers tapping the post as she does. Then she jogs, hitting imaginary forehands, trying to find her rhythm. Juliette shakes her head, but the fluid movement of Kacic's body is stuck in her brain.

Antony would say Kacic was doing it as an intimidation tactic, but it's distracting in a different way. Juliette tosses her bottle down onto the ground harder than she means to and tries to focus instead on imagining herself winning this set, feeling the triumph that would surge through her veins, sharp and sweet. Just three more points, and it's hers.

She doesn't make the mistake of looking up at Kacic before she serves.

Juliette hits a low slicing serve, and Kacic nails it into the net. A free point. Kacic twists sharply on her heel, braid smacking against her sweaty shoulder. When Kacic returns to the baseline to serve, she's icy calm; no nerves flicker across her face. Kacic takes the next two points with ease, putting the score at 5–4, and Juliette knows she has to take a chance now. No risk, no reward. She can hear Antony urging her behind her but doesn't spare him a glance in the audience. She must focus.

She hits a hard serve in the middle of the box and Kacic cringes out of the way, catching the ball awkwardly on the frame.

6–4, set point.

Juliette steadies her breathing, plucking at the strings of her racket. She simply needs to hit a good serve to win this point and the set. It's always easier to win from ahead than to fight to get even. She'll be able to breathe a sigh of relief if she only has one more set to win. She rolls her shoulder and goes for her usual high-kicking serve into Kacic's backhand.

Kacic must be expecting it, because she moves before the ball hits the ground and slices it deep into Juliette's forehand. She rolls the ball back into the court, but Kacic is already moving, predatory, into the center of the court. She smashes Juliette's weaker shot for a winner.

6–5.

Kacic pumps her fist for the first time, and the crowd roars. It's almost deafening. Juliette smacks the edge of her racket against her calf. It isn't over and she can still win the set, but she feels the momentum swing like a pendulum. Pressure tightens her shoulders, and she huffs out a breath in an effort to lower them from her ears.

There is always another chance in a tiebreak. This late in the set, fatigue and nerves could compromise even the most composed player.

Juliette crouches, eagerly waiting. So far, Kacic's serve hasn't been predictable. Her motion is so fluid and even, regardless of what kind she hits. Juliette has to get lucky, trust her gut. Sometimes, that's all tennis is. Better lucky than good.

The serve is hard and cuts down the center service line. Juliette barely gets her racket on the ball, but it floats over the net. Kacic's racket draws back, and instead of pounding the weak shot for a winner, she slices the ball. A drop shot.

Juliette runs toward the net before Kacic's swing even comes through the ball. The shot barely drops over the net, but Juliette is there, rolling the ball into the open court. It should be a winner. She skids to a stop, every nerve in her body on fire. It bounces once. If it bounces again, it'll be Juliette's point to win the set.

But Kacic's racket cuts beneath the ball just before it bounces twice, tossing the ball up in a high lob that arcs into the lights. Juliette hops back, pulling her racket back like an archer draws their bow. She should let it drop and bounce once before smashing the overhead into the middle of the court. It's what Antony would tell her to do, but she *needs* this point *now*.

Juliette's heart hammers, and she can hear her breath harsh in her ears. She angles herself under the ball, but the bright light blinds her. The ball drifts farther right than she anticipated.

It drops into striking range. She drives with her elbow, snapping her wrist and racket over the ball. She connects, but not cleanly. Her shoulder tweaks as she hits it slightly off-center.

The line calling system shouts, "*OUT.*"

Too much angle. Not enough spin.

Juliette drops into a crouch, pressing her forehead onto the hilt of her racket. Her chest aches, lungs begging for air. She wants to scream. She lifts her head to watch the big screen declare it a CLOSE CALL, showing everyone how she missed the overhead by a fraction of a centimeter.

Juliette straightens and walks back to the baseline. She can't look up at Antony. She knows he'll be shaking his head in disappointment.

They're back even, and Juliette has squandered both her chances to win the set. 6–6. Her stomach churns, uneasy. She shakes her head, trying to force herself to have a terrible short-term memory. She can't think about what could've happened. She can only be here in the present.

Kacic's serve again. Juliette barely gets into the point, but once she's in it, neither of them wants to lose it. They smack the ball back and forth, forehand to forehand. Kacic hits harder than Juliette does, and it takes all of her concentration and years of training to keep the ball in and not overhit.

This is the exact type of point Juliette has been trying to avoid. The moment she eases off the speed, Kacic changes the trajectory of the ball and clips the baseline for a winner into the opposite corner.

6–7. Another point and Kacic wins, but Juliette is serving. She can control the point. Juliette is used to this. This is what she practices for. Juliette swirls the balls in her palm. Both are equally fluffed up, so she chooses randomly. She keeps only one in her hand. It's gotten to the point in the match where she's soaked with sweat; the ball will be too damp if she has to pull it out from her skirt to hit a second serve.

She won't be hitting a second serve.

Juliette steps a little farther wide than she usually stands. It gives a better angle for her wide serve. Hopefully, it'll spin out too far for Kacic to hit.

Juliette breathes in and out, sharply. She runs her wristband over her forehead. It's barely any use. It's too humid, and it's soaked through. Juliette glances up and sees that Kacic has moved farther back, anticipating.

Juliette cuts her serve to angle wide and short. Kacic lunges, the ball barely ticking off her strings. It should go straight into the net.

It doesn't. It clips the top of the net and rolls along the edge, tantalizingly slow. Juliette nearly sees it in slow motion as it dribbles over to her side. There is nothing she can do. Not even the fastest person could get to it.

"Game and first set, Kacic."

She was so close. Less than an inch from taking the first set. Tennis is always a game of inches, and this time, Juliette lost.

The whole crowd goes wild, and Kacic holds up her hand in apology. Still, there is no regret in her face. She doesn't even celebrate winning the first set, simply strides back to her bench with her hand up. She stole the first set from Juliette, and she doesn't even *celebrate*? As if it doesn't matter to her, as if this isn't the biggest match of their careers. Kacic doesn't fucking deserve it.

Juliette can barely swallow her rage until she gets to her bench, and then she smashes her racket onto the ground. It splinters and cracks, paint chips scattering across the court. The crowd gasps and then boos.

It doesn't make her feel better; if anything, the fury skitters across her every nerve like fire. She tosses the broken racket onto her bag.

It isn't over. Not until Kacic wins another set, but she's halfway there. Juliette grabs her small bag of clothes and heads off the court to change and go to the bathroom before set two. She needs to splash her face with cold water. As she walks toward the tunnel, she passes the Daphne Akhurst Memorial Cup, the trophy for winning the Australian Open. The lights glint off the gold tennis rackets crossed at the top, the silvery surface shining, almost mocking Juliette.

It *will* be hers. She won't let Kacic take it from her.

THREE

LUCA

Luca never understood the reasoning behind the nickname Lucky Luca, and although she's never said anything about it, she doesn't like it. If she were a man, she might've been touted as Legendary Luca, because it would've been her skill that was attributed to her rise through the rankings.

But as her shot rolls on the edge of the net, dribbling over onto Ricci's side, she is thankful for her so-called luck.

Her legs tremble like jelly as she sits down on the bench. It is surreal to be halfway to a Grand Slam win. She can almost taste the victory on her tongue. Or maybe that's the blue Gatorade.

Crack.

Luca glances to her left and sees Ricci's racket in splintered pieces. The crowd's cheering ripples into boos and jeers.

Brat.

Luca hides her smug smirk with a sip of water. She has been diligent in not thinking about Ricci's press conference comments. Vladimir told her that what happened off-court didn't matter and to talk with her racket.

So far, the advice is working out in her favor.

When Luca is in a point, it's easy to ignore the butterflies in her stomach. Then those butterflies make her sneak glances at Ricci during the changeovers. She is softly pretty, her delicate features hiding the sharply competitive spirit beneath. But every time her dark gaze snags on Luca's, she sees how much Ricci wants this. Or maybe Luca is simply seeing her own desire reflected back at her.

Luca sinks back into her chair and watches Juliette stalk off the court. She knows the crushing feeling that comes from losing a tight set.

Luca reaches into her bag for new wristbands. She makes quick work of her right one, but the stadium lights reflect on the silver of her soulmark. As she fiddles with her left band, she assesses the set. Despite all the nerves and glances and missed shots, this is undeniably *fun*. Ricci is tactically a different player than Luca, relying on her speed and high-percentage shots to keep her in the rallies. Luca has to take points from her with pinpoint accuracy and raw power. It's like playing against a ball machine at times. They're evenly balanced, as soulmates should be.

If they *are* soulmates.

Luca swipes sweat from her brow with her towel and pushes that thought far from her brain.

By the time the umpire calls time, Luca's legs have stopped shaking and she's regained control of her breath. Ricci will serve first in the second set, and Luca bounces on her toes at the back of the court.

She looks at her box. Others might say it's sad to have only a single person in it, but Luca prefers it. She doesn't know how Ricci plays with her entire family in her box. The pressure on her shoulders must be immense, especially with Claudia and Octavia Ricci being professionals too. Surely they'd be sitting there thinking they could do better, they should be the ones on court battling for the title. By contrast, Vladimir is front and center, calm and serene. He dips his chin at Luca as their gazes meet, and she nods back to him.

Ricci arrives back on court with her wild curls now twisted into a tight knot at the crown of her head instead of spilling freely down her back. It brings a sharpness to her, with the locked set of her jaw and a burning intensity in her eyes. Juliette wins her first game without Luca winning a single point, which isn't unusual, but it does put Luca on her back foot. Luca always plays better when calm. Once her emotions spiral out of her control, she's lost. The opposite seems to be true for Ricci. Yet another key difference between them.

Luca knows, logically, that her serve is her best asset. The smooth, fluid, and simple motion makes it reliable but also hard to read. She flexes her wrist a certain way and the ball snaps in an entirely different direction. So, when Ricci starts smacking her serves for winners, it's unsettling. Ricci is good at returning to begin with, but the way she's stepping into Luca's serves is different, more aggressive.

And she's more vocal with grunts and yells of *come on!* whenever she hits a good shot. It's deeply irritating, and Luca doesn't want it to bother her, but it does. The fun she was having evaporates and a coil of panic closes a fist around her lungs.

She gets broken at zero and has lost all eight of the first points of the second set. She glances at Vladimir, who claps encouragingly at her. "You have this, Luca. Settle in."

"I know, I will," Luca says as she towels off her face.

She does, eventually, get a grip on her strokes and her serve, but Ricci is like a dog with a bone—she refuses to give an inch. Even if Luca can win a few points on Ricci's serve, it's never enough to get back the game she lost.

Ricci holds her serve for a final time to take the set six games to three. And when she does, Luca watches her raise her arms and wave them, egging the crowd on and bringing more yells and jeers. She cups her palm against her ear and listens to the screams. Luca tries to block it out, but it grates against her nerves. Many players use the crowd and antics to pump themselves up, but as Ricci turns around, she smirks at Luca. It's mocking, meant to rile Luca up and throw off her focus.

Luca's heartbeat thunders in her ears. There was nothing sporting or fair about that taunt. When Luca sits down, she throws her towel over her head. It blocks out the bright blue court, the shouts and screams, the fact that this is the Australian Open final and whoever takes this last set will be the new champion. But she can still see Juliette and the wicked curve of her mouth when she blinks.

Champion. The word rings in Luca's head. Sharp and metallic. She forces her jaw to unclench, and her breath hisses through her open mouth. She has played plenty of tight matches in her life, both in other tournaments and in college. Here, the pressure is all on her.

The only person she'll disappoint is herself. It doesn't matter if Juliette Ricci is her soulmate. Either she will be or she won't, but Luca won't know until the match ends. And when it does, Luca will be the winner. And if she is, they'll figure it out in the aftermath of the match; not now.

That thought steadies her more than she thought it would. This is her match to win. This is who she is and what she was built for. It doesn't matter what Ricci does; Luca will fight for this win.

She pulls the towel off her head and crams an energy bar into her mouth, washing it down with her water. She switches rackets and leaves the other one on her bag. It's superstition, changing rackets after the loss of a set, but if they're going to insist on calling her Lucky Luca she may as well lean into it.

They exchange games back and forth. It seems Ricci has cooled off in between the second and third set. At 3–2, they switch sides again for Ricci's serve. Luca tightens her ponytail, the braid starting to fall loose around the end from swinging around so much. It bothers her, the way it clings to the sweaty skin on her shoulders, but there isn't time to fix it.

Luca towels off her face, and Vladimir nods at her again. "Come on, right here, Luca." It isn't much encouragement, but it settles the burgeoning annoyance in her chest.

She manages to fight her way into the points and gets the game to a critically even point. Two more points in Luca's favor and she'll be up 4–2. Win two more games after that, and she'll be the Australian Open champion. She'll know if Juliette Ricci is her soulmate.

Ricci's next serve goes, predictably, into the widest part of the service box. Luca sidesteps into it, rolling the ball high. Ricci's next shot is in the opposite corner. Luca skids into it, barely hitting the ball when she feels her ankle roll underneath her and she stumbles, dropping her racket and planting her hands on the ground to stop from falling.

Her ankle hurts, but it isn't sprained or broken. Still, as she tries to walk on it, pain lances through her leg. "I need a trainer," she says, hobbling to her bench. She can't breathe, her chest tight. This can't be how her first Grand Slam final ends. She holds on to the throbbing ankle, trying to roll the pain away, but it doesn't work.

Luca catches sight of the scoreboard.

That can't be right. No way she got her ball in. No way is she about to win this game. She can't believe it, and for a moment, it distracts her from the pain.

"Trainer will be out in a moment," the umpire says.

"This is bullshit. It's the middle of my service game!" Ricci complains at the top of her lungs from her side of the court.

"Luca is entitled to a medical timeout, Juliette. You know that," the umpire says.

The trainer jogs out from the side court and crouches in front of her. "How badly does it hurt?"

"It throbs." Luca winces.

The medical trainer peels off her shoe and sock. Her ankle pulses as his fingers press into the tender spot on the outside of her foot. "Oh, right there." The trainer continues to place pressure on different spots, but the edge of her ankle is the worst.

"How does it look?" Luca asks. She is vaguely aware of Ricci still having a meltdown with the umpire, raging about the match being paused.

"It's not swelling." The trainer looks up at her. "It might get worse, though," he warns.

Luca nods, thinking. If she loses this match and her ankle gets worse, it won't be worth it. But she cannot give up the opportunity to win her first Grand Slam. She can't stop now. She is *so close* she can taste it.

"This is poor sportsmanship! I'm serving. Make her wait until the end of the game!" Luca is half-surprised that Juliette isn't stomping her foot.

The umpire sighs. "There is nothing I can do, Juliette." He speaks slowly, as if talking to a child. "I would be saying the same thing if you'd hurt yourself."

Ricci groans and storms away, off to the box where her family sits. She waves her racket in the air, clearly ranting to them.

Luca can't believe Ricci is still having a temper tantrum over this. She would never want emotions to throw her off her game, but maybe blowing off steam is how Ricci keeps her focus.

She waits a few beats, deliberating and rolling her ankle from side to side. The pain is already a low-level ache, barely anything worse than a tweak. "Can I have a pain tablet and a wrap around it?" she asks.

The trainer nods, pulling out a blister pack from his bag and a roll of bandages.

Luca swallows the pain tablet and watches the trainer's sure hands wrap the bandage around her ankle. By the time he's done, her adrenaline is rushing back, blocking out any residual pain. She slips her sock back on and laces up her sneakers.

"I'm okay," Luca says, flexing her foot. Her ankle aches as she stands, but it isn't a spiky pain like before. "I can play." She stands, bouncing on her toes. The pain is worse than when she was sitting, but bearable. She knows this could hurt her more in the long run, but she doesn't care. This is the Australian Open, and she'll never quit.

So, she picks up her racket and strides back around the net. When she jogs, she doesn't feel the pain. The more that she moves, the less it hurts. She may limp in between points but she can move to the ball, so it won't matter.

Ricci glares at her as she stands at the baseline, her chest heaving as she tries to steady her breathing. Luca steels herself against the heat in Ricci's gaze and looks down at her racket. This moment isn't about Ricci, even though every inch of her body wants to focus on Ricci. Even if her pulse skitters around Ricci, skin flushed hot under her gaze, she tightly packs every thought away. This moment is like every regular practice. She adjusts her grip and finally looks up, a sense of calm settling on her shoulders. Ricci's serve is good, but her next shot isn't and Luca pounces, angling a short shot down the line to win the game. She doesn't allow herself to celebrate yet, but when she looks up at Vladimir, he's smiling.

Her service game and Ricci's next one go quickly. 5–3, and Luca needs only to hold her serve.

Yet, as she stands at the baseline and bounces the ball, nerves flutter to life in her chest. She inhales, trying to silence the swirling thoughts in her mind, but her fingers still tremble. Her lungs burn from playing for over two and a half hours. The realization that she can win this match is beginning to sink in, buzzing in her bones. She looks at her wrist, the soaked black wristband.

Luca cannot think about the score or whether Ricci is her soulmate. Instead, she visualizes her toss and her serve.

Even though her shoulders and forearms are aching, her motion is as easy as ever. With her height and the snap of her wrist, the serve goes precisely where she wants it. Three serves and well-placed forehands and it is championship point. Just one more and she is a Grand Slam champion. She swipes her palm down the edge of her skirt but it's no use, she's drenched in sweat. Her racket nearly slips out of her hand.

The crowd chants Luca's name. She would try to ignore it, but it rings in her ears. She steps up to the line, the pain in her ankle throbbing in time with her pulse. She watches Ricci at the towel box, wiping off her arms and hands. She doesn't look at Luca as she goes to the baseline. A calm settles in her. With a final deep breath she hits her favorite serve.

Ricci tries to hit it cleanly, but it skips off the frame.

Luca doesn't breathe as Ricci's shot coasts through the air. She shuffles back, racket poised at the ready. Her breath is ragged in her throat, her ankle aches, but she moves anyway.

The ball could spin in. She still could have to hit it.

OUT.

Luca's legs give out. The racket slips from her grasp as she slumps to her knees and then onto her back. The lights are blinding above her, and she can't see. But it doesn't matter. She covers her face with her hands, all of the tension draining from her body as laughter bubbles up into her throat.

She's done it.

"Game, set, and match, Kacic. Two sets to one. 7–6, 3–6, 6–3."

Luca looks at her shaking hands. She can't believe it. Her eyes fall to the wristband around her right wrist, soaked through and heavy with sweat.

The moment of truth. It sparks on her tongue, mingling with the delicious taste of victory. Luca gets to her feet slowly, trying not to limp to the net. Ricci is already there, leaning on it with one hand. She looks like she is going to be sick, her mouth a thin, flat line. Luca holds out her hand, and Ricci stares at it. For a brief moment, Luca wonders if Ricci will snub her. Then, slowly, Ricci reaches out and they clasp hands.

Luca breathes in and out once more before she knows.

Touching Ricci feels even better than winning. Luca's veins light up golden, and her breath catches. Their palms slide against each other, warm and clammy, but Luca knows this Juliette is *her* Juliette. If she ripped off her wristband at this moment, she would see the name scorched black on her skin.

"Oh," Luca says.

Then she looks up at Juliette Ricci and sees her face contorted in barely concealed rage. Her lip curls in disdain, and Luca feels the radiant heat of Juliette's hatred.

Juliette rips her hand from Luca's. She flexes her fingers, as if she can get the feel of Luca off her.

The world is a blur as Luca shakes the umpire's hand and collapses onto her bench. She buries her face into the towel, overwhelmed. All of her expectations lay in tatters, all hope for her soulmate crushed into powder beneath Juliette's On tennis shoe.

Luca is a Grand Slam champion. She's the number one player in the world. But the tears burning in her eyes aren't tears of joy.

Her soulmate hates her, and that hurts more than if she had lost.

FOUR

JULIETTE

When Juliette was a child, her sisters said she was more bird than girl. Light on her feet and always climbing the olive trees in their Naples backyard in Italy, higher and higher until she imagined her fingers touching the velvet blue of the sky and peeling it away to see what lay behind the marble atmosphere.

Then, when she was eight, she fell.

Juliette remembers the way her stomach punched into her throat, the melting of the sky and ground as she plummeted. Then, when Juliette read the fable of Icarus, she dreamed of falling again. She still has the nightmares. Only in her sleep, it never stops. The bone crush of reality doesn't snap her arm, she never hits the ocean and drowns; she's always caught in the limbo of falling.

But knowing Luca Kacic is her soulmate is like finally hitting the earth and snapping every bone in her body.

The trophy ceremony is a blur of color and motion and sounds. Juliette doesn't remember what she says. She knows she is too stiff with her wooden congratulations to Kacic. It feels like a lie rolling off her tongue. She can't even look at Kacic. She imagines she will see her glowing with pride and triumph, lording this win over Juliette, and a rocklike ball of anger lodges itself behind her ribs.

Once back in the locker room, Juliette rips her wrist wrap off, hoping it is simply a fluke. Some kind of cruel cosmic joke. A terrible dream, like she's falling again.

Her fingers trace *LUCA*. The letters are starkly black and strangely bright against the pale skin of her fragile inner wrist. It's almost shiny, like a burn mark. It takes all of her restraint not to punch the lockers. Instead, she twists her wrap back on.

She storms into the shower stall and yanks the curtain closed. With frantic tugs, she throws her clothes off. She wants to immediately get on a plane and fly somewhere far from Australia. Maybe somewhere snowy and cold so she can bury herself in the ice. The best she can do is twist the shower to cold and stand under it. She shivers violently, but it's enough of a shock to stop thinking about anything.

It is torture to stand under the cold water, but it's what she deserves for losing.

She isn't gentle as she wrenches a comb through the sweat-tangled knots. She scrubs her body harshly with soap, wanting nothing more than to wash this loss down the drain. Cold water soaks through her wrist wrap; she can't bear to take it off. Maybe if she doesn't look at her mark, it'll go away.

By the time she's done, she's freezing. Goose bumps trail across her skin, just like they had when she first touched Kacic. Would it be better if she didn't know? Maybe she should have snubbed Kacic and dealt with the consequences of being known as the tour bitch.

She wraps her towel around her and storms back to her stuff. Her hair drips cold droplets down her back, so she tosses on a hoodie and sweatpants as fast as she can.

The locker room door swings open with a creak that says no one's ever oiled it.

Juliette is grateful she pulled clothes on because in comes Luca Kacic—sweaty, flushed, and happier than ever.

For a heartbeat, they stare at each other. She has her bag over her shoulders, her trophy in her arms.

"Hi," Kacic says softly, her eyes wide. She still has her visor on. The fluorescent lights cast odd shadows over her face because of it.

Juliette doesn't know what to say. She doesn't want to talk to Kacic.

"Can we talk?" Kacic asks, her voice wavering.

Juliette rakes her gaze over Kacic. She crosses her arms over her chest.

"I know we started on the wrong foot," Kacic says.

"Don't you mean ankle?" Juliette sneers. God, the irony. "You said I only won my 1000 because of Chen's ankle injury."

Kacic flinches as if Juliette struck her. "I didn't mean it like—"

Juliette cuts her off. "And then you took a medical timeout to break my rhythm."

Kacic blinks. "What? No, I twisted my ankle. It's not like that. None of that is like that." She looks . . . hurt. It's strange to see it peek through the usual smooth, impassive shell she wears. "Whatever. That doesn't matter. What does matter is that we're—"

"Don't say it, Kacic," Juliette hisses, cutting her off. As a kid, she never worried about finding her soulmate because her parents were madly in love and perfect together, despite not having each other's name on their wrist. Tennis became the love of her life at a young age, and all she's ever wanted is to be the best—to win Grand Slams and be number one, even if for a brief moment. Tennis success is so fleeting, and for a second, Juliette had it within her grasp. But now? She's lost the biggest tournament of her life, and she's cosmically tied to the woman who beat her for the Australian Open title.

"But—" Kacic starts, but Juliette shakes her head.

"I don't want this. I didn't choose this, or *you*, so just fuck off, Kacic."

Kacic's mouth falls open, and she blinks rapidly. She looks shell-shocked, sputtering as she tries to find words to refute Juliette.

But Juliette won't be beaten again. She grabs her bags and slings them over her arm, storming out of the locker room on bare feet. The door creaks as it shuts, leaving Kacic alone with her trophy.

It isn't until Juliette makes it back to her hotel room that the numbness breaks and her eyes sting with tears. She buries her head under the pillows and lets herself sob. Luckily, none of her sisters come and try to comfort her. They will in the morning, commiserating over the loss with room service waffles. Sure, Octavia and Claudia have lost Grand Slam finals in the past, but never to their soulmate. This is a specific kind of humiliation that burns in Juliette's throat.

Before the match, Juliette knew she wanted to beat Kacic, of course, but her need to be *better* now runs far deeper, burrows into the marrow of her bones.

Juliette forces herself out of bed and to the desk. She knows what she's doing is childish, but she grabs the marker out of the drawer and scribbles over the name on her wrist. And for a moment, she feels lighter. She knows it will wash off, but she also knows she doesn't have to be with her soulmate. She may not be able to control who her soulmate is, but she can control her career. She *needs*, more than air and water, to win.

And she will. No matter what it costs.

FIVE

JULIETTE

Two and half weeks after the horrific Australian Open final, Juliette loses to Kacic again in the quarterfinal in Dubai.

It is a humiliating loss. One that Juliette would be ashamed of if she wasn't so sick. She coughs and sneezes her way through the match, her lungs burning whenever she has to run too much. At least it gives her an excuse to keep the handshake at the net brief, if anyone in the press asks about it. Still, as Kacic's hand, slick with sweat, clasps hers for a brief moment, lightning knifes through her veins. A wave of tingles sprawls from her palm across her body. For a moment, the ache in her neck and the stuffiness in her nose eases.

"Hope you feel better," Kacic says, her gaze pinned above Juliette's head. Juliette lets go of Kacic's hand to sneeze into her elbow.

Phantom tingles linger as Juliette goes through the abbreviated steps of her postmatch routine. It reminds her of the TV-static feeling after lying on her arm too long. A shimmer of pins and needles whenever she flexes her fingers.

She blames the feeling on her fever.

Juliette is still sick when she arrives in Mexico to play the Monterrey 500. She watches the replay of Kacic's match, skipping straight to where Kacic loses the tight third set tiebreaker. It should be satisfying to see her rival lose, but it only makes envy swirl in her chest alongside the raucous cough. It should be *she* who beats Kacic, not some young upstart barely old enough to drive. She smacks her laptop closed and fluffs the starchy hotel pillow beneath her cheek. When sleep eludes her and boredom makes her too acutely aware of her own misery, she opens her phone. A message from Antony drops in; a strategy document about her first round match.

Juliette ignores it in favor of Twitter.

On the top of her feed is a post from Kacic's brand-new account. With a considerable amount of likes and reposts, it's clear the algorithm thinks this is the perfect content for Juliette to consume.

Unlike most players, Kacic only made a Twitter after the Australian Open. Most likely to soak in all the praise from fans after she showed her resilience and beat Juliette through an injured ankle. Which clearly wasn't that bad if Kacic kept winning in the tournaments after Australia. Juliette clenches her jaw as anger roils in her again, and pain shoots through her ear because of her headache.

She clicks on Kacic's post, curious about the responses to it. She has to click the translate button, since Kacic wrote it in Croatian.

@luca_kacic
Congratulations to my fellow countrywoman @lana_ivankovic! You played incredibly today, and I hope we share the court many more times. Good luck in the rest of the tournament! Amazing night for Croatian tennis!

Juliette rolls her eyes at the responses.

@lanadelkovic
You are a true class act @luca_kacic

@goatkacic
kind words from my champ!

@flopicci
nice words! Now go win the next one, Luca!

@idemoluca
queen shit

Juliette knows it isn't good for her to dwell on Kacic, but her thumb presses Kacic's profile, and she scrolls through the mundane and frankly boring tweets. Maybe Kacic has a PR person run her account for her, and that's why there is little to no flavor in any of her posts. Eventually, Juliette returns to her main feed, but her mind keeps snagging on Kacic. She's like a scab that won't heal. She doesn't always bother Juliette, but occasionally if Juliette twists a certain way, she feels her. If she closes her eyes, she can almost feel the luminous and staticky feeling of Kacic's touch on her skin.

It's annoying.

A knock on her door puts an end to her thoughts. "Go away," she croaks, not wanting to get up.

A key card swipes and the door beeps as it unlocks. Antony steps into the dim room, carrying a plastic bag hopefully full of food and Gatorade. Everyone except Livia calls him by his first name. A habit they picked up as a result of him being their coach. Now, it almost feels wrong to call him *Dad*. "How are you feeling?" he asks, setting the bag down on the bedside table and twisting it open.

Juliette shrugs, her arms like noodles as she tries to lift herself into a sitting position.

"I would say to pull out, but you won here last year," Antony says, handing her a plastic shot glass of scarlet cough syrup. Juliette pinches her nose as she swallows it, but the bitterness still pools on the back of her tongue.

"I know," she says around a half-stifled gag. Antony grimaces and hands her a blue Gatorade. "But it's early in the season."

Antony sits on the end of her bed, looking at her. He presses the back of his hand to her cheek, humming, as if it tells him something vital about her condition. "It is."

Juliette can see him arguing with himself internally. As a coach, he wants to encourage her to keep going, but as a father, he's clearly worried. So, he stays silent and lets her make the decision. She knows he wants her to play. He always does. She also knows he hates watching her lose.

She looks down at her phone, swiping her thumb over it. The

screen unlocks and opens onto one of Kacic's tweets. With every win she has over Juliette, she pulls farther ahead in the rankings. The five hundred points awarded to the winner of Monterrey would certainly help Juliette's overall ranking. There aren't many top players besides Juliette playing, so she could sweep through and claim the points easily if her lungs weren't swimming in mucus.

"What do you think?" she asks finally, still teetering on the edge of a decision.

Antony's mouth thins. "I think you should play. Anything to boost your ranking."

Juliette swallows, her throat scratchy, and nods. "Okay, I'll stay in."

Antony smiles and pats her shoulder. "Good. Now, eat this soup and then rest up."

LUCA

March is home to Luca's favorite tournament: Indian Wells. The dry California air, wide-open sky, and skyline of palms and mountains combine to create a sweeping atmosphere that Luca looks at with stars in her eyes.

On the night before the tournament starts, Vladimir drags her out to dinner at a surprisingly nice restaurant.

"I admit I have an ulterior motive," Vladimir says as they're brought to the back patio by a hostess who smiles at Vladimir as if she knows him.

"What do you mean?" Luca asks, wishing she had worn a nicer pair of pants instead of jeans. Vladimir only smirks at her, a glint in his eyes that makes her stomach churn. She starts to protest when the hostess stops next to a table that is already occupied.

"Vladimir." The woman at the table rises, sweeping her shining golden hair off her shoulder and down her back. Luca knows she's gawking, but she can't stop. Karoline Kitzinger is one of the best tennis players of all time. "Lovely to see you as always."

Vladimir kisses her cheeks like they're old friends. "It's been too long, Karo." He turns to Luca, and she snaps her mouth shut. "As you know, this is Luca Kacic."

"It's amazing to meet you," Luca says, breathless as Karoline shakes her hand firmly.

Karoline is retired now, but in the late 1990s and early noughties, she was a part of a rivalry nicknamed the Fierce Four. They always compelled Luca because of how different they were. Each one excelled at a different Grand Slam because of their distinctive play styles: Victoria Ferreyra at the Australian Open, Karoline at the French Open, Aurore Cadieux at Wimbledon, and Payton Calimeris at the US Open. There was tennis drama around the head-to-head matchups and the arguments in court, but it was the off-court scandals and incidents that Luca ravenously consumed. The cutting words tossed carelessly in press conferences, celebrity exes, and the infamous fountain incident all created a tapestry of what the public knew of them. Karoline had multiple nicknames throughout her career. Her tennis one was the Dancer, but off the court she was called the Heartbreaker and the Swiss Miss. Now, face-to-face with Karoline, Luca understands why. She is chic and sultry, distinctly feminine, and pretty in a way that conceals her predatory ambition.

Luca sits down at the table with Vladimir next to her and Karoline across from her.

"You are an excellent player, Luca," Karoline says, lacing her hands together in front of her.

"Thank you," Luca says, trying not to stutter. "That means a lot coming from you."

Karoline's smile tightens at the corners. "I apologize that I'm not much for small talk, so I'd like to simply state why I asked you to meet me here."

Luca reaches for her water and nods.

"I would like to invite you to be the fourth member of my team for the Connolly Cup."

Luca is glad she didn't take a sip, because she definitely would have spit it out. "Really?"

Karoline smirks. "You are number one in the world and the reigning Australian Open champion. Frankly, I'm surprised neither Aurore nor Victoria reached out to you earlier. It's between Roland-Garros and Wimbledon, the third week in June. You'll have to miss Birmingham, unfortunately." Karoline does not make it sound like it'd be a great misfortune.

And Luca does agree. It's a small warm-up tournament, and she'd make so much more money just showing up to the Connolly Cup than winning Birmingham. "It's in Naples this year. An indoor hard court, so I know it won't be helpful for preparing for Wimbledon, but it's like this."

Luca swallows. The Connolly Cup is a charity exhibition event put on every year by the Fierce Four members in honor of their rival, Diana Connolly. She had won every Grand Slam in 2004, dethroning them and blazing through tournaments and the rankings like a meteor. Then, to the shock of all, at the end of the year, she died of a drug overdose. Now, the Connolly Cup is a charity organization that raises money for addicts and mental health organizations. This year, Karoline partnered with Payton Calimeris to set up their team to face off against Aurore and Victoria's team. And over the last few years, Luca has enjoyed spectating from the safety of her apartment. Even though it's technically low stakes for players, there is a hot spotlight shining on them, the entire tennis world watching as if they're on a reality show. They're all waiting for another scandal, although Luca doesn't know how anything will top two years ago, when Claudia Ricci slapped her then boyfriend (and coach) after finding out from a rogue post that he was still married.

The glass slips in her fingers, and she puts it down before it shatters or she spills water everywhere. "I'm honored."

Karoline tilts her head, dark eyes glittering in the setting sun. "I fear a 'but' coming," she says, leaning back and unlacing her hands. "Say yes, Luca, you won't regret it."

Luca chews on her lower lip. She knows the rest of Karoline's team, and unfortunately, Juliette Ricci is one of her picks this year. A weekend of playing on the same team as Ricci, attending events, and pretending not to hate each other sounds like torture. Still, longing hooks into her stomach, and she finds herself nodding despite the twist of anxiety in her chest. "Okay. I'd love to."

Karoline grins, softer than before. "Perfect."

By the time the dinner wraps up, the news of Luca being the fourth and final member of Karoline's team has broken over Twitter. While in the car back to the hotel, Luca scrolls through the excited posts below it. A notification pops up, and Luca sees she's been added to a group chat by Karoline. As expected, it has Claudia Ricci and Zoe Almasi, the two other players of their team, and two numbers she doesn't know. One must be Juliette Ricci and the other is the team's cocaptain, Payton Calimeris. A flurry of *welcome to the team* texts pour in from everyone except Juliette Ricci.

Typical.

SIX

LUCA

Clay season rolls around after Indian Wells, and Luca dreads it. She doesn't like sliding and slipping on the red dirt. Her game isn't built for the slow balls and grinding rallies. She doesn't win any of the tournaments, but at least she doesn't embarrass herself. Eventually, the clay swing finally culminates in the French Open, Roland-Garros.

It rains on and off during the first week of the tournament. Playing tennis in the rain on clay should be a crime. Still, Luca considers herself lucky because she gets scheduled early and on the court with a roof.

With the court enclosed, it's humid and sticky. The clay clumps beneath her shoes and the ball moves even slower through the air. Luca still wins but it takes hours, and she's drenched like she just stepped out of a pool by the time it's over.

Sweat slides down her temples and cheeks as she bends down to put her racket into her bag. She impatiently brushes it away, irritating her skin and making her throat tight. She rips off her wristbands and tosses them at a cluster of girls cheering her name. She smiles at them, and they squeal to each other in rapid French. She grabs her Rolex out of the side compartment of her bag and shimmies it onto her wrist, snapping it closed. She likes the money that comes from the sponsorships, but it has been a hassle remembering to put on the watch after her match.

A tournament manager approaches her with a purple pen and a smile. Luca takes it and turns to the camera. In quick scrawling letters, she signs her name on the plexiglass over the lens and adds a smiley face that is objectively terrible. She tries to fix the edge of the smile but smudges it. She shrugs and hands the pen off. As she glances up at the jumbotron, she sees herself signing the camera, a few seconds delayed.

Ice sears through her. She's forgotten to put on her wrist wrap and her watch isn't nearly wide enough to hide her soulmark. It stands out, brilliantly black. The first three letters wink from behind the gilded edge of her Rolex band.

She wraps her left hand around her wrist and hurries back to her bag, crouching down and shoving her hand into it so no one can read more letters. She finds her real wrap, a strip of black wide enough to cover the black block lettering, and twists it around the mark with trembling fingers. Sweat trickles down the back of her neck, prickling and itchy.

Slowly, Luca stands. She rubs her face with her towel again, trying to calm the rattling nerves in her chest. The last thing she wants is someone prying into her private life or even intimating that her soulmate is Juliette Ricci. Spiky panic cuts into her lungs like shards of glass, but she forces herself to throw her towel into the crowd too before heading onto the court again for another interview.

Luca's phone buzzes, and she swipes it open.

A screenshot sits beneath a message from Nicky. Her stomach twists, humiliation and anger spiraling in her throat. Ricci has quote-tweeted the grainy, blown-up image of Luca's soulmark with a winking face. Nicky's only message is a few grimacing emojis. He'd been the first one she called after winning the Australian Open. Even jet-lagged and yawning, he'd consoled her about how terrible Juliette Ricci had been and talked through every second of the interaction with her until she finally let him go to sleep.

The sound of her name snaps her back into the room, staring at a sea of faces.

Unfortunately, this fourth-round win means she has to sit in another dreadful press conference and pretend she doesn't hate the clay. And pretend she didn't notice that her soulmark was halfway on display after her match. A careless mistake she is still agonizing over even though no one has mentioned it to her face so far.

Luca has been diligent in trying to ignore Juliette Ricci. Sometimes when she sees Ricci, she's right back in that locker room. She can feel the hand-warmed metal of her trophy against her arm, smell the light citrus and coconut of whatever products Ricci used, and remember the hope that maybe Ricci would apologize for her words and want to get to know Luca.

Then the bile of humiliation rises in her throat, and she has to forget the rest.

"Sorry, can you repeat the question?" Luca stares at the bright phone screen showing the audio waveforms rippling with her voice, capturing its slight quaver.

"Have you seen Twitter yet? The speculation about your soulmark?"

Luca swallows, trying to keep her expression neutral. At least she had a heads-up from Nicky. Still, her heart hammers against her chest like she's been in a long rally. Which, in Paris, is unfortunately often. "Why would I want to comment on that?" she asks, glancing away from the reporter audacious enough to ask it. "What does that have to do with my tennis?" She wishes Twitter didn't even exist. Maybe she should delete hers—not that it matters, now that the picture is out on the internet.

"There is speculation that your soulmate is your most competitive rival, Juliette Ricci. That must make playing tennis complicated. Especially after the Australian Open and the rest of the hard court swing."

Luca wishes the ground would open up and swallow her whole. No other reporters jump in to save her, which isn't surprising; they're all sharks with gleaming, hungry eyes.

Even the sound of Ricci's name makes Luca's skin prickle. She stares down at her hands and spots freckles of red clay on her forearms that she didn't wash off properly. Juliette Ricci loves the red clay of Paris. She basks in her moniker as the Princess of Clay, and the luxury of being an expected favorite at Roland-Garros. Luca scratches at her itchy skin and swallows the sharp, unpleasant feeling nagging in the back of her throat.

"We're both professionals and nothing outside of tennis matters. I do not wish to comment on my soulmark. It is no one's business but my own." Luca hopes the answer satisfies the hungry reporters.

No such luck. The reporter narrows his eyes, latching on to something that Luca must've stumbled over without realizing it. "Well, with the Connolly Cup coming up, I'm sure we all would love to know how it feels to be on the same team together. Do you feel as though you're rivals?"

Luca sucks in a breath through her teeth. She should play it cool and even, but unless she's on a tennis court with a racket in hand, Luca has never been cool or even. "I don't care. In order to be rivals, I would think that Ricci would have to beat me first."

The reporter grins. "Thank you, Ms. Kacic. That's all."

Luca hates herself for snapping back, even though it's true. She doesn't want to care, and she doesn't want to talk about Ricci. There's no point. Ricci has made it clear that she has no interest in any type of relationship.

JULIETTE

"As your PR manager," Livia begins, and Juliette groans.

"You're my publicist, not my—"

"I have to say this is stupid," Livia plows on as if Juliette never spoke.

Juliette lets her phone fall to her stomach as she lies on her ridiculously plush hotel bed. For the last two hours, she's been scrolling through posts about Luca Kacic's accidental soulmark reveal.

@HewittLover_69
wouldn't it be ironic if kacic's soulmate was ricci?

@idemoluca
there are millions of people with JUL- names. it'd be such a scam if it were ricci

@riccisbackhand
nah y'all remember AO? their faces after that handshake? there is something going on 👀

Soulmarks get revealed all the time, even if people are diligent in hiding them. It's especially hard for sweaty athletes with watch brand contracts to keep. What Twitter seems to find the most fascinating is that there aren't that many *Jul-* names, and Luca had seemed very eager to cover hers up.

Juliette simply posted a winky face.

Now Livia has taken up residence on the adjacent love seat and is staring at Juliette, thoroughly disappointed by her choices.

"Come on, you have to admit it's kind of funny," Juliette says after a beat of deliberate silence. She kind of likes that Kacic had her soulmark revealed and will probably have to answer awkward questions about it. It might throw her off her rhythm, and Juliette isn't above fanning the flames a little hotter.

Livia levels her with a brow raise that would make their father proud. She lifts her blue light blockers and nestles them in her messy bun. "I don't like it."

"Why not?" Juliette asks.

Livia sighs. The frown is not at home on her face. Usually, she's into Juliette's antics. It's Octavia who frowns intensely at any sign of fun, taking her role as the oldest seriously.

"It'll come back to bite you in the ass, for one. Also, I still don't understand why you don't like her." Livia's voice warms, her deep brown eyes becoming soft and inquisitive—a surefire way to get anyone to do whatever she wants, but Juliette holds firm as her good mood sours.

"You don't understand, Livie," Juliette says, bitterness like ash in her mouth.

Livia huffs and pulls her glasses off her head, but they catch in her wild curls, and she has to thread them out of the loose strands, skewing her messy updo. "But you never even gave Luca a chance," Livia says as she returns to the laptop resting on her knees. "What if it's worth it?"

Livia can't understand. She isn't a tennis player and never has been. Juliette fiddles with the bracelets on her right wrist, ignoring the wrap on her left one. "Nope," she says stubbornly, popping the word in a way she knows frustrates Livia.

"You're impossible," Livia says, snapping her laptop closed and swinging her legs off the chair.

Juliette wriggles into the downy pillows. "Bye!" she calls after her, and she doesn't need to look up to know Livia's flipping her off as she stalks out of the room. She reopens her feed and scrolls through unhinged fan posts to amuse herself.

In the months since the Australian Open, Juliette has won a few tournaments, including Monterrey. As much as she enjoyed the early season, this is the portion of the season that she loves the most. She feels at home on the clay, and she has no time to think of Kacic. She has a French Open to win.

SEVEN

JULIETTE

Juliette does not win Roland-Garros.

Luckily, neither does Luca Kacic.

They both lose in the quarterfinals, narrowly avoiding a Grand Slam rematch.

Juliette grinds through the press conference with no quippy remarks for Twitter to blow out of proportion. She sticks to the script, even as the questions grate on her last exhausted nerve. Livia told her she would cut all the strings on her rackets if she didn't follow the perfunctory bullet points.

Whenever she has to take a breath to compose herself, she thinks of her sisters' latest messages in the group chat.

CLAUDIA

shit luck, Jules. finish your presser quick and we'll eat ice cream.

OCTAVIA

We have matches tomorrow. Eat whatever you want, I'll be sleeping.

CLAUDIA

more for us! 😜

She wishes she could breeze through, but it's hard to talk about how high her expectations were for the French Open. She wishes she would have had a new chance to beat Kacic, get to another final, and prove she is just as good—no, *better*—than Lucky Luca Kacic.

Juliette fumes the entire way back to her hotel room and slams the door open.

"Uh oh, here she comes!" Claudia's singsonging voice carries through as Juliette shuts the door with more grace.

"Shut up!" she shouts back, letting her bag drop by the door despite the tripping hazard.

She stomps into the living space, bombarded by the scent of skincare products. Her hotel room has been overtaken by her three sisters. Octavia glowers on the couch, ice wrapped around her slightly bum knee. She looks like a ghost with the sheet mask on her face. Her dark hair is expertly braided—courtesy of Livia, no doubt. Claudia is on the floor in front of the coffee table, putting together a puzzle with a painful-looking charcoal mask on her face. She looks up as Juliette arrives and grins, cracking the mask around her cheeks. Livia lounges in the desk chair, still on her laptop. She's sans face mask, but she has a large glass of red wine, which she delicately lifts to her lips as if she's sixty-five and not twenty.

"What is happening here?" Juliette asks.

Claudia rolls her eyes. "A girls' night, obviously," she says, waving her hands. "Take off your shoes, you heathen. Who raised you!" She shoves the coffee table back and fishes her long legs out from underneath it.

"She's on a warpath," Octavia bemoans with her eyes closed.

Juliette shucks her sneakers off before Claudia shoos her into the love seat. She plants her hands on her shoulders. "Sorry about your loss today," Claudia says, so sincere that Juliette feels her eyes prickle again. "We'll get them next year. You'll win Roland-Garros, I know it."

Claudia is almost a carbon copy of their mother. Her hair is wild and curly, soft golden-blond, and streaked naturally by the sun, whereas the rest of them have variations of their father's brown curls.

She even has their mother's long legs, ski slope nose, dip in her chin, and soft sage-green eyes.

She is also the one who appears in headlines the most, either because she's won another doubles title with Octavia or because she was sleeping with a married man. Even if she didn't do it on purpose.

But they don't talk about that.

"Now, chocolate or vanilla?" Claudia asks, leaning away from Juliette and heading for the minifridge in the corner of the kitchenette.

Juliette is in the mood for a shower and sleep, but she humors her anyway. "Chocolate."

Claudia barks out a haughty "HA!" and points at Octavia.

"Thanks, Jules, you lost me thirty bucks," Octavia grumbles.

"I thought you would've been with Leo. *He* won today," Juliette says, trying not to sound too bitter but failing miserably.

"Claudia dragged me here," Octavia says. She's never one to flatter. "She says I need to '*relax*' more." She dramatically flips her hands.

"You do, Octo," Livia says. "And do not say you can *relax* with Leo." She makes a gagging motion, and Octavia huffs.

Juliette snorts and curls her legs beneath her.

"We need to talk about your problem," Livia says, because apparently Juliette isn't allowed to have any time to simply mope.

"What if I don't want to talk about it?" Juliette whines.

Claudia balances four bowls in her arms, and Juliette relieves her of a chocolate one. "Absolutely not. This is gossip, and that is the tenet upon which these girls' nights were founded." She flops onto the floor in front of them, puzzle abandoned.

Juliette stabs her plastic spoon into a mound of ice cream.

"This is about Luca, isn't it?" Claudia asks.

"Shut up."

"Why do you insist on getting distracted by what Luca is doing?" Octavia asks through a mouthful of vanilla.

Juliette sighs into her ice cream. "I'm not!" She can feel their eyes on her, intense and curious but not malicious. They aren't journalists. Still, they don't understand how *irritating* Kacic is. She shoves ice cream into her mouth and nearly gags. "Is this sugar-free?"

Claudia shrugs, trying to appear innocent. "Livia says we can't completely ruin the diet Antony put you on."

"Traitor." Juliette glares at her and sets her bowl on the arm of the chair.

"Come on, Jules, spill it. You're obviously bothered by Luca. What's going on?" Claudia insists, gentler this time.

Juliette rubs her left wrist, the wrap that hides Luca Kacic's ink-black name. They know Kacic is her soulmate, they saw the Sharpie on her arm the next morning, but Juliette has successfully managed to avoid talking about any of it until now.

Kacic has been an irritant these last few months, with her perfect and quiet excellence. She coasts through every tournament as the one everyone needs to beat, but in the media, she's understated and coy. Juliette hates her for it.

"I don't understand why you hate her," Octavia says, fiddling with her braid. "She's very polite."

"She beat me in Australia! In Dubai! Defeated *us* in Indian Wells!" Juliette points to Octavia and Claudia. "I don't *hate* her, I just want to beat her. Don't you?"

"And so you play mind games in the media? Jules, you know that's dumb," Octavia says.

"And you did kind of start this," Livia adds. Juliette glares at her, and she shrugs. "Just saying. Telling a press conference full of reporters that her game was 'wholly unoriginal' and that her serve was over-hyped did not help." She tilts her wineglass at her, most of it already gone.

Juliette winces. "They asked me what I thought, and I was honest." She shakes her head. "Plus, *she* started it. She acted like I only won against Xinya by default."

Livia sighs. "Honesty doesn't mean being a bitch. And wanting to beat someone doesn't mean you have to be cruel. Especially to your—"

"Don't you fucking dare," Juliette snaps. They know how she feels about soulmates. She doesn't want hers, and she won't be told what to do. If Juliette never speaks her name, never looks at her wrist, and never acknowledges what Kacic is to her, it won't be an issue.

"We just want you to be happy, Jules, and holding this grudge is not going to help your game," Claudia says.

"I know we've always put our ambitions before our romantic lives, but that doesn't mean you can't be civil to Luca," Octavia adds solemnly.

"You guys are supposed to be on my side," she pleads. Her sisters piling onto her after her loss just adds insult to injury. Tennis has always come more naturally for Octavia and Claudia. They have worked hard to be the best players, but they don't understand the pressure of being the third professional player to come up the ranks in a family, especially considering their early success. They don't *understand* how much Juliette has had to sacrifice to get to this point, how much she's had to chase just to get within sniffing distance of their accolades. And even then, she isn't close.

"We are on your side," Octavia says. "It just seems unfair that you just write Luca off without knowing her."

Frustration bubbles in Juliette's stomach. "Easy for you to say. You had a chance to grow your career early *with* Leo. Plus, he isn't your rival," she snaps.

"Fair point," Octavia concedes with a tilt of her head.

"And you're the lucky one! You don't have a soulmate to worry about." Juliette waves her hands at Claudia, wishing for not the first time in the last few months that she could switch places with her and not have a soulmark.

"Why do you let Luca bother you so much?" Livia chimes in, drawing Juliette's attention.

"She's annoying! A fact that all of you seem to ignore," Juliette grumbles.

"An opinion none of us hold, more like," Octavia says primly.

"I'm just trying to be pragmatic." Livia finishes her wine and sets the glass down with a loud click. "The more you fuck around with mind games, the less focused you are. You don't care that she's your soulmate?" Juliette winces at the word. "Fine. But don't let it get in your head." Livia taps her temple, swaying a bit in her seat.

"I've already had a bad day, can we stop now?" Juliette whines.

She knows they mean well and want what is best for her, but their feelings about soulmates are different. Octavia is able to commit to tennis and Leo. Claudia can have a vast and fluid love life without the worry of tying herself down. And Livia doesn't have a single competitive bone in her body; she doesn't have to worry about a rival in any aspect of her life.

"Fine, we'll let it go," Octavia says soothingly. "Do you want to talk about your match?"

"Not really," Juliette mutters, slumping farther down into the love seat. She already knows she's going to get a lecture from their father. His silence is concerning. He should've sent a document of all her failures already, but it's suspiciously absent.

"Why don't you go to Naples early?" Livia suggests, her purple acrylics tapping away on her keyboard. "I can get you a flight tomorrow." Three more clicks, and before Juliette can reply, she's cooing, "Oh look at this cute apartment near the water!"

"But what about you two?" Juliette gestures to Claudia and Octavia. They're still alive in the women's doubles draw together.

Claudia waves her off. "Don't stop on my account. I'd rather you clear your head before the Connolly Cup." Juliette fights her grimace. The last thing she wants is to think about being chummy with Kacic. Is it too late to quit the exhibition? But bad publicity is the last thing Juliette needs. Plus, she *wants* to play, to be coached by Karoline Kitzinger and Payton Calimeris. She'll be damned if she lets Kacic ruin that chance for her.

Octavia nods. "Don't sulk because we're here. Go home if you want."

"Antony will kill me if I leave," Juliette says.

Claudia frowns and then winces. "Ouch, my mask is dry, hold please." She scrambles off the floor and disappears into Juliette's bedroom.

"Where is he?" Juliette asks, glancing around as if he'll appear from behind the couch.

"I told him to lay off tonight," Octavia says as she sits up and unwraps the ice from her knee.

Juliette sinks even lower into the cushions. "Is he really that mad?" she asks, voice raspy and soft.

"Not mad, more upset." Octavia rips her mask off and crumples it into a ball, tossing it toward the trash can and missing horrifically. She rubs the serum into her skin. "You know what he's like. He thinks you should never lose."

Sometimes, despite how much she loves her sisters, they make her feel worse. "Great."

"I've got a plane ticket on standby, just say the word," Livia pipes up.

Octavia sighs. "That is why I fired him as my coach. Not that he ever acts like a dad, but it's better now. Maybe you should do the same." She turns her gaze to Juliette. She has their mother's piercing and knowing sea-glass green eyes, brighter than Claudia's. At least now her brows are lifted and the corners of her mouth soft, her overall bitch-face toned down to be sympathetic. "No one plays well under all that pressure."

Her words are loaded with a lifetime of trauma and scars and ambition. Juliette rubs the thin scar threaded along her wrist from surgery last year. It was to try to prevent the eventual ruination of her career; if her doctor hadn't been successful in patching her slipped tendon, she would've had to put down her racket forever. She hasn't had a break since she was forced to because of that surgery. Months she suffered without tennis, and she had been so eager to return to play, she didn't even consider taking any time off. That it might be *good* for her.

"Book it, Livie," she decides. A smile tugs at the corner of Octavia's mouth, sparking warmth in Juliette's chest.

Livia dramatically slaps the enter key. "Done."

Juliette picks up her sugar-free chocolate ice cream and digs in without a grimace.

EIGHT

JULIETTE

Coming home to southern Italy is the balm Juliette needed on her aching heart. She cannot imagine a better way to spend ten days than sinking into the familiarity of her native tongue and basking below a sky so clear she swears she can see the heavens through wisps of delicate pearl clouds. The salty air coils playful fingers in her hair, the sand scorches her feet, and the sun melts away any of the lingering disappointment about Paris. It burnishes gold into her caramel curls and further bronzes her olive skin. The sea cradles her tenderly, healing her worn-out muscles and quieting her mind.

Her father's voice nags in the back of her head that she should pick up a racket, but it's easy to ignore that voice with a cocktail in her hand and sunglasses on her face.

Before she knows it, the vacation slinks to a close and the Connolly Cup is upon her. The Cup isn't always held in Naples, but with nearly half of the participating players being Neapolitan, it wasn't hard for their father to convince the Fierce Four to hold the tournament in their hometown. Especially with their sponsorship connections. Juliette should be excited about this week—Octavia still talks about how fun the previous year's festivities were in Shanghai. Unfortunately, due to karma, Juliette has found herself on the same team as Luca Kacic.

On her last evening as a solo woman, she makes her way to Karoline's villa, where all the players will be staying during the Cup. It sits off the water, a white-sand path leading to a hidden stretch of beach and delicate waves. She finds the keys under a welcome mat and lets herself in. She claims one of the larger rooms, a boon for arriving a day before everyone else.

The sun sets late, and leaf-patterned shadows creep across the terra-cotta floors. The final rays of gold flash across the expansive kitchen island Juliette doubts any of them will use. She pours a limoncello neat, the icy burn of it sweet against her tongue and down her throat. She shivers, grinning as she pours another into a tulip tasting glass to enjoy on the patio. She slides into a lounge chair, staring up at the blushed lavender sky and watches as it slowly bleeds into indigo. Her eyes slip closed, and she listens to the cries of cicadas, the distant burble of the water, and the sweet rustle of branches. The day's heat lazes on the dark slate of the patio, radiating onto Juliette's skin and bringing the suggestion of sweat to the back of her neck beneath her curls. Tomorrow the villa will echo with shrieks of laughter and accented conversations, but tonight, Juliette enjoys the quiet.

She is half done with her second limoncello when the rumbling of tires on gravel stirs her from her peace. Juliette sits up, glancing down at her phone. The group chat has been silent for two hours, ever since everyone confirmed their flights and arrival times for tomorrow.

Only Luca Kacic hadn't said anything. Her number is the only unsaved one—a petty choice, but she's blocked Kacic everywhere else, so why would she give her the time of day in her phone?

Annoyance prickles beneath her skin as Juliette swings off the lounger and pads back into the house. Light slices across the front windows, and she frowns.

For a moment, Juliette wonders if she's about to get murdered. Panic flashes through her at the thought, and she dives for the kitchen, ripping a knife from the block and holding it in front of her. It isn't unusual for these things to happen; another player was stabbed in the hand by a home invader years ago.

Several quick knocks break the silence.

Juliette narrows her eyes. Intruders don't knock, but maybe they would if they wanted to know if anyone was home. Something heavy hits the ground and Juliette swallows hard, edging closer to the door.

Frosted glass lines both sides, and she can see a shadow pacing back and forth.

Her phone buzzes.

Juliette shrieks and drops the knife. The figure outside stops and Juliette fumbles to get her phone free.

It's the random number she assumed was Kacic's. She declines the call because she's not above being childish.

The knocking begins again in earnest, more akin to pounding. Juliette weighs her options, picking up the knife off the floor. She decides it's much too much of a coincidence for it not to be Kacic at the door, but she keeps the knife in her hand as she swings the door open.

"Oh my God!" Kacic cries, nearly swinging into Juliette with her fist. "Is that a knife?!" She recoils sharply, her mouth agape.

"You're not supposed to be here," Juliette says instead of answering, still brandishing the knife.

Kacic stares at her, blinking so many times she reminds Juliette of a lemur she saw at the zoo once. "What does that mean?" Her voice is rusty and quiet, her brows pitched together in confusion.

Juliette fumbles for her phone, switching the knife to her non-dominant hand to grab it out of her pocket. "Everyone gets here tomorrow," she says. Of course, of all the people to arrive early, it's *Kacic* who shows up without warning. Juliette hadn't planned for her final night of peace to be disturbed, and she certainly hadn't mentally prepared for the sight of her. It's just like Kacic to ruin all of Juliette's best-laid plans.

Kacic opens her mouth to say something and then closes it. Her eyes fall to the phone and Juliette glances at it. She holds it in her left hand, and she remembers, with regret, that she isn't wearing her wrist wrap.

LUCA is exposed to Kacic for the first time.

Juliette shoves her hand back into her pocket. "The door was unlocked, you know," she says, heading back into the villa. She sets the knife on the kitchen island and considers racing upstairs to get her wrist wrap. Kacic grumbles behind her and Juliette glances over her shoulder. She drags her suitcase up the stairs, her tennis bag slung over one shoulder. Juliette wonders how she doesn't tip over the railing, so wildly off-balanced.

Annoyingly, Kacic is several inches taller than Juliette, but thin as a rail. Lanky, lean, and bony in the shoulders, with an awkwardness that hides her agility on court. She vanishes upstairs, grunting and banging the wheels of her case the whole way. Juliette's stomach swoops with the realization that she is here, *alone*, with Kacic.

Juliette digs her fingernails into the stupid name on her wrist and wonders if there's ever been an anti–soulmate—a soulhate. Maybe she and Kacic are the first. She steps onto the patio again and breathes in the humid air, her lungs sticky in her chest. Even though she never goes high in skyscrapers, never lingers near windowsills in hotel rooms and never, ever, climbs another tree, she is still stuck in that same feeling of falling she experienced as a child.

Warm light from the kitchen spills suddenly across the flagstones. Juliette unglues her feet from the ground and rushes back to the lounger, getting adjusted back into it as the sliding door eases open. She stares at the sky, her eyes tracing the patterns of stars in the inky darkness. She grits her teeth as sneakers scuff across the tile.

"Is this the path to the beach?" Kacic asks, her voice a rasping whisper.

Juliette's eyes flick to Kacic, more out of instinct than anything else. She looks exhausted, with deep purple shadows beneath her eyes, a furrow between her brows, and her lips pressed into a thin line. She rolls a water bottle between her palms, her body swallowed by a cozy creamy white sweatshirt. Her hair is twisted into a bun on the top of her head, but strands are falling out of it, floating around her face in honeyed brown frizzes.

"What?" Kacic snaps. Her shoulders cave, a protective gesture that Juliette looks away from.

"It's that way," she says, jerking her chin to the winding path into the trees.

Kacic heads off, arms wrapped around herself as if she's freezing.

Juliette finishes her limoncello, now too warm for her taste. It swirls in her churning stomach like a typhoon. There was something wobbly in Kacic's voice, something Juliette hasn't heard before.

She should leave Kacic alone.

She should go take a shower and wash the sand, sweat, and sunscreen off.

Muttering to herself, she grabs another tulip sipper from the kitchen and pours two fresh glasses of ice-cold limoncello. She continues to mutter to herself about the stupidity of this as she treks down the sandy path to the beach.

The trees shiver and whisper to each other, the lapping waves gossiping right back. The path curves away into a ridge that plunges into a dune and a stretch of uneven shoreline.

Kacic sits on the beach, about halfway to the frothy waves. A crescent moon splashes silvery highlights on the water, and her white hoodie is a beacon against the night.

Juliette jogs down the dune with ease, the sand cupping her and rolling with each step. Kacic doesn't look up as she skids to a halt next to her. She's wrapped her arms around her knees as if she can crunch herself into a tiny ball and disappear into the sand.

"Welcome to Naples," Juliette says, holding out the limoncello.

"What's this?" Kacic asks, glaring incredulously at the glass as if it's going to bite her.

"A drink. Take it." Juliette shakes it in front of her face. The drink splashes along the rim.

Kacic frowns but takes it. "Damn, you're bossy," she mutters, staring down at the liquor.

With a huff, Juliette flops down onto the sand next to her. Nowhere near close enough to touch, but angled so she can see Kacic's face. It's too dark to make out many of her features. Just the silhouette of her face, the curve of her cheek, the little button of her nose, her tongue as she licks her lips.

"Drink it," Juliette demands, setting her glass into the sand. "Slowly!" She grabs Kacic's wrist without thinking as she makes to drink it like a shot of vodka.

An electric jolt rushes through her, lightning-bright, and heat scorches across her skin. She drops Kacic's hand as she flinches away.

Kacic freezes, like a deer caught in headlights. Her breath comes in uneven pants, as if she can't expand her lungs fully for fear of breaking.

Juliette flexes her hand, hating how dizzy she is. For a moment, the roller coaster twists of her stomach that had started with Kacic's arrival had halted. It's the first time she's ever touched Kacic outside of a tennis court. "It's meant to be sipped," Juliette says, her voice too strangled for her liking. She picks up her glass, letting it cool her warm palm.

Kacic doesn't look at her as she slowly lifts the glass to her mouth and sips. Her throat bobs and Juliette licks her sun-chapped lips, a strange heat gathering in her stomach like a storm.

The moment breaks when Kacic recoils back from the glass and screws her eyes shut, tongue darting out as she almost spits the liquor back out. "Lemon?" she accuses.

"What the hell is wrong with you? Too good for citrus?" Juliette snaps, defensive.

Kacic grimaces and sets the glass into the sand. "I hate lemon." She unscrews her water bottle and chugs half of it, then shudders and smacks her lips like a drama queen.

"Whatever. More for me," Juliette says, finishing her drink in two long, slow drags. She grabs Kacic's glass and takes a sip. It only occurs to her then that her mouth is lying where Kacic's had been a moment ago, but she shoves the thought away. Kacic may have ruined her night but she will not ruin a perfect glass of limoncello.

"How many of those have you had?" Kacic asks, a judgmental note to her voice that makes Juliette seethe.

"A couple," she says defiantly, grateful her voice doesn't slur.

She should be pleasantly tipsy. She should be going out into Naples and finding a young, hot thing to bring back to her room and make love to in the salty air.

Instead, she's on the beach with her biggest rival and soulmate. The soulmate she never chose and doesn't want. Juliette grits her teeth, her face blotchy with angry heat. "Why did you come tonight?"

Juliette snaps, turning to face Kacic fully. This is her fault. She ruined Juliette's last night of freedom, and she deserves to know why.

There is another kind of heat boiling low in her stomach. This is the longest she's ever been near Kacic, and something inside of her coils tight at the thought.

Kacic shrugs. "I have nowhere else to go," she says. If she was aiming for nonchalance, she misses by a mile.

"Lonely, Kacic?" Juliette sneers. "None of your friends want to deal with you?"

Kacic glowers. "Something like that," she mutters.

Juliette's breath hisses in and out of her open mouth. Maybe Livia is right. Maybe she is being unreasonable and bitchy, but Kacic makes her blood boil.

Kacic pulls her sleeves over her wrists, fingers curling tightly into the hem. "Why are you here?"

"I'm playing in the Connolly Cup, dumbass," Juliette says, realizing after it comes out of her mouth that Kacic hadn't meant Italy, but rather the beach.

Kacic shoots her a loathing glare. Juliette doesn't back down and stares right back, forcing Kacic to specify. "I meant," she grits out, "why are you here on the beach with me? I thought you couldn't stand me."

"Maybe I'm here to bask in your self-pity?" Juliette snipes.

Kacic twists her head away. "Then go away," she mutters, almost too low for Juliette to hear.

Juliette should leave. She brought Kacic a drink. They exchanged more than ten words. She can scurry away without the guilt of being a bad host. But her limbs are drunk-heavy, and the sand is warm, making it impossible for her to lift out of its soft cocoon.

"I won't apologize for winning," Kacic says suddenly.

Juliette stares at her. "I wouldn't believe you if you tried."

Kacic meets her gaze evenly, her eyes burning with such intensity that Juliette can't find her breath. "What is wrong with you?"

Juliette blinks rapidly, trying to regain her composure, but her brain is sluggish. "What?" she asks stupidly.

Kacic's breath heaves. "I don't know what I did to make you hate me so much."

"You're not the one who lost a Grand Slam final!" Juliette snarls. "You get everything, and for what? You win a few good matches and suddenly everyone says that you're going to be the greatest of all time. The second coming of Aurore Cadieux and Payton Calimeris!" Juliette's hands shake, and she wants to hide them in the sand.

"You think I want this attention?"

"Oh, spare me the pity party." The wind snaps against Juliette's face, crisp compared to the fire that burns on her skin. "I'm sick of it, Kacic. And I'm sick of everyone saying you're the perfect professional and I'm the asshole."

"You started this!" Kacic hisses.

"I did not! You said it was such a shame that I only won because Chen sprained her ankle. Don't pretend that wasn't bitchy."

Kacic blinks. "I was being honest. I wanted to see you guys play a good match. Didn't you want to win fair and square?"

Juliette doesn't deign to respond, glaring at her.

Kacic's lower lip wobbles, a sheen on the edge of it that Juliette can't help but stare at. "Whatever. Why don't you just continue existing as if I don't?"

Juliette shakes her head. "Unbelievable." She watches as understanding flickers over Kacic's face. Her mouth falls open, and she exhales like Juliette punched the air out of her.

"You're jealous." Kacic says it like a revelation, as if she can't believe it.

Now it's Juliette's turn to be sucker punched in the stomach. She can't scoff or deny or even say anything at all. So, she does the next best thing.

She runs away.

NINE

LUCA

"You're jealous," Luca says, the realization illuminating Ricci in sudden and spectacular light. It's strange, the relief flooding through her chest as she swallows the idea that maybe Ricci doesn't hate her just for the sake of hating her.

Ricci's jaw snaps shut, and then she scrambles to her feet. Just like six months ago, in the locker room, Ricci is running away from her. This time, Luca leaps to her feet and chases after her. "Hey, wait, we're not done," she says, grabbing Ricci's shoulder without thinking.

Heat flares across her palm, scalding her skin, but she can't let go. A tug deep in her gut threatens to overwhelm her.

The moment breaks as Ricci spins around and knocks her hand off. "Don't touch me," she snarls. Her curls are frizzy and wild around her face, begging Luca to run her fingers through them. "Why are you here?" Ricci demands. She shoves at Luca's shoulders, not hard, and Luca only sways.

Luca doesn't know what to say. She can't admit that she came to Naples early because she messed up her travel schedule and booked the wrong flight then promptly had a panic attack at the airport because she can't speak a lick of Italian and the only thought that didn't cause her to want to die was coming to Karoline's villa, even though Ricci would be there.

Although seeing Ricci wielding a knife when she'd first opened the door had almost made Luca turn tail and run. Especially seeing her name scrawled black across Ricci's pale wrist for the first time.

The humidity smothers Luca and her pulse throbs, a familiar

tightness in the center of her chest starting to swallow her. "I told you. I have nowhere else to go." But now that Ricci has unintentionally shed light on her feelings, Luca latches onto it. "I want to move past whatever this is," she adds, gesturing between them.

"Why? Why do you care if I'm jealous or hate you? You don't like me either—and don't even try to lie about it," Ricci snaps, running an impatient hand over her hair and shoving strands off her sweaty forehead.

"I don't care how you feel about me," Luca says, knowing it's a lie. Ricci's cheeks blaze pink. Luca is surprised by how easy it is to rile Ricci. Before, she was cold, her words clipped and sharp. Now, her composure is unraveling before Luca's eyes.

"Then what?"

"I don't like when you act like a spoiled brat," Luca says without thinking.

Ricci somehow manages to turn an even darker shade of red. "Fuck you," she hisses through clenched teeth.

"We're soulmates," Luca says, forcing her voice louder, even though it catches in her throat. She has waited so long to say those words. They've been burning a hole in her throat since Ricci cut her off in Australia, and to finally say it out loud is such a relief, like swallowing an ice cube on a hot summer day. "Whether you like it or not, we're going to be bound together." In a fit of wild temptation, Luca almost rips her wrist wrap off and waves Ricci's name in her face.

Ricci jerks her chin away. Luca's heart hammers in her chest, the silence between them suffocating. Then she licks her lips and looks back at Luca. For a moment, Luca lets her hopes rise that perhaps, finally, Ricci will see sense. Luca has longed to find her soulmate for years. Alongside her dream for a Grand Slam, one of her deepest desires has been to find the one woman designed for her, the one who will love her unconditionally. And soulmates are meant to be evenly matched, opposite puzzle pieces that fit together and make each other better. Maybe Luca does need more of Ricci's fiery passion, just as Ricci needs a bit of Luca's calm focus.

"That wasn't my choice, and even if it was, I never would have chosen you," she says, the furious heat of her voice pitching low.

The words are a cruel knife, slicing through Luca's carefully maintained armor and carving through the softest, most vulnerable part of her. And suddenly Luca is back in the locker room. Rejected by her own soulmate, again. It shouldn't hurt as much as it did the first time, and yet it does. Instead of getting easier to swallow, the pain compounds on itself, threatening to crush Luca into a fine powder.

This time, when Ricci walks away, Luca does not follow.

JULIETTE

Despite chugging an entire bottle of water and popping more painkillers than would be recommended by a doctor, Juliette still wakes up with a massive hangover.

The headache throbs behind her temple, and she throws her arm over her eyes, trying to protect them from the sun's violent assault.

She forces herself to sit up, and the bedroom spins. She swears and clutches her head. What had happened last night?

She flails her arms out, but there is no other warm body in the bed. There goes that theory.

Juliette is halfway to the bathroom when fragments of the previous night flicker through her head. She splashes cold water on her face and stares up at herself. Her hair is a tangled nest, falling out of the bun around her shoulder. It'll be annoying to brush out.

"You are never drinking again," Juliette tells her reflection, pointing the finger at her face. "Never." She winces, remembering the poor choice of words she spat at Kacic.

I never would have chosen you.

Juliette groans and drops her head to her forearms as pain blisters through her skull. Before she can even think about making amends with Kacic, she needs painkillers.

She barely makes it down the stairs without falling head over heels. She stumbles into the kitchen and freezes. Kacic is standing there, a glass of water in one hand. She's either soaked with sweat or she dove into the pool fully clothed.

"You're up early," Kacic says coolly, her eyes pinning Juliette to the spot. Her shoulders are stiff, and her knuckles are white around her glass.

"Headache," Juliette mutters, finally making her feet move in the direction of the medicine cabinet. The sun slaps her in the face and she squints at it, offended by its audacity to shine when she feels like this.

"Too much to drink last night?" Kacic asks with a self-satisfied smirk.

Juliette huffs. She would rather not be reminded of the previous night. She grabs the ibuprofen and slams the cabinet door closed. It's too loud and she winces, rubbing her aching eyes.

Kacic opens the fridge and ponders its contents for a moment before letting it fall shut with a frown.

"Hungry?" Juliette asks. Kacic turns back to her and crosses her arms over her chest, leaning on one hip. Her gaze is unreadable. Juliette pops a few painkillers dry, not wanting to step around Kacic to get a glass.

Kacic stares at her as if she's waiting for Juliette to offer a solution. Juliette had planned on visiting her favorite café this morning. She decides not to invite Kacic. She may feel bad for what she said to Kacic last night, but she'd rather have a peaceful morning without Kacic's scrutiny.

Juliette wishes Kacic had picked a shirt that was a different color, preferably one that wouldn't turn see-through the moment it got wet. Sweat runs down her temple, and sticky strands of her drenched hair cling to the curve of her throat and her shoulders. It's distracting, especially the beads of sweat on her shoulders, her collarbones . . .

Juliette turns and heads out of the kitchen, trying to ignore the uncomfortable knots in her stomach. "Go take a shower." Juliette pauses, glancing over her shoulder. "You're very sweaty," she adds at Kacic's furrowed brow.

Kacic looks down at herself as if she's just realized she's dripping.

Juliette follows her eyes and tries not to swallow too obviously as her gaze traces the dip of Kacic's waist and the strip of skin above the band of her loose black shorts, the lines of her abs.

She snaps her gaze back to Kacic's before she says something stupid and then she realizes she's been caught staring. Kacic's eyes widen, and Juliette watches her swallow, clearly startled.

Juliette scowls and storms away with as much dignity as she can muster.

TEN

JULIETTE

By the time Juliette has showered the sweat from the previous night off, detangled her hair, and flopped into the pool lounger, her headache is almost entirely gone.

She apologizes to the sun for hating it earlier and tilts her face into the rays, soaking in the happiness. She almost misses the soft hiss of the sliding door opening and the rustle of someone stepping out. She waits, wondering if Kacic is going to say something. She can feel Kacic's eyes tracing her face, and she fights the urge to swallow, suddenly self-conscious.

"Take a picture, it'll last longer," Juliette says finally.

Kacic inhales sharply.

Juliette opens one eye, glancing sidelong at her. Kacic is picking at the skin around her thumbs, a faint blush across her high cheekbones and the bridge of her nose. It could be from the heat, but Juliette lets a smirk curve on her mouth.

"Like what you see?" she asks, just to see Kacic's teeth clench.

"You have an eyelash on your cheek," Kacic says primly.

Juliette rubs her cheek, which makes Kacic click her tongue and step forward.

"Wrong side," Kacic murmurs, leaning down. Her hair swings over her shoulder, curtaining them. The sun glints on the silky strands, her fair lashes white in the light, her lips slightly parted and a delicate pink. *She's so pretty.*

Juliette tenses, her eyes widening as Kacic tenderly brushes her thumb across her cheekbone. Juliette's every thought blanks as heat

pools in her belly. Kacic holds out her thumb, a long dark lash clinging to the tip.

"Make a wish," Kacic says, soft as if sharing a secret, close enough
to be heart-poundingly intimate.

Juliette closes her eyes, and she gently blows the lash away.

I wish I could stop falling.

It's a strange wish, one that comes out of nowhere, but those are
the words in her head as she watches the lash flutter away. Luckily,
Kacic doesn't ask and retreats a safe distance away, tucking her hair
behind her ear.

"I didn't really mean to be such a bitch last night," Juliette blurts
out, the uncomfortable knots in her stomach tightening to nausea.

Kacic scuffs the toe of her sneaker against the sandy gravel.
"Well, you're pretty good at it."

Juliette rises.

"I was drunk," she says, knowing it's not an excuse, but she
doesn't have the words to apologize.

The full force of Kacic's narrowed gaze lands on her, and all her
words die in her throat. "What do you want me to say? Let's be best
friends and frolic in a field somewhere? You've made it very clear how
you feel about me."

There is a scathing finality to the words, and Juliette winces.
"Listen, I didn't—I don't—" she stutters, unsure what to say.

"Don't what, Ricci?" Kacic demands.

She doesn't like the scrutiny of Kacic's gaze, as if she sees through
Juliette's skin and bones to the rotten edges of her. Her stomach
twists and she swallows, tasting bile in the back of her throat. It's
strange hearing her name on Kacic's tongue. She can't formulate any
thoughts when Kacic is staring at her like that.

She can't tell Kacic that she said those things because her drunken
self has no filter and saying those mean things betrays how much she
hates and wants Kacic in equal measure. That she makes Juliette hot
under the collar, her skin prickly, and her throat tight. So instead she
says, "It's complicated." It's a bad excuse, and shame snares in her
chest.

Kacic scoffs. "Complicated?"

"Whatever," Juliette mutters, giving up for now. She needs a coffee to even attempt to be coherent.

Juliette storms into the house, yanking her satchel off the counter and hiking it over her shoulder. She pulls out her pair of rounded John Lennon sunglasses from the pocket and slides them on her face. She pauses in front of the mirror hanging by the door and scrapes her curls into a scrunchie, fiddling with a stubborn curl that's trying to go rogue.

"You're so vain," Kacic says from where she stands at the sliding glass doors.

"Thank you," Juliette says, flashing her a smile that is all teeth. She slams the door on her way out, playing with the keys as she heads for the bikes around the side of the villa.

An SUV pulls up in the drive, bouncing along the gravel, and all Juliette's seething anger and guilt vanish the moment the car stops, the doors pop open, and her sisters spill out. Claudia bounds over to her, wrapping her in a hug with a squeal. "Surprise!"

"I thought you were coming later?" Juliette asks as she melts into the hug. Claudia pulls back but keeps an arm around Juliette's shoulders.

"Livia got us earlier flights," Octavia says, tossing her dark hair over her shoulders. Unlike the rest of them, she straightens her curls. The humidity is working hard to bring some of the curl back in the form of frizz, even though she's done her best to tame it into chic, long layers and curtain bangs.

"And we come bearing coffees and breakfast," a familiar voice says, the backseat door closing to reveal Leonardo Mantovani. Ranked number ten and one of the men's tours' biggest heartthrobs, Leo has been dating Octavia for nearly six years. He slings a tattooed arm around Octavia's shoulders. He's more handsome than sin, and Juliette has certainly heard enough grumbling about how unfair it is that ice queen Octavia Ricci pulled him.

Hell, Juliette had a crush when she first clapped eyes on him. Until she found out that Leo had her sister's name on his wrist. Then her desire to jump his bones had fled and she only saw him as a brother.

The front door opens and Juliette freezes. Claudia looks behind her and Juliette catches the edge of her mischievous grin. "Hello there, Luca!" she says, slipping into English.

Sometimes Juliette really hates her.

"Hello, Claudia," Kacic says. "How are you?"

"Oh, I'm just fine," Claudia purrs, and Juliette rolls her eyes. "How are you? Hope Jules didn't bite. She's testy before her coffee."

Juliette glances back at Kacic, who is awkwardly loitering on the step.

She looks at Juliette, and for a moment, Juliette thinks Kacic is going to say something snippy and mean. Or perhaps tell Claudia that Juliette was a giant bitch.

Instead, Kacic flashes a secretive half-smile at Juliette, and her stomach swoops. "She welcomed me to Italy with limoncello, so I can't complain." Juliette notices a dimple pop on the corner of Kacic's mouth. It's strange to see it in real life.

"Oh, how sweet of her," Claudia says, nudging Juliette's side.

"Enough chitchat, the coffee is getting cold!" Octavia says, now balancing four to-go cups in her arms. Leo has several brown bags in his arms. "Sorry, Luca, we didn't know you were here, otherwise we would've asked what you wanted. You can have Claudia's coffee; she doesn't need any more caffeine."

"Hey!" Claudia protests.

Kacic laughs. "Not a problem. I don't drink coffee."

Juliette busies herself by relieving Octavia of two of the cups. "Come on, let's eat on the patio," she says, brushing Kacic's shoulder as she moves around her and into the house. In the whirlwind of dumping out the pastries and fruit, somehow Claudia has maneuvered it so Juliette is at the end of the table across from Kacic.

"What is this exactly?" Kacic asks, looking down at the lobster tail–shaped pastry on her paper plate.

"It's *sfogliatelle*, a pastry, obviously," Juliette says. "It has ricotta and candied orange peel in the custard." Juliette's mouth waters. The ridges are dusted with sugar, flaking off as she cuts through the shell with practiced ease and the custard cream seeps out along the rich brown pastry. She groans softly as she eats each bite, the sweet and tangy taste vibrant across her tongue.

When she looks up at Kacic, she has an odd look on her face. Her eyes trace down Juliette's throat and she has stopped eating. "Kuna for your thoughts?" Juliette asks, drawing Kacic's gaze. Surprise flickers across her face and Juliette tries to smother her smile.

"That's pretty cheap," Kacic says, sounding oddly delighted.

"Is it?" Juliette tilts her head. She doesn't know what the conversion rate is, her knowledge only extends to knowing that Croatia doesn't use euros. "Anyway, you looked deep in thought."

Kacic's mouth thins and she shoves a forkful of pastry into her mouth. Cream catches on the corner of her mouth and Juliette suddenly wants to lick it off, heat burning in her stomach. "How do you like it?"

Kacic shrugs, her tongue swiping along her mouth. "Citrusy," she says.

"Try the coffee. It balances the flavor." Juliette pushes her cup across the table to her. "I think you'll like it."

Kacic carefully takes the coffee, ensuring their fingers don't touch. "How would you know what I like?"

"It doesn't taste like lemon," Juliette says, smirking.

Kacic rolls her eyes and takes a sip. Juliette watches her lips curve over the edge of the cup and she tries not to think about how her mouth was there a moment ago. Kacic's lashes flutter as she briefly closes her eyes, considering the taste. She doesn't screw up her nose or shudder in disgust. Then she sets the cup down and slides it back to Juliette. "It's good," she concedes.

Juliette lifts a brow. "Just good?"

"As I said, I don't like coffee that much."

Juliette cannot fathom that. "Is it the flavor? Not milky enough? Not sweet enough?"

Kacic's eyes flash, her jaw ticking. "It makes my anxiety worse."

Juliette startles, then shocks into stillness at the admission. "Oh."

She searches for words, guilt pulsing in her chest at having pressed Kacic too hard. "I'm sorry, I didn't know."

"Why would you?" Kacic grits out through her teeth. "It's not like you choose to know me."

Juliette flinches, her own words thrown back in her face. She looks down, shame making her flush. "I'm sor—" she starts, but Claudia smacks her hands down on the table and brings everyone to attention.

"Let's go get the bags and then, I think it's beach time!"

ELEVEN

JULIETTE

Juliette avoids Kacic and busies herself with throwing out the trash. When she gets back outside, the familiar bickering she's known all her life washes over her and she pushes the breakfast conversation out of her head.

"I swear to god, Claudia, we're here for five days. Did you need your entire apartment?" Octavia is saying. Her words are immediately followed by a heavy thump and a flurry of curses.

"You did that on purpose!" Claudia accuses in a high-pitched voice.

"I did not! But serves you right, bringing all of your shit from London."

Claudia whines and bounces up and down on one foot, her giant green suitcase tipped over after having presumably fallen on her other foot.

"Come on, I thought you wanted to get to the beach," Juliette grouses, crossing her arms over her chest.

Octavia rolls her eyes. "Tell her to stop being so dramatic."

"Can I help at all?" a timid voice asks from behind Juliette. Goddamn Kacic.

"Oh, of course!" Claudia grins, her foot landing on the ground as she gives up on the ruse of being exceedingly dramatic.

Juliette forces her shoulders down from her ears. She refuses to jump every time Kacic is near. Claudia shoves her backpack into Juliette's arms, a slyness to her smile that Juliette hates. Once they're laden with various bags and gear, Juliette bolts to the villa and heads upstairs.

"Put me as far away from those two as possible," Claudia says, heading up to the third floor. "I do not want my beauty sleep disturbed by their fucking."

"Claudia!"

Juliette snorts at Octavia's outraged yell.

Claudia smirks over her shoulder and takes the room on the top floor with a view of the water. She drops her stuff unceremoniously onto the ground and rushes to the balcony, tossing the doors open and stepping out onto it.

A bag drops to the floor, and Juliette glances behind her. "I assume this is hers?" Kacic has another bag over her shoulder, black and monogrammed with the number eight. But the one she dropped is vibrant red and covered with various pins from Claudia's favorite anime.

"Yeah," Juliette says, her mouth dry as she stares at the soft blush that covers Luca's cheeks and the bridge of her nose.

"Okay, bye," Kacic says, shuffling from the room awkwardly.

"I still don't see why you hate her. She's very pretty."

Juliette spins around. Claudia leans against the bedpost to kick off her shoes. "You don't know her," Juliette says flatly.

"You don't either." Claudia rips the scrunchie out of her hair and her blond curls tumble around her shoulders, wild and messy. "Come on, tell me, why is she here with you? We were supposed to arrive first as a surprise. It's why Livia changed the flights." Claudia shimmies out of her sweatpants, tossing them onto her bed as she goes to her suitcase.

"She got here last night," Juliette says, leaning back against the wall. She nearly knocks down a painting in her effort to remain cool and collected.

"Last night?" Claudia's eyes spark and her brows raise. She pulls out her bikini and Juliette turns around.

"She said she didn't have anywhere to go."

"So she came to you?" There is thinly veiled excitement in her voice.

Juliette rolls her eyes. "No, Karoline probably told her she could stay."

"All right, you can turn around." Juliette does as Claudia shrugs on an old T-shirt over her head. "Well, I'm going to rally everyone to go to the beach. You want to come?"

"Someone has to be the greeting party," Juliette says. "You go with Octavia and Leo. I've been at the beach all week."

Claudia slides her flip-flops on and loudly clomps over to her. She tucks a loose curl behind Juliette's ear and smiles. "I can tell. You're very tan." She taps the tip of her nose. "Sunscreen?"

"Always," Juliette says, rolling her eyes. "Stop mothering me and go swim." She lightly shoves Claudia out the door and can't help but smile as Claudia cackles with glee.

Octavia tries to play hostess, but Juliette uses Leo to shoo her to the beach. She probably should have ordered groceries the night before, but Kacic's arrival rattled her. Or so she tells herself, because she could have ordered them earlier, but she isn't in the mood to be responsible for that.

The rest of the players chosen for the Connolly Cup trickle in slowly. The youngest of the women is Bulgarian phenomenon Nadia Valcheva. Or maybe it's her twin, Tatiana. Juliette can't tell, because she's never played against her before. Nineteen and quiet, there's something about her wide eyes as she takes in the villa that makes Juliette think of a ghost.

Arriving right after her is the second best player in the world, Zoe Almasi. She's Claudia's close friend, and Juliette greets her warmly.

"Claudia is at the beach if you want to see her," Juliette tells her as they bring the last of her bags in.

"Oh," Zoe says quietly. Despite being a fierce competitor, she's soft-spoken. The direct opposite of Claudia in every way, and sometimes, Juliette wonders how they even get along. She fixes Juliette with a neutral smile. "Thanks." She rubs her neck as if it aches. "See you later." Then she heads up the stairs.

Now that the majority of the women have arrived, Juliette sits on one of the many couches in the lounge and kicks her feet up with her laptop. She needs to edit the photos she took during her week-long solo vacation. She usually prefers to use film, since the first camera her mother ever gave her was from the 1980s, but Livia has been pestering her about more content for her Instagram, and it's easier to use a digital camera.

She pops her headphones on, listening to her newest curated playlist. It's mindless work, moving all the files off her camera and into the correct folders, so her mind slips into thinking about Kacic. In the kitchen, glistening with sweat and lightly panting, how would she taste after her run? Of sunscreen and sweat, washing off easily with whatever soap she uses. Instead of sweat, Juliette pictures water splashing down the curve of Kacic's throat, across her collarbones, running down her sternum to her belly and lower . . .

Juliette blinks, recoiling out of those thoughts. She *can't* think of Luca Kacic like that. Maybe if they weren't rivals, she could consider sleeping with her and then moving on. Maybe if they weren't soulmates, she could pursue a sexual relationship, but Juliette knows most people have *expectations* about their soulmate. They want the romantic relationship, and Juliette won't commit to that.

Hands land on her shoulders and Juliette startles, ripping her headphones off. "What the fuck?!" she screams, twisting around to find Remi Rowland smirking at her.

"I've been trying to get your attention for like, fifteen minutes, Jules," Remi says, skirting around the couch to plop down on the opposite one.

Remi Rowland is the golden girl of the United States and, infuriatingly, a spot ahead of Juliette in the rankings. Remi was the first of their generation to shoot to the top of the rankings, hitting the Top Ten before her nineteenth birthday. The only ding on her career so far is her inability to close a Grand Slam final, but at least she always chokes in spectacular fashion. Like when she won five straight games in the second set of her first Grand Slam final and then double faulted four times to give one of the breaks back. Then, her nerves got the best of her and she lost thirteen straight games, gifting Zoe Almasi the French Open and the number one ranking.

Unlike Juliette, though, Remi has never been anything but easy-going about her big losses. Gracious in defeat and oozing charm no matter the scenario.

She grins with her perfectly shaped and plush mouth like she knows something Juliette doesn't. They haven't always been friendly. Juliette's temper clashes too much with Remi's outgoing and bright persona for them to be anything more than acquaintances. But in the last six months, Remi has seemed to be on a mission to be chummy and friendly with her. "So," Remi drawls in her sweet southern accent. "You and Kacic, huh?" Remi toys with one of her box braids.

Juliette tenses. "What about us?" she asks through gritted teeth, and Remi's smile, somehow, widens.

"How long has she been here with you?" Remi asks, leaning forward. The sun warms her deep brown skin and catches on her high, chiseled cheekbones, illuminating her sparkling brown eyes. Juliette itches to take a picture. This slant of light highlights her features so beautifully, and her fans, the "Rowdy Rowlanders," would love to see it. No wonder she's always featured in sports magazines and New Balance commercials.

"Since last night," Juliette says, crossing her arms over her chest.

"Have you two slept together yet?"

Juliette's jaw drops. "What?"

Remi waggles her brows like she's twelve again. "Did you?" she asks impatiently.

As if she has any right to know.

"Why would you ask that? And why would I tell you?" Juliette grinds out.

Remi grins. "So, you did."

"No!" Anger burns in the back of her throat, and she's sure a flush is crawling across her face. "I will not be sleeping with Luca Kacic," she clarifies sharply.

Remi raises an eyebrow, judgmental and thoroughly unconvinced at the same time. "She is your soulmate, isn't she?" Her chin jerks down to Juliette's left arm.

"None of your business," Juliette snaps. So this is why Remi is suddenly interested in her. All for the gossip and drama.

Remi, having perfected the art of looking extremely skeptical and also completely sympathetic, gives her a look. "Sex with your soulmate is nice, that's all I'm saying."

There is a sudden quiet tenderness to Remi's voice that makes Juliette pause. She blinks, suddenly uncomfortable with how weirdly open Remi is being. She has been dodging questions about her soulmate for years, even though she's confirmed she's in a relationship. "You found your soulmate?"

Remi shakes her head. "Oh, no. You do not get to ask questions about me when you're in denial."

"I hate Kacic," Juliette says, but it sounds lame, even to her.

"Right," Remi says slowly, drawing out the word.

The sound of footsteps approaching ends the conversation, so Juliette doesn't dignify Remi with a response.

Zoe rounds the corner with Kacic, her hands moving animatedly as she tells Kacic something. As if drawn by magnets, Kacic's eyes slide to Juliette and her lashes flutter as she blinks rapidly. She's wearing a bikini now, stark black against her pale skin, and Juliette forces herself to look away.

"Hey, girls," Zoe says, leaning on the couch back, close to Juliette. Her long, sable-black hair tumbles over her shoulder. Her dark brown eyes are brighter now compared to before, and she arches one bushy but artfully manicured brow.

"How was your flight?" Juliette asks.

Zoe shakes her head. "Didn't take a flight. A train from London." She fiddles with the gold rings on her fingers. "Long but peaceful."

Maybe Juliette could do that to avoid planes.

Zoe looks from Juliette to Remi. "We're heading to the beach. Want to come?"

Remi hops to her feet. "Oh, hell yeah. I need some sun." She stretches, her crop top riding up. Juliette glances behind Zoe to see

Kacic standing by the kitchen island. She fidgets with her fingers, a nervous tick, perhaps. One Juliette has never noticed because she usually sees Kacic with a racket in her hand.

"I'll join later. I need to get something to Livia." Juliette glances down to see her files have loaded and Lightroom is up and running.

"Don't wait too long. It's gorgeous out," Zoe says.

Juliette glances back at Kacic, noticing all the uneven tan lines that fade from cream to tan, a gradient in some places. "Don't forget sunscreen," she tells Kacic. "You'll need it."

Kacic frowns, a wrinkle appearing between her brows. "I haven't forgotten." She sniffs, looking away. She shuffles her straight honey-brown hair over her shoulder, pulling her sunglasses down from the top of her head and onto her face.

Juliette rolls her eyes and pulls her headphones back on, cranking up the music. She feels the heat of Kacic's gaze on her, even long after she leaves.

TWELVE

JULIETTE

Juliette doesn't go to the beach. The idea of having to interact with others when her head is stuffed to the brim with confusing thoughts of Kacic seems like torture. Especially when Kacic is going to be there, sweaty and wearing hardly any clothes.

Instead, she finishes editing her photos and shoots them off to Livia, who responds within nanoseconds with the winky face emoji. Then she spends time on the loungers by the pool, soaking in the sun. She must have fallen asleep, because she wakes up to the sound of laughter carrying up the path, and the sun has slunk beneath the trees, honeyed orange rays blinding her.

She rubs her eyes and sits up in time to see Leo carrying Octavia on his back. She is grinning more than Juliette has seen in months, and her usually straight ironed glossy hair is curling from the sea salt. Claudia has her arm threaded through Remi's, and they skip toward the house.

Zoe is talking to Kacic, and she says something that makes Kacic laugh. A sharp feeling carves through Juliette's stomach, like she's missed a stair. Kacic's smile is luminous, something carefree in the honking noise of her laughter.

"Jules!" Octavia shouts, sounding surprised. "Why didn't you come to the beach?" She hops off Leo's back, but he wraps his arm around her to keep her close.

"Didn't want to get sandy," Juliette says, which is partly true.

"Where is a great place to eat? I'm starving," Remi says, untangling herself from Claudia. She sits down on the lounger next to

Juliette and flops dramatically across her lap. "I'm slowly dying," she says, laying a hand over her forehead and lolling her tongue out of her mouth.

Juliette considers shoving her off, but she pinches her side instead. Remi squeaks, jolting upright. "You'll be fine until we shower," Juliette says, brushing a patch of sand off Remi's shoulder.

"It has to be a vegan place," another voice says.

Juliette twists around to see the final member of the team slip onto the patio. Chen Xinya is the oldest player at this Cup at twenty-eight years old, and she's been on tour since she was thirteen. Like many top players, her meteoric rise to the top has been well-documented, especially as one of the best Chinese players in decades. Then, at twenty-two, she dropped out of the tour and into oblivion. No one knew what happened. And no one dared to ask when she returned two years later with chopped bleach-blond hair, dozens of piercings, and a completely new team.

Now, Xinya seems to be back to her natural color and minimal jewelry, with her long, silky black hair and only an industrial earring remaining in her left ear. More recently, her ankle has healed well from when she twisted it against Juliette in Guadalajara.

As Claudia and Octavia argue about which restaurant will be best for all the dietary restrictions they have, Juliette leans back and catches sight of Kacic standing a bit apart from the group. She is looking into the rippling pool water, facing away from Juliette. Kacic's whole back is red, from the dip in her spine up to the nape of her neck. Clearly, she hadn't taken Juliette's warning about sunscreen seriously.

Serves her right.

Still, Juliette can't help but feel the odd desire to cup her hand over the back of her neck, to feel the heat. Perhaps dig her thumb in to see Kacic's skin blanch white and count how long it takes to return to the burnt ruddy color.

Kacic turns and Juliette looks away before she is caught staring.

LUCA

She should have listened to Ricci.

The Italian sun is brutal. She thought she'd be fine with the sunscreen she'd slathered on after her shower that morning, but Luca is burnt to a crisp.

Regardless, the sun has sunk pleasantly into her skin, warming her muscles and loosening the tension from her body. She loves the way the sun glazes her skin, even if she knows it'll hurt later. By the time they reach the restaurant, her skin is uncomfortably tight.

Luca can't remember the last time she was on vacation. And while this technically isn't a vacation, it certainly feels like one. She finds herself between Chen Xinya and Octavia Ricci at dinner, the food and wine flowing as everyone talks over each other.

After the first course, Octavia leans into her space. "I am sorry if my sister's been rude," she says, grabbing a hunk of Parmesan focaccia and delicately ripping off a piece before dipping it into a bowl of herbs and olive oil.

Luca struggles to find words, and Octavia takes her silence with a wry curl of her lips. She thinks of earlier, when Ricci had encouraged her to take a sip of her coffee. It had seeped across her tongue, bold but sweet. Slightly bitter, but not enough to be unpleasant. That's what Ricci's personality is like, but she can't explain that to her sister. "She's fine," Luca says finally, wishing Xinya would lean over and save her from having to talk to Octavia. Unfortunately, Xinya isn't very talkative on the best of days and ignores her.

"Look, I know it's none of my business," Octavia continues, pausing to dust bread crumbs off her hands, "but for what it's worth, she isn't all bad and I hope you don't think less of us because of her. Juliette is . . . " She trails off with a wince.

Perhaps she's had too much wine.

"Well, you and Claudia don't have to worry. I can be an adult and professional, even if she can't," Luca says, reaching for her water.

Octavia sighs. In the low lamplight of the restaurant, her eyes are even more piercingly green, especially with her flutter of ink-dark lashes and smoked-out eyeliner. It's hard to look away from her. She has an intensity that doesn't fade, even when she's off the court. "Good," she says, finally looking away from Luca and releasing her from the gravity of her gaze.

Luca glances down the table at Ricci. She's deep in conversation with Remi, listening intently and then chuckling at something she's said. As if she knows Luca is looking, her head twists and she catches Luca's eye.

Ricci raises an eyebrow and Luca bites the inside of her cheek, looking away sharply.

"Octavia," Luca says, curiosity outweighing her anxiety.

Octavia cocks her head, brows lifting in silent question.

"You were saying that Juliette was something. What were you going to say?"

Octavia's expression remains smooth and unreadable. Her gaze flicks over Luca's shoulder to the end of the table, presumably to her younger sister. It's quick, subtle, and if Luca wasn't staring at Octavia, she would have missed it.

"She's complicated." Octavia pauses, pursing her glossy lips. "No, that's not quite it. Juliette has always been a little different. Maybe because she's younger, maybe because she's been babied, maybe because she was born that way. She may not act like it, but she's sensitive, and she doesn't like that about herself."

Luca furrows her brow, unsure of why Octavia is telling her this. Perhaps this is how siblings behave with other people, spilling details about their personalities without thinking. Luca wouldn't know; Nicky is the closest thing she has to a sibling. "Okay," she says slowly, and Octavia gives a little shake of her head, pieces of her bangs falling across her cheek. She brushes them back impatiently.

"Juliette is tough to get to know, Luca. So, don't feel bad that she won't let you in." Octavia gently pats her hand, and when Luca says nothing else, she turns back to Leo.

Luca sips her water, glancing at Ricci again. She looks carefree and happy here. Her head tilts back as she laughs, her eyes scrunching up and her nose doing an adorable little wrinkle. Maybe she shouldn't find it as endearing as she does, but Luca's stomach does a funny little flip.

She forces her gaze away. She cannot be distracted by Ricci, not even on vacation.

THIRTEEN

LUCA

Later that night, when she finally collapses into bed, Luca is pleasantly sun-sleepy. However, every time she starts to doze, her burnt skin protests and wakes her.

"Ugh," she mutters as she pads downstairs for ice. She had scoured through the villa's cabinets earlier for aloe but found none.

The downstairs is quiet and still. The air is cool, making her shiver. It's both pleasant and unnerving. It isn't the worst burn she's experienced, but it is beginning to ache, as all sunburns do after a few hours.

She slips the loose straps of her pajama tank top down her shoulders to dangle against her biceps. She fumbles through the freezer, wincing as she bends and causes the burn to ripple, but she manages to gather a bag of ice.

"What are you doing?"

Luca turns too sharply and winces. Ricci flicks on the light, and Luca squints. She fights the urge to cover herself and hide her shameful sunburn.

"I told you to wear sunscreen," Ricci says quietly as her eyes trace over Luca's collarbones.

Luca shrugs and hisses through her teeth at the movement. "I know, I was stupid."

"Supremely," Ricci agrees. She's barely wearing any clothes, just like earlier that morning, except her silk sleep shorts and button-down are navy instead of plaid.

Luca looks away and rests the bag of ice on one of her burnt shoulders but instantly regrets it.

She gasps out in agony, and the bag slides from her skin as she lets go. The ice is too cold, doubling the burn. It crunches as it smacks against the terra-cotta. She curses, waving her hand over the burn as if that will help ease the sting.

"Sit down, dumbass," Ricci says, striding into the kitchen and ripping the refrigerator open.

Luca stays standing. She won't be bossed around by Ricci, especially not when she's insulting her.

Ricci turns back to her. They're quite close now. "Sit," Ricci demands again, gesturing to the stools. There's an edge to her voice that has goose bumps prickling along Luca's arms. She's holding a clear bottle of what looks like gel.

Luca narrows her eyes at Ricci but pulls out one of the stools and sits with her back to Ricci. "Is that aloe?" she asks, trying to distract herself from the jitters coming to life in her stomach.

"It is." She hears the cap opening and the squelch of gel. "It's going to hurt for a minute," she warns.

Luca breathes in deep but tenses, curling her fingers into her knees. It hits her that Ricci is going to touch her, to *help* her.

Ricci's touch is electric against her skin.

Luca jolts almost off the stool, pain slashing across her sensitive skin, blotting out everything. But Ricci keeps her palm pressed firmly against her shoulder, holding Luca down, grounding her. She hisses through her clenched teeth and swallows the tiny whimper that threatens to undo her.

"Are you all right?" Ricci asks, her voice a low rasp.

"Yeah." Luca breathes out, relief relaxing the tension out of her shoulder. Now that the shock of the cold aloe is over, Ricci's palm creates a patch of soothed skin. She can't help but wonder *why* Ricci is helping her.

Ricci's hand moves slowly, gently, circling over her left shoulder blade first. It's safe territory, but even that causes an undeniable burst of desire and agony in Luca's chest. She remembers Octavia's words at dinner and wonders if this is what she meant. Perhaps Ricci is all talk and no bite.

Well, the bite from Ricci's words still hurt, even if Luca wishes they wouldn't.

But these actions are sweet, almost caring. So different from when Ricci taunted her, digging into Luca and hitting her deepest insecurity. She can almost trick herself into believing that Ricci is doing this because Luca is her soulmate, not just because she's in pain and Ricci feels bad.

She breathes harshly through her teeth. Ricci's free hand moves Luca's hair over her shoulder, her thumb sweeping across the back of her neck. Every inch of Luca's body buzzes, as if Ricci's touch reverberates through every nerve ending. She is grateful that Ricci can't see her face as she nearly crumples into thousands of pieces, a cry half-caught, strangled, in the back of her throat. Luca doesn't want Ricci to stop touching her and that want cleaves through all of her defenses.

Ricci makes a soft humming noise, her aloe-covered palm cupping the back of Luca's neck, her thumb arcing up to curve below her ear.

Luca bites her lip and hunches forward. Ricci's thumb digs in, and she closes her eyes, pain and pleasure twisting together in an elegant dance.

And then her hand is gone. The gel bottle squeaks, then both of Ricci's hands land on her shoulders. Lightning sizzles through every nerve, and Luca exhales heavily, lower lip viciously caught in her upper teeth. The sensations ripple through her, and Luca wants Ricci to touch every part of her, to unravel Luca with this same tender care.

Ricci stills.

"Come on, Ricci," Luca urges, but it feels wrong to use her last name in this intimate moment.

Juliette. Her thumb sweeps across her wrist wrap. Heat builds beneath it even though that patch of skin was protected from the sun.

The ache of the burn returns, twice as bad as before now that she's come to expect the soothing gel to distract her.

"How far down does the sunburn go?" Juliette's hands curve along her shoulders.

Luca breathes out softly. Then, with more courage than she usually has, she pulls her tank top off, clutching it to her chest to cover her breasts.

Juliette whistles. "Oh."

Heat blooms through Luca that has nothing to do with the sunburn. She holds her breath, closes her eyes. Juliette pauses and both of them hang on the edge of this moment. Is it too much? Luca's eyes sting as she tries to brace for another rejection.

Then, Juliette's hands move down her back, still so achingly gentle, the gel making them glide. Juliette's fingers skate down her ribs, her sides, to her hips. Luca bites her lip, sighing through her nose as the cool gel soothes her inflamed skin.

Juliette's thumbs brush across the dimples at the base of her spine, and Luca whimpers. She never wants Juliette's hands to leave her skin.

"Feels good, doesn't it?" Juliette's voice is a low purr, her breath a hot puff against the back of Luca's neck. She doesn't even know when Juliette got that close, but she can feel her body heat, hear the whisper of her silk shirt. Luca wants to curl up against her and be held.

The best she can do for now is lean back. With each panting gasp, she can smell the suggestion of whatever citrus-scented haircare product Juliette uses. "Keep going. Please," Luca whispers.

Juliette's breath catches, ragged and rough. Luca isn't the only one effected by this. She hadn't considered that Juliette might be enjoying this too. Excitement zips up Luca's spine, and she shudders.

Juliette rubs more gel onto Luca's shoulders. Her thumbs rub tiny circles into her skin, and Luca goes boneless. The gel has sunk in and taken most of the sting out of the burn.

Luca's breath evens out as Juliette continues to caress her skin. She doesn't know how long they stay there, indulging in this moment, but for the first time in days, the buzzing in Luca's head quiets.

Juliette slowly slides her hands over the crest of Luca's shoulders, sliding across her collarbones. Luca holds her breath and silently pleads for Juliette's hands to continue their exploration. Juliette sucks in a sharp gasp, and heat boils in Luca's stomach at the thought of Juliette's hands elsewhere.

Juliette's hand splays and treks down Luca's sternum. The gel is tacky now, and the slide isn't perfect. The calluses on Juliette's palms catch on her skin, and Luca gasps, lowering her arms and exposing herself to Juliette's hands. Juliette's fingers and palm curve to cup Luca's left breast, so close to her nipple that Luca whimpers with need.

"Juliette," Luca whispers, desire bleeding into her voice. Her name fits perfectly on Luca's tongue, as perfectly as it fits on her wrist.

Juliette jumps, and in a rush of cool air, her hands are gone.

The moment shatters, and Luca's eyes fly open. She clamps a hand over her mouth, embarrassment coating her in a fresh wave of heat. Now that she's had a taste, she wants more. With just her hands, Juliette has stripped Luca bare. A pang of longing ripples out like radar from her chest, making her whole body feel like a bruise.

Juliette slams the aloe bottle onto the counter next to Luca, and it's like a splash of cold water over her head.

"I trust you can reach your chest and stomach." Juliette tosses the words over her shoulder, not even looking at Luca as she flees.

Luca pulls her tank top over her head, and it sticks to her skin. Her throat tightens with a lump. She cannot let that happen again, even if she desperately wants it. Juliette touched her for barely fifteen minutes and it unfurled something inside her that she has to keep buried. Juliette may have *liked* touching Luca, but Luca can never have something that is just physical.

Not again.

Luca snatches up the aloe, glaring at it. Her hands shake as she applies the gel to her own stomach. Her touch is nothing like Juliette's.

And she's never craved anything more.

JULIETTE

Juliette cannot stop her hands from shaking.

She stares down at them. They look normal apart from the tremor in each of her fingers and the tacky, half-dried aloe gel caught on the ridges. She half expects them to be bright red and gleaming, making a mockery of her. How could she think that she wouldn't feel something the moment she touched Kacic?

She had convinced herself that she was helping Kacic in an effort to be nice. However, once her hands started moving, she couldn't stop. And she *wanted* Kacic to feel better; not just physically, but also emotionally. She had bared herself, given in to the feelings that Juliette had evoked in her and that felt too much like a fragile gift. One Juliette doesn't want. Or deserve.

She shoves into the bathroom, slamming the door closed with more force than she means to. She washes off her hands, roughly scrubbing the gel from her skin. Then she stares at herself in the mirror. She looks wild. Her cheeks are flushed, her lips red and bitten, her arms shake where she holds on to the sink, and her pupils are blown wide and dark.

She splashes ice-cold water onto her face, the rivulets running down her cheeks like tears, streaking down her throat, and making her shiver. "Get a grip," she mutters to her reflection.

Still, no matter how much she tries, Juliette can't stop hearing Kacic's strangled moans, her soft whimpers growing more audible as Juliette stroked her burning skin. She felt the heat of Kacic's burn seeping into her hands as she drew the sting away. She can't stop seeing the way Kacic shivered uncontrollably, as if she couldn't decide whether to lean into the touch or pull away. Juliette knows what she wanted.

It's driving Juliette crazy. She could get drunk off the way Kacic had whispered her name. A wild, desperate part of her wants to race back downstairs and pounce on Kacic. Wrap her up in Juliette's arms and kiss all of her reddened skin better.

She clenches her jaw and forcibly stuffs the sudden yearning for Kacic into a box, locking it away behind the wall of her ribs.

She pushes off the sink and retreats into her bedroom, closing the bathroom door behind her and sliding down it. Moonlight mingles with the amber lamplight, twisting together and casting shadows across the length of the cold floor. She digs her fingernails into the grooves of the wood and breathes in through her nose.

She hates Kacic. She hates the way she stares and sees everything. She hates her clinical demeanor as she dispatches her rivals on court with brutal efficiency. She hates that Kacic has dug herself under Juliette's skin like a leech and distracted her from what she actually wants. And she hates that with a few touches, Luca Kacic's walls had seemingly crumpled. This is simply a mind game—one Juliette will not lose.

She doesn't want her soulmate, she doesn't want to be told by God or the universe or karma who she should love. She wants to be a Grand Slam champion. It's all she's *ever* wanted.

She desperately holds back the intense feelings that threaten to wrangle loose and complicate her very uncomplicated dream. When she closes her eyes, she feels like she's tumbling into a free fall, and no matter how she pinwheels her arms, she can't slow the descent. She curls in on herself, wrapping her arms around her middle.

Slowly, Juliette regains control over her harsh breathing. Tonight was simply an . . . anomaly. She doesn't *want* Kacic romantically, she just hasn't gotten laid in a week.

The words ring hollow in her mind.

Her throat hurts like she's been screaming, her eyes are gritty, and she knows she needs to go to bed and sleep this off. But as she looks up, arms still tight around her stomach, she doesn't really want to get into the king-size bed alone. It's a sea of cold white sheets that threaten to drown her.

She gets up and stumbles downstairs. The lights are off, and the living room is silent. She crawls onto one of the couches, wrapping the too small but fluffy blanket around her shoulders. It's almost like she's a kid again, napping before her next tennis practice. So, she curls into a tight ball and, with her lashes wet, falls asleep.

FOURTEEN

JULIETTE

The early morning sun and a gentle shake wakes Juliette.

She blinks blearily up, her vision fuzzy around the edges. She can't quite make out who is gently touching her shoulder.

"Jules, are you all right?" a familiar voice asks in Italian.

"'m fine," Juliette mutters, even if she isn't. She somehow feels more exhausted than when she fell asleep. Her neck aches, her back muscles bent the wrong way, and her nose is stuffy.

"Jules?"

Juliette lifts her head, rubbing her eyes so she can see Leo clearly. He looks concerned, his warm brown eyes searching Juliette's face and his lips curved into a frown. "I'm fine," she says again.

"Why are you on the couch?" Leo asks, his brows scrunching in confusion. He's switched back to English, now that Juliette is awake. His Italian is better than before they met but still limited. At least it's better than Octavia's rather poor attempts at Portuguese.

Juliette shakes her head, but her temples pound at the movement and she winces. "I don't know," she lies, not wanting to talk to her sister's boyfriend about her problems. "What time is it?"

Leo straightens from his crouch. He's still wearing his pajamas, a pair of sweatpants and a Brazilian fútbol T-shirt, so it can't be too late. "Half-six," Leo says. "You want coffee?" He gestures to the kitchen.

Juliette uncurls her limbs and shoves the blanket off her lap. "That'd be great."

Leo pads into the kitchen, leaving Juliette to drop her head into her hands and collect her thoughts. She allows herself a moment to wallow in the pain caused by sleeping on the couch before forcing herself to her feet. She stretches her arms over her head, letting the near orgasmic relief of the early morning stretch ripple through her.

"Do you take cream and sugar?" Leo asks.

"In espresso? Hell no." Juliette twists around to stare at Leo, who is making coffee from a *packet* of all things. Juliette shakes her head. "How does Octavia stand you?" she mutters as she pads over to the kitchen and slides onto one of the stools beneath the island.

Leo starts to smile. "We don't do a lot of standing," he says innocently.

Juliette gags. "Now *I* can't stand you."

Leo stirs his cup and takes a sip.

"Please, do not tell me that's instant coffee." Juliette might have to die if it is.

Leo smiles apologetically, and he's almost handsome enough for Juliette to forgive him.

Still, death is more preferable than dealing with an instant coffee lover.

"I'll make you an espresso, don't worry, Jules," Leo soothes as he turns to the espresso machine sitting on the counter behind him. "I have to make one for Tavvy anyway."

Juliette looks Leo over. "You're up very early. And very chipper."

Leo shrugs. "I'm a morning person." The conversation pauses as Leo grinds a double shot and takes his time tamping it down. "Sort of comes with the territory."

"I mean, yeah, I have to be up early a lot, but that doesn't mean I like it," Juliette grumbles. None of the Ricci family are morning people—the only trait they all share.

Leo turns around and slides the double shot over the island to Juliette. "It's nice to be up with the sun," he says as he starts making another for Octavia. "And I meant I got up early as a kid to work in my parents' shop."

"Oh, right," Juliette says, realizing she should have remembered. Unlike a lot of the people on the tennis tours, Leo hadn't come from money and a fancy club.

The conversation cuts off as Octavia comes stumbling into the kitchen. She blinks, confused at seeing Juliette. "What the hell are you doing up?"

"Good morning to you too," Juliette says, sipping her espresso delicately.

"I was going to bring this up to you," Leo says, holding out the demitasse cup to her.

"Thank God for you," Octavia says, tugging on his wrist and dragging him into a quick kiss.

Juliette busies herself by taking another sip of espresso to ignore the uncomfortable wriggling in her stomach. It seeps over her tongue, hot and bitter, waking up her body and mind. Sometimes she wishes she could inject espresso straight into her veins.

"No, seriously, Jules, what are you doing awake? Usually we have to drag your ass out of bed."

Juliette looks up at Octavia, who lifts a dark brow, as if she knows what Juliette was doing last night. She tries not to flush at the memory of Kacic's skin beneath her hands, hot and trembling. "Maybe I wanted to wake with the sun," she lies, glancing sideways at Leo.

Leo, wisely, keeps his mouth shut and sips his coffee again.

Octavia rolls her eyes. "Whatever. Keep your secrets." She turns to the fridge and pulls it open. "Did you get Claudia her energy drinks?"

Thanks, Juliette mouths to Leo, who winks. "Not the peach flavor she loves, but there is a blue raspberry one."

"She'll have to deal then," Octavia says, grabbing it and sauntering out of the kitchen.

Leo leans on the kitchen island. "Are you all right?" he asks again, so achingly sincere that Juliette's guilt triples, swelling in her gut.

"It's nothing that I can't handle," Juliette says, brushing her thumb along the edge of her cup.

Leo sighs. "But you don't have to deal with it alone. This week is supposed to be about having fun, and you seem off."

Juliette looks back up at Leo. Even though Leo is like family, she won't even tell her sisters what happened with Kacic. "I'm fine, really.

Don't worry. You need to focus on your next tournament. Queens, right?"

"Is this about clay season?" Leo ignores her question. "Because those losses were—"

"No," Juliette cuts Leo off sharply, even though she can't help but feel that Leo is partially correct. "No, it isn't. Thanks for the coffee." She slides off the stool, effectively ending the conversation.

LUCA

For the first time in months, Luca wakes up refreshed. It's a strange sensation. She glances at her shoulders and back and blinks.

There are no blisters, no scabs, no peeling. It's as if she was never burnt at all; only lightly tanned skin is left behind.

She rips her phone off the charger and immediately searches the internet for answers, fingers shaking.

Can a soulmate's touch cure sunburn?

She clicks on the first article from a nonsponsored site and reads through the research. Most of it is the theoretical hypothesis of soulmates being able to cure each other's ailments. One couple claimed that by bathing each other every day, they'd been able to rid themselves of cancer.

Luca doesn't know if she believes that, but she finds another reputable site that does say there is evidence that the touch of a soulmate heals superficial injuries like cuts, bruises, and burns, as long as there isn't serious damage. There's more scientific jargon about how the physical connection energizes cells or something, but Luca feels satisfied with the answer.

She knows that Juliette is her soulmate. It shouldn't be strange that Juliette can heal her burn with her touch. There is nothing significant to this and so she won't give it any more thought.

But that's the thing about trying not to think about something; it invades Luca's brain and twists in on itself. She thinks about it from every angle until it's unrecognizable from the original thought. Her brain focuses on the way Ricci's hands had been so sure on her skin, but careful. Just enough pressure to feel, but not enough that her calluses scratched against the burn. Then Juliette's hand had coasted down Luca's sternum, fingers spreading to nearly touch her nipple. Almost as if Juliette wanted to touch Luca lovingly, instead of just to help get rid of a nasty sunburn.

She shakes off the thoughts as best she can and heads downstairs. Most of the villa is awake and moving around. A basket of fruit sits on the island, and Luca snatches a banana even though she doesn't feel particularly hungry.

She leans against the counter, feeling awkward and out of place. Octavia, Claudia, and Remi are at the stove, scrambling eggs and chopping fruit. Well, Octavia is scrambling eggs, Remi is chopping, and Claudia is pounding an energy drink at an alarming rate. Juliette and Zoe are drinking coffee in the lounge, and from the snippet of conversation she hears, Zoe is complimenting the espresso, which makes Juliette's whole face light up.

Luca isn't used to being in a room full of other players. Especially not in such a casual setting. She shrinks into her hoodie, peeling her banana. She pulls out her phone to distract herself and sees a message from Nicky.

NICKY

good luck today! remember to try to make friends! 😊

LUCA

Okay, Mom 😏

Luca hesitates over the call button. Part of her wants to tell Nicky about the previous night, if just to ask about the healing touch of a soulmate. But a larger part of her wants to keep it a secret. Not out of shame, but because she wants to tuck that nice moment close to her chest. Nicky would probably scold her for not using sunscreen, then be annoyed that she let Juliette close to her. He would remind her of her other relationships that had started with small gestures like that, and how they had ended.

Claudia tosses her empty can into the recycling bin, and it rattles, startling Luca out of her brooding.

"Good morning, Luca," Claudia says with a yawn cutting through her words.

"Late night?" Luca asks, her throat sticking around the words awkwardly. She shoves her phone into her pocket and shovels half the banana in her mouth to distract herself.

Claudia shakes her head as she pulls another drink out of the fridge. "No, early morning. Can't believe they'd make us practice this early."

Luca shrugs. "Gets it out of the way. I like it."

Claudia snorts. "I'll let you get all the balls and take a nap on the back of the court."

"I can see the tweets now. 'Claudia Ricci caught sleeping during the Connolly Cup! Is philanthropy a snooze?'" Luca jokes.

Claudia cackles, and Luca's chest warms with satisfaction. She can be friends with other players. She doesn't have to stand awkwardly on the side like she does in the locker room. Maybe this weekend won't be so bad.

The rest of their conversation is cut off by the front door opening.

"Good morning, ladies!" a bright voice calls, the vowels wrapped in a coiling French accent.

"Oh, excellent, they're actually awake," a distinctly American voice drawls.

The Fierce Four enter in a whirlwind, led by the youngest, Aurore Cadieux. She looks like she's hardly aged a day from her debut on the tour. Payton Calimeris has her arm thrown around Aurore's neck, a paper bag under her other one. Seeing her in real life takes Luca's breath away. Luca modeled her game on Payton Calmeris. She always said it was because Payton was the best on a hard court, but really it was because she had an intense crush on her when she was a teenager.

In person, she looks even taller, especially with her thick and wildly curly black hair fluffed up around her, streaks of silver in a few of the ringlets. She is the oldest and retired first, but she is still thick with solid and corded muscle. On the court, she was calm and icy, but now she's grinning. Even though she had three months to prepare to meet the rest of the Fierce Four Luca can't breathe.

"Who is ready to play some tennis?" Karoline asks as she sweeps in next, Victoria Ferreyra on her heels. She winks at Luca and a bit of her nerves melt away. They want her here. She was specifically asked to be a part of this team, and that means that Karoline Kitzinger believes in her.

"I'll be ready once I have one more caffeinated drink," Claudia mutters.

The four of them integrate into the kitchen, as easy as breathing. "We brought—what are they called again, Karo? Malozolli?" Payton asks, hoisting the bag up and dropping it onto the island counter.

"*Maritozzi*," Karoline says patiently.

"Oh, God bless you," Juliette says. She takes the bag and starts dishing out fluffy buns dusted with powdered sugar. She doesn't even look at Luca when she hands her one.

Luca takes it even though she's not even halfway done with her banana. It is soft and light in her palm, much more appealing than a banana, and she won't refuse a sweet treat gifted by the best tennis players in the world.

"All right, we're having team meetings before we go to practice," Karoline says, but she cuts off with a squeak as Payton pinches her side.

"Let them enjoy a bite of their food before going into business mode," Victoria says, the rough rasp of her voice more pronounced, as if she just rolled out of bed. Karoline glares at her.

The ease between them is palpable, and while she shouldn't be surprised, Luca is. Seeing the four of them standing in a kitchen, laughing and chatting like they're all friends meeting up for brunch, makes Luca think. She glances sideways at Juliette, who is staring at Karoline like she hung the moon and the stars. Maybe even if their start has been rocky, much like the Fierce Four they too can have a happy ending.

"Eggs are ready!" Octavia says, turning around and sliding the pan into the middle of the island. Remi sets down a fruit salad and plates.

"Very healthy," Victoria says. "Your team needs the protein." She elbows Karoline.

"Everyone needs protein," Karoline says primly. "Dish up. We have a busy day!"

Luca appreciates being able to throw herself into practice without having to worry about conversation. She doesn't have to be flustered with jokes or try to get people to like her. She can just *play*.

Practice is also easier than matches. There are no external stakes in practice. All the pressure is in the preparation, and there is no room for anger or whining or ego. It's almost too easy.

Which is why she doesn't love the Connolly Cup.

It's a spectacle, even practice. The press is invited, and they're constantly taking pictures from the seats. Each team has to pose together. Luca is forced to awkwardly stand next to Juliette and smile as they snap hundreds of photos.

After being handed a tiny microphone and made to answer inane questions about which player would make the best pizza or who would cry at a sad movie, Luca finally stands at the bench with her racket in her hand, spinning it impatiently.

"Ugh, I'm so jealous that the other team gets blue," Claudia says, holding up a red tennis dress and inspecting it thoroughly. "Blue would look so much better on our complexions," she says to Luca, holding the skirt up to her arm. "Don't you think, Jules?"

Luca freezes.

Juliette sidesteps around the net from behind Luca and stands next to her sister. "Sure," she says, her eyes lingering on Luca's face but not meeting her gaze.

Luca is saved from responding by Payton clapping loudly and calling them over for a meeting about the actual start of practice.

For most of practice, Luca avoids Juliette. She plays a couple of singles sets against Octavia and then Remi. Luckily, Karoline doesn't ask them to play against each other or even with each other.

When they're done and back in the red team's locker room, Payton urges them to gather together. Luca shuffles awkwardly to stand in between Claudia and Zoe, trying to ignore Juliette across from her.

"All right, Karoline and I decided on the roster for tomorrow." Luca swallows, hopeful that she won't have to play doubles. "Claudia, you'll be the first singles match. Zoe, the second. And Juliette and Luca, you two will play doubles."

Luca grimaces and Juliette makes a similarly disgusted face. "Why?" Juliette asks, clearly struggling to keep her voice even.

If Payton notices their discomfort, she doesn't comment on it. "Everyone has to play at least one doubles match and one singles match. Sorry, Jules, but you're the weakest doubles player, so we'll get yours over with first." She points at Claudia. "And I want you to play mostly doubles, so let's get your singles match done."

Luca can't argue with that logic. Every match is worth a certain number of points. One per match on Friday, two on Saturday, and three on Sunday. If they fail spectacularly together, it won't cost the team as many points. Still, the idea of playing doubles with Juliette under the scrutiny of thousands of fans makes Luca's stomach lurch into her throat.

Juliette's glare is hot on her face, and Luca dares to look at her. But, for once, Juliette keeps her mouth shut and doesn't argue.

FIFTEEN

JULIETTE

Sitting on a bench and watching her sister lose is not Juliette's definition of a good time. It's only marginally worse than getting interviewed in between sets and asked how she feels about her teammates. She tries to stick to light trash talking about the blue team, but the interviewers make thinly veiled comments about playing with Lucky Luca, her rival. *Potentially something more,* a journalist threw out casually. Juliette brushes it off as best she can but makes an effort to praise Kacic's enthusiasm in cheering for their team.

By the end of the match, annoyance is bubbling beneath her skin. Claudia, at least, is in surprisingly good spirits as she comes off the court. Juliette follows her back into the locker room.

"I can't believe how rusty I am," Claudia says as she slides her bag onto the bench and strips her dress off. Even though the event is held indoors, it's humid and hot on court.

"Remi is hard to beat on this surface. Her serve is too good," Juliette says, and Claudia shrugs.

"Are you ready to play with Lucky Luca?" Claudia's mouth quirks into a playful smirk.

At the mention of Kacic's name, Juliette's stomach flips. Juliette has done her best to ignore Kacic throughout the afternoon. On changeovers, when Claudia collapsed onto the bench and sucked down water, Juliette had leaned over the bench to try to give her tips for the next games against Remi. Kacic had hovered on Claudia's other shoulder, suggesting similar tactics, but Juliette had avoided giving her more than a few sidelong glances.

Not that it had worked. Remi Rowland's serve could not be touched, and it was hard to win a match without any sniff of a break point.

"We're gonna kick their asses," Juliette says, tossing Claudia another towel.

Claudia yanks her hair out of its tight bun and spirals fall around her face, clumped and damp with sweat. "Oh, are you now? Are you two on talking terms?"

Juliette shrugs, hoping she's kept her face neutral, even though she's definitely thinking about the heat of Luca's skin against her palm, the curve of her breast as she cupped it . . .

Feels good, doesn't it?

Juliette's cheeks flush at her own audacity.

Claudia grins. "Good luck, Jules." She disappears into the showers, and Juliette returns to the court where Zoe is warming up against Octavia. To the left is a designated area for both teams. No one is sitting on the blue side. They're probably still in the locker room with Remi. On their couch, Kacic sits alone. She is a bright spot in a red tracksuit. Her knees bounce up and down. Juliette sits down, leaving a cushion between them. "How good are you at doubles?" Juliette asks. Out of the corner of her eye, she sees one of the cameras swivel to stare at them.

Kacic shrugs. "Fine. I don't like being at the net."

Juliette fights against a sigh. "Which side do you prefer?"

Kacic glances at her sidelong and shrugs again. "Doesn't matter."

"Fine. You take deuce. I'm left-handed and your backhand is better," Juliette says, shifting to lean against the armrest. It's going to be an incredibly long day.

Juliette watches Zoe win from the locker room as she stretches out before her match. It's a tough match, and Juliette feels strange about rooting against Octavia, but at least their team has a point now.

Kacic emerges in her red tennis dress and visor, her braided ponytail swinging over her shoulder. She pulls her jacket on to keep her muscles warm. "Ready?" Juliette asks, focusing back on her reflection as she ties her headband tight around her forehead.

"As I'll ever be," Kacic says. She fiddles with her sweatbands, making sure they're covering Juliette's name on her wrist.

Juliette doesn't know what to say to break this awkward tension lying between them. Maybe she should mention Kacic's sunburn and how perfectly it's healed. Discomfort twists in Juliette's throat at the thought. That would make it even more awkward. So far, they've done a great job at pretending that night never happened. She could say something about playing doubles, but they both prefer singles.

So, in the end, she says nothing at all.

Juliette drags herself onto the court, dread making her feet heavy and her shoulders slump. She breathes in deep, trying to harness the electric energy of the crowd.

She doesn't say anything to Kacic as they stand together for the coin toss. She gestures to Kacic to decide whether she wants heads or tails. The coin glints in the light, landing on heads when Kacic had chosen tails—of course.

Remi grins at them, deciding that they'll serve first. Juliette barely restrains sticking her tongue out at Remi as they go back to the baseline for the warm-up.

The announcer goes over each of their achievements and Juliette shanks a forehand into the crowd at the mention of Kacic's Australian Open title.

She holds up her hand in apology at Remi and ignores the smirk on her face.

The umpire calls time and Juliette positions herself at the net. It takes all of her energy not to look back at Kacic. Instead she focuses on Remi and Nadia. They're a comical pair, because Remi is so much taller than the other girl, so she has to bend her head, hand over her mouth, to talk to her.

Remi's serve is blistering, but Kacic manages to block the ball back, popping it over Nadia's head. Juliette freezes as Remi moves for the ball, smacking a forehand straight at Juliette. Her instincts keep her from being bludgeoned in the shoulder. The ball clips off the edge of her racket and sinks into the bottom of the net.

Juliette swings around. "Sorry," she mutters to Kacic as she passes. She can't even look at her. First point and she can't even hit a reaction volley. She can almost see her father typing *poor volley footwork* in a document.

This is an exhibition match, it shouldn't matter. But as Juliette bounces on her toes at the baseline she realizes she wants to impress *Kacic*. The thought is so stupid that she wants to smack herself in the face. She is supposed to have *fun*.

Juliette shoves her thoughts away as Remi's first serve sails out. The second kicks up into her forehand, but she manages to tick it down the line. Nadia moves, angling a volley at Kacic's feet to win the point.

At least Juliette isn't the only one who is uncomfortable at the net.

As they pass each other, Kacic holds out her hand. Juliette hesitates, surprised by the gesture. High fives are a normal gesture for a doubles team, but Juliette doesn't know how to make her hand move.

Kacic drops her hand and doesn't look at her as she moves to the baseline.

Juliette's heart sinks and she's so unfocused on the next point that she misses another volley into the net because she didn't move in enough.

Remi aces Juliette to win their first game and she tries not to stomp over to the bench.

"I'll serve first," Kacic says as they stand at the bench and take quick sips of water.

"Fine," Juliette grumbles, waiting for Remi and Nadia to pass them as they go to the opposite side of the court. Jealousy slinks in Juliette's stomach as she watches them giggle together.

Juliette jogs toward their side of the net, spinning her racket in her hand.

"Hey!" Kacic says and Juliette looks up at her.

Kacic gestures to the ball kid for the balls. "Look, you're good at the net, Juliette." Juliette swallows, falling still as Kacic's hazel eyes land on her. "Trust yourself. You know how to volley. You've practiced for this."

Kacic's gaze is sweetly earnest. She believes in Juliette, and that warms Juliette from the inside out, chasing away all the jealousy.

"I got it. Thanks, though," Juliette says, starting to turn away.

"Juliette."

She spins on her heel. "What now?"

Kacic frowns, covering her mouth with the ball. "I'm going to serve down the center. You cover the center of the court, okay?"

"Got it," Juliette says and holds out her fist for Kacic to bump. She does it and sparks jolt up her arm briefly.

It doesn't matter because Kacic hits an ace.

"Nice serve," Juliette says once she's back at the baseline with Kacic.

"Thanks. I'll try to do it again."

"You got this," Juliette says, even though the words feel foreign in her mouth. Kacic blinks, biting her lower lip briefly.

Juliette tries not to think of Kacic's mouth as she goes to the net again. Instead, she thinks of Kacic's words. It fills her with a strange, warm confidence. And when Nadia hits a sharp backhand at Juliette, she steps into the ball and angles it away beautifully.

"Knew you could do it," Kacic says, and when she holds out her hand this time, Juliette smacks it with conviction. Maybe they aren't so terrible at this.

Juliette puts away two more volleys to even the games at one all. "We're not doing too bad for a couple of singles players," Juliette says as Luca falls into step with her at the back of the court.

"No, but we'd be done for if we were playing doubles specialists." Kacic plucks at her strings.

Nadia holds easily with Remi up at the net to put their returns away with ease and Juliette nearly running into Kacic to get a ball that was not on her side.

As they go back to the bench, Juliette shrugs off the last game.

They haven't been broken yet, at least, and Remi and Nadia haven't run away with the set, even though they're much more coordinated.

They sit, a respectable distance between them, but Juliette's skin prickles from being so close to Kacic. She can ignore the feeling on the court because she's focused on playing, but it's harder here without distractions. Juliette cracks her banana open and pops half of it into her mouth.

"Any words of wisdom for my serve?" she teasingly asks Kacic.

"Hit it hard?" Kacic says, her voice ticking up in a question. Her eyes are a little wide as she glances at her.

"Always excellent advice," Payton says with a teasing grin as she leans between them on the bench.

"Thanks. I never would've guessed," Juliette says, but she isn't annoyed. If anything, she's amused that she caught Kacic slightly off guard.

The umpire calls time and Juliette shakes out her wrists, ready to take on her serve. "Kick serve out wide," she tells Kacic, who nods before she sprints to the net, crouching down.

Juliette doesn't mean to, but her racket connects awkwardly with the ball and nails Kacic in the shoulder.

A gasp ripples through the crowd and Juliette smacks a hand over her mouth in shock. Kacic straightens, but when she looks back, she's laughing. "Guess I should've clarified. Hit it hard *at them!*"

Giggles rise in Juliette, and even though she tries to stifle them, she can still hear them in her voice as she yells, "Sorry!"

The rest of the service game is just as messy. Juliette has to duck twice to avoid getting smacked by Kacic's racket. But they pull it together to win the game.

"You're both doing well," Payton says, leaning in between them, elbows on the back of the bench. "I think you can break Remi if you aim most of your returns at Nadia. She is weaker at the net, so try not to hit the return back crosscourt to Remi."

Juliette nods and pops the last of her banana into her mouth.

"Be mindful of each other. You've almost run into each other multiple times," Karoline says, appearing next to Kacic.

Juliette nods. "We'll get into it. Right, Kacic?" She holds out her fist for Kacic to bump, and she does. A bright burst of tingles zings against her skin, giving her a boost of energy.

"You're not serving so I think my shoulder is safe," she says, and Juliette laughs.

"I really am sorry about that."

"Sure you are," Kacic says, her eyes glittering with amusement. Juliette's stomach swoops, unsure of how to navigate this odd truce they've shakily built on the court.

Just keep playing.

"Time," the umpire calls. Juliette grabs her racket, jogging around the net. At the baseline, Juliette bounces on her toes.

Remi lines up on the baseline and bounces the ball as the crowd murmurs fall away, leaving only quiet. Remi's eyes flick up for a brief second before she rocks back and serves.

Kacic drills the ball back at Nadia, who barely gets her strings on it and pops the ball. Juliette moves in and punches the volley cleanly, angled and short, winning them the point.

The crowd claps, and Juliette pumps her fist.

"Nice volley, Jules!" Payton cheers from the bench. Karoline sits next to her, elbows on her knees as she watches with her intense gaze. She nods slowly, but her face is impassive.

Juliette moves back to the baseline and catches Kacic's hand as they move past each other. Remi is already ready by the time Juliette crouches in position. Remi switches up her serve and kicks it into her forehand, wide and unexpected.

Juliette slices it back crosscourt, too caught off guard to attempt to hit it at Nadia.

Remi hits a near-perfect drop shot, but Juliette is faster. She slides on the hard court, her shoes squeaking as she pops the ball over Nadia's head.

"Switch!" Nadia calls out, shuffling to the opposite side as Remi skids into the ball, throwing it up into a high lob.

With her and Kacic at the net together, Juliette is very aware that they are slightly out of position and definitely awkward. She backs up.

So does Kacic.

The ball arcs across the lights, aiming for the middle of the court.

Juliette doesn't think about it. She's unused to sharing the court with anyone.

"Got it!" Juliette says just as Kacic calls out, "Mine!"

Juliette split steps, about to move forward and slam the overhead when she collides with a warm, solid body.

It happens so fast that Juliette doesn't even process falling, but suddenly she's on the ground, tangled with Kacic, and there is pain.

Bone-jarring and horrific pain.

"Fuck," she whimpers, holding on to her wrist. She squeezes, and the pain triples.

Juliette rolls to her side, cradling her arm to her chest. Pressure points of pain on her back and hip make her curse a litany of *fuck*.

"I'm so sorry, Juliette. What's wrong?" Kacic asks frantically, pale-faced and stricken.

Juliette rolls onto her back and gasps as the pain sparks up her spine. "Ah."

Warmth engulfs her knee, and she feels Kacic drawing little circles with her thumb against her skin.

The moment stretches out, lingers, as Kacic stares down at her. Then the world snaps back to full speed, and suddenly Karoline is crouching next to her, touching her shoulder.

"Is it your wrist?" Karoline asks, her voice low and calm. She rubs Juliette's shoulder.

Juliette nods. "Yeah. And my back." Lying on it makes it pulsate with the beat of her heart, but she can't move anymore.

She pants as the pain in her wrist starts to dissipate. She looks down at her palm and the flecks of blood from tiny cuts on her skin.

"I'm sorry." Kacic's voice is low and laden with guilt.

Payton is at Kacic's shoulder, gently tugging her up and away. A trainer swarms where Kacic has left, and Juliette's knee feels cold without her touch. A camera looms closer, focusing on her misery.

"Jules!" Claudia's face blocks the camera's eye, and Juliette sighs in relief.

"It'll be okay, Jules," Octavia says, her voice near the side of her head.

It takes every bit of Juliette's self-control not to burst into tears, but her eyes prickle with heat. She becomes hyperaware of the crowd's concerned murmurs, with a few people yelling encouragement in Italian. The lights high above are so bright, and when she looks away, her vision swims and black spots bloom.

Her fingertips find the scar on her wrist, lacing up the edge of her pinky. With help from the trainer and Karoline, she sits up, but her back spasms and pain ricochets up her spine. She can barely stand without shuddering.

"Kacic?" she asks once they get into the locker room.

"She only scraped her hands," Payton says as the trainer prods at her aching back. The pain has started to dissipate, but with each jab it ripples outward.

"We should get scans to make sure nothing is damaged."

Juliette flinches. *Damaged.* The word cuts into her, sharp panic winding around her ribs. "The match," Juliette gasps out between clenched teeth.

"Don't worry about it," Karoline says. "It doesn't matter." Her eyes are warm and crinkled with concern. "Your health is more important."

"We were playing well," Juliette laments, shaking her head.

Karoline chuckles. "Maybe you two aren't so bad together after all."

Juliette's stomach jolts and the phantom feeling of Kacic's hand on her knee, shoulder, palm tingles on her skin.

Maybe they aren't so bad together.

SIXTEEN

LUCA

Luca digs her knuckles into her sternum, wishing she could release the anxious pressure building in her chest as she stands in front of Juliette's door. She wants to turn tail and run.

Karoline had told them that Juliette's scans came back negative for any injury, but she was put on bedrest. Still, she knows if she avoids Juliette and the role she played in her fall, the guilt will consume her. It already eats at her stomach, an acidic inferno that makes her palms slick with sweat. So after dinner, her guilt drives her upstairs, followed by the wolf whistles and cheers of the other women. It's unfortunate that their tenuous relationship has been on display for months. It's like a soap opera, and Luca wants to turn the channel.

With a final deep breath, Luca gathers her courage and knocks.

For a moment, there's only silence. She wonders if Juliette is sleeping or if she's purposefully ignoring visitors. She leans closer, trying to listen for snoring or soft sounds of life beyond the door.

It opens, and Luca nearly tumbles into Juliette. Again.

They're close, too close, her head curved down slightly and Juliette leaning against the doorframe. For a hesitant beat, they stare at each other. Juliette's eyes are wide and red-rimmed, such a deep brown that Luca is reminded of the espresso Juliette loves to drink.

Luca steps back and clears her throat. She doesn't want to intrude, especially because Juliette doesn't look great. There is a barely there tremble to her shoulders as she gazes up at Luca, her cheeks are ruddy, and a pillow line slashes across her cheekbone. She's wearing an oversize T-shirt that exposes the long column of her throat and the edge of her collarbone.

"Are you all right?" Luca asks softly as her gaze roves over Juliette's face.

Juliette shrugs. "Why are you here?" she asks, equally quiet.

Luca glances into the room. "Can we talk?"

Juliette blinks at her, slowly, as if she's processing the words at half the speed. "What about?"

Her knotted stomach lurches. It's now or never. "Are you still hurting from earlier?"

Juliette narrows her eyes and shrugs.

Luca slips her hand into her pocket and pulls out a slender gold glass bottle. Juliette's brows furrow. "Erm, it's massage oil. I read online this morning that a soulmate's touch can help heal superficial cuts and bruises. My back is almost entirely fine from the sunburn, so I thought I'd return the favor." As the words pour from her mouth, she realizes how strange this must seem. "It's fine if you don't want—"

"Sure," Juliette says, turning around and vanishing into the room, leaving Luca slightly openmouthed.

She did not think that would work.

Fear and desire fight in her stomach, and she is suddenly very aware of how scratchy her breath is in her throat. She tries to swallow around the dry lump and follows Juliette into the room, gently shutting the door behind her.

"Luca," Juliette starts, and it sounds like her name is punched out of her. The sound of it on Juliette's lips brushes down Luca's spine, and she shivers.

"Yes," Luca says as the silence stretches awkwardly.

Juliette's arms wrap around her middle, and she shifts on her feet. "I'm sorry," she murmurs, looking up. Her expression is a mix of guilt and tenderness, her big dark eyes flickering in the low light from the amber lamp.

Luca hadn't expected that, hadn't prepared a response for an apology. There is too much space between them, too many unspoken words that Luca doesn't know how to say, so she swallows them.

"Okay," she says finally, because it's the only thing she can make herself say.

"It's not okay," Juliette says, her arms falling loose at her sides. She takes a deep breath, as if bracing herself. "The other night, on the beach, I—I . . . " She stutters, pauses, and collects herself before resuming. "It was cruel and insensitive. I know we're rivals, but you didn't deserve that."

Luca picks at the label of the massage oil bottle, still entirely baffled as to what she should say. She should be used to this. She's never been anyone's first choice. Not as a kid, not as an adult, not even with Vladimir. The only reason Vladimir even considered being her coach was because the kid he was supposed to train with was sick that day at the club in Zadar.

But Luca can't tell Juliette any of that. She doesn't know how to voice how badly it hurts to not even be chosen by the one person who was supposed to choose her. "It's fine," she lies.

Juliette's eyes cut through her, and she shakes her head. Her curls tumble around her jaw. "It isn't." She moves another half-step closer, and a cramp of longing spasms across Luca's chest. "It isn't fine. It was horrible, and I had no right to say that to you."

"Was it true?" Luca asks, because apparently, she's a masochist.

Juliette's gaze drops, and she heaves out a rattling sigh. "I don't know. I don't think so," she murmurs, looking up at Luca, her eyes shining. "I think I may have been wrong about you."

Luca's breath hitches, and she can't breathe. "About what?"

"I've watched you, Luca. I see you," Juliette says with such sincerity that Luca's eyes sting. "I think we understand each other, even if I don't know how to feel about you. About us." She looks down again.

"We don't need to know," Luca whispers, latching on to the sliver of hope that maybe they don't have to hate each other and exchange scathing words. "We can try to be ourselves. Try to be friends."

"Friends?" Juliette asks, tasting the word as if it's foreign to her.

"Yeah, friends," Luca repeats.

"I'm messed up, Luca." Juliette chews on her lower lip. Luca suddenly has the urge to reach out and brush her thumb against Juliette's lips to stop her from adopting that nervous tic.

"Me too," Luca says instead, and she gives Juliette a half-smile. "But that's okay." Regardless of—and perhaps because of—who they are, their relationship will never be storybook-perfect.

Juliette stares at her, as if searching her face for something, and Luca is suddenly certain Juliette can see through her skin and bones to the wriggling mass of anxiety in her chest.

"So," Luca says, inhaling deeply, "how about that massage?" She holds up the bottle again, and Juliette gives her the barest hint of a smile before she nods.

JULIETTE

Juliette never thought she'd feel like a virgin again.

It's ridiculous. She's trembling like she's about to crawl into bed with her first boyfriend and have sloppy, uncoordinated, and frankly dreadful sex. The best part of that experience had been the anticipation before it. The way he'd slowly lifted the shirt over his head and Juliette had lost her mind staring at the expanse of his perfectly imperfect acne-pocked skin.

But now, as she grabs the hem of her shirt, she feels like she is back in that moment. She is facing away from Luca—she absolutely *does not* analyze the fact that Kacic has changed to Luca in her mind—and she's trembling.

She shucks her shirt to the side, grateful she put on a bandeau before opening the door. She twists her curls into a bun on the top of her head so they're out of the way.

Juliette glances over her shoulder. Luca is hard to read at the best of times, hidden behind a wall of iron and snark. But now, in the half glow of saffron light, she looks mesmerized. Her honeyed hazel eyes, dark and shaded, trail down the line of Juliette's back.

"Like what you see?" Juliette asks, trying to tease, but her voice is too shaky for it to be convincing.

Luca's gaze snaps back to her, and pink floods her face. "Erm," she stutters, and then she licks her lips, and heat pools like magma in Juliette's gut.

"I hope this works," Juliette says, trying not to think at all as she gingerly gets back into bed. She arranges herself facedown on the pillows, curls her arm beneath them, and turns her head to one side, angling her wrist so it doesn't ache. "My back hurts like a bitch."

The air is thick and heavy around them. She twists her head to the other side to look at Luca. She blows a rogue curl off her face and sees Luca sitting on the very edge of the bed, rolling the oil bottle between her palms. "You'll need to be a lot closer than that," Juliette says, letting her voice dip low. It's not quite a command, but Luca shivers anyway.

When she looks at Juliette, she's hesitant. "You want me on top of you?" she asks quietly.

Heat explodes in Juliette's stomach, and she nods, not trusting her voice. She didn't expect Luca to phrase it like *that*.

Luca moves slowly, giving Juliette plenty of time to tell her to stop. She swings her long legs up onto the bed and gets onto her knees. Juliette twists her head the other way, and her neck protests.

A light touch to her midback has her tensing.

"It's just me," Luca says, as if it would be anyone else. But the lilt of her voice loosens some of the tension in Juliette's chest, and she shifts, letting her legs fall slightly open. Her belly softens, and she sinks deeper into the mattress.

Juliette is very aware that Luca has her knees on either side of her hips, the warm weight hovering just above her. The bottle clinks, loud in the stifling silence. Maybe she should suggest putting on music, but her jaw is wired shut, her body cemented beneath Luca's.

She hears the oil slick between Luca's palms, rubbing back and forth as she warms it. Juliette clutches the pillow under her chin and tries to remember how to breathe.

It feels like an age before Luca's hands touch beneath her shoulder blades, cupping them gently. Just like Juliette did for her the day before. For a moment, Luca is still. Her hands are warm, slick with massage oil, and then she moves.

Juliette never paid too much attention to hands, but maybe she should have.

Luca's are long and spindly, much like the rest of her. Calluses from years of holding a racket shape her palms and fingers, but as she applies pressure and slides slowly down from Juliette's shoulder blades, they couldn't be more perfect.

"Can I go underneath your bra?" Luca asks.

Juliette nods, her skin tingling.

Luca dips her hands underneath and kneads into the tense muscles in the center of her back before she caresses her hands down the dip of her spine, stopping before her lower back.

"Is this okay?" Luca asks, kneading her thumbs into twin tight knots on either side of her spine.

It is *glorious*. Juliette moans something entirely incoherent.

Luca chuckles, sweeping her hands up and digging her thumbs into the meat of Juliette's aching shoulders.

Juliette buries her face into the pillow and closes her eyes. Luca's warm hands don't move from her shoulders until the knots come loose and Juliette's shoulders sag.

"There we go," Luca whispers, so quiet that Juliette almost misses it. "Relax, Jules," she murmurs. The curve of her nickname on Luca's lips sends a shiver down her spine. It's familiar, but far more intimate being said by Luca than anyone else. Juliette's thoughts go fuzzy, every defense slackening.

More oil, slightly cold, drizzles onto her back, and Juliette sucks in a sharp breath. Luca's warm hands are quick to return, splayed wide. Luca follows the contours of Juliette's body, hands gliding across her skin tenderly, reverently. She uses her thumbs to drive a hard line on either side of her spine, but her fingertips stroke against her ribs.

Juliette twitches and bites the pillow to keep from squeaking.

She sucks in a breath, trying to keep her ribs from Luca's imploring fingers.

"Ticklish?" Luca asks teasingly, and Juliette stubbornly shakes her head.

Luca does the motion again, fingertips digging into Juliette's skin, and she gasps out a laugh, more fluttering against her chest as she desperately bites it back. Luca chuckles too and finally takes mercy on her, returning her splayed hands to the arc of her shoulders.

Luca is careful. Slow. Deliberate. She works along the subtle grooves of Juliette's muscles, the dip of her waist, and the knobs of her bones. Her fingers sweep beneath the thin fabric of the bandeau, and her touch causes sparks to scamper across Juliette's skin. It's intimate, soft, but Juliette longs for a return to her lower back, where tightness is becoming more apparent.

Luca turns her right hand over, and her knuckles drag down the ridge of Juliette's spine, entirely too light. Juliette's breath hitches as Luca's hand goes lower and lower until she stops at the band of Juliette's shorts.

"Is this okay?" Luca asks again, her knuckles lifting to barely touch.

Juliette hums her approval.

"I can't hear you," Luca says, voice gravelly and teasing. Her thumb traces random shapes against her skin.

A shiver ripples up Juliette's spine, desire snaking through her, and she turns her head to look at Luca. She's staring at Juliette, intensely focused, like she's on court.

"Luca, please," Juliette rasps.

Luca inhales sharply and swallows. She lays her hands flat on Juliette's lower back, her thumbs dangerously close to sliding beneath her shorts.

Juliette wishes she would.

Luca digs in and presses her weight into the tense muscles spasming there. Juliette bites the pillow as the heat builds beneath her skin, pushing the tension and agony out.

She can't stop moaning. It's torturously good. She knows what this must sound like, but she doesn't care. And just when she thought Luca's fingertips couldn't dig deeper, they do. It's like she's carving out the hurt herself, encouraging warmth to grow instead.

Luca's fingers skim right, toward her hip, and pain blooms where there was once exquisite pleasure. Juliette jolts, head jerking up so fast her vision bursts with black spots.

"Hey," Luca says, her hands soothing down her back, grounding Juliette. It's comforting as the pain fades away. "Tender spot?" she asks, her knees shifting as she finds a better position to look.

"Yeah, that hurt," Juliette says.

Luca clicks her tongue, and the pad of her thumb brushes over the spot. It's a light touch, not enough to hurt, but Juliette flinches anyway. "There's a bruise," Luca says, "I'm sorry I missed it." Her other hand is still tracing looping circles up and down her back.

Juliette drops her head back down into the pillow. "It's fine."

"Tell me if this hurts, okay?"

Luca waits until Juliette gives a verbal confirmation and then she begins to trace the outline of the bruise. She spirals out, gently applying more pressure as she goes.

"It's all right. I think the pain startled me," Juliette says, swallowing hard. Her body is nearly boneless, but her mind is struggling with the intimacy of this. The tenderness and softness.

Luca hums softly and doesn't stop her soothing touches up and down her back. Her other hand spirals away from Juliette's bruised hip, and she starts another line up her spine. She doesn't stop at her shoulders, though; her hands cup the back of Juliette's neck. "I can feel you thinking," Luca whispers, her breath warm against Juliette's shoulder.

Juliette starts to grit her teeth, but Luca's thumb scoops into the base of her neck and wriggles upward. It's such a shocking sensation that her jaw drops, pleasure clouding her mind, and she can't stop the way she mewls under Luca's touch. It's hot like an oven and Juliette is butter, melting into liquid.

Luca maneuvers her thumbs to curve in the dips behind Juliette's ears, and her eyes roll.

This is orgasmic.

Juliette tries to turn her face away, heat burning on her cheeks, but Luca's oil-slick fingers catch her chin. She could easily turn away, but she doesn't want to—not with Luca staring at her with naked, unbridled longing.

Luca's chest rises and falls shallowly. Then her thumb reaches up and brushes against Juliette's lower lip, and without thinking, Juliette's tongue darts out. She just misses, but she gets the not entirely unpleasant taste of coconut.

"Oh," Luca whispers, "you're beyond gorgeous, Jules."

When Juliette turns her head this time, Luca lets her. The compliment is like whiskey down her throat—it's pleasant but still stings. She isn't shy about her looks, and she knows she's conventionally attractive; enough men and women have fallen all over her to ensure she has no self-confidence issues. But the way Luca says it . . . it's as if she's seeing the sun for the first time. Awed, beguiled, completely taken aback by the depth of beauty.

The power they hold over each other is an intimidating anchor, and Juliette never realized it until this moment.

Luca *wants* her.

Juliette realizes she wants Luca too, with every fiber of her being. She wants Luca's hands on her skin, caressing her, warming her, relaxing the tension out of her.

Juliette's eyes water, and she bites the pillow again. This has to be purely physical. Her body is reacting to whatever magical connection soulmates have. She knows it's natural to feel this way, enhanced by their proximity.

Luca doesn't stop massaging her neck, but she doesn't say anything else, and Juliette is grateful. Despite whatever tension hangs between them, Luca must sense how overwhelmed Juliette is. It's building in her chest, and she nearly chokes on it.

Maybe being physical with Luca wouldn't be the end of the world or her career. Juliette is no stranger to no-strings sex and friends with benefits.

Luca adds more oil and does another luxurious pass over her

back. All coherent thought flakes away. When Luca gets to her hip, she swirls in gently, the pressure lessening as she reaches the edges of the pained area.

Heat grows, white-hot and all-consuming, and by the time Luca moves her hands to Juliette's other hip, it's as if she never had any pain. She smooths her hands over Juliette's left hip, taking as much time and care in warming and loosening as she did with the injured one.

Her hands lift and Juliette melts into the bed, certain she'll never be able to move again. Frankly, she doesn't want to.

"Thank you," Juliette murmurs, and Luca shifts off her, plopping down beside her. "I think you turned my limbs to jelly," she says into the cotton, and Luca laughs. Warmth blooms in her stomach at the sound.

She turns her face toward Luca. "I feel like I should return the favor," she murmurs, watching Luca fiddle with her fingers, picking at the skin around her thumbs. Juliette groans as she gets to her knees and then sits beside her.

"You technically started this by helping with my sunburn." Luca refuses to look at Juliette. "Want me to massage your wrist?" she asks, disarming Juliette again.

Juliette doesn't know what to say. Her instinct is to plead, *yes, God, please yes*. But she's terrified of this raw feeling in her chest. And terrified that something could happen to her wrist again.

"It's okay if you don't want me to touch you anymore, I can go," Luca says quickly, misunderstanding Juliette's silence.

"No," Juliette says, fumbling with the word, so she lays her hand over Luca's knee.

Luca's eyes widen as she freezes. There are flecks of green in the gilded hazel of her irises that Juliette never noticed before. They've never been this close.

"I would like that," Juliette says, slowly lifting her hand from Luca's knee and holding out her aching wrist.

SEVENTEEN

LUCA

Juliette surprises Luca, again, by extending her hand. "Why are you letting me do this?" Luca asks as she takes Juliette's right hand.

"You did offer," Juliette says, amusement laced through her voice. Her cheeky smile has returned.

Luca doesn't start with Juliette's wrist but instead slides her thumb across Juliette's palm. Juliette's fingers open like a flower toward her. "I know," she says, finally, "I was more asking why you even let me in your room. Every other time I try to talk to you, you tell me to fuck off."

Juliette winces. "Are we going to talk about that now?"

Luca shrugs and presses her thumbs into Juliette's palm, arcing out toward the edges of her hand before taking her time to work out the kinks in each of her fingers. She memorizes the details of Juliette's hand. Her hands are smaller, but she has identical calluses. Her nails are clipped short, painted a creamy gold. "What happened to your wrist?" Luca asks when the silence starts to freak her out.

Juliette's breath catches, and Luca dares to glance up at her. She is so achingly beautiful, especially as her perfect mask slips and pain etches across her features. "There was a rupture in the tunnel that holds it in place, and the tendon slipped out of the grooves. I had surgery to repair it."

Luca traces circles on Juliette's palm. She can see the curve of a tiny scar on the pinky side, a ridge that tells a tale of pain and fear.

"I thought I'd never play again," Juliette admits with a shaky sigh.

Luca looks up. Juliette's head is turned away from her, as if being this vulnerable pains her. Luca slowly trails her thumb across Juliette's inner wrist and caresses the scar.

Juliette flinches out of Luca's grip and cradles her arm to her chest. Her breath is rapid. "Sorry," Juliette mumbles.

Luca's chest aches. She understands, on some level. She has no idea what she would do without tennis to keep her sane. Even the idea of injury has her thoughts spiraling into circles of anxiety. So, Luca does the only thing she can think of. She reaches out and curls her fingers around Juliette's wrists, tugging them away from her chest.

Juliette looks up, surprised and confused. Suddenly, Luca is aware of how close they are to each other. "You don't have to hide. I get it. And I'm sorry for knocking you over. If you'd hurt your wrist again . . . " Luca trails off and closes her eyes, unable to voice aloud the guilt she would have felt.

Juliette gently twists her right hand and interlocks their fingers. "Thank you," she breathes.

Luca remembers what Octavia had said at dinner, about how Juliette is sensitive. Maybe all her bravado is simply another barrier to keep herself safe.

Barriers are a sentiment Luca can relate to. If she keeps her inner circle small, there is less chance for being hurt, disappointed, or abandoned.

She starts to say something, but when she looks up, every word in every language she's ever known flits from her brain. Juliette's mouth is slightly parted, her eyes clear and bright, burning with a desperation that Luca's never been on the receiving end of before.

"Erm," Luca says, because she's intelligent.

Juliette snorts out a laugh, the minty coolness of her breath drifting over Luca's face. She's so close, close enough to kiss, close enough to devour. A featherlight touch to her cheek has her gaze lifting to Juliette's, a little taken aback. Juliette's fingers curve against her jaw, her thumb caressing her cheekbone.

"Don't," Luca breathes, and she can't stand the fragility in her voice.

"Don't what?" Juliette asks, her face dipping closer. Luca can count her freckles from this close. She can't stop staring at the beauty mark above Juliette's lip. "Luca." The sound of her name on Juliette's tongue sends a shudder down her spine. "I can feel you thinking," Juliette says, echoing Luca's words from earlier.

Luca isn't really thinking; her thoughts are mangled beyond comprehension. Juliette's head tilts, and their foreheads press together.

This is the closest they've ever been to kissing. Juliette's eyes are big, pupils blown black to nearly eclipse the whiskey heat of her irises. Their breath mingles, and if Luca tilts her head, their lips would press together.

"Tell me what you're thinking," Juliette says.

"Why?" Luca is so distracted by the unbridled look of wild longing in Juliette's gaze.

"I don't know how to read you," Juliette whispers back, her gaze flickering, as if she's trying to rob Luca of her thoughts through her eyes.

Luca lifts her other hand and places it on Juliette's cheek. Her skin is soft and warm as she skims her hand through Juliette's gold-touched curls. The tie holding them back loosens, and the silken feel of them is even better in real life than in her dreams.

"I'm thinking about how much I want to kiss you," Luca says finally. It's the only way she can make sense of the wild pounding in her heart and the electric sparks between them.

Juliette starts to smile. "Really?"

Luca looks away, tempted to shift away. "Don't mock me," she whispers, curling her fingers tighter into Juliette's hair.

"I know it might be hard to believe, but I'm not," Juliette breathes. "I was thinking the same thing."

Luca freezes and looks back at Juliette, the frenzied beat of her heart stuttering. "Well, why don't you?" Luca challenges.

Juliette smirks, her eyes gleaming as she tilts her head and their lips brush.

It's barely a kiss. It's the most delicate touch of their lips, the tremble of their collective breaths so fragile between them.

It lasts only for a heartbeat.

Luca lunges, capturing all of Juliette's mouth. It isn't neat or even particularly good. It's hungry and driven by the marrow-deep need to feel Juliette against her.

Juliette gasps as Luca knocks them backward. Her fingers dig into the back of Luca's neck, driving her closer. Luca shudders, reminded viscerally of Juliette's hands on her burned skin.

Luca licks into Juliette's mouth, drawing a breathy gasp from her. She lifts the hand she still has a hold of up over Juliette's head. She trails her fingers down Juliette's wrist, brushing down the length of her forearm and bicep before she stops on her heaving ribs. Juliette's skin is hot beneath Luca's hands. She kisses the corner of Juliette's mouth, the beauty mark, the dip of her chin, the hinge of her jaw. She sucks lightly at her skin, addicted to the way Juliette's breath hitches and her chest heaves. She soothes every bite with a swipe of her tongue.

Juliette whines and hauls Luca up by the back of her neck to cram their mouths together. It's needy and desperate, but so incredibly hot that she rolls her hips down and presses the length of their bodies together.

Juliette rakes her fingers across Luca's shoulders, a strangled moan caught in her throat. Juliette arches into Luca, and her free hand slides beneath Luca's T-shirt, fingers splaying across her back, dipping beneath the straps of her sports bra.

It's too much, these sloppy kisses and frantic touching. Luca rips herself from the velvet heat of Juliette's mouth and gasps for air. Her head spins like she's drunk, and she can't find her breath.

Juliette cups her jaw and tries to reel her back in for more heated making out, but Luca grabs her wrists. "Stop," she whispers, staring at where her hands engulf Juliette's wrists. "I can't do this." Luca lets go and scrambles off the bed.

"What, why?"

Luca risks turning back to her. Juliette is tangled in the sheets, her chest heaving, and her curls spill down her shoulders in spirals. Her lips are kiss-swollen and scarlet, her face blotchy with a flush. Luca is desperate, tempted even, to dive back in the sheets and finish ravishing Juliette. Heat pulses in her core, slick and wet already.

"You don't have to leave. We could be, like, soulmates-with-benefits?" Juliette frantically pushes her hair out of her face. "The health benefits of touching each other cannot be understated."

Luca's fingernails dig into her palms, tiny crescents of pain. "You don't want that," she whispers, desperately wishing it wasn't true.

"What if I did?" Juliette scrambles off the bed.

Luca scoffs, stepping back from Juliette. She sways, hitting the wall. She swore she would never let herself land in another solely-physical relationship, especially with another player. But this is her soulmate

"I know it's hard to believe—" Juliette starts.

"You're right," Luca cuts her off, "and even if I did believe you, I can't have a purely physical relationship. I can't do it again." Luca steadies herself against the door, fingers curling around the doorknob. Her body clearly wants one thing, but she knows she can't keep her feelings from tangling in a messy knot. She can't trust Juliette with her heart—even if she is her soulmate, she's also her rival. One who has been hell-bent on playing mind games in the media and distracting her for months. "And once you get what you've always wanted, will there be any room in your life for me?"

Luca needs to focus. She has tournaments to win and a number one ranking to keep. If she loses herself and looks away from her goal for one moment, all she's worked for will be ruined. The resulting spiral will destroy her. A tight, thorny feeling latches around Luca's lungs, a familiar panic she knows more intimately than any lover.

Juliette blinks and stammers, trying to come up with words, but ultimately she fails.

"I hope your wrist feels better," Luca says as she shoves out of Juliette's room.

EIGHTEEN

JULIETTE

The rapid flicking of the overhead light on and off wakes Juliette from a fitful slumber.

"What the hell?" She tosses her arm over her eyes.

The bed rocks and bounces. "Time to wake up!" a familiar voice singsongs.

"Fuck off, Remi," Juliette mutters. She feels hungover, even though she hasn't had a drink since that night on the beach. Her eyes burn, her throat is sore, and there is an unpleasant and frankly annoying ache in the center of her chest.

She would never admit it to any living soul, but after Luca left unceremoniously, Juliette had fallen asleep crying. She allowed herself the grace to wallow in her self-pity and overwhelming feelings. She didn't know what she was crying for after a while. She tells herself it was the fear of hurting her wrist again, a catharsis after an emotional day.

But she knows that it has everything to do with the way Luca had behaved—all over her one minute and pushing her away the next. She wouldn't put it past Luca to try to mess with her head, but she didn't expect herself to fall for it so thoroughly.

"Come on, Jules," Remi says, nudging her hip.

"Leave me alone." Juliette lowers her arms and finds Remi lying next to her on her stomach, her head pillowed on her arms, and her soft dark eyes sparkling with barely contained mischief. She looks happy with herself, like she knows something Juliette doesn't.

"Nope," Remi chirps, kicking her legs back and forth like a teen girl from a 1990s commercial.

"What?" Juliette isn't in the mood for Remi's games. She stretches out her leg and kicks Remi's calf.

Remi leans closer, undeterred by Juliette's attempts to shove her away. "You and Luca Kacic?" She wiggles her brows.

"Nothing happened," Juliette lies, turning on her side to grab her phone. She has a few missed calls and messages from Livia. She winces as she reads through them, the panic evident in her rapid sending of the texts. By the time she gets to the end of them, clearly someone had called and finally soothed her.

PICCOLA POLPETTA

> you better be okay or I will kill Luca.

> (I don't care if she's your soulmate btw.)

> hope you feel better soon though xoxo

"I'm sorry, Jules," Remi murmurs.

Juliette glances at her. "For what?"

Remi nudges her again. "Luca was going to come up here last night. I guess she didn't."

"Oh," Juliette says, swallowing hard. "Well, she did." She is grateful her voice doesn't crack.

"Oh," Remi says, interest piqued.

Juliette curses herself. "Shut it. Nothing happened. She just gave me a massage."

"A massage!" Remi's eyes widen, and a smile sprawls across her face. "You're kidding! Then what?"

"Nothing!" Remi is the last person she wants to talk to about Luca and their kiss.

Remi's pout is nearly compelling. "Come on," she whines.

Juliette huffs out a sigh. Even if her head is swimming and her heart aches, her body thrums with a renewed, electric energy. "She gave me a massage because a soulmate's touch cures little ailments. Like bruises and cuts."

Remi's mouth quirks into the start of a smile and Juliette looks away. She doesn't know why she admitted it to Remi, but it's not like Remi didn't suspect it already. Still, saying it aloud makes it feel like her ribs are too tight around her lungs.

"It's true," Remi says, nodding solemnly.

Juliette raises her brows, seeing this as an opportunity to divert attention away from herself, but she's also curious. "Oh, yeah?" She touches Remi's wrist, closely wrapped in black and bracelets.

Remi rolls her eyes, equal parts annoyed and amused.

"Why are you keeping it a secret?" Juliette asks, looking up at the ceiling.

For a couple of heartbeats, Remi remains silent until she finally sighs, long and heavy, as if the weight of the secret lies on her shoulders. "She wants to keep it a secret."

"Why?" Juliette turns over, stuffing a pillow under her head so she can look at Remi fully.

"She just wants to wait for the right time, y'know?" Remi rolls over onto her back, flopping back with a heaved sigh.

"Is she on tour?" Juliette asks.

Slowly, with her lower lip caught in her teeth, Remi nods. Some of the tension in Juliette's chest unwinds. Maybe Remi isn't as much of a gossiper as she thought. Maybe Remi is looking for someone to confide in about the complexities of having a rival tennis player as a soulmate.

"Are you happy?" Juliette asks softly.

Remi tilts her chin back, her grin genuine and utterly luminous. "Yes," she breathes, as if saying it too loud will snatch the happiness from her.

"That's all that matters then, right?" Juliette asks.

"Yeah," Remi says, her smile softer, but she still glows with incandescent happiness.

Juliette swallows the sudden bile of jealousy in her throat and rolls onto her back to open Twitter.

"Oh, no," she mutters as she scrolls through about a dozen tweets about her collision with Kacic.

 @sexyalmasibae
i'd say this is sabotage before wimby but we all know ricci is shit on grass xD

 @cozyclaudia
there is no "charity" between luca & jules it seems lol

"What is it?" Remi asks, and Juliette tilts her phone to show her the feed. "Yikes."

"That's an understatement," Juliette grumbles, tossing her phone to the end of the bed, as if that'll rid her of the internet gossip. She presses her knuckles into her eyes to try to block out the thoughts of the media scrutiny.

At big events, like WTA 1000s and Slams, the spotlight is glaring and stressful. It's hard not to shy away from it, and Juliette is not the best at keeping the media from spinning her words and intent. Some players, like Remi, are better at it, but even she isn't immune to the media's criticism—of her inauthentic schmooze, of the way she reacts after games. They definitely lay into her more harshly than the white players, and while Juliette has certainly rolled her eyes at Remi's tendency to be openly arrogant after a particularly thorough win, she has never been worse than Juliette. And sometimes, Remi deserves to be a little cocky. She's one of the best players in the world, and Juliette rarely sees any of the same criticism lobbed at the men.

A rapid knocking on the door pulls her from her musings. "Go away," she calls, recognizing Claudia's annoyingly loud knock.

"Too late!" she chirps as she throws open the door. The bed creaks as she jumps onto it.

Juliette lowers her hands to her chest to glare at her. Claudia wriggles her way between her and Remi, lying on her belly. "Who pissed in your oatmeal today?" she asks, pouting at her.

"Cornflakes," Remi says, exasperated.

"What?" Claudia asks, scrunching her nose.

"It's 'who pissed in your cornflakes?' Y'know, forget it." Remi shoots Claudia a look that says *don't ask about Jules*, and Juliette huffs.

"I'm right here. I can literally see you making that face."

"Is it your wrist?" Claudia asks, her playfulness dissolving into concern.

Juliette rubs her wristbone, but there isn't even a dull ache anymore. "No, it's fine. It's Twitter."

"Oh, hell, Jules, I told you to delete it. They've been hounding you this year." Claudia shakes her head and pushes off her belly to sit cross-legged at the end of the bed.

"I know, but you know Livia. She won't let me." It's a poor excuse, and Claudia's eyes immediately narrow.

"Livia isn't even five feet four and hasn't worked out a day in her life. Don't tell me you're afraid of her."

"She's surprisingly terrifying," Remi chimes in.

Juliette looks at her, thoroughly confused.

"Oh, I see her in y'all's box." She shrugs, as if that explains anything at all.

Claudia rolls her eyes. "You two are ridiculous." She swings off the bed. "We're leaving in an hour." She swats Remi's leg as she passes. "Do not be late!" she calls over her shoulder.

LUCA

Juliette insists she's well enough to play her singles match. Luca keeps her mouth shut because it's none of her business.

The Italian crowd chants Juliette's name when she comes out for the first match. She soaks in the praise, glowing in the bright lights.

Luca is entranced by her. She keeps trying to look away, but every time she does, her chest tightens. She *needs* to look.

It'd be weird if she didn't look at her teammate, though. Luca decides to just look at her as much as she wants. She can almost convince herself it's so that she can give advice to help Juliette win.

Not that it matters because Luca hangs back during the change-overs, letting Karoline, Payton, and Claudia encourage Juliette as she loses horrifically to Xinya.

Luca's advice probably wouldn't have been helpful anyway. *Stop double faulting. Get your second serve in. Don't push the point too early and miss. Move your feet.*

All things she's sure Juliette is thinking herself and would fix if she could.

Luca is saved from sitting on the bench for the second set because she has to prepare for her match against Octavia. But she can't escape the televisions in the locker rooms, even if she tried. From using the arm bands to stretch out her shoulders to warming up her legs on the bikes, she's forced to watch Juliette lose.

Once the game is over, Juliette seems in good spirits, grinning as she hugs Xinya at the net. Aurore and Victoria pat Juliette on the shoulders, sympathetic to her loss. It looks like Victoria asks about Juliette's back and she shrugs it off.

Luca shakes out her wrists and hands, sinking into her competitive headspace. Because Juliette lost, they're down 4 points to 1.

The crowd screams for Octavia like they did for Juliette, loving all the Italian representation. The match begins slowly. While Luca wants to win, this is still just an exhibition game, and that lack of pressure keeps her loose as she plays.

On the first changeover, Karoline hands her a water bottle. "Keep doing what you're doing."

"Any advice?" Luca asks as she takes a swig.

"Hit drop shots," a familiar voice brushes against the back of Luca's neck.

Luca tries not to startle, but her head snaps to the side. Juliette leans over the bench to Luca's left. Her dark eyes glitter in the light, a smile playing on the edge of her mouth. "Octavia is struggling with her knee. If you can get a drop shot to her backhand side, you could get some easy points. But you gotta follow it in and put away some volleys."

"Okay," Luca says dumbly, her eyes falling to Juliette's mouth.

"You can do that, can't you, Kacic?" Juliette teases, her voice full of uncharacteristic warmth.

"I'll manage," Luca says thickly, her brain frazzled by the proximity of Juliette Ricci.

She brushes her fingers over Luca's bare shoulders, leaving goose bumps in her wake as she walks back to the couch.

"You got this, Luca!" Zoe calls. The sound of her clapping breaks Luca from her stupor.

Luca hits twenty-eight drop shots throughout the match and wins twenty-five of them.

Juliette gives her no more advice, but she does cheer whenever Luca hits a good shot. And she's the first one to high-five Luca when she wins.

Juliette and Claudia put together their sister energy and win their first set while Luca is showering and eating.

It takes Luca until halfway though their second set to step behind Juliette. "Try to hit a kick serve into Xinya's backhand. She's weaker on that side," Luca says.

Juliette glances up from under her devastatingly long lashes. "Are you my coach now too?" she asks coyly, before bouncing off the bench and onto the court.

An embarrassed flush creeps up Luca's neck. She hides behind her phone, but Nicky sends her a steady stream of tweets about how uncomfortable Luca looks.

 @paytoninafountain
kacic and ricci are giving payton and karoline vibes circa 1998. they can't stand each other, and I can't wait for the chapter in one of their tell-all memoirs that describes how much they HATED each other.

@storiesofwoe
jules got run into but luca is the one giving butthurt

@NIKEFEMME
Go on kacic, give us nothing queen!

Claudia and Juliette win their doubles match, giving their team their first lead. 7–4 heading into the final day.

It is, unfortunately, their last win of the Connolly Cup. Luca decides she's just going to avoid Juliette, but it's hard to stay away from her. Every time she turns, they're scraping elbows and shoulders, always next to each other, no matter how Luca tries to maneuver to have Zoe and Claudia between them.

Eventually, Luca either succeeds or Juliette finally takes the hint to let Luca just try to be. The mood on their side is thoroughly crushed after Nadia beats Zoe to put Aurore and Victoria's blue team up 10–7.

And when Claudia and Zoe lose a heartbreaking tiebreaker to Xinya and Remi, the last thing anyone wants to do is hang around and tease playfully.

"Aurore is never going to let this go," Payton grumbles as they head back to the locker room on Sunday after the trophy ceremony. "She's so annoying when she wins."

Once they're back at the villa, Luca wants to crawl under the covers and sleep, but unfortunately there is still one more mandatory event. Her legs are aching and her left shoulder is tight after so many matches in a row, so she stands in the shower under the hot spray until it unwinds the tension from her tired muscles. She doesn't want to think of Juliette, but it's hard not to. Juliette has wriggled her way under Luca's skin, and there's no escaping her, now that Luca knows Juliette wants her too. The kiss circles in her head, the feeling of Juliette's body against hers making heat flush across her skin.

After her shower, Luca crams an energy bar into her mouth and stares at the tailored suit hanging on the back of the bathroom door.

The ending gala is where rich tennis fans buy seats at tables so they can stare at their favorite players like zoo animals. And Karoline made it clear that they had to be on their best behavior and charm the billionaires into whipping out their checkbooks. Maybe if her team had won, Luca would look forward to this celebratory gala. Her stomach roils at the thought of *another* social event, but she wrangles herself into the suit.

"You are utterly hopeless," Luca says to herself as she takes in the sight of her still hapless and woefully crooked bow tie. She tries one final time to get the bow tie right. It's not the worst attempt, so she leaves it, shrugging on her cropped suit jacket before leaving her room.

Downstairs, the rest of the women are dressed and ready to impress. Immediately, Luca's eyes search for Juliette. As expected, she's standing between two of her sisters, and Luca has to exert a considerable effort to keep her mouth shut.

Juliette always looks incredible, especially in casual athleisure, but in a beautiful dress, it's impossible not to stare. The dress is shimmering and deep blue, strapless, and cupping her body, cinched tight to leave nothing to the imagination. A high slit shows off one of her long golden legs, the other covered by a rippling flow of silken fabric. The setting sun gilds her curls, which fall loose around her shoulders, only a few pieces pulled back and held with a sapphire pin. Her elegant hands hold the sleek body of a vintage camera, and her nails are trimmed short and painted the exact color of her dress.

When Juliette glances at her, Luca's gaze drops, unable to meet her eyes. She doesn't want to see what Juliette's reaction to her will be. If she'll be angry or hurt—or worse, indifferent.

Luca is distracted by the sight of Juliette's bedazzled blue Adidas tennis shoes with lighter blue satin ribbon for laces. It's cute.

"You look nice," a silken voice purrs in Luca's ear, and she jumps. Octavia has abandoned her family to stand next to Luca. "I like the suit. Bold choice." She brushes invisible lint off Luca's shoulder.

"Thank you. It's more comfortable than a dress."

Octavia glances down at the black satin dress clinging to her slender frame. It's simple, but with her dark red lips, blown-out, glossy hair, and shining diamond jewelry, she looks ready to be the center of attention at this gala. "I'm sure it is," she says with a smile. "Maybe next year we'll all wear them."

Luca isn't sure what Octavia wants from her, but she's saved from responding by Karoline ushering them out of the villa and to the cars. Luca finds herself crammed in the far backseat between Octavia and Remi. Juliette, Claudia, and Nadia sit in front of them.

As soon as they enter the city proper, Remi presses her face against the glass to try to see Vesuvius against the skyline. Claudia points it out in the distance, a dark rising mound on the horizon.

The car weaves through Naples traffic with vigor and speed. Luca presses her fingers into the seat in front of her to keep from swerving into Octavia. She must use a similar perfume to Juliette's, because Luca's senses are invaded by the intoxicating sweetness of grapefruit. She tries to focus instead on the bright lights laid out like winking fairies that weave between ancient structures and modern builds.

Not a moment too soon, their destination comes into view through the front windshield. Museo Archeologico Nazionale di Napoli, or MANN, is a long, rectangular building painted deep crimson, framed by weathered gray stone. The cars stop in front of it, and Luca tries to climb out without stepping on Octavia's dress.

"This city is extraordinary," Octavia says, turning to her. "I always miss it when I'm away." She is even more extraordinary in the shimmering lights strung from the palms above them. She is long and graceful, her high cheekbones painted an artful and rosy pink, her brows arching and elegant, but she is completely impassive.

Luca is aware she's staring, and Octavia lets her for a moment before holding out her arm. "Shall we?" she asks, her crimson lips lifting at the corners for a barely there smile. Her eyes, almond-shaped and piercingly green, see through her, and Luca suddenly panics that Juliette told her sisters about their kiss.

Luca nods, unable to find her voice, and links their elbows together. In heels, Octavia is the same height as Luca.

"Have you been to the museum before?" Luca asks as they walk up the stairs through the flashing cameras and into the lobby.

"I have, yes. My mother is a historian in Rome. I imagine that will explain our unusual names," Octavia says.

"Oh, yes, Octavius became Augustus, didn't he? First emperor of Rome?"

"Very good. I didn't pick you as a history buff," Octavia says, clearly impressed.

Luca ducks her head. "I watched the TV show *Rome* over Christmas."

Octavia chuckles, and Luca counts it as a win.

"Octavia Minor was also the wife of Mark Antony. There is a porticus named after her in Rome," Octavia says. "I guess I should be thankful she didn't name me Cali."

Luca doesn't get the joke and Octavia pats her arm. "Caligula. The worst emperor in Roman history? Well, at the very least, his name meant Little Boot, so I'm grateful it's not my name."

"Octavia seems to fit you," Luca says. It feels like marble in Luca's mouth—strong and uncrackable, but beautiful and polished.

Octavia shrugs. "One grows into their name, I suppose." There is a soft bitterness in her voice that strikes Luca as odd. Before Luca can ask any questions, they're ushered into the museum's grand entrance hall. Austere white walls rise to show off the beautifully painted ceiling. A wide staircase guarded by two lounging statues leads their group into another hall. Starlike bulbs gleam from the ceiling, engulfing them all in a glittering warmth. It's as if they are the city's first inhabitants from thousands of years ago, lit by the glow of torches.

Luca can't help but fall silent in the face of such an expansive history as she takes in the sculptures that are artfully guiding them down the long, narrow hallway. The marble pedestals display ancient Romans—soft-bellied women and lean men, the color chiseled away by time or design, their faces cold and dull. As they pass a naked man with his arm up, Luca catches sight of a carving on his wrist, etched in a language that Luca can't read but assumes is classical Latin.

She pauses and Octavia lets go of her arm without a word, sliding away to continue through the museum.

"Wonder what his soulmark says?"

Luca startles and twists around to see Juliette next to her. "I do, yes."

"I bet it was difficult to find your soulmate back then. Everyone had the same name. His is Aelia, I think," Juliette says, tilting her head. The lights catch on the honeyed gold flecks in her irises.

"I hope they found each other," Luca says, shoving her hands in her pockets.

Juliette looks at her, eyes tracing her face, as if searching for something. A sad smile plays on her mouth. Luca swallows, wondering how to bridge the gap between them. She hates that all her words tangle and clog in her throat.

Juliette breaks the silence. "Come on, we've lost the others." Then, she spins on her heel and continues down the hall as if they'd never spoken.

She follows Juliette through the entryways until they reach one labeled THE GABINETTO SEGRETO. Luca doesn't understand but as she steps inside, she's greeted by a rather spectacular collection of phallic iconography.

"Oh," Luca says, blinking. The room is dimly lit, but the cases show off dozens of erotic artifacts, while quite raunchy frescoes and mosaics dominate the walls. Heat floods her face, and she clears her throat, which makes Juliette laugh.

"Welcome to the Secret Cabinet."

"Secret Cabinet, I guess that makes sense," Luca says, gesturing to the expressions of human sexuality everywhere. She moves around the gallery, some of her embarrassment starting to fade. It's *art*, not a porno.

She pauses in front of a painting of a man with an absurdly long cock. "Well, that guy must have thought highly of himself," Luca says.

Juliette snorts, as if surprised by the joke. "That's Priapus," she says, and Luca turns to look at her.

"Don't tell me you're a history buff too?" Luca hopes Juliette doesn't hear the fondness in her voice.

Juliette shrugs. "I might be." Her gaze falls to Luca's throat.

Luca swallows.

"Your tie is uneven," Juliette says. "Let me fix it." She moves in before Luca can stop her and gently unravels the knot at the base of her throat.

Luca runs her fingers through her hair, gathering it into her hand so it doesn't get stuck in the tie. Juliette loops the tie around Luca's neck with ease and fluffs her collar. Her fingertips are warm as Juliette presses them flat against the back of Luca's neck. Luca lets her hair fall and then shoves her hands into her pockets to hide their trembling. Juliette doesn't look at her, entirely too focused on the task of securing the perfect bow.

It allows Luca the opportunity to study Juliette's face, all her features up close for Luca to memorize. Who knows when they'll be this close again? Even if Luca won't allow herself to be with Juliette, she can still indulge in this moment. Juliette's long lashes are covered in mascara, her thick dark brows relaxed out of their usual pinch, and the straight slope of her nose has shimmer on the end of it. Her lips are light pink, plump, and full, begging to be kissed. Luca forces her eyes away from Juliette's mouth, and the light catches a rogue speck of glitter on Juliette's cheekbone, most likely from when she wriggled into her dress.

Without thinking, Luca reaches up and brushes her thumb against it. A spark of warmth makes the pad of her finger tingle.

Juliette freezes. Luca wants to step away, but Juliette is only halfway through the knot. Her eyes flick up and she blinks, having caught Luca staring.

"Sorry. You just . . . never mind." Luca looks away from Juliette but comes face-to-face with Priapus and his massive dick, so she looks back at Juliette. It's torturous to be so close and yet so far. To smell the warm sweetness of Juliette's perfume and still be able to pick out the grapefruit slice fragrance on her caramel-brown curls. To remember the sensual heat of her mouth on hers and not be able to re-create it.

"Priapus was actually a good luck symbol. He used to scare off thieves, apparently," Juliette says, a blush high on her cheeks, deeper than before.

"Really? Can't imagine what's so scary about a massive cock," Luca says, trying to keep a straight face.

"Have you seen his?" An unabashed smile spreads across Juliette's face. "I'd be intimidated." She glances up from under her lashes, then finishes tightening Luca's tie.

"Right, well, erm, thank you," Luca stammers. She expects Juliette to step out of her space, but instead she smooths her hands down Luca's chest.

Heat courses through Luca's veins and her skin prickles as her throat goes dry. Juliette is still wearing a teasing smile. She's sure that Juliette can feel her heart throbbing in her chest, hammering a frantic staccato that reveals her every thought in Morse code.

Juliette's hands linger, and Luca barely remembers to breathe. Her eyes, shining with warmth, search her face. For days, Luca has been trying to figure out the precise color of Juliette's irises. In most lights, they're dark, like earthy silt. But in this direct slant of golden light, they're an intense chestnut pool of mahogany and honey. Luca feels the flush creeping up her neck at the scrutiny. Then, Juliette's hands drop, and she takes a step back. Without the spotlight, her eyes return to their shaded dark brown, like autumn. "May I?" Juliette asks, lifting her camera. It hangs on a silken cord around her neck.

Luca's breath hitches. "Ah, sure," she says, trying to appear casual. She reaches up and tucks her hair behind her ear.

"Don't smile." Juliette lifts the camera, her thumbs easily fiddling with the buttons, knobs, and lens, adjusting the settings. "Act natural."

Luca scoffs. "How am I meant to do that? You just put a camera in my face."

Juliette's eyes narrow into a playful glare over the top of the camera. Something about her smile becomes wicked. "Do you trust me?"

"No," Luca says immediately.

Before Luca can react, Juliette reaches out and runs her fingers across Luca's cheekbone, in a similar gesture to what Luca had done to her a few moments ago.

Luca tries not to seize up, but she can't help but gasp. The camera clicks and Juliette lowers it, grinning. "Got it."

"Can I see?" Luca asks, running a self-conscious hand over her hair.

"No," Juliette says silkily. "Let's go. We have rich people to schmooze." And then Juliette slides around her and out of the gallery, leaving Luca in front of a wall of penises, alone and flushed.

Luca huffs as she hurries after Juliette.

NINETEEN

JULIETTE

The first time Juliette entered the Museo Archeologico Nazionale di Napoli, she was four, clutching her mother's hand and afraid of the crowds surrounding the statues and art. Her mother had distracted her by positioning her in front of each statue and telling her stories about the subjects, even adding funny voices to make her laugh.

Now, in the empty halls, the museum is a lonesome sight. Juliette hears Luca's footsteps catching up to her as she lifts her camera to snap a photo of the *Farnese Bull*. It's a complex carving of Dirce, the first wife of the King of Thebes, tied to a wild bull. It's a horrific image, one Juliette has never forgotten. She circles the sculpture to see Dirce's face; strangely serene considering the bull's hooves are about to crush her.

"Do you know Dirce means 'double' in Greek?" Juliette asks. She snaps a photo before turning to Luca. "You see she has a carving on her right wrist?"

Luca nods, stepping closer and lacing her hands behind her back. She leans forward to inspect the chiseled letters. "If you peak around the edge here." Juliette points to Dirce's left hand, clutching the leg of either Amphion or Zethus; Juliette can never tell. They're twins. "You can see another carving here. She has double soulmarks."

Luca blinks. "How did they know? Is it written?"

Juliette shakes her head. "She most likely didn't. This is a Roman copy from the Greek original. And, I know you don't speak Greek, but this second name is Dionysis."

Luca's nose scrunches in confusion. "What?"

Juliette grins, glad she retained something from her mother's endless history lessons. "It's believed that people would carve their gods' names onto their wrists as a sign of devotion."

"Oh," Luca says, "so it doesn't mean that Dionysis exists and was soulmates with this woman?"

Juliette shrugs. "I mean, he might've been. But the point is, a lot of art reflects the world's beliefs of soulmates. It's fascinating."

"Fascinating is one way to put it," Luca says, grimacing. "Carving into your own body still isn't very pleasant."

"A lot of history isn't very pleasant."

Luca's head tilts, pondering Juliette with her intense eyes.

"Come on, let me show you something," Juliette adds, hoping the exhibit she wants is still in the same place.

Luca follows quietly, a step behind. Juliette wants to say something to try to mend the broken pathways between them. She wants to shove Luca against a wall and demand that they can just enjoy each other without feelings or soulmate nonsense getting in the way. What had Luca meant by *not again*?

Juliette knows Luca doesn't owe her any answers, but it nags at her anyway, like a blister.

She fiddles with her camera, her stomach tied into a complex labyrinth of knots. Why had she taken that photo of Luca?

Juliette feels like a fool.

She knows in the heat of the moment, she'd wanted to capture the softened, vulnerable look on Luca's face. When she'd touched her cheek, so quick, barely there, featherlight, Luca had flushed, a blotchy stain of heat, and her eyes had darkened with something akin to lust. Maybe it was only temptation. God or the universe or fate making fun of her. So what if Luca had unwound every tense muscle from her back? So what if Luca had slipped behind the barriers she'd built and seen the rot but decided to hold her hand anyway? So what if kissing Luca was like an ice bath after a long match, painful in its exquisite torture, but comforting in how right it felt?

Juliette finds the Maidens precisely where she remembers them being. They're displayed front and center within a case, surrounded by their plaster brethren.

"Oh," Luca says.

Juliette watches Luca take in the room, the gravity of the phantoms of death. "Are these . . . ?" Luca breaks off, swallowing. She looks almost guilty, as if it's her fault that Vesuvius erupted and covered thousands in his acidic ash.

"Yes," Juliette answers. The exhibit is dim, the air heavy and somber, even though all it holds are plaster molds of what used to be real, living people. Now those people are nothing but decayed dust, lost to the unforgiving nature of a volcano.

Luca follows her to the heart of the exhibit. "The Maidens. Although, not really maidens, because they're actually men," Juliette explains.

"What does the plaque say?" Luca asks, her shoulder brushing Juliette as she leans in to try to read it. Juliette shivers at the silky touch of Luca's jacket against her bare arm.

"It's discussing the discourse of whether the two were soulmates." Juliette has heard it all before, especially her mother's rant about it being unlikely because the actual percentage of soulmate matches in the ancient world was quite low without social media to foster connections.

Juliette looks at Luca's face as she studies the two figures, embraced together with one's head angled into the other's chest.

"It would be nice if they were," Luca says. She meets Juliette's gaze.

"Does it matter if they were?" Juliette challenges. Luca's brow scrunches, as if the mere thought distresses her. "Can it not just be that they were two humans who, knowing the end was near, clung to each other because they wanted comfort?"

Luca blinks and whips her head back around to stare at the plaster replicas of the bodies long gone.

"Isn't that more romantic?" Juliette asks, her throat tight.

Luca shakes her head, still staring intently at the sculptures. "No."

Luca falls silent and brushes her knuckles over her sternum, pressing in, as if she's trying to relieve pressure. "Maybe."

"I believe we have some choice over who we love," Juliette says fiercely. She wants a response, a crack in the armor. "And that love is more powerful because it's *real*."

"Soulmate love is real," Luca snaps.

"But is it? If the only reason you're with someone is because they're your soulmate?" Juliette presses.

Luca's mouth twists into a delectable pout as she considers. "What does it matter, if your soulmate doesn't even want to give it a chance?" Luca spins on her heel and marches out of the exhibit.

"Luca!" Juliette stares after her. A wriggling, greasy feeling unfurls in her chest, and she looks up at the ceiling. It's cool inside the museum, but suddenly she is far too hot.

Why had she said that? Why had she said it like *that*? She had wanted to open the barriers between them, not snap them shut with a half-condemnation of soulmates and love.

Juliette wonders if she's the stupidest person on the planet. Maybe she should crush herself under one of the statues. She would genuinely consider it if it weren't unethical and illegal.

She heads out of the Pompeii exhibit and follows the noise of chatter into the Great Hall of the Sundial. Tables are artfully arranged in a spiral around a raised dais in the center of the hall, all the chairs filled with glamorous rich people swirling wine and whispering to each other. It's a sharp contrast to the naked statues standing sentinel along the walls. The organizers of the gala and the Connolly Cup are giving their usual spiel, joking about the competition and making the crowd chuckle politely. Juliette barely hears it, her stomach twisted into knots and her camera heavy in her hands. She lifts her gaze to the warm twinkle of the lights strung around the ceiling that alternate casting the frescoes in red and blue.

Juliette slides along the back wall, finding Claudia's mass of golden curls and the shimmer of her emerald dress. When she sidles up, Claudia's fingers curl around her wrist and squeeze. Juliette gives her a reassuring smile, and Claudia lets go with a nod.

Slowly, Juliette lifts her camera and snaps candid photos of their group, freezing them as they are in this moment. Claudia glows, rosy and wild under a particular shaft of scarlet, while Octavia gleams like ink and ivory under the blue. Remi is half-and-half, red and blue carving her features into elegant slices of each, her dark eyes reflecting pools of ruby and cerulean. Her teeth flash as she laughs with Nadia. In shadow is Xinya, but Juliette catches the softest half-smile as Remi glances in her direction.

The Fierce Four are onstage, glistening in the full spotlight. Karoline Kitzinger and Payton Calimeris in crimson and maroon respectively. The Dancer and the Wolf, side by side, sharing glances. Karoline with her lashes lowered, mouth moving as she whispers something to Payton that makes her giggle into the back of her hand. Juliette snaps a photo just as Karoline skates her fingers along Payton's bare shoulder, pushing her curls away.

Aurore Cadieux is speaking, her French accent ribboning over her words with effortless charm. She glows as she smugly talks about their hard-fought victory. Her cocaptain, Victoria Ferreyra, is not looking at anyone onstage but instead at their cluster at the back of the hall. She wiggles her fingers in a wave at them, and Juliette catches it in a photo.

She's the only one so far who notices Juliette taking photos, snapping them in rapid succession. She knows they might be blurry when she gets them developed, but it will reflect the whirlwind nature of their lives. Time rushes by in flicks, but when she turns the camera to Luca Kacic, it grinds to a halt.

She is a bit distant from the rest of them, eyes upturned to the gleaming lights. She looks pensive, soft in a way she rarely is on court, but often is in real life. The planes of her face are bathed in warm crimson, soaking her hair in red like it's blood, and her lower lip is caught in her teeth. She releases it just as Juliette clicks, catching the slight parting of her mouth. She selfishly goes to snap more, but Luca catches her, looking right into the lens.

Juliette jolts, unsure if she caught the photo or if it'll be as blurry as the rest of them. She lowers the camera and looks away.

Juliette barely has any time to think before they're swept into a line and walked up to the dais single file. The cameras flash and generous rounds of applause echo through the cavernous hall. She goes to their side of the stage, bathed in crimson light. She stands beside Karoline, who winks at her. Juliette flushes, wondering if Karoline caught her taking pictures too. She glances to her other side and finds Luca. The bright lights thread through her hair and make it gleam like bronze. She squints through the spotlight, and Juliette sees her swallow, fingers shaking before she shoves them in her pockets. They're close, but the distance feels immense between them.

Juliette forces herself to smile, sucking in her stomach and angling her body to be perfect as thousands of pictures are taken from every angle. Nausea swirls in her stomach, her pulse so loud in her ears that she doesn't hear a single word from the tournament directors.

Juliette looks up at the ceiling, at the wash of grays and whites surrounding angelic figures, the riots of red mingling with cool blues to show off the sleek religious imagery nestled in the clouds.

It is right then, in this Great Hall, surrounded by her friends and family, by thousands of eager strangers, that Juliette realizes she's never felt more alone. It's as if she's in the fresco, a painted portrait of herself being stared at and admired, but never heard, never seen for who she is.

A touch to her wrist brings her back to the gala and she looks down to find Luca staring at her. She isn't smiling, her face a carefully blank mask, but she tilts her head, and her eyes soften with concern.

Juliette wants to point up at the ceiling in explanation, but she knows she'd look like a lunatic. There's nothing up there, and she can't convey her thoughts in a few short words. Luca dips her chin, brows raising, and Juliette nods.

She may not be alone, but she is lonely.

She locks that thought away to explore later.

For now, she has rich people to impress, smiles to give, and money to collect for mental health and addict charities. There is no room for loneliness here.

After hours of charming the pocketbooks off glamorous women

and laughing along with the stupid jokes from cigar-smoking men, the gala winds down and they're ushered back to the cars.

Juliette stares out the window, the conversation around her crashing and rolling like the waves, but she stays on the shore, quiet. She turns her thoughts over and over again, pondering them like some kind of puzzle.

Against all of her notions about Luca, Juliette can no longer deny that she wants more. Maybe that is the key that needs to be slid into the lock of her loneliness. She's had a taste of Luca, and now her body needs more. It might be some biological response to kissing your soulmate.

Whatever it is, Juliette will satiate the urge and be done with it. She can return to her normal life and play tennis and win. She doesn't have to make this a big deal to herself or to Luca. It can be exactly what this weekend was meant to be—silly, low-stakes fun.

Her thoughts are settled by the time their half-hour drive is done and they're piling out of the car. Claudia corners her at the stairs, grabbing onto Juliette's shoulder as she peels off her six-inch heels. "Oh, no, you're not going anywhere. It's the last night, we're playing games." There is a mischievous quirk to her mouth that has Juliette deciding to play the role of annoying little sister.

"No, Claudia, I'm tired," Juliette whines, laying it on thick.

Claudia shakes her head, pearl earrings jangling. "It's tradition." She pinches Juliette's cheek, and she swats her away. "Don't make me sic Remi on you."

Juliette rolls her eyes. "Fine. Give me five to get out of this." She plucks at her tight bodice.

Claudia kisses the cheek she pinched. "I love it when you cooperate nicely with my plans," she says with saccharine sweetness.

TWENTY

LUCA

The dusky night is stifling. The cicadas howl, and the distant roar of the ocean beckons Luca for a late-night dip.

She knows she should be enjoying nights like these. It's hot and beautiful, and the stars are an epic tapestry of fate and riotous light. In an ancient city like this, it's a night for nymphs and forgotten gods. For wild love and laughter, to be reckless and foolish and young and give in to temptation.

And yet Luca can't dive into the beckoning abyss of abandon when her heart weighs so heavily in her chest, an anchor that drags her mood down.

She wanders out to the side patio, surrounded by lush greenery. Someone has flicked the string lights on. It's barely enough to combat the shadows, but it creates a warm sphere. The terra-cotta is still sunwarmed beneath Luca's socked feet.

Claudia and Remi slide out of the villa laden with bottles of wine and cases of beer, which they lay out on a half-wall protecting the patio from an overgrown swath of plants.

"Chug this," Claudia tells Remi, shoving a bottle at her.

"What, why?" Remi asks, but she obliges anyway, downing the beer in a couple of quick swigs.

Claudia plucks the bottle out of her fingers and places it in the middle of the table. "We're playing Truth or Drink. Gather the others. And, Luca, don't you dare think about sneaking off."

Dread spreads in Luca's chest, but she goes over to the cases of beer, grabs one, and cracks it open. She's going to need it. Claudia grins at her. She changed out of her dress and into a pair of tiny jean shorts and a crop top quickly, but her makeup is still intact.

Luca pulls out one of the chairs surrounding the table and flops down into it. She shrugged off her jacket and bow tie earlier; now, she rolls up her sleeves. She scoops her hair up, twisting it around her fist. A cool, salty breeze whispers through their private grotto, disturbing the heavy heat that has settled upon Luca's skin.

The rest of the players Claudia wrangled into her game start to fill up the table. Octavia wanders over and flops into a chair, listless. Her boyfriend, Leo Mantovani, left the previous night for a tournament in London, and Octavia seems adrift without him.

Zoe Almasi sits next to Octavia and smiles over at her. Zoe's dark silky hair is thrown into a high bun and wrapped with a scarf. Remi hands her a cocktail of some sort before she takes the seat next to her. Only one chair remains between Luca and Remi.

"How does she manage to do this?"

Luca startles and turns as Payton Calimeris slides into said chair, beer in hand. "Who?" Luca asks.

Payton gestures to Claudia, who is arguing with Juliette over the music.

"Seriously, Claudia?" Juliette is saying, hands on her hips.

"What? 'Pompeii' is the perfect song for Naples, Jules," she says, turning up the volume a few ticks.

Juliette shakes her head. "It isn't even Bastille's best song," she grumbles.

"She is very adept at putting us under her spell." Karoline takes the seat on Luca's other side. Now Luca is flanked by two absolute legends, and her palms start to sweat.

Karoline is as chic as ever, but she lets her golden hair fall loose around her shoulders. She runs her fingers through the top, fluffing it with one hand as she holds a half-drunk glass of white wine in the other. "I'm surprised you guys even want us here."

Luca stares at her. Even in this casual setting, her back is ramrod straight and her lipstick is impecable. She turns her dark brown eyes toward Luca, a corner of her mouth lifting in a small approximation of a smile that's more of a smirk. There's something intimidating about the way she holds herself aloof.

"Don't mind her," Payton teases. "She's just talking shit." Luca turns her head to look over at Payton, but she is staring at Karoline, totally at ease in her chair. Payton has tamed her curls back with a clip, but they spill out the top, the ends beginning to frizz in the Italian heat, a playful grin on her full, lush lips. This close, Luca can see freckles on the bridge of Payton's nose, faint against her warm brown skin.

Luca starts to say something, but Claudia cuts her off by spinning the bottle in the center of the table with a flourish and clapping loudly to get everyone's attention.

"The name of the game is Truth or Drink. Whoever the bottle lands on gets a question from the spinner. Don't want to answer? Drink up. I'll go first."

She flicks the bottom of the bottle, and it whirls wildly, wobbling until it lands on Payton Calimeris.

"Oh, no," Payton says in mock dismay, but she's still grinning.

"Come on, live a little," Claudia presses, leaning forward and planting her elbows on the table so she can properly stare at her.

"The point of the game is that if you don't want to answer, you must drink," Karoline says evenly. "And you never say no to that."

Payton leans forward, staring at Karoline, who lifts her feathery blond brows in a challenge. Payton sighs and turns to Claudia. "Go ahead, then," she says, resigned like a teacher humoring her young students.

"Have you met your soulmate?" Claudia asks, and everyone's eyes fall to Payton's left wrist, wrapped in black to hide whatever name is etched into her skin below it.

Payton pauses, holding her beer halfway to her mouth, as her dark eyes dart around the table. They're like liquid ink in this light. Then she looks at Claudia and says, "I haven't."

Claudia's spine straightens, and her face is a mix of confusion and shock.

"I thought you were married?" Remi chimes in, now that the game has gotten juicy.

"That's what I thought!" Claudia exclaims, pointing at Remi.

Next to Luca, Karoline snorts.

"Not that it's any of your business, but I was engaged," Payton says, rubbing her thumb along the slender neck of her beer bottle. "Never married."

"What happened?" Juliette asks, leaning forward in tandem with Claudia.

Payton smirks at them and shakes her head. Then, with deliberate slowness, takes an exaggerated drink of her beer.

Payton revealed more than Luca would have expected her to. As she mulls over Payton's candid response, Luca takes a drink from her own bottle and instantly regrets it. She hates beer.

"Thank you for indulging me, Payton," Claudia says, saluting her with her wineglass. "You get to spin next!"

"Oh, how fun," Payton drawls, but she's grinning as she spins the bottle. It wobbles, nearly falling off the table. Luca holds her breath as it comes close to her, but stops on Karoline.

"Amazing," Karoline says dryly. "Don't even bother asking. I'm not answering." She cheers her wine to the air and drains the whole glass.

"Boo, you're no fun," Payton says.

Karoline nudges the bottle with the tip of her acrylic and it does a lazy half-turn before landing on Remi.

"Oh, bring it on, Kitzinger," Remi says with a wicked grin.

Karoline tilts her head, her gaze searching Remi's face. "What's your opinion on open relationships? Polyamory? Polycules?"

Remi blinks, taken aback. It's quiet for a beat, then Juliette breaks the silence. "You do love to be in other people's business, Remi. Might be the perfect arrangment for you."

Remi chokes on a laugh. "Fuck off, Jules," she says.

"Being nosy and polyamorous are not mutually exclusive," Karoline says mildly, a smile tugging at the edge of her mouth.

"I've never thought about it," Remi says. Her gaze slides toward the villa, higher to one of the windows above. "But I doubt my partner would be a fan." Luca glances around the table. They're missing two members of the Connolly Cup—Xinya, because she didn't want to be outdoors in the heat, and Nadia, because she doesn't drink. She files that thought away for later.

"Why not?" Octavia asks, twirling a lock of her hair around her finger. "Jealousy? Posessiveness?"

Remi clears her throat. "You'd have to ask her."

"We would if we could," Juliette chimes in, "but *someone* won't spill." Luca frowns. So Juliette is close enough to Remi to even ask about her soulmate? Luca grits her teeth; that level of familiary is foreign to her.

Remi shrugs nonchalantly, but her gaze keeps darting to the villa. "That is also her doing."

"Ah, your hands are zipped," Claudia says with a sage nod.

Remi lowers her forehead to her palm. "My lips are zipped? Or my hands are tied?"

Claudia blinks. "That's what I said, no?"

Karoline hums. "Satisfactory answer, I suppose." She shrugs.

Remi eagerly spins next and it whirls on the table so fast the bottle is a green blur.

"Aggressive much?" Juliette teases, but she's laughing so her nose scrunches adorably. A cold pit opens in Luca's stomach, at odds with the tightness in her throat; an unpleasant mix of a desire to see Juliette laugh like that and a jealousy that Remi made Juliette laugh so easily.

Remi giggles. "I was excited for my turn! I already have my question."

The bottle finally slows, pointing at Juliette. She groans, running her hands over her hair. "I guess I deserved that."

Remi cackles. "Perfect. Now, describe your last intimate encounter in three words." Her eyebrows waggle, and the bridge of Juliette's nose flushes red.

Juliette holds up her hand. "Unfufilling." She ticks off a finger. "Short." She pauses, her gaze sliding purposefully to Luca. "And oily." She smirks.

Panic freezes Luca in place. Of course Juliette would talk about the massage night and not the last time she had sex. Anything to make Luca squirm. She didn't say Luca's name, but as her gaze lingers, she knows all the others at the table are looking at them. Did Juliette tell Remi about that night? About the massage and the kiss and Luca freaking out?

"Sounds boring"—Claudia yawns—"your turn now, Jules, spin." Claudia smacks Juliette's shoulder lightly, uncoordinated now that she's finished her drink.

Juliette rolls her eyes and swats the end of the bottle, sending it spinning wildly. Luca watches as the light catches off the deep green glass and sends a shower of emerald light shards across the table. It seems to spin forever, time suspended as Luca prays it doesn't land on her.

The wind picks up, ruffling Luca's hair and making the bottle do one additional rotation. Then it stops, pointing directly at Luca's chest. Her gaze connects with Juliette's, who is staring at her with intense dark eyes.

Luca looks away and sees that everyone's gazes are bouncing among them, riveted spectators waiting to see what Juliette will ask and if Luca will respond. Heat prickles Luca's neck. She waves a hand at Juliette. "Ask, then."

Juliette's eyes narrow. "I'm thinking."

"Really? I didn't think you ever thought before you spoke," Luca snaps back. Though her retort came quick and sounded confident, she feels like she wants to peel her own skin off. She's too warm, the prickling sensation growing to an irrepressible itch.

Juliette's knuckles blanch as she tightens her fists on the table. "Would you ever sleep with another player?" Her question burns through Luca. Every eye is on her, and Juliette knows, without a doubt, the answer. Luca was inches from crossing that line with Juliette the other night.

The longer the silence stretches between them, the more smug Juliette looks. Luca snatches her beer and sips it. It's an answer in and of itself. Tightness winds itself like a spring around her chest, a screw twisting again and again—and it snaps. Luca puts down her beer.

"Excuse me." She pushes out of her chair and it takes every ounce of her control to not run off the patio.

The night presses in, suffocating Luca. Of course Juliette wouldn't care if her answer to Remi's question and her own question humiliates Luca in front of their friends and two incredible tennis legends. Now they'll all think they slept together. And Luca can't even refute it because she can't very well explain that *"No, actually, we didn't sleep together, And I wouldn't sleep with any other player. But my very pretty soulmate? Yes, actually, I want that very much."*

It's all just a game to Juliette. One that Luca doesn't want to play.

Even though she wants to throw up after that conversation, her mind supplies her with thoughts of being with Juliette. The moment in bed when they could trust each other to be vulnerable without the fear of rejection. When Juliette had told Luca of her fear of being injured again. In that moment, Luca hadn't wanted *just* sex, but also Juliette's emotional vulnerability.

And Luca doesn't trust Juliette to put aside her jealousies and games to give Luca that. All she wants to give is the physicality, and that is something Luca can't give away.

Luca ducks behind the thick foliage that creates a secluded path down to the beach and swerves into the tree line, away from the water. A faint citrus scent tinges the salty sea air, causing Luca to pause by one of the many potted lemon trees and breathe in deeply to ground herself, but the tangy aroma reminds her of silky curls between her fingers, now just out of reach, and she winces.

Footsteps slap against the path behind her and Luca turns, her anxiety spiking. It's dark under the foliage, almost too dim to see, but she still recognizes Juliette's lithe silhouette and curly hair.

"What the hell is your problem?" Juliette yells, stumbling to a stop. There is nowhere for Luca to go except deeper into the trees toward the beach or back toward the house.

Juliette followed her. For some reason, maybe to toy with her again. That thought roots Luca's feet in place. "I don't have a problem," Luca says, hating the tremor in her voice.

Juliette sways. She must be drunker than Luca thought. The wind picks up and a shimmer of light cuts through the leaves and catches on Juliette's high cheekbones, the curve of her jaw, the flutter of her lashes. Luca's stomach clenches as she remembers her fingers skating across that smooth skin, her mouth rough and hot. She's been avoiding thinking about it for two days, and as much as she tries to forget, the memories sear through her.

"No? Then why do you keep running away from me?" Juliette demands, taking a half-step closer.

The irony is a slap in the face. All Juliette's ever done is run away from Luca. The locker room in Australia, the beach that first night, when she put aloe on Luca's shoulders.

"Says the queen of running away from uncomfortable conversations," Luca snaps.

Juliette flinches, having the grace to at least look away, chagrined.

"And I'm not running away. I know when I'm not wanted," Luca adds. She wishes she wasn't trembling, that she could remain cold and steely—like ice, like her father had been.

Juliette shakes her head with a wry laugh. "No, that's not it. I kept kissing you the other night. I wanted you. I still want so much more." Desperation coats her tone, but Luca can't fool herself into thinking it's earnest.

Luca wonders if this is what being lit on fire is like. The itchiness crawls across her overheated skin, and it only burns more, knowing that Juliette might be the only balm. "I realized I don't want you at all," Luca says, turning her face from Juliette so perhaps she won't see how much the words hurt to say.

"You're such a liar, Luca Kacic." Juliette steps closer, nearly nose-to-nose with Luca now.

The use of her full name has Luca reeling, and she is suddenly too aware of the throbbing beat of her too-fast heart. Anger flashes through her, hot and searing, burning in her throat and pooling on her tongue.

"So are you!" Luca snaps. "You say you want me. Why? And if

you do, why do you say things that make me think you don't? If you're just messing with me, Juliette . . . " Luca can't even finish the sentence. Juliette shakes her head, curls bouncing wildly around her. She breathes out heavily, and Luca feels Juliette's breath across her face. They're so close now, chests heaving and anger radiating between them.

Luca rakes her eyes over Juliette's ruddy cheeks, the curls falling into her eyes, the intense heat of Juliette's gaze threatening to light Luca into a burning inferno. Her fists are clenched, as if Juliette's keeping herself from grabbing Luca and crushing their mouths together.

"Go back to hating me," Luca says finally. "It's better for both of us." She stumbles a halfstep backward.

Juliette licks her lips, drawing Luca's gaze. The motion is hypnotic, pulling her eyes to the glossy sheen on her lower lip. Luca clenches her fists tighter, palms stinging, the pain the only thing keeping her from lunging at Juliette and stealing another taste of her lips. The air is charged and electric around them, burning hot and about to catch flame. All they need is a match. The craving to lick every inch of her beautifully tanned skin is driving Luca mad. Desire and anger and arousal—it's hard to distinguish between them, and Luca is dizzy.

"I don't think you want that," Juliette snarls, she strides forward and Luca backs toward the trees, but there is nowhere to run now. Juliette thrusts up her jaw. They're almost nose-to-nose again, but this proximity feels so different from the night before, when they had been trembling *together* rather than *against* each other.

Luca attempts to shake the memory of last night from her mind. "Well, I do. And you hate it. You hate that now I don't want you."

Juliette shakes her head minutely, her eyes slowly skating down Luca's face to her throat . . . her chest . . . and hips. When her eyes snap back up to Luca's, they spark with triumph. "Oh, you want me."

Luca stops breathing for a second. She takes a step back, but Juliette follows, staying just inches away. "I don't want you and I don't need your mind games. Why do you think I stopped? I don't have space for you and your baggage." Her nerves are raw and frayed, centimeters away from snapping and sending her spiraling.

Luca knows Juliette Ricci will be the death of her and her career. She has achieved so much, but she craves even more. Her career has just begun, and she has worked too hard to give it up. Now she has a target painted on her back, the world number one ranking hanging around her neck like an albatross.

Juliette, regardless of what she says, is caustic and volatile, unpredictable in her whims. So even if Luca itches and desires more than anything to kiss and touch Juliette, she won't. She *can't.*

"I don't believe you," Juliette breathes, desperate and shaky.

Luca's back hits a tree, and suddenly Juliette's hands are planted on either side of her waist, trapping her against the tree. She is thoroughly trapped. She wants to snap her body into Juliette's like they're puzzle pieces, release the tension from her body, and get some much-needed friction on her itchy skin and throbbing core. "You believe we have power over who we love."

Juliette shivers. "And what does this have to do with love? You drive me crazy. I want you, you want me, why can't it be that simple?"

Juliette's words are a shower of cold water that extinguishes the passionate heat threatening to overwhelm Luca. "It is never that simple," Luca hisses, and she shoves Juliette away from her.

Juliette stumbles back, and Luca traipses down the path. This time, Juliette doesn't follow. Luca doesn't realize she's back in the villa and upstairs until she slams her door shut behind her.

She sinks against the frame, pressing her fists into her eyes so hard she sees sparkling ribbons of color. She wants to scream. Luca considers for an unhinged moment abandoning all her common sense and dragging Juliette up to her room to release all the steam burning inside her.

She chokes on a laugh. It's always been pathetic how wrapped up in her fantasies she's been. Even if she wants Juliette to pleasure her, she can't give in to temptation. She can't have that sort of relationship again. She has too much to lose, and she isn't certain she could put herself back together again.

Luca's legs shake, but she gets off the floor. She doesn't need Juliette Ricci. She doesn't need a one-night stand. Especially not one with the woman cosmically designed to ruin her.

She might not need one, but she definitely wants it.

TWENTY-ONE

JULIETTE

Juliette wakes to a flurry of texts from her father about Wimbledon prep. For a moment, that's all she has to worry about. Then, as she sits up, she thinks of Luca Kacic, even though she doesn't want to. Luca's rejection stings, and Juliette knows she's sulky and licking her wounds, but it's impossible not to. Luca has wriggled her way under Juliette's skin, and the aching cavern in her chest keeps expanding because of it.

Luca is already gone by the time Juliette is packed. Trying to channel her hurt into annoyance, Juliette says goodbye to the rest of the women and gets into the backseat of Octavia's rented SUV. On the road to the airport, Claudia and Octavia happily chatter about what junk food they're going to indulge in once they're in London, but Juliette's stomach twists in unhappy knots. She presses her forehead against the cool glass and watches her home pass by in a blur of color. She has always loved being in Naples, she will always say it is her home, but as her stomach flips over and over again, she realizes it's never actually been her home. She loves Italy, of course, but her feet are never on the same soil long enough for her to become settled.

Sure, she has her apartment in Monaco, Claudia's flat in London, and Octavia's house on the French Riviera, but none of those places have ever satiated the hungry loneliness in her chest. Not even lifting a trophy had done that.

But Luca's soft and plush mouth on hers, sun-chapped and tasting of pomegranate lip balm, the feel of her calloused palms against her ribs, the silk of her hair crushed in Juliette's fingers . . . that had calmed the raging thoughts in her mind.

It is so deeply mortifying that Juliette puts her head in her hands. She really needs to get a grip.

The night is young and bursting by the time they land and cram in the back of a cab to go to Claudia's expensive Hackney townhouse. It's on the opposite side of London from Wimbledon, but there was no talking her out of the charming space with the glossy hardwood floors, natural light, oak built-ins, and quaint garden.

Juliette always feels calm in Claudia's space. Despite Claudia's extroverted and riotous personality, her apartment is clean, tranquil, and full of quirky bits of her that no one else sees. Juliette almost feels like a teenager again when she walks in, especially as Claudia cranks up some pop song and opens the windows to let in a fresh breeze to air out the stale apartment. The sky is vivid-bright still, even as the sun sets beneath the building line in a flash of gold and persimmon.

It isn't long until Livia arrives, a whirlwind as always, with her hair twisted into a messy bun. She's wearing stylish wide-leg trousers and a silk shirt instead of her usual leggings-and-oversize-tee combo. Juliette raises an eyebrow at her.

"Were you on a date?" Claudia squeals as she yanks Livia into a massive hug.

"No, of course not. I had a meeting with your watch brand." She smacks Claudia's shoulder as she lets go. "I did send you notes." Then she launches herself into Juliette's arms, slamming into her so hard that they almost teeter off-balance, both of them laughing as they swing around.

They order more food than four people could ever possibly eat. And on plush couches the color of spilled wine, they talk and gossip like they're normal sisters.

"Hey, why isn't Leo here?" Livia asks eventually as the gossip peters out.

Octavia shrugs. "This is a Ricci Sisters Night." She wiggles her fingers. "And until there is a ring here, he isn't invited."

"Harsh," Claudia says with a pout from where she sits, with her head hanging upside down and her feet over the back of the love seat. "He's been with you for years. He's practically one of us."

Storminess enters Octavia's face, and Juliette winces internally. Octavia hates being argued with. "Well, it's always been my rule." Three of their phones ping in unison, and they all groan.

There is only one group they're all a part of that Livia isn't.

"Antony," Claudia says, as if they don't already know. "He wants to know about practice schedules."

Octavia rolls her eyes. "I should block him."

"Don't," Livia says, ever the diplomat. "He's trying his best."

"He's irritating," Octavia mutters darkly, "especially since he isn't my coach anymore."

Juliette hovers her thumbs over the keyboard, staring at the message. It's a cold reminder that Wimbledon starts next Monday. Still a week to get ready, but the bubble of girls' night has been thoroughly popped. "I'm going to take a shower," she says. She leaves her phone on the couch, text unanswered.

She can feel Octavia's eyes on her as she goes upstairs to one of Claudia's many bathrooms. The hot water loosens her muscles and washes the airport smell and feeling off her skin, but her thoughts refuse to unwind. By the time she returns downstairs with one of Claudia's curl creams in hand, Claudia and Livia are nowhere to be found, and it's suspiciously quiet.

"They went to get ice cream." She follows Octavia's voice into the kitchen. An electric kettle starts to bubble, and Octavia leans against the island, her back to her.

"Why didn't you go?"

Octavia shrugs with one shoulder.

The kitchen light is warm, the cabinets painted a lovely sage green. Juliette spots one of their mother's many cookbooks on the shelf. Of all of them, Claudia has tried the hardest to capture the vibe of their childhood home, although the floors are wood, not terra-cotta, and the layout is all wrong.

The kettle flicks off, and Octavia pours the hot water into a mug that proudly states I MAY BE LEFT-HANDED BUT I'M ALWAYS RIGHT. Juliette chuckles at the sight of it. Octavia is right-handed, but Claudia will be annoyed at her use of her mug, so it feels almost like a joke.

"You want me to?" Octavia asks as she turns around.

At first, Juliette is confused, but then Octavia gestures to the curl cream in her hand, and she nods. "If you wouldn't mind."

Octavia ushers her into the living room. "I won't be nearly as efficient as Livia, but I'll do my best." She grabs a claw clip off the side table and twists her hair up into it. She hadn't bothered straightening it again before they left Naples, and the natural curl is stubbornly trying to return.

Juliette sits on the couch, and the cushions dip as Octavia arranges herself behind her. Her fingers thread through her hair, gently detangling without breaking apart her natural curl.

Juliette closes her eyes, focusing on the scent of grapefruit and sunshine now permeating the room as Octavia finger-rolls her curls with cream. And when she remains quiet, Octavia starts to hum, slightly out of tune, like their mother, but Juliette recognizes the lilt of the old lullaby anyway.

"I keep fucking up," Juliette says once the lullaby tapers off.

Octavia pauses in her finger rolls. "What do you mean?" Her voice is surprisingly gentle.

Juliette breathes in deeply. The weight of the last few days lies heavily on her shoulders. "You know how Luca was already at the villa?"

"Yeah?" Octavia twists a section of already rolled curls over Juliette's shoulder. She closes her eyes, letting herself get lost in the sensation.

"She showed up the night before and we got into a spat. Well, actually, I antagonized her and said awful things." A rock of guilt lodges in her throat.

"What did you say?" Octavia asks.

"Don't." Juliette shakes her head. She can't say the words again. "I apologized, and Luca said we could try to be friends. Then she gave me a massage to help after we collided."

Octavia clicks her tongue. "And you didn't tell us?"

Heat crawls over Juliette's face. "I didn't know how to talk about it," she mumbles.

Octavia sighs. "Okay, so what's the issue? You two are friends now, no?" Octavia scrunches more cream into her curls, gently squishing them into their spirals.

Juliette's throat closes. "It's just . . . we kissed. Multiple times." She feels stupid, like she's thirteen again and admitting that she kissed a girl down by the beach.

This time, though, Octavia doesn't laugh but instead sighs pensively. "Yes, groundbreaking, Jules. Kissing your soulmate."

Juliette spins around, and Octavia stares at her with her impossibly green eyes, a brow raised, as if challenging her. It reminds her so much of their father that she cringes back. "I don't want to feel like this, Octavia!" she says, throwing her hands up. "I can't feel like this, I have a Grand Slam in front of me. But I feel like I don't have a choice. I don't understand how I can miss her and want her when—" Juliette cuts herself off.

Octavia's hands land on her shoulders, grounding and steady. "Look, I know this isn't what you want to hear, but have you ever considered you might be wrong about Luca? That you might actually *like* each other, given the chance to get to know one another?"

Juliette inhales sharply, but it isn't enough to bring relief to the burning sensation in her lungs. "That's—what—I'm—worried—about!"

It isn't until Octavia's hands grab on to her shaking ones that she realizes she can't breathe, can't think.

"Jules," Octavia says, squeezing her hands rhythmically. "Look at me."

Juliette does, and she's dizzy. "Fuck," she whispers, and she tips forward into Octavia's arms.

Her sister holds her as she sobs, unable to breathe and shaking so much she thinks she might vibrate out of her skin. Octavia strokes her hair and whispers soft words into her temple, rocking Juliette gently as she falls apart.

Her world rocks on its axis. Everything wobbles and threatens to collapse, to break. Juliette loses track of time as the perfectly constructed circles of her life warp and twist into unrecognizable shapes.

She has no idea how long she cries, but eventually, it tapers off. The panic is still there, a snake curling around her lungs, threatening to crush them, but she's run out of tears. Now she's left with hiccupping sobs and strangled breath.

Octavia pulls back, rubbing Juliette's arms vigorously. "One moment," she says suddenly, getting up and striding out to the kitchen.

Juliette wraps her arms around herself, suddenly cold. When Octavia returns, she has a blister pack in her hand and a fresh glass of water. She pops out a pill. "Open," she commands, and Juliette does, like she's a strung-up puppet. Octavia puts the pill on her tongue and holds the glass to her mouth.

Juliette drinks and doesn't question her, swallowing with a bit of difficulty. Octavia keeps the glass pressed to her lips, forcing her to drink the whole thing. She does, grateful because her mouth is parched, and her hands are shaking too badly for her to take it.

When the glass is empty, Octavia fills it again and sets it on the coffee table.

"I'm sorry," Juliette hiccups, rubbing her face with her hands. She grabs a hunk of napkins and blows her nose.

Octavia waves her hand. "I've definitely done that a few times."

Juliette blinks wetly at her.

Octavia smiles, a little sardonic, and sighs. "Oh, well," she says as she tucks a still-wet curl behind Juliette's ear. "We are more alike than I'd care to admit. And I know you're close with Claudia and Livia, who isn't? But we're cut from the same fucked-up fabric."

"You and Leo?" Juliette asks dumbly.

Octavia leans back and curls her legs beneath her. "Leo has two soulmarks."

"Two?" Juliette can't believe she'd never noticed. It's more common for someone to have no soulmark than to have two. Juliette didn't even know it was possible.

Octavia nods. "So, for a while, I tried to convince him to find his other soulmate. I thought there was no way I could make him completely happy and that he wouldn't make me happy. It hurt Leo to have me repeatedly push him away. No matter how badly I wanted him, I thought I couldn't have him." She pauses to shake her head, barking out a wry laugh.

"I didn't know that," Juliette whispers.

Octavia looks up, her features softening in a way Juliette hasn't seen in years. "I didn't tell anyone. It's my job to protect you all. I know Claudia's sensitive about soulmarks, since she doesn't have one. Livia is the baby, I can't burden her with that. Mom and Dad aren't soulmates. You have always been anti-soulmate. I didn't have anyone to talk to about it."

Guilt swells in Juliette's chest, and her eyes prickle again. "I'm sorry."

Octavia touches her cheek, sweeping a tear away with her thumb. "Don't be. I didn't tell you this to guilt-trip you when you already feel like shit."

Juliette takes a shaky breath. She doesn't like the crystalline feeling in her chest, as if her heart is fragile and with too deep a breath she'll dissolve into feelings and tears again.

"Look, I know you and Luca had a rocky start. You both are dealing with a lot. There is so much pressure in this stupid sport, but I think happiness is worth pursuing." Octavia smiles, small and tender, as if she's barely daring to hope. "And I don't mean just a one-night stand." Her voice is knowing, not quite judgmental, but Juliette drops her gaze to her wrist, where a strap hides Luca's name.

"And you know you can find love with anyone," Octavia continues when Juliette remains silent. "I mean, look at Mom and Dad. Not perfect, but they do love each other. And in their own ways, they love us. Sometimes a choice is a burden, and even though your soulmate is predetermined, you still have to choose love, choose happiness. With your soulmate, or not."

Juliette stares up at Octavia from under her lashes. "What do you mean?"

"I mean, give it a shot with Luca. There is more to life than this silly game we play, and maybe life will be better if you're happy." Octavia takes her hands and squeezes. "You may be rivals, but you have a lot in common. Maybe that's why you're soulmates."

Juliette frowns but understands the logic of that. Still, the ugly feelings in her chest have sharp edges. Want and desire refuse to leave her alone, a ravaging and physical passion that threatens to scorch her to ash. The only cure for her loneliness is to give in to those desires and melt into Luca Kacic.

"She doesn't want me. She won't have me," Juliette says finally, deflating as she admits her nagging worry.

Octavia shakes her head, a cheeky smile tugging at the corner of her mouth. "I wouldn't be so sure about that. I've seen the way she watches you. She wants you too, she's just afraid."

Juliette chews on the inside of her lip. "You think?"

Octavia laughs, fully grinning. "Oh, Jules, I know it."

TWENTY-TWO

LUCA

The persistent drizzle of London refuses to let up. After the bright warmth of sunny Naples, Luca isn't thrilled by the prospect of several days of dreary rain. She stares out the car window, watching condensation gather on the glass. She draws a frowny face in it before wiping it away with the edge of her hoodie.

"Luca?" Vladimir asks. "Are you listening?"

"Sorry, what was that?" Luca twists around to look at her coach.

Vladimir sighs. "I was saying you have Ricci as a practice partner today."

Luca grimaces before she can stop herself, a pinch of panic threading through her chest. "Which one?" She prays it isn't—

"Juliette."

Of course. Luca snaps one of her bracelets against her wrist.

"Your first round is a qualifier you've never played before, but she's left-handed and very quick."

Luca nods. Juliette is quick, left-handed, and twice as good as the qualifier, which is precisely why Vladimir requested Juliette to practice against.

"Luca?" The cab skids to a halt, and Luca glances at Vladimir. "Are you all right? You seem unfocused." Vladimir strokes his dark goatee, pensive rather than upset.

Luca shrugs. "I'm fine. I just know Twitter will have a field day with this practice." It isn't a lie, but her feelings are tangled in complicated knots when it comes to Juliette. It's more than just media concerns. She *wants* Juliette, but she isn't naive enough to think that

Juliette wants anything more than physical pleasure with her. She can see being entangled with Juliette is a bad idea from miles away. But her body yearns to be near Juliette, to twine their fingers and bodies together.

Vladimir hands a wad of cash at the driver, and Luca flees from the car, her heart beating too quickly. Droplets of rain land on the back of her heated neck and slide underneath her collar. She shudders and lifts her hood over her head, smacking her cheek with the end of her braid. Vladimir takes her bag over his shoulder, and they rush into the side entrance of the club.

"Damn rain," Vladimir mutters, shaking his thick, dark hair off his shoulders. "I hate London."

Luca huffs. She doesn't hate London as much as she hates rain. Vladimir leads the way through the labyrinthine halls of the country club. She prefers to play outside, but it's better to practice inside than not at all.

Their court is a secluded, lonesome one on the opposite side of the club. The vivid fluorescent lights irritate Luca's eyes. The revolving glass door sticks as if it hasn't been oiled in a while, and she has to shove through it. Dozens of balls litter the court, about half of which are lying at the base of the net, mocking whoever hit them.

Rapid Italian flies through the air, and she glances to her right to see Juliette Ricci repeatedly bouncing a ball on the baseline while her father yells something from the opposite side. She knew she wouldn't be able to avoid Juliette forever. That would be an impossible endeavor, but she had hoped she wouldn't have to run into her so soon after Naples.

Instead of Juliette, Luca focuses on Antony Ricci. This is the first time she's seen him close up. He's taller than Luca expected, but she usually only sees him in Juliette's box at matches. His hair is dark, streaked with white at the temples and cut short to reveal tight ringlets. He is tan, much like Juliette, like he's spent his entire life lounging in the sun. Like Octavia, he's right-handed, but a brace keeps his arm immobilized.

Antony's eyes snap to Luca and narrow, annoyed that she's entered the court. Does he know that she's the *Luca* named on his daughter's wrist? She shrinks into her hoodie, hating how his gaze pierces through her.

"Ricci," Vladimir says, breaking the moment.

Luca glances at Juliette, who has paused the bouncing ball to stare at her. She's clad in all-white with her hair tied up into a tight bun and a headband tied around her forehead, the ends brushing her shoulders. Luca quickly looks away, not knowing how to handle Juliette's scrutiny.

"Orlic. We still have an hour and a half," Antony Ricci says in a clipped tone.

"I'm aware," Vladimir says calmly, dropping Luca's bag before joining the Ricci patriarch on the other side of the net.

Luca forces herself to move to the unused bench. She busies herself with peeling off her sweatpants and withdrawing both her and Vladimir's rackets.

"I thought you didn't have space for my baggage," Juliette says, and it takes all of Luca's self-control to keep from looking up.

She shrugs, trying to come off as nonchalant despite how much she's sweating. "I don't pick my hitting partners. Vladimir does." She sets her racket on the other side of the bench and lifts her foot to tighten her shoelaces.

Juliette thunks a ball rhythmically against the grass. "I see."

Luca hums because she doesn't trust her voice.

The ball stops abruptly.

"I thought we were going to be friends," Juliette says, her voice so close that Luca flinches.

She looks up to see Juliette leaning in close, a tightness to her jaw that Luca wants to smooth away with a brush of her lips. "Aren't we?" she whispers back, and Juliette's lips press into a flat line.

"You tell me, Kacic."

It's jarring hearing her last name when all she wants is to hear the way Juliette's lilting accent curves around the vowels in *Luca*.

"Luca. You can call me Luca," she says, finally meeting Juliette's eyes. Juliette blinks, startled. "If you want," Luca adds in a rush, the tightness in her chest forcing the words out.

"Do you want me to?" Juliette asks, the edge of her mouth twisting into a smirk.

Luca shrugs. "It is my name."

"So is Kacic."

Luca looks down and switches feet to distract herself. She fiddles with the loops of her laces. "Okay, but you don't call your friends by their last names, do you?"

"Depends on the friend, I guess. I call Rowland by her last name." Juliette sounds thoughtful.

"Just call me Luca, okay?" She says, even though it feels dangerously intimate. Her last name could nearly be a barrier, but it's just too *weird* to have Juliette call her by her last name when they've kissed.

Heat strikes Luca in the stomach and she tries to distract herself by grabbing her racket.

"Whatever my soulmate wants," Juliette says and Luca's whole body jolts.

Soulmate.

The word carves through her and she snaps her gaze up to Juliette. Is she messing with her again? Before practice to make her play terribly?

"That's not funny," Luca says, crossing her arms over her chest, racket strings pressed against her as a shield.

Juliette tilts her head, face unreadable as she studies Luca's face. "No, it isn't, is it?" She sounds pensive, as if she's doing this to try to test the boundaries, see where she can press and where she has to back off.

"Enough chitchat over there!" Antony Ricci calls from across the court. Vladimir must have been successful in getting Ricci to relent to actual match play against each other for the remainder of Juliette's session.

Juliette tosses her the ball, and Luca barely snags it before it flies over her right shoulder. "Good luck, Luca," Juliette says with a smirk before she brushes past her and onto the other side of the court. "Hi, Vladimir," she says brightly as Vladimir joins Luca.

"I don't know what you were so worried about. Ricci is very strict about media around his player." Vladimir grabs his racket. "You and Juliette should be practicing against each other more. It's good for you both."

Luca ignores the pointed look from Vladimir and jogs over to her side of the court. The grass is firm and browning beneath her shoes on the baseline. She scuffs her heels over the white lines.

Her knees are like jelly, but after a few rallies, Luca eases into the routine of practice.

The problem, however, lies with Antony Ricci, who will not stop shouting in Juliette's ear and let her play. Luca knows it would drive her insane if Vladimir tried to micromanage every aspect of her game. Her favorite part of tennis is sinking into the quick-time instincts of strategy. There is no time to overthink when she has a fraction of a second to decide. The muscle memory kicks in, and she only needs to live in the moment.

After twenty minutes, Luca sheds her hoodie and tosses it to Vladimir, who appears pleased.

Told you, Vladimir mouths, and Luca purposefully turns away and smacks a ball back at Juliette.

They move into actual points, a couple of tiebreakers, and Luca starts with a serve. As she's tossing the ball into the air for the first point, an alarm blares and she flinches. Her shoulder twists through the air and she connects awkwardly with the ball, sending it into the ceiling.

"This thing!" Ricci yells, and he stomps across the court to the revolving door. "It's been blaring off and on all session. I thought they'd fixed it." Ricci snarls something else in Italian before he vanishes through the revolving door.

"I better make sure he doesn't kill the club manager," Vladimir half-shouts over the pulsating noise. "You can handle this, right?" Vladimir pauses.

Luca waves Vladimir off, even though her throat constricts. She certainly would not want to be the employee dealing with the hot-headed Antony Ricci. Vladimir dips his head and jogs away.

The blaring alarm feels like it's throbbing in the back of Luca's neck, irritating and too loud. She can't even hear herself think. Juliette jogs to the net, her bun flopping and her curls nearly spilling free. Sweat drips down her cheeks, gathers in the hollow of her throat and gleams on her arms. Luca forces herself to look away as she joins her.

She grabs water from the cooler behind the bench and rips it open.

"That's irritating!" Juliette shouts.

Luca nods. Juliette's gaze is hot on the back of her neck.

The alarm cuts off midscreech, and Luca touches her temple where a thorough headache has burrowed itself. "And it keeps going off?" Luca asks to make conversation.

When she turns, Juliette reaches around her for the cooler, even though there's one on her side of the net. Juliette grins up at her as she yanks a bottle free. Luca freezes, unable to step out of the gravity of Juliette, even as she straightens. Heat climbs up Luca's neck. This isn't very different from the night among the trees after the disastrous Truth or Drink game. Juliette smells like sweat, and Luca has the absolutely unhinged urge to lick her.

"Yep," Juliette says, popping the *p*. She cracks her bottle open and lifts it to her lips. Her head tilts back as she drinks, and Luca's eyes trail down her throat to her collarbones, the straight line of the top of her shirt and where it stretches across her breasts. Juliette sighs as she lowers the bottle, chest heaving. She wipes sweat from her brow. "Good excuse for a break."

Luca swallows and gives a noncommittal sigh as her focus slips away from her. She wants to lean into Juliette, thread her fingers through her loosening bun, and tug until it all tumbles free and gives Luca the leverage to drag their mouths together.

"Do you want to get lunch after this?" Juliette asks. Luca blinks, returning to the present. "You like tea, right? There's a shop my sister loves we could go to."

"How did you know that I like tea?" Luca asks, caught off guard by Juliette remembering something about her—even something as innocuous as her love of tea.

Juliette tilts her head, a smile playing on her full lips again. "I do pay attention to you." She shifts on her feet. "Occasionally."

"Right," Luca drawls, a surge of warmth flooding her stomach. "And when do you pay attention to me?" For once, being under the scrutiny of Juliette's dark, smoldering eyes doesn't feel so scary.

Juliette shakes her head. A stray curl, soaked limp with sweat, brushes her cheek. "Anytime I can," she says.

Luca can't resist reaching up and gently twisting the strand off her face, tucking it into the headband. "You're sweaty," Luca comments, even though it's obvious.

Juliette's fingers brush her wrist, and she is so close that Luca can almost count all the faint freckles speckling her cheeks, brought out by months in the sun. "It seems like you're paying attention too."

Luca's fingertips brush against the shell of her ear. "And if I am?" Luca murmurs. Once again, she tells herself this is a bad idea. She said she couldn't do this in Naples, and that hasn't changed. But no one could possibly trust Luca to make good decisions when faced with a sweaty, hot, and incredibly close Juliette Ricci.

Juliette doesn't get a chance to reply.

The alarm chirps and Luca jumps, stumbling back from Juliette a moment before the sprinklers flick on with a hiss, and water rains down on them. "Seriously?" Luca mutters as she's soaked through with water within moments. It's warm like spring rain, but it still makes her feel slimy and gross.

She zips her bag closed, the zipper slippery against her fingertips, and hoists it onto her shoulder.

Juliette's palm slams into the glass of the revolving door. "It's stuck."

"Great," Luca mutters, feeling like a drowned rat. She shakes her now wet braid off her shoulder and straightens her visor. It's drenched and a few droplets slide underneath it. She brushes them off and blinks a drop out of her eye, then looks at Juliette.

Droplets of water slide down her cheeks and drip off her nose.

Her white tank top and shorts cling to the dip in her waist, her sculpted abs, the flare of her hips.

"You never gave me an answer," Juliette says.

"What was the question?" Luca asks, every coherent thought in her head drowning at the sight of Juliette in a see-through tee and shorts. She flexes her fingers, intimately reminded of Juliette's warm skin beneath her hands, the shift of her muscles as she massaged the tight knots from her back.

Juliette steps closer, and Luca takes a half-step back on instinct.

She does not have the energy or strength to do this while her brain is overwhelmed. She shakes her head. "Sorry, you're—it's—the water, I mean. It's distracting," Luca says, waving her hand at Juliette to try to explain that it isn't so much the water as it is that Juliette is in front of her, dripping wet in see-through white clothes.

Juliette moves into her space, and she holds her hand over Luca's visor, as if to protect it from getting any more rain on it. Her lips twitch into a smile, and Luca can see a shimmer of hope in Juliette's expression. Luca should crush it and move away, but her limbs are numb, and she can't make her lead feet move. She wants nothing more than to run away, but she can't. She's trapped without any way out. Her breath constricts, and she shakes her head.

"Luca, are you okay?" Juliette's playful hope softens into concern.

Luca shakes her head again. The water against her skin feels like needles, too much stimulation. "I . . . " She trails off with a hitched breath. She closes her eyes and tries to gather her spiraling thoughts.

For months, the pressure has been mounting, bending her bones and threatening to crush her beneath the weight of her own expectations and dreams. She knows, intellectually, that Juliette would be the final weight that would snap her in half, and she would fall apart.

She opens her eyes, feeling as though she's standing on the edge of a precipice, staring into a whirlpool that would drown her. But just as she's about to step away from Juliette, her fingertips lightly brush Luca's temple, down her cheek to her jaw, cradling her face with more gentleness than Luca ever thought Juliette was capable of. "What can I do?" Juliette asks, barely audible above the hissing sprinklers.

"Kiss me," Luca murmurs on impulse. Juliette's touch is like a ray of sun, and while she's touching her, Luca isn't thinking of the prickling anxiety that's about to collapse her lungs.

Juliette blinks. "Really?"

Heat from a mixture of desire and embarrassment coils in her stomach. Luca nods, unable to form a simple yes.

The sprinklers cut off, and Juliette shifts forward, her eyes closing. Her lashes are thick and dark, clumped with water. Relief washes through Luca along with the glittering sweetness of excitement.

"Juliette!"

Antony Ricci's voice cuts through the moment.

They snap apart. Luca breaks out of the dizzy, feverish haze that possessed her. Antony is speaking in loud, rapid Italian, his hands flying as he complains. Luca is sure her face is bright red if the heat scalding her cheeks is anything to go by, but Antony doesn't even look at Luca as he grabs Juliette's shoulder and drags her toward the revolving door.

Within a few seconds, Juliette is gone, vanishing with a whoosh of air.

Vladimir replaces her as the door swings around. "Oh, shit, Luca, sorry about the sprinklers."

Luca swallows. "Not your fault." She stares after Juliette.

Vladimir says something else, but Luca's mind is replaying the last few moments on a loop.

She never did respond to Juliette's lunch question.

TWENTY-THREE

LUCA

Other than her anxiety, the only trait Luca got from her mother is the tendency to avoid uncomfortable things. Which is most likely related to her anxiety, but Luca refuses to acknowledge that.

Luckily, Juliette is easy to avoid after the sprinkler incident. They're on opposite sides of the Wimbledon draw, so they don't even go to the grounds on the same days. She tracks Juliette's progress through the tournament, but she is diligent in never turning on her matches.

The Connolly Cup was an anomaly. She never spends time with other players, unless it's Nicky, and usually, Nicky is the one barging into Luca's life unannounced and occasionally unwanted. But Juliette doesn't attempt contact, for which Luca is grateful.

Maybe a part of her is oddly sad. But now that she's back into the groove of her routine, her anxiety lessens, and she can almost forget the complicated web Juliette entangled her in.

Wimbledon shouldn't be difficult for Luca, but the pressure of playing on grass when everyone tells her that her game is suited for it gets to her head. After winning the Australian Open, she feels like Wimbledon is hers to take. At Roland-Garros, she could excuse her poorer performance because clay isn't her surface. And even though her game *technically* is made for grass, she feels awkward and graceless on the slippery surface, perhaps even more so than on the uncontrollable clay. The only good part is that Luca can serve dozens of aces and win free points. With that tactic, she manages to skate by the first three rounds of Wimbledon without dropping a set. She doesn't feel great about any of the wins, her body aching in familiar ways. She knows Twitter must be talking about how lucky she is to have won six straight tiebreakers thus far, most by the skin of her teeth.

On her off day, she wakes up early for a morning practice session with Vladimir. The courts are quiet, and the grass is a little slippery with morning dew. By the time Luca warms up her legs and unzips her sweatshirt, the sun gleams overhead and burns away any remaining slickness.

They start slow. "Focus on your hit point on the forehand side," Vladimir tells her. After a few easy balls, Vladimir starts to hit harder and farther out into the court.

The muscles in her legs ache. She stretches her racket out for one of the balls that is slightly too far from her reach, taking a full swing and regretting it immediately. A muscle spasms in her back. She had assumed her aches were just fatigue, but this is so much more.

Luca grabs the offending muscle and digs her fingers into it in a desperate hope that the pain will go away. Of course, injuries don't work like that. Her body lashes out, the throbbing pain radiating up her spine now.

"Oh, God," Luca mutters with a sharp intake of breath, leaning on her racket as her muscle spasms again.

"Luca?" Vladimir's worried voice washes over her. His warm hand lands on her shoulder, grounding and gentle. He crouches, coming into Luca's line of sight. "What's wrong?"

"My back," Luca says through gritted teeth. She forces herself to straighten, but the muscle winces again, and she gasps. "Just a twinge."

Vladimir's mouth thins into a flat line. "It does not look like that." He straightens and waves for someone to get a trainer.

"How long has it been hurting?" he asks, his mouth twisting. Luca's guilt grows as she swears she sees a hint of hurt in Vladimir's eyes.

"I don't know. A little while. I thought it was just stiffness," Luca says. It's the truth, but she also knows she should have said something sooner.

Luca leans on Vladimir as they hobble over to the bench. The pain isn't too bad, now that she isn't lunging for a ball, but the muscle still throbs. A trainer drops a bag next to her and crouches down to examine her.

Vladimir turns away and Luca reaches for him, wincing in pain at the movement. "Don't leave," she whispers, and Vladimir blinks. For a moment, Luca hangs in suspended panic.

"I'm getting your water, Luca," Vladimir says gently, and Luca forces her fingers to loosen from his forearm.

Vladimir isn't leaving. Not yet at least. If it turns out she can't play anymore, he'll move on to another player.

She can't breathe until Vladimir sits next to her and takes her hand.

By the time the trainers are done with her and have sent her scans off for a doctor to review, Luca has taken enough painkillers that she's numb. Vladimir takes her back to the hotel and forces her to lie down on her stomach instead of pacing. He plants a bag of ice on her lower back and reads out her texts from Nicky. She can almost hear Nicky's panic in the tone of the texts, but she tells Vladimir to leave them unanswered. She doesn't know what to say—to Nicky or herself. Luca's stomach twists in nauseating knots. She wants to throw up, but she buries her face into the pillows instead. She curls and uncurls her fingers into the sheets, trying not to think about this catastrophic injury.

"You probably won't be able to finish Wimbledon, Luca," Vladimir says, sitting next to her. One of his hands cards gently through her hair as he says what Luca's unable to admit to herself. Luca feels like a failure. After not winning the French Open, Luca had hoped she could prove she wasn't a one-Slam wonder during Wimbledon. That she is more than just *lucky*. Too often she sees the comments online saying that she had an easy draw in Australia, or that she won because she broke Juliette's concentration. She knows, intellectually, both of those things aren't true and that she won fair and square. But the thoughts still seep into her mind as she wallows about having not won *another* Grand Slam. To cement her place in history, she'll have to win much more than just one Australian Open.

She groans and claws her fingers into the mattress.

"I know," Vladimir says, his fingers never stopping the slow and even track over the top of Luca's head and to the back of her neck.

Luca breathes in the fresh scent of cotton and lavender and wonders if she should smother herself. She turns her head instead and tries to look up at Vladimir. He's sitting back against the pillow, and she can't see his face from this angle, which is probably for the best.

"What if my career is over?" Luca whispers, finally voicing the worst of the thoughts that have been nagging in the back of her head since she first sat down and realized this wasn't just a sore muscle. She hates the way her voice shakes, small and fragile. Tennis is the glue that keeps her life together; has been since she was six years old and realized it made her father look at her with pride instead of disappointment.

"Don't think like that. Which I know is easier said than done, but it'll be okay, I promise." Vladimir's rumbling voice is soothing, and even though the thoughts don't disappear, they do shrink. "A back strain is relatively minor. And you're young."

"Hardly," Luca scoffs. Twenty-four is young by a "normal" life's standards, but she still feels like time is slipping through her fingers. She'll be twenty-five in October and theoretically in the twilight of her career.

"Some of the greatest players were in their midthirties when they retired, and they were still playing at the topmost level," Vladimir points out. "Karoline played until thirty-seven."

"What if I'm not one of the greatest?" Luca hates saying one of her biggest fears out loud.

"You probably won't be." It's the stark, hard truth, and *oh*, it hurts. "But as long as you do your best, then you'll be happy." Vladimir squeezes her neck gently.

Luca huffs. Vladimir is right, as always. Even now there are articles over which of the Fierce Four was the best. But the greatest of all time isn't a single statistic or match. And it's much more than winning championships. The Fierce Four are great outside of the court because of their philanthropic endeavors and continued efforts to help their communities. Maybe if she couldn't play tennis anymore, she could coach. Find another young Croatian girl with big dreams and help her get to the topmost level. Perhaps that could be enough, even if it isn't what Luca wants right now.

"Thank you," she whispers after several beats of silence.

Vladimir's hand pauses, resting on the crown of her head. "What for?"

"Being here," Luca whispers. Her throat is tight and clogged, her eyes prickling with an aching sting that she doesn't want to give in to.

Vladimir hums, and Luca falls asleep with her coach's hand grounding her to reality.

JULIETTE

Juliette gets roped into another late lunch with Remi after practice. Remi is the last match on Center Court today, so she's scarfing down food like she's been starving for weeks.

"Do you think that collision at the Connolly Cup has anything to do with Kacic's injury?" Remi asks as she devours a bagel smothered in avocado and salmon.

Juliette's fork clatters to the plate. "What?"

Remi chews as she stares at Juliette. With deliberate slowness, Remi swallows before asking, "You didn't hear?"

"Hear what? What happened to Luca?" Juliette demands, half-tempted to reach across the table and throttle Remi for dragging this out.

It was only a week ago that they'd been forced to practice against each other at the indoor club. Juliette had taken a chance, tried to reach out and get to know Luca as Octavia suggested. And for a moment, staring at each other, Juliette was convinced she'd broken through to Luca. But then her father had dragged her away, and she hadn't been brave enough to reach out again.

"She pulled out of the tournament. Back injury." Juliette jerks her attention back to Remi. She licks her lips and sets down her sandwich. "I thought you knew. You guys seemed . . . closer," Remi says, trailing off into silence. "You've been mentioning her a lot recently."

Juliette winces. *Close* isn't quite the word she would use. She takes a sip of water to avoid answering. Remi's brows rise. "Well, I didn't know," Juliette says finally, setting her water glass down a bit too heavily. A few droplets splash onto her wrist.

Remi, finally having the self-preservation skills to know Juliette will probably punch her if she continues down this path, tries to navigate to another topic. "Anyway, um . . . " Remi avoids finishing her sentence by inhaling the rest of her sandwich. Juliette wonders how Remi doesn't choke. "How did she seem when you practiced with her?"

Heat spikes through Juliette's stomach as she remembers Luca's warm, wet skin against her fingertips, the heat of her flushed cheek, the flecks of green in Luca's eyes brought out by the luminous fluorescent light and mist of water around them. She can picture the frantic bobble of Luca's head as she asked Juliette to kiss her.

"Fine," Juliette says after a lingering silence. "Not injured, if that's what you mean."

Remi tilts her head, the sun slanting through the windows and lighting her usually dark eyes to warm brown, shining with striations of copper, reminding Juliette of Livia's tiger's eye crystals. "What else was she like? Anything you want to talk about?" Remi wriggles her brows.

Juliette rolls her eyes. "Shut up."

"Come on," Remi whines.

Juliette hesitates. She isn't used to considering Remi as a potential friend. Juliette doesn't have any real friends beyond her sisters and Leo. Too busy and too focused on herself and her career. But now after the Connolly Cup, she understands Remi. Even if she doesn't love Remi's tendency to gossip.

Remi kicks her under the table.

"Ow!" Juliette complains, even though it didn't really hurt. "You tell me first. How is it going with your soulmate? Are you two ever going to be public? Or even tell your friends you're together?"

Remi blinks, caught off-guard. She rubs the back of her neck, brushing her fingers along the bun of braids there. "It's fine." She sighs and tilts her head back. "She doesn't like media attention, and she doesn't think being public is important. We know, and that's all that matters to her. And like, I get it. I agree that it doesn't really matter." Remi stares out the window at the leafy green trees of the park surrounding them.

There are words Remi isn't saying. Words Juliette isn't capable of saying herself when it comes to her complicated relationship with her soulmate. And even if Remi acts nonchalant, Juliette knows this matters a lot to her. It's a matter of the heart, a delicate balance that Remi seems afraid of upsetting.

Juliette sighs. Remi's gaze snaps back to her, eyes wide and uncertain, a strange vulnerability to her. "It's clear that this matters a lot to you," Juliette says finally. "Anyone can see that. If it's making you unhappy to keep it a secret, you should bring it up to her and have a serious conversation about it."

Juliette is surprised by her own capacity to give advice. She's terrible at taking it for herself. Maybe Octavia is rubbing off on her.

Remi's lips twist as she chews on the inside of her cheek. She seems to be holding her breath. Then she exhales and slumps, letting go of the facade of composure. "You're right." She leans on the table. "But I don't want to upset what we have. I can't lose her." She traces rings on the table, pointedly not looking at Juliette.

Juliette's chest cramps, a feeling of understanding and empathy hitting her so hard she's knocked breathless by the feeling. "I get it," Juliette says, "but in the long run, won't it hurt you both more to keep this problem festering?"

Remi looks up from under her lashes, frowning. "I hate you," she mutters without any heat or anger behind it.

Juliette smirks. "Why? Because I'm right?" She kicks Remi under the table as retaliation for earlier.

It earns her the beginnings of a smile. "When did you get so good at giving advice? Your life is a disaster."

Juliette shrugs. "Do as I say, not as I do?" she offers, and Remi laughs. Juliette counts it as a win.

"So, are you going to see Luca?" Remi asks, her playful smirk returning. It's more at home on her face than her dejected hopelessness.

Juliette blinks. "What do you mean?"

Remi looks at her like she's the biggest idiot in the world. "Uh, she's injured. Don't you think you should go hang out with her? Comfort her? I mean, wouldn't that be a good place to try to rebuild trust with each other?" Remi tilts her head, considering Juliette with appraising eyes.

Juliette opens and closes her mouth like a silly guppy. How had she not considered that?

Well, she knows how. Because she's a coward. Juliette is afraid of pain and rejection, and she knows there is a very big chance that Luca will slam the door in her face. But Luca might also consider that Juliette would understand. She's had an injury sideline her from a big tournament; Juliette knows how isolating an injury is.

Juliette scratches her wrist and makes up her mind.

"You're right," she tells Remi.

Remi smirks. "I always am."

Juliette glares at her, but a smile tugs at her mouth traitorously. "Don't push it."

Remi laughs, boisterous and infectious, and Juliette gives up and joins in.

Approximately two hours and thirty-seven minutes later, Juliette stands outside of Luca's hotel room, laden down with shopping bags. Luckily for Juliette, Luca has been advised not to fly to America yet with her strained back. She shifts, anticipation and excitement swirling in her stomach. She's grateful for all her sisters' help at the grocery store, but she's acutely aware that she probably bought too much.

After a bit of bullying over text—more like a lot of groveling and begging—Nicky had given her Luca's room number.

She shifts the bags to one hand and knocks on the door. She

bounces on her toes while she waits, time stretching uncomfortably long. What if Luca is asleep? What if she's at physiotherapy? What if she's with her friends or Vladimir?

Finally, Juliette hears the familiar click of the dead bolt sliding back, and the door swings open. Luca glares into the bright light of the hallway, her brow scrunched, and blinks. Her long and lanky frame is swallowed by an oversize black sweatshirt, the hood pulled over her hair. "Juliette?"

"Hi," Juliette says lamely.

"If you're here to try to have sex, I'm out of commission for today," Luca says dryly.

Juliette chews on the inside of her cheek and shakes her head. Then she hoists up her haul. Luca's eyes lower to the bags, staring at them like Juliette brought a live snake to her door. "I brought snacks. And games." She tugs on the strap of her backpack. "I figured if I can't beat you on the court, I might as well kick your ass at Mario Kart."

Luca tilts her head and, without a word, pulls the door open wide to allow Juliette into the gloom of her hotel room.

Juliette weaves through the suite to the kitchenette, where she puts down the bags and her backpack. "How's your back?" she asks tentatively as she starts to pull out snacks. There are several varieties of popcorn and chips, raisins, nuts, and about a dozen different chocolate bars.

Luca hunches against one of the high-top chairs on the opposite side of the counter. She shrugs with a single shoulder. "Hurts," she mutters.

Juliette winces. She should have expected that. "I didn't know what you liked, so I kind of bought everything." She pulls out a bag of chocolate rice cakes, a staple of the Ricci household, even though Octavia and Livia hate them.

"I don't usually eat this stuff," Luca says stiffly, her eyes roving over the candy bars.

Juliette starts unloading the cheese.

"God, Jules, did you buy the entire store?" Luca asks, sliding into the chair and surveying the truly heinous amount of junk food.

Juliette turns away to hide her blush and opens the minifridge to stack the cheese away. "Maybe." Antony would kill her if he could see her now. She shouldn't eat *any* of this.

"Why?" Luca asks, a touch sharp.

"Ah, I wanted to make you feel better?" She clears her throat as it comes out as more of a question. Switching gears, Juliette turns back to Luca and leans on the counter, closer to her, so she can look at her face. "I know how shitty it is to be injured. Pain is isolating, and I didn't want you to be alone in that," she says, surprised by how quiet and tender her own voice sounds.

Luca looks away, biting her lip. "Well, thank you," she murmurs.

"No problem," Juliette says, trying to slough away the sudden urge to wrap Luca in a blanket and a hug. "So, what do you want to start with?" She grabs the bag of Jelly Babies and rips them open, popping two into her mouth. They're almost too sweet. She isn't used to having this much sugar anymore.

Luca blanches, looking overwhelmed by the choices. "Erm, I don't know. What's your favorite?" She fiddles with her hands, picking at the skin around her thumbs.

Juliette taps her chin as she thinks. "Close your eyes," she says as she decides. It isn't her favorite, but she thinks Luca might like it.

Luca stares at her, incredulous, but with a huff she does as she's told. Juliette peels open a Bounce Hazelnut Praline bag and maneuvers around the kitchenette to stand next to Luca.

"You're not allergic to nuts, are you?" Juliette asks, suddenly worried she might accidentally kill her. Luca startles at Juliette's proximity, but turns her head toward Juliette's voice, obediently keeping her eyes closed, then shakes her head.

"Open your mouth," Juliette says softly.

Luca's lips part, and Juliette carefully slips the chocolate into her mouth, her fingertips barely brushing her lips.

Luca chews and her brows twitch together as she tries to determine the flavors. Then, she starts to smile as she savors the bite. "That's good," Luca says, opening her eyes.

Juliette holds up the bag. "I read that praline is popular in Croatia, so I figured you might like it."

"I do." Luca grins, a dimple popping up at the corner of her mouth. Juliette wants to brush her thumb across it.

"It's probably no Bajadera chocolate, but it'll work," Juliette says, fully aware she's butchering the pronunciation, but it makes Luca laugh. Juliette pops one into her mouth and sighs as the deliciously smooth chocolate melts over her tongue and the almond butter blooms with a nutty sweetness.

"Thank you," Luca murmurs, and when Juliette looks at her again, Luca is staring at her with a softened expression.

Juliette's stomach flips as if she's falling. She's nearly used to the sensation. "All right," Juliette says, leaning away from the sudden sappiness that threatens to overwhelm her. "I doubt it's good for you to sit on a metal chair. Go lay down." She shoos Luca out of the chair and to the couch, grabbing a handful of snacks and two bottles of orange Lucozade.

"You don't have to stay," Luca says, arranging herself on the couch, two pillows supporting her back and a bag of half-melted ice on the coffee table.

Juliette dumps the haul on the table. "Do you need a new ice bag?"

Luca shakes her head. Juliette takes the ice bag to the sink so the water doesn't ruin the wood. "I don't have anything else to do, but if you want me to leave, I can," Juliette says, facing away from Luca. She doesn't want Luca to see the disappointment on her face if Luca asks her to go.

"No, you don't have to leave," Luca says quickly, and Juliette lets out a sigh of relief. "I just don't want you to feel like you're obligated to stay."

Juliette returns to the living room and plops down on the love seat adjacent to Luca's couch and unzips her backpack. "We're friends," Juliette says. Maybe if she says it enough, it'll become true. "So, movies or games?"

TWENTY-FOUR

LUCA

Unfortunately, Luca realizes quickly that trying to play Mario Kart isn't going to help her strained back. It's impossible to turn off her ultracompetitive nature, and when she flinches the wrong way turning to avoid sliding off Rainbow Road, her back protests.

Juliette pauses the game. "It hurts, doesn't it?"

Luca throws herself back among the pillows and is rewarded with Juliette snorting at her dramatics. "Of course it does." She huffs, annoyed. She'd spent the last day and a half trying to find a comfortable way to exist. She can't sit up, because none of the chairs have enough support. Standing is fine, but eventually if she shifts on her feet, the twinges return. So, she has to lay on a plethora of pillows and ice.

"Movie, then?" Juliette asks, navigating out of the game menu to an array of streaming services.

Luca shrugs, noncommittal. She doesn't really want to watch a movie. She knows the minute it starts, she'll fall asleep and then Juliette will leave and she'll be left in her lonely hotel room with nothing but her pain again.

Luca pushes those thoughts away and stretches her legs over the edge of the couch, wriggling down so her feet hang over the armrest.

Juliette glances at her, face half-illuminated by the TV. Her legs are curled beneath her, and she's staring at Luca with a question on her face.

"Do you know how long you're out for?" Juliette asks, clicking the controller. Luca watches her open up her Spotify and turn on a random playlist, lowering the sound to a background murmur.

Luca chews on the inside of her lip. "The rest of Wimbledon, at least."

Juliette frowns. "I was looking forward to beating you."

Luca scoffs. "Yeah, right. Maybe you would have a chance now."

Juliette chuckles, and her eyes glint with enjoyment. "I would've won anyway."

Luca crosses her arms over her chest. "Bold of you to think you would make it to the final," Luca says, and Juliette extends her foot out to lightly nudge at Luca's calf.

"I'll show you," she says.

"I look forward to it," Luca says, surprised to find it isn't a lie and feeling an odd warmth in her chest. Now that she isn't playing, Luca is tempted to watch Juliette's upcoming matches.

Juliette runs her fingers through her hair, twisting the curls over her other shoulder. She doesn't look at Luca as she speaks. "Do you want to see if my soulmate hands would work on your back?" She does jazz hands as she says it.

Luca chokes on a laugh, even as her low-level anxiety spikes from the buzz in the back of her head. She curls her fingers into the sleeves of her hoodie.

"I don't have to," Juliette says quickly. "I just thought it might help. For Miami."

Luca isn't sure what to say. Her whole body aches to say yes, but she knows she should say no. She doesn't know how to fight the surge of want that she feels every time Juliette comes close. She's never been one to stay away from temptation after indulging.

Too sensitive, too emotional, too soft. All things she heard throughout her childhood until the hard courts toughened her and she found an escape through tennis. Though that doesn't change her nature and how quickly she falls in love.

Her mother once described the pull toward her father as being parched in a scorched desert. And his love, however painful, was always the water she desperately craved.

Luca can't need Juliette as if she'd die without her. Even if they're tentative friends, Luca doesn't know if she can trust herself to let Juliette close.

And yet, despite her misgivings, she sets down her drink and nods. This is a compromise. This is Juliette helping her so she can play tennis, the one love that has never betrayed or hurt her. "Okay." Luca's voice comes out raspy and she sits up. "We can try it."

"It worked for me," Juliette says, swinging her legs around on the love seat. "And on your sunburn."

Heat punches through Luca's stomach as she carefully turns around. She really should not have said yes.

The couch dips, and suddenly Juliette's hand is on her shoulder. "I think it'd be more effective if you weren't wearing a heavy hoodie," Juliette says, a teasing lilt to her voice.

Luca swallows. "Right," she says, too frozen to move.

Juliette's other hand touches her hip, her thumb sliding beneath the hem of the hoodie and brushing across her skin. Luca grits her teeth against the light sensation. "Which side?" Juliette asks.

"Left," Luca says. "It flares when I twist on my forehand."

Luca laces her fingers together in her lap to avoid fidgeting. She is equal parts grateful and annoyed that she isn't wearing a bra. Juliette's knuckles graze across the offending muscle in her back. Luca tries not to tense, but slivers of pain cut into her.

Juliette's palm splays across her back, cool against her warm skin. Luca shivers. "Sorry. Cold hands, warm heart, as my *nonna* always said," Juliette says.

Luca snorts despite herself.

Juliette remains quiet as she focuses on gently running her fingers along Luca's spine, her fingertips dipping to brush against the dimples adorning Luca's lower back.

The silence is oppressive, and Luca struggles to breathe through the soft and tender way that Juliette feels her aching muscles and tries to soothe them with gentle pressure. Soon, the noise in her head quiets, and the tangle of thoughts she's been trying to ignore slowly starts to unwind.

"Can I ask you something?" Luca asks, and Juliette hums in agreement. "Would you ever quit tennis?" Luca has been thinking about her career, her own choices, and the fact that the choice might be stolen from her by an injury one day.

She expects Juliette to scoff and say no immediately. Instead, her fingers still. Then she sighs, her warm breath skating over the back of Luca's neck. "I don't know," she admits.

Luca waits and gives Juliette the space to continue.

"I've been fighting for my ranking for years, so I feel like I can't give it up. My family is so entirely wrapped up in the sport, and it would feel like such a waste to throw it all away."

Luca swallows. "But does it make you happy?" Juliette's fingertips press into her skin, and pain flares. Luca hisses through her teeth, and Juliette flinches away. "Don't stop," Luca whispers. "It's working." She doesn't know if it is, but she doesn't want Juliette to stop. Her touch is addicting.

"Erm, sometimes," Juliette answers, her fingers returning to Luca's skin, as if drawn by a magnet. "Sometimes I hate it so much I want to quit. The highs are incredible but the lows . . . they threaten to break me in half. I've seen it break both of my sisters, and yet they keep coming back. I do love this silly sport, but I don't know if I want it all the time."

This time, when Juliette presses in, there is no pain, only a burning warmth that unwinds each of her tense muscle fibers. Luca sighs as relief sprawls through her body, relaxation taking over. She didn't realize how much lingering pain was lacing through her back and how tight it was making her.

"It's so stupid to talk this way," Juliette says with a croaky laugh. "I'm so lucky to get to do this for a living. I travel the world and meet incredible people and make a lot of money. I'm in amazing physical shape. I know I'm privileged to have this life." Juliette pauses, breathless and suddenly quiet, but her fingers keep rubbing against Luca's aching back.

"Tennis is a fickle mistress," Luca says.

"She really is."

Luca tips her head back, staring at the ceiling. Her hood falls back and her hair bunches in it, tickling her neck. Juliette's fingers brush her hair out of the hood, letting it fall down her back. Luca means to say thank you, but what comes out instead is a question.

"Did you choose tennis, or did you do it because your older sisters were doing it?"

Juliette remains quiet, and Luca is grateful she can't see Juliette's face. She worries she's pushed too far, asked too much of this tenuous trust built between them.

"I think I chose it, yes," Juliette says finally. "I love the competition, the challenge, and the fact that I have full responsibility for the outcome of the match. It's tough to swallow after losses, but the pride after winning is worth it, I think." Juliette trails her knuckles up the knobs of Luca's spine, and it takes her breath away. "What about you?" Luca feels her lean in closer, warmth radiating over her.

"No, I didn't." Luca wants to swallow her own tongue, but the words keep spilling out anyway. "My mother put me in lessons when I was six years old, and I kept doing it because it made my father proud. And I do love tennis, but it's also the glue that keeps my life together." Luca draws in a deep breath despite how tight her chest is and admits, "It's all I have."

Luca doesn't know who she is without it. She could go find out, but she's worked too hard for this career to abandon it now. Now that she's finally reached the top, she can't let go.

"I think that's why I've envied you so much. Beyond just your ability. You have a drive that I don't," Juliette sighs.

Luca fiddles with the strings on her hoodie. "Is survival really a drive?" She hates that the words come out of her mouth at all, but especially because they're so soft and fragile.

"Survival?" Juliette whispers.

Luca shakes her head. "Never mind."

"Luca," Juliette murmurs, and Luca shifts, ready to get off the couch as discomfort washes over her like a wave.

But then Juliette's arms wrap around her stomach, and her chin rests on Luca's shoulder as she squeezes her into a hug. For a moment, Luca forgets to breathe; she's so surprised by the sudden gesture.

"You'll play again, Luca," Juliette says, her breath warm against the shell of her ear. Luca shudders. The words are a salve pressing precisely where it hurts.

"How do you know?" she dares to ask, uncertainty twisting like a straitjacket around her lungs and heart.

Juliette hums, and Luca feels the rumble of it against her back. "You're an incredible player, Luca Kacic, and I know this won't stop you. If anyone can continue your amazing trajectory, it's you," she says with such sincerity that Luca's eyes sting. The hard core of anxiety wrapped around her lungs melts into goo.

"You think so?" Luca doesn't know how to believe her. A nagging voice threatens the relief Juliette's words gave her. "You said I was overhyped and unoriginal," she adds, and even now it aches to say, though she tries for a teasing tone.

Juliette's breath is warm against her throat. "I lied."

She closes her eyes, dizzy and overwhelmed, but she curls her fingers around Juliette's, holding on as if she is her lifeline. She can feel Juliette's wrist wrap press against her stomach, hiding her name.

"Thank you," Luca says, her voice thick.

Juliette squeezes again and Luca relaxes against her, sagging back until she can tilt her head against Juliette's. The scent of her washes over Luca, fresh citrus and something rosy in her perfume, with the lovely lightness of freshly washed cotton.

Juliette's nose presses against her throat, and Luca feels her breathe in. "What are you wearing?"

Luca blinks, the tenderness of the moment cracking as she can't help but laugh. "What do you mean?"

"You smell nice. Herbal. What is it?" Juliette shifts her head, and a curl tickles against Luca's skin, making her scrunch her shoulder at the sensation.

"Lavender," she says. "I was trying to sleep before you showed up."

"Oh." Juliette lifts her head, and Luca almost leans back into her again. "Should we watch that movie now?" Juliette asks, her arms loosening from around Luca's waist. "Do you need pain medication? Did my hands help?"

Despite the warm relief that Juliette's hands had provided on the surface level of her pain, the lingering echoes of her injury sit deeper in her muscles. "Yeah, but I still need something. It's just irritating now."

Juliette's arms vanish from around her waist, and Luca barely stops herself from whining. She turns back around to rest on her pillows as Juliette heads for the kitchenette. The pillows aren't as warm and comfortable as Juliette, but Luca will live.

Juliette returns and hands Luca a blister pack. "You can stay on the couch," Luca murmurs. She wishes she could lie across Juliette so she can't leave quietly if Luca falls asleep. She pops two of her painkillers with the rest of her Lucozade and tosses the pack on the coffee table among the discarded chocolate wrappers.

Juliette drops onto the couch next to her. "Are you flying out of London soon?"

Luca looks away and wriggles her toes beneath Juliette's warm thigh. "Tomorrow night. We're going to Miami to rest and see if I'll be healthy enough to play." The strain isn't too bad, and while a long transatlantic flight won't be great for her muscles, Vladimir convinced her to splurge on a first-class flight.

She swears she sees Juliette's face fall. "I hope you can. I'd love a rematch on a hard court." Then she curls her fingers around Luca's ankle, and heat ripples up her leg. "You can stretch out if you need to."

Luca does not need to be asked twice. She slides her feet out from under Juliette and guides them over her lap. She wriggles down on the couch, settling her thighs over Juliette's lap in order for her head to be on a pillow. Immediately, she yawns.

"Bored of my company already?" Juliette teases, one hand resting on her knee and drawing circles against her skin.

"Of course, you're the least interesting person I know," Luca says, crossing her arms over her chest and snuggling into her pillow.

"Well, shall we watch an exciting movie to liven things up?" Juliette asks.

Luca shrugs. "Play whatever you want. I don't think much will keep me awake now," she says, a wave of exhaustion hitting her as the remaining pain dissipates from her back.

"Sleep, then. I'll wake you up later," Juliette reassures. Luca's view of Juliette is already getting blurry around the edges.

Luca yawns again as she nods. "Don't leave, please," Luca murmurs, and she isn't sure Juliette even heard her before she sinks into dreamless black.

TWENTY-FIVE

JULIETTE

Juliette watches with overwhelming fondness as Luca succumbs to sleep. Her head tilts to the side, her lashes fluttering, and within moments she's snoring lightly. Luca is peaceful in her sleep, without her usual frown or iron-hard exterior. She looks nearly girlish, sweet in a way that Juliette has never seen before.

She sinks farther into the couch, one hand on Luca's knee and the other on her thigh, content to sit and trace little circles against Luca's skin with her thumb.

Juliette flips through her catalog of favorite movies and lands on the 1999 version of *The Mummy*. She knows it front and back, and the lilt of the Egyptian music is always comforting. She sneaks little glances at Luca every once in a while, but she never stirs, even as Imhotep steals the American's eyes and tongue.

As the credits roll, Juliette gently nudges Luca's knee. "Luca."

"Five more minutes," Luca mutters, eyes still squeezed tight.

"It isn't good to sleep on the couch all night." Juliette glances at her watch. It's barely past seven, but she knows Luca will try to keep sleeping in her drugged-out haze. "Luca," she repeats with fond exasperation.

Luca grumbles and curls her face into her hood. "What do you want?" she whines. Her eyes crack open, and she blinks against the light.

"I don't want you to hurt your back more," Juliette says gently. "You should sleep in your own bed."

Luca shakes her head. "No."

"Yes."

Luca closes her eyes.

Juliette changes tactics. "It'll be easier to cuddle in bed."

Luca opens one eye to glance at Juliette askew. The start of a smile betrays Luca. Juliette lets her fingers trace up the inside of Luca's knee to her thigh, drifting just beneath the hem of her shorts. Goose bumps pucker along her skin. Finally, with a swallow, Luca nods.

Juliette maneuvers herself out from under Luca's legs and holds out her hand. Luca takes it, and Juliette helps lift her off the couch.

"Ouch," Luca mutters and grabs her back. Juliette wraps her arm around Luca to keep her upright, taking a majority of her weight as her knees buckle.

"I got you," Juliette says, and Luca's free hand clasps around Juliette's bicep, fingertips digging in.

"Sorry," Luca murmurs, "I'm okay."

Still, Juliette holds on to Luca as they hobble together into the bedroom.

Juliette is about to ask if she can lie down with her when she hears the familiar click of a key in the door.

Luca lets go. "Vladimir," Luca says, climbing into bed with a groan.

"Stay lying down. It's better for you," Juliette says, touching Luca's shoulder. She leans on the doorjamb. "Hey, Vladimir," she calls, and Luca's coach startles in the center of the abandoned living room.

"Oh, erm, hello, Juliette," Vladimir says, a comically shocked expression on his face.

"Luca's in her room," Juliette says, unsure how to explain why she's here.

Vladimir tilts his head, blue eyes scrutinizing Juliette's face. Like Luca, he gives absolutely nothing away. "I brought food. I didn't know you'd be here." Juliette glances down at the white bag bursting with takeout containers.

"Neither did Luca. I showed up unannounced," Juliette says.

"Anyway, I should go. Early practice time." It's a lie, but she's uncomfortable under Vladimir's impassive scrutiny.

She glances over her shoulder and meets Luca's eyes. "I'll see you in Miami, then, yeah?" It's a hope, a promise, even if it feels too far away. Still, she smiles at Luca.

Luca nods. "Good luck."

"Thanks, Lucky Luca," Juliette teases as she backs out the door and Luca grins, that adorable dimple popping out again.

Juliette gathers her gaming console, shoving all the cables into her backpack haphazardly before stepping out of Luca's room and sagging against the door. She knows her sisters will want an update, but she stands in the peace of knowing she hasn't messed up this time. And, for once, she isn't afraid of the butterflies tickling the inside of her stomach.

She heads out to the lobby and orders an Uber to take her back to Claudia's apartment. She shoots their group chat a quick text to tell them she's on her way back. She expects one of them to call, but Octavia responds first.

OCTAVIA

Antony is pissed you skipped practice.
He's here. Brace yourself.

Juliette's stomach drops and all of her giddy joy freezes into immediate dread. The Uber arrives, and Juliette climbs in the back.

JULIETTE

Thanks for the warning D: <

She fidgets with her phone as the lights of London blur together. She should have answered her father's million questions about why she was skipping practice, beyond a simple *I am*. At the same time, though, Antony Ricci wouldn't have understood. He has never been good at oscillating between being a father and being her coach.

Juliette wonders which Antony she'll have the pleasure of arguing with tonight. Probably both at once. Or, whichever one will lay the most guilt onto Juliette's shoulders.

Too soon, the Uber turns onto Claudia's quiet street and stops in front of her building. Slowly, as if her joints are made of rusted metal, Juliette gets out of the car and heads into Claudia's apartment. She lets the door bang shut, announcing her arrival, and hears the murmur of conversation die.

Juliette winces. She slings her backpack around the banister of the stairs and takes a deep breath before wandering into the living room.

"Hey, Jules!" Livia says, lying across the bay window seat. She grins, but it's too wide and uncomfortable. Octavia is nowhere to be seen. Claudia is sitting across from their father in her usual love seat, but this time she's upright, feet flat on the floor.

"Juliette," Antony says, staring at her from the couch she and her sisters had gossiped and snacked on just a week ago.

"Hey," Juliette says.

With deliberate slowness, Antony rises from the couch. "Let's talk," he says, calm and even-toned. He won't yell at Juliette in front of her sisters.

Livia flashes her a sympathetic thumbs-up, but Claudia doesn't even look at her as she follows Antony into the back garden. The plants are growing wild, their blooms full of color and warmth, much like Claudia.

Antony plucks one of the flowers and twirls it in his fingers. "Do you want to win, Juliette?" he asks.

"Wimbledon?" Juliette asks for clarity.

Antony's eyes snap to hers. "Anything. Wimbledon. Miami. Cincinnati. The US Open."

"Yes," Juliette says firmly.

"Good." Antony sighs, a long-suffering and disappointed sound. "It does not seem like you do."

"I missed one practice," Juliette says, barely restraining an eyeroll.

"One practice during one of the most important weeks of the year," Antony hisses, his voice low but harsh. "I have been lenient with you over the years. Perhaps too lenient, but you almost won the Australian Open."

Juliette flinches. She doesn't want to be reminded of that failure.

"You're almost twenty-four years old, Juliette. It is time to stop being irresponsible and take this seriously." Antony's eyes are as sharp as a shark's, his voice pitched low, even though there's probably no one in this area able to understand Italian.

"I am taking this seriously!" Juliette exclaims. "Missing one practice does not mean I don't care."

Antony's eyes narrow. "Where were you?"

Juliette considers lying, but she thinks one of her sisters probably already spilled about where she was. "With a friend."

"Which friend?"

Juliette swallows. "Luca Kacic."

Antony scoffs. "You are not friends with her." He shakes his head. "Do I have to remind you who took your Australian Open win away from you?"

"No, you do not," Juliette says, heat burning along the back of her neck. "But you have no control over who I'm friends with."

"Juliette," he says slowly, his eyes boring into her. "Please, let's not be naive. I only want what is best for you." Juliette grits her teeth as Antony stares at her. Then he stalks across the lawn and plants his hands on Juliette's shoulders. He gently taps Juliette's cheek like she's a child. "And *Luca Kacic* is your enemy." He spits her name as if it is poison. "Even if she is your soulmate."

Juliette shakes her head. "She isn't my enemy. And I'm not throwing away my career by having friends." For years she's kept herself busy and away from other people. She has let friendships and potential partners slip through her fingers for the sake of tennis. "I still want to be the best," she says. "I can balance friendship and tennis."

Antony frowns, as if he doesn't believe her. She wants to shout and shake his shoulders. Force him to understand that she still loves this sport and she won't disappoint him again. Juliette's stomach turns unpleasantly. "As long as you still work hard." There is an assumed question at the end of his statement.

Juliette nods. "Always," she murmurs. She knows it's true, deep in the marrow of her bones. But tennis isn't the only thing she's allowed to care about.

Antony doesn't look convinced, but he nods before stepping past Juliette and back into Claudia's apartment.

He's ceded ground, but somehow, Juliette feels worse.

TWENTY-SIX

LUCA

Vladimir insists on joining Luca at her hotel to watch Juliette play in the Wimbledon quarterfinal. It's stressful watching her play Chen Xinya and near impossible to keep her face neutral. Every missed backhand and randomly thrown-in double fault has Luca flinching.

She hasn't talked to Vladimir about her tenuous friendship with Juliette Ricci. She hasn't told anyone about it. Nor about the sudden appearance of Juliette in her dreams, or the longing that has buried itself between her ribs. Luca swallows around the realization that Juliette has subtly intertwined herself in Luca's heart without her even realizing it. It is possible Juliette wants to screw her over, but despite everything Juliette has said, her actions say something completely different. And in a rush of unstoppable desire and the absolute knowledge that this *is* right, Luca has let herself fall. If she thinks about it too much, she'll panic, so she chooses to trust her gut.

Watching Juliette does nothing to lessen the feelings. It's thrilling to revel in Juliette's fluid grace, her toned body, her sweat-slicked olive skin tanned by the sun, her tousled mess of highlighted-brown curls that darken with sweat as the July sun beats down on her. . . .

"Are you sure you should play Miami?" Vladimir asks as Juliette breaks to win the first set.

Luca can barely breathe, she has been so invested in the match. It's a weird sensation, to be rooting for her rival. Especially when Juliette winning Wimbledon would mean she's a step closer to overtaking Luca's number one ranking.

"Yes," Luca says belatedly, mentally cursing the TV as they cut to a commercial even though Juliette is lifting her shirt to wipe the sweat off her brow and lip.

"Luca," Vladimir admonishes.

Luca looks over at him, reclining on the adjacent couch. She doesn't understand why a penthouse living room needs three couches, but at least both of them can lie down to watch the TV. His hands are clasped behind his head, showing off the plethora of tattoos that snake across his pale skin. Luca never dared to ask what they meant, even though she knows Vladimir would tell her.

"What?" She looks back at the television. "I have a lot of points to defend."

"It's going to be so hot. You'll be cooked! The pavement will melt."

Luca frowns. "I'll be fine." The doctor gave her the all-clear for playing in the next tournament.

"You shouldn't have to be. I don't know why they made Miami the beginning of the US hard court swing." Vladimir heaves out a resigned sigh. "April was better."

Luca shrugs. "It's a cruel summer." The broadcast returns to Juliette serving in the first game of the third set.

"I thought you disliked her," Vladimir says suddenly, and Luca snaps her head to look at him.

"Dislike who?" She blinks, and Vladimir's lips curve into a barely there smile.

"Ricci," he says, gesturing to the television.

"Oh." Luca looks back to see Juliette acing Xinya to even the game at thirty-all.

"Are you two getting closer?" Vladimir presses, and Luca plants her cheek on her hand to hide her blush. She shrugs, aiming for nonchalance, but Vladimir laughs.

Whatever is brewing between them, Luca knows it's too delicate. She's afraid that any misplaced word will break the tentative strings holding them together, and she can't lose Juliette. Not when she's only had the briefest taste of her. Luca wants to explore the boundaries of this relationship, and it seems Juliette does, too. If that means they get closer, so be it.

"I don't know," Luca says, fiddling with her phone. For two days, she's been texting Juliette. It's different from talking, easier, since she can't see Juliette's face or read too much into her reactions.

Although, sometimes it's worse. Luca often has to swallow the itching desire to respond within seconds.

"Really?" Vladimir's voice drips with incredulous snark.

Luca is half-tempted to throw a pillow at him. "You know I'm not good with feelings," she mutters.

"Oh, so there are feelings involved?"

Luca smashes the pillow into her own face and groans. "No!" she shouts through the fabric.

When she lowers the pillow, Vladimir stares at her with a knowing look. "Be serious, Luca."

Luca picks at the peeling skin around her thumb and says nothing. She doesn't know what to say.

"I will always advocate for your happiness. I may be your coach, but I also love you as if you were my own child," Vladimir says, achingly sincere.

Luca's eyes sting, and she swallows around the sudden lump in her throat. Vladimir has never been the sentimental type. He is a quiet listener, a gentle soother, but never someone who outright says what Luca needs to hear.

"And I know how much tennis means to you," Vladimir adds. "I love seeing you play at this level, and if you hated it, I would tell you to quit. But you do love it, Luca. And I don't know if this relationship is good for you." His tone is pointed, and Luca understands why.

Her last relationship had not ended well. Mae was another tennis player and had known that Luca wouldn't always prioritize her. They had agreed to keep their relationship to "just sex," but Luca's heart hadn't gotten the memo. When she expressed that she wanted more, that she was *in love*, Mae had recoiled.

Luca doesn't blame her, not anymore.

Still, after the breakup, she didn't win a match for three months. She lost touch with her friends.

Except Nicky. He held tight and didn't let her disappear. He and

Vladimir rebuilt Luca from the demolished rubble and helped her suture up her fractured heart and feelings. She started winning again. Clawed her way into main draws of important tournaments, got notoriety and sponsors and a nickname from tennis fans.

Now, she's on that precipice again and hoping she won't be crushed.

Luca looks up at Vladimir, a gentleness to his pale gaze that Luca is still uncomfortable under. It has taken years to build a tennis career and she has sacrificed relationships, friendships, and family to be in this position. Several of her exes hated that she didn't prioritize them.

"I know." Luca's heart has never been particularly adept at compartmentalizing, and a part of her still worries that Juliette is only messing around to try to throw Luca off her game. "I'm figuring out the boundaries," she says finally.

Her life is nearly perfect now, except she can't keep her nagging anxiety from telling her that Juliette is only going to hurt her in the end. Her heart feels like a grenade, ready to explode after any rejection. She needs to be careful, outline the boundaries of whatever this is, and not implode her life from the inside out. This won't— it *can't*—be like last time.

"If Juliette makes you happy, I will be happy. I want you to reach your goals, so if they've changed, I need to know," Vladimir says.

Luca heaves out a sigh. "I want everything."

"Life rarely gives you that," Vladimir says with a rueful smile.

Luca leans her head back against the couch and lolls it back toward the television. Juliette has lost her serve, and Xinya is poised to win her next game.

"Ugh," Luca mutters. She turns her attention back to Vladimir. "I know I can't have my cake and eat it too, but for once, I want to."

Vladimir shrugs. "Maybe it'll work out. Maybe it won't. But I want you to make the best choices for yourself, and even if it all falls apart, Luca, you won't be alone."

Luca has to bite the inside of her cheek and stare at a spot on the floor to hold back her tears. "Thanks," she says, her voice raspy.

Vladimir simply hums, giving Luca the space to collect herself. By the time she does, Juliette's serve is about to be broken again.

The camera flashes over to Xinya's box after she crushes one of Juliette's weak returns down the line. Luca squints, almost certain that Remi Rowland is in the second row. It's hard to tell with a hat pulled low over her face. Seeing other players in someone's personal box is unusual, but Luca shakes it off. If anyone could get away with it, it would be a social butterfly and extrovert like Remi. It isn't *that* weird.

Although . . . maybe, eventually, she could sit in Juliette's box. Antony Ricci might kill Luca for even attempting it, but she doesn't mind the thought of watching Juliette courtside. Anticipating the hypothetical Twitter response does make her shiver, though.

The rest of the set does not go Juliette's way. Xinya is one of the best returners on the tour. She is lightning-quick with decent volleys. Any ball Juliette leaves short, Xinya attacks and puts away with either a featherlight drop shot or an angled volley. Juliette loses the second set 6–2, with one final set for the match.

It's grueling. Xinya holds easily, but Juliette struggles to keep the score even. Eventually, Juliette hangs on to send it to a tiebreaker.

"She's playing too passively," Vladimir says as Xinya prepares to serve. "She needs to move in, make Xinya defend instead of letting her play aggressively and dictate from the center of the court."

Luca frowns. "Her forehand is misfiring, though," she says.

"The best way for her to gain confidence is to hit out, to trust her muscle memory," Vladimir says. "She will lose either way—by letting Xinya dictate the points or by hitting the ball out, but only one of those could lead to a win."

Luca considers Juliette as she loses the first point to Xinya serve-and-volleying. Her shoulders are tense as she holds out her racket to the ball kid. She lets two of them roll behind her as she steps up to the baseline.

Luca has been on the wrong side of that serve during a tiebreaker. At first, she couldn't figure out how to adjust to the strange lefty spin

Juliette hooks onto her kick serve. Finally, Vladimir had urged her to step in and take the ball on the rise.

Which is exactly what Xinya does to take the point. Juliette should move forward, but she doesn't. She hesitates, keeps the ball in the middle of the court, and hopes Xinya makes a mistake.

She doesn't.

Xinya has Juliette on strings, moving from one side to the other until she whips a crosscourt angle and steals the minibreak. The crowd roars in awe, and Luca bites her already worn-down nails.

"Come on, Jules," she mutters to herself.

As Juliette gathers her composure for the next point, Luca thinks about Vladimir's tennis advice. It explains a bit of Juliette's behavior in real life. All aggression and passion until she starts missing, then her confidence drains away.

Juliette doesn't win another point, and the match ends on a rather anticlimactic ace from Xinya. Juliette slides the white headband off her forehead and shakes out her sweaty curls as she jogs to the net. She clasps Xinya's hand and touches her shoulder. The announcers and the roar of the crowd keep Luca from being able to hear what they're saying to each other, so she switches the broadcast to Nicky's match. Guilt worms its way into her throat at the thought of the string of messages he's sent that she hasn't replied to yet. She should text him, but she clicks on Juliette's name instead.

She knows Juliette won't respond for a couple of hours, but she types out a message anyway. Perhaps this is her way of being more aggressive, going for what she wants. They won't get anywhere by playing passively.

LUCA

> Tough loss, Xinya's a top player. You did play well.

> If you're looking to drown your sorrows in some bright sun, you could join me in Miami

Maybe she should add a winky face? Or is leaving it without a period better, more open-ended? Before she can overthink it anymore, she hits send and tosses her phone to the end of the couch, so she'll have to sit up to get it again. Her chest constricts, but she stares up at the ceiling as if nothing is wrong.

Vladimir shuffles around the kitchen, ice clinking.

Luca's phone buzzes and she lunges for it. It's only a message from Nicky's soulmate and on-again, off-again boyfriend, Magnus, about the match. She sighs and watches the lucky loser—a player who lost in qualifying for the main draw but got in because another player pulled out—march onto the court for his first quarterfinal. Nicky follows with a sunshine-smile, waving at the crowd as the announcer lists off his accomplishments.

As expected, it isn't until Nicky is almost through his third set that her phone buzzes. She stares at where it lies facedown, hiding whatever message is waiting.

With a deep breath, she flips it over and opens the message.

JULIETTE

are you serious?

I mean that earnestly.
like are you fucking with me?

LUCA

I'm not. If you want to come early for Miami, we can have some fun? It's fine if not, but I thought I'd offer.

Luca does not have to wait long for Juliette's response.

JULIETTE

have fun, huh? 😒 😉

Luca's cheeks heat, and she fiddles with the fringe on a pillow, the blinking cursor laughing at her as she tries to parse precisely what she wants to say.

LUCA

Another massage perhaps?

Get to know each other better?

"Way to break back, Nicky!" Vladimir's voice is too loud and too close, and Luca slams her phone onto her chest.

"Yes! He's playing well," Luca says, even though she wasn't paying attention. Her phone buzzes, and as Vladimir arranges himself on the couch again with a sandwich, she sneaks a glance at the text.

JULIETTE

gimme the room # and I'll be there

Luca smiles to herself as she texts her room number. Warm tingles spread out from her stomach, excitement taking root alongside her low-level buzz of anxiety.

For once, the idea of exploring something physical with Juliette doesn't make Luca want to vomit from fear.

Well, it does, but Luca is not going to sit and play passively until they both lose.

TWENTY-SEVEN

JULIETTE

Juliette is not in the habit of lying to her family, but she does not want her nosy sisters checking in on her when she's with Luca. They've already harassed her enough about the snack experiment, which Livia keeps insisting on calling a "date."

So she tells them she's going to practice early in Miami. All the Ricci girls lost Wimbledon. Claudia and Octavia both lost in the third round, while Juliette made it to the quarterfinal. Claudia is staying in London, putting off going to the next tournament as long as possible. Octavia, on the other hand, is vehemently against playing Miami in July.

"It was acceptable heat in April. I will not be dying for this stupid sport," she said when Claudia complained about being left without a doubles partner.

There's still a week after Wimbledon ends before the Miami Open starts, but her father still insists he come help Juliette train. At least she'll get two days of Antony-free time. And even though she has an ulterior motive for coming to Miami, she does intend to get a few decent practices in so she can grow accustomed to the heat.

And *have fun*, as Luca put it. Her hands shake with jitters, and a nervous excitement refuses to leave her body, even though she should be exhausted from her flight.

It's easier to focus on these emotions rather than the devastation of losing to Xinya in the quarterfinals. It hurts more than she wants to admit. She should have won. It felt within her grasp after the first set, but one bad bounce off the chalky line and suddenly her forehand was off.

And now fans online keep saying her quarterfinal curse is back in full effect.

Maybe she should delete the apps from her phone.

Now she's in an Uber to the hotel where all the players are staying. The hotel sits off the Biscayne Bay and has a sleek modern style that matches the glitzy Miami aesthetic. Juliette admires the deep reds and lush ocean blues that accent the elegant curves of modern architecture and give a youthful flair to the otherwise gold and white hotel. Despite the late hour, a bellhop takes her luggage up to her room, even if she won't be sleeping there tonight. It's only been a few days since she last saw Luca, and she's surprised that Luca initated this. Her snack experiment worked out better than she could've anticipated. And this invitation feels like an olive branch extended by Luca, one Juliette is hopeful works out.

She gets her key and makes a beeline to the elevator. She pulls her hood up, sunglasses perched on her nose, and keeps her head low. She doesn't want anyone to catch her going up to the floor where Luca is and potentially start a rumor.

The glass walls of the elevator reveal the sprawl of Miami, and her stomach twists at how high up she is. The expanse of rippling water shimmers with lights from party boats and the other high-rises. She curses. She should have turned around and taken the stairs, but it's too late. The dizzying height makes her vision swim, the blur of starry lights disorients her. The elevator eases to a stop, and the doors ping open. She stumbles out and leans against the wall, taking a few steadying breaths. Then, once her heart rate has slowed, she glances around the empty hall. Colorful photographs depicting Miami nightlife clash with the riotous black and navy wallpaper speckled with pink flamingos.

She bows her head, overstimulated by the brightness of it all, and jogs down to the correct door. She shakes out her hands before shoving her hood back. She dangles her sunglasses in her fingers as she lifts her other hand to knock on the door. She swallows and taps three times. Juliette's skin prickles. Her stomach is in knots, and her heart is pounding as if she's *falling, falling, falling.*

The anticipation builds, a roaring crescendo that cuts off as the door opens.

Luca leans against the doorjamb, her hair smoothed back into a ponytail. She's wearing a white T-shirt that shows off how tan she's gotten. Her gray sweatpants hang low on her hips, and Juliette has to force her eyes up to Luca's face.

"Hi," Juliette says, sounding breathless.

Luca's lips twist into a smile and she steps back, allowing Juliette to enter. "Hi."

"Holy shit," Juliette says as she enters the equally bright room. The walls are creamy white, but abstract shapes are painted in teals, oranges, and pinks all over. Weird, crystalline-like lights shower the room with sparkling white light.

Luca laughs, a huff of air. Nerves, perhaps? Juliette can't tell. "It's not really my style, but the hotelier insisted."

Juliette pauses in the center of the living room, and her backpack slides off her shoulder to her feet. Floor-to-ceiling windows show off the sterling skyline and beautiful bay, the water rippling like the metallic hide of a car. The glare from the indoor lights makes it worse. It's almost as if Juliette is standing above the water, like she could reach out and touch the skyscrapers. She sways on her feet.

"Jules?" Luca moves into her line of sight, and Juliette tries to smile, but it stretches foreign across her mouth.

"Yeah?" Her voice wavers and sounds faraway.

"You look a little pale. Are you okay?" Luca's brows pinch together in concern.

Juliette glances over Luca's shoulder at the window, and another wave of dizziness threatens to topple her. She looks down and sees her hand wrapped around Luca's forearm. Warmth sparks beneath her fingertips, and she tries to focus on that sensation instead. "Erm, I forgot to mention this before, but I am not a fan of heights."

"Oh," Luca says, but it sounds like she's underwater. "Come on." She tugs on Juliette, who keeps her eyes on her feet until she is guided into a chair.

It's a stool at a short kitchen island with no windows around it.

Juliette swallows and tries to breathe evenly through her nose, but she can hear how harshly she is sucking in air.

"Here, drink this. The curtains are closed. I don't know if that helps, but we could go to your room?"

Juliette fumbles with the water bottle but manages to twist it open. "No, I'll be fine, as long as I can't see how high we are," she gasps out before taking a few careful sips of water.

Luca's hand curves around her right wrist, and her thumb sweeps in soothing circles against Juliette's hammering pulse point. Juliette glances up, but Luca is staring at Juliette's trembling hands. Then, as if Luca feels Juliette's gaze, her eyes lift, and Juliette tries to smile. "Thanks," Juliette whispers.

"I'm sorry, I didn't know," Luca says.

Juliette shakes her head. "How could you know? I never mentioned it. It's not like this is new." Her tremors lessen and then fade until her hands are still. "I wasn't always afraid of heights."

"No?" Luca prompts, her thumb never stopping the soft caress.

Juliette's breath evens out and the tension in her chest releases. "I used to climb all the trees in our backyard when I was a kid. But when I was eight, I fell and broke my arm."

Luca hisses through her teeth. "Ouch."

Juliette nods. "I haven't climbed a tree since, and I can't stand heights."

"Luckily you picked a profession where you never have to fly or end up in high-rise hotels," Luca says with a smirk.

"Shut up," Juliette says without heat, and Luca laughs. "All right, I told you a secret, tell me one of yours."

Luca's thumb falters on her skin, and she chews on the inside of her cheek. "I have anxiety, I'm afraid of everything."

"That is not a secret," Juliette says.

"Of course it is. No one knows except Vladimir and Nicky."

"And me," Juliette says. "You told me in Naples."

Luca frowns, and Juliette flips her hand over and starts tracing Luca's palm and fingers. It's barely a touch, but Luca looks up at her with a hitch in her breath, her cheeks tinged pink.

"All right," Luca says, her lower lip wet from where she was biting it. Juliette wants to kiss her again, taste if she's wearing chapstick. "I like you more than I should."

Juliette's whole body jolts. "Do you really?"

Luca looks away. Juliette slides out of the chair, her legs wobbling, but she steadies herself. She joins Luca on the other side of the counter. Starlike silver light weaves across Luca's face, highlighting her high cheekbones. Juliette can't read the emotion in her face, but Luca leans closer, as if they're being pulled together.

"Yes," Luca whispers, her voice rough. She clears her throat. Juliette twists their fingers together, her heart pounding. Juliette tilts her head toward Luca, and they're so close that Luca's breath skates across her face. Herbal, like she's been drinking tea.

Juliette raises her free hand and skims her knuckles over Luca's flushed pink cheek. "Tell me what you want."

"*Everything*," Luca breathes, squeezing Juliette's hand so hard it stings.

Juliette's stomach swoops, punching into her throat. It is so hard not to kiss her. It is like soaring and somehow, Juliette isn't afraid.

"Be specific," Juliette insists. Luca's head dips, trying to kiss her, but Juliette turns her head away and chuckles. "Tell me, Luca."

From this angle, she can see Luca's eyes, dark and sultry, burning with a smoldering heat that Juliette can't look away from. "I want everything from you. Kiss me. Touch me. Fuck me. Make me come, or don't. Let me lick every inch of you. Let me worship you." Luca's eyes never leave Juliette's.

Juliette never expected Luca Kacic to know how to dirty talk. She is stunned into silence, but the air between them crackles with the electric heat of untamed arousal and want. Then, Juliette lunges.

They crash together, desperate, hungry. Their hands unclasp as they scramble to touch every inch of each other's skin they can. Luca's hands thread through Juliette's hair, tugging her close. Juliette grips Luca's narrow hips, and they snap together like puzzle pieces. Their mouths clash together in a wet heat, fighting not for dominance, but because the pain hurts so beautifully.

Juliette crowds Luca against the counter and slides her hands down to Luca's thighs, fingers digging into soft cotton. Luca hoists one leg around Juliette, hooking it around her waist. The hot cut of her body burns every other thought out of Juliette's head.

Luca claws at whatever patch of Juliette's skin she can find with one hand while the other roots into her curls, holding Juliette's head close and where she wants it. Heat pools and centers in Juliette's stomach as Luca whimpers in the back of her throat. Juliette breaks off their kiss and tilts her head to nip at Luca's jawline. Her lips are raw and tingling as she methodically sucks kisses onto Luca's pale skin.

She snakes a curving lick up to her earlobe. The scent of her hair, her skin, the perfume at the hollow of her throat, it all drives Juliette up a wall. "Is this what you meant by *have fun*?" She asks.

Luca breathes hard, nearly hyperventilating. "Even better."

Juliette smiles against her skin, and Luca shudders. "Good."

Luca tugs on her hair and they kiss again, noses dragging against each other. Luca's tongue sweeps across the seam of her mouth. Juliette slips her hand beneath Luca's shirt, her skin hot and tacky with sweat. Her fingers trace the dip of her waist, brush along the ridges of her ribs as she realizes Luca isn't wearing a bra. "Eager, aren't we?" she asks as she pulls back.

"Efficient, I'd say," Luca says. Her eyes are glazed, her pupils blown wide. She wriggles against Juliette.

"Bedroom?" Juliette asks.

Luca nods frantically. Her leg drops from Juliette's waist, and she mourns the loss. But Juliette will have it wrapped around her again soon anyway. Luca twines their fingers and leads Juliette through the suite to the bedroom.

"Lay down and spread out," Juliette orders, and Luca takes a shaky breath, flopping onto her bed. Juliette joins her, straddling Luca's waist. Luca leans up onto the pillows and Juliette indulges in kissing her. Softer now, less frantic. They have time to relax.

Luca tries to intensify the kiss, hooking her arm around Juliette's neck to drag her down and closer, but Juliette catches her wrist and squeezes hard. Luca winces out of the kiss and Juliette loosens her grip, realizing it was too much. "I only have one rule," she whispers, and Luca blinks, staring up at her with tender trust. "If you need to stop, if you're uncomfortable for any reason or you're done, you say Margaret Court."

Luca's eyes widen, and then she snorts. "Australian tennis champion and Christian minister Margaret Court?"

Juliette bites the inside of her lip to keep from laughing. "Yeah," she says, "because you better not be moaning her name while we're together."

Luca smiles, and Juliette can't resist swooping down to kiss Luca's dimple. "Got it," Luca says, laughing against Juliette's cheek. "Safeword is Margaret Court. And that goes for you too."

Juliette nods and then shifts back, stroking her fingers over Luca's clothed stomach before she splays her hand and pushes the fabric away. The material catches on the underside of Luca's breasts and Juliette keeps it there, held taut. Luca's nipples press against the fabric, already tight and hard.

"Come on, Jules," Luca whispers, her eyes heavy and hooded as she stares at Juliette.

"So impatient," Juliette teases.

Luca's chest heaves, and Juliette gives in and slips her other hand beneath Luca's white T-shirt, cupping her right breast and sweeping her thumb in broad strokes across her nipple.

Luca stops breathing, and her mouth falls open as her head tilts back. Juliette leans down and mouths kisses onto Luca's trembling stomach. "Lift your hips," she says, slipping her fingers beneath the band of her sweatpants.

Luca thrusts up, back arching, and Juliette peels Luca's sweatpants off.

And when Juliette looks down, she gasps.

Luca Kacic is naked from the waist down and *dripping*.

TWENTY-EIGHT

LUCA

Earlier, Luca had cringed while putting on her sweatpants without underwear, afraid she'd maybe misread what could happen after Juliette arrived.

But now, seeing Juliette's eyes widen and her mouth fall open in an audible gasp, Luca can't help but squirm under the appraising look.

"Efficiency," Luca says with a smirk.

Juliette's dark eyes flick up to hers. "Oh, you are a miracle, Luca Kacic. I want to touch every part of you."

Luca's pulse quickens. Juliette's words are like a scorching hot iron, pressing against her skin and making it impossible to decipher feelings from reason.

Juliette's hands skate up her ribs again. "Arms up," she commands, and Luca obediently helps wriggle her own shirt off. Now, Luca is completely naked, left vulnerable beneath the woman who could easily hurt her. Juliette is still in her hoodie and shorts, but there is reverence in Juliette's eyes, a hot want that makes something oily squirm in Luca's chest. Without thinking, she drops her arms over her chest.

Juliette's hands capture Luca's wrists, peeling them away from her breasts. Juliette leans forward, pinning her hands above her head. Luca's skin tingles, the cool air sweeping over her skin. "Don't hide. Let me admire you." Juliette's voice is soft, and she frees one hand to trace a finger across Luca's cheekbone. "You're so beautiful," she breathes.

Luca can't meet Juliette's gaze, her cheeks heating. The heady rush of desperate desire is so overwhelming, she wriggles one of her hands free to anchor onto Juliette's shoulder.

"Take this off," Luca whispers, tugging on the fabric. She finally looks up at Juliette. Her face is flushed, lips kiss-swollen, and her curls are in disarray, a frizzy halo where Luca had been pulling. Juliette lets go of Luca and obliges her. She leans back and in one swift move, she shucks the sweatshirt over her head and tosses it away. She is wearing a sports bra and Luca runs her fingers beneath the strap. "This too."

"Bossy," Juliette says fondly, before she wrangles herself out of it and her breasts spill free, dusky brown nipples already pebbled in the cool air. "Don't hide your face. I want to see your reactions." She wriggles out of her jean shorts and tosses them over her shoulder.

Luca hates that a flush spreads across her face and down her neck. She grabs Juliette's waist, holding on to her. For weeks Luca has been overwhelmed by want and desire, but now she is being crushed under the anxiety of what is currently happening between them.

Juliette pauses, her fingers trailing up to Luca's jaw, cupping her face gently. "Do you still want this? We can stop," she whispers, her eyes big and kind.

Luca does want this, but she is terrified. What if Juliette hurts her like her ex did? Luca wants love. What if Juliette only wants sex?

Well, Luca also wants sex. Her skin is buzzing, and she thinks she might die if Juliette doesn't touch her soon. "I don't know. I can't." She can't seem to form full sentences.

Juliette pulls back, giving her space to breathe. "Are you okay?"

Luca nods, collecting her spinning thoughts. "Be careful, okay?"

Juliette's eyes soften and she nods. "Of course." Her head tilts and she brushes her lips across Luca's cheekbone. Every thought in Luca's brain goes mushy and fuzzy. "Trust me, I want to take care of you."

Juliette's words are like honey over her aching heart, and Luca can't help but believe her. Juliette presses her face into the curve of Luca's neck, breath hot on her ear. "And even if I break you into pieces, I'll put you back together."

Luca leans back and nods. "Okay," she murmurs, feeling a little dizzy and far too hot. She squirms and Juliette moves with her, giggling.

"I haven't been able to stop thinking about you," Juliette says, peppering kisses across Luca's face.

Luca's eyes pop open. "What do you think about?"

Juliette's breath hitches. "Your lips," she murmurs, her fingertips brushing across Luca's lower lip. "Your eyes, your accent." Luca laughs. "The way you looked that first morning, soaked in sweat and your shirt transparent and showing off your perfect body." Juliette's fingertips drift across Luca's sharp shoulders, her thumbs brushing her collarbones. The touch is light, but it's like being struck by lightning. "I've been thinking about how I want to know you. Every part of you," Juliette continues, taking her time to explore Luca's skin.

Luca wants to say that Juliette is lying, that she can't possibly want to know her. That Luca's only talent is tennis, and she is a coward too terrified to live and love. But Juliette's fingers coast across her ribs and it almost tickles, which cuts off every coherent thought.

Luca's muscles twitch and she wriggles, unable to stay entirely still. Juliette clicks her tongue and flicks Luca's nipple. The sting is instant and sharp, and she gasps, unsure if she should arch her chest up or curl away. Juliette flicks the other before she soothes the slight burn with a brush of her thumb across the tip.

"Fuck," Luca breathes.

"And you said *I'm* sensitive," Juliette says, her thumb making lazy circles around one of the buds. Luca's eyes nearly cross, spikes of pleasure roil through her, and she rocks her hips up. Juliette leans down, her hot breath brushing across Luca's breast. "You're trembling," Juliette whispers against her skin.

"You're good at this," Luca whispers back, digging her fingers into Juliette's shoulders to anchor herself.

Juliette slides to the side, pressing one leg between Luca's and nudging her knee against her center. Pleasure jolts through Luca, and she knows she's dripping onto Juliette's leg. The thought is agonizingly hot.

"I've had a lot of practice," Juliette murmurs. Then her head dips down, and she swipes her tongue across Luca's hardened nipple as if she's eating ice cream.

It has been an embarrassingly long time since Luca had any form of release beyond her hand and vibrator. She shudders as her clit throbs, barely enough stimulation on it, but enough that she tilts her hips and widens her knees for more.

"Could you come from this?" Juliette asks, pensive as if she's just considering what to eat for dinner. Then she swirls her tongue, and Luca curses.

"I don't know," Luca whispers, the edges of her mind becoming hazy. It could have been thirty seconds since they started or six hours, she has no idea.

Juliette shifts to Luca's other nipple, sucking her mouth over her breast, while rolling her fingers over the nipple she's just abandoned. The competing sensations have Luca arching and squirming. "God, you're soaked," Juliette says as she lifts her head.

Luca can't figure out a response in any language, and she's barely able to keep a whine from escaping her throat. Juliette shifts down between Luca's parted thighs and slides her arms underneath, fingers bruising against her skin. Juliette looks up at her with a gleam in her eyes and seductively tracing her lips with her tongue.

"Juliette," Luca breathes as Juliette dips her head and breathes over her hot core. Luca whimpers. Juliette kisses and swipes her clit with her tongue, keeping the touches light.

"Fuck," Luca moans as Juliette's tongue plunges into her, curling and curving against her walls. Luca claws her fingers into Juliette's hair. The pleasure builds, impossible to stop, like a tsunami of sunlike pleasure.

Her hips buck, her thighs trembling, but Juliette doesn't let up until the waves crash and Luca is shot into oblivion. Pleasure sears every nerve, and she arches so hard she thinks her back might snap in half. Juliette sucks and licks and tongues her through every wave before pulling back.

"God, Luca, you should see yourself. You're so sexy."

Luca's skin is on fire, and she only wants to douse herself in more gasoline. This must be what people mean when they say soulmate sex is the best.

Juliette slowly lowers her thighs back to the mattress and massages Luca's trembling muscles. Luca whines, grabbing Juliette's shoulders until she finally leans up to kiss her. Luca didn't think tasting herself on Juliette's tongue would be hot, but her stomach coils and she groans against her mouth.

Juliette nuzzles their noses together. "You're so loud."

Luca's eyes fly open, and she knows she's blushing all the way down her neck to her chest. "Sorry."

Juliette shakes her head. "You are so fucking sexy. I want to hear it all." She kisses her again, soft and tender, a barely there brush of their lips.

Then, Juliette's fingers are sweeping across her clit, tapping with gentle pressure, and Luca gasps. "Please."

Juliette smirks. "Patience, Luca Kacic."

TWENTY-NINE

JULIETTE

Watching Luca fall apart, writhing and whimpering and unable to form a coherent sentence, is immediately addicting.

Luca's head twists from side to side, mouth bitten bright crimson and shredded by her own teeth. She keens and mewls, begging for more, begging for less. At some point while she's edging Luca, a distant part of Juliette realizes that she is thoroughly ruined for anyone else. She's becoming attuned to Luca's whimpers and moans, to the flex of her stomach and the tremble of her thighs, to the way she likes to be touched.

And more importantly, Luca never asks her to stop. Juliette can't help but lean down and lick Luca's mouth, swallowing all the tiny sounds she's making. In a streak of heat, she realizes she never wants anyone else to hear Luca make those beautiful sounds. She never wants anyone else to touch Luca like this.

She is mine, Juliette thinks, strangely possessive.

The thought should scare her, but it doesn't.

"Juliette, please," Luca whimpers as Juliette grinds the heel of her hand into Luca's clit and brings her to the edge without pushing her over. Luca's face is blotchy, sweat dewed on her forehead and in the hollow of her throat, but Juliette has never been so turned on in her whole life.

Luca is beyond gorgeous. She is sex-hazed, needy, and desperate for Juliette to touch her. "Please, let me," she rasps, blunt nails scratching into Juliette's scalp. She wishes Luca would pull.

"Yes," Juliette whispers, dotting kisses along Luca's hips. "Come on, you've earned it." She lets it build slowly this time, making note of the way Luca's thighs shake so hard she's almost vibrating, and her breathing stutters. Juliette drives three fingers into her, and Luca clenches down on them. Her lashes flutter, clumped together, and her mouth opens into an obscene moan.

Her hands clench into the sheets, the muscles and veins in her forearms popping, her back arching like a bow off the bed as the tension snaps, shimmering tears streaking down her temples. Juliette strokes her through the orgasm with her thumb angled against her clit. Her wrist cramps, but she doesn't care when Luca looks that good coming around her fingers, gushing hot and beautifully slick. Juliette can almost feel the phantom sensations as she strokes Luca through her orgasm.

Luca slumps, boneless and relaxed. Juliette roots around in her backpack for wipes and cleans them both, quickly but gently. Luca is completely lost in the drifting clouds of postorgasm haze.

"I'll be right back," she says, kissing Luca's sweaty forehead.

Luca's whimper makes Juliette freeze.

"No, wait. Don't go."

There is something in the hitch of Luca's voice that chills her bones. She turns, swiftly leaning down into her line of sight. She kisses her, gently caressing her face and wiping the tears away on one side. "I'm right here. I only want to get water for you." She smooths her hair back, trying to assure Luca that she isn't leaving.

Luca's breath hiccups, and she nods. Juliette's heart wrenches, and she indulges in tracing the curves of Luca's face until her breathing steadies and she relaxes against the pillows again, eyes closing.

Juliette would like to think she doesn't sprint to the minifridge, but she does. "See, right here," Juliette says as she tosses herself back into the bed with a water bottle. "I need you to drink this before we continue," Juliette says.

Luca's head lolls. "I want to eat you out," she says.

Juliette shudders. Fuck. She wants that too. "Drink this first," she says.

Luca struggles to lift herself onto an elbow and tips the bottle back. "Is this the end of the fun?" she asks after draining half the bottle, glancing sidelong at Juliette.

Juliette plucks one of Luca's nipples, and she nearly shoots water up her nose. "Oh, I'm not done," she says, then adds, "unless you are."

Luca shakes her head, hair tangled against her skin, sweaty and clinging to her cheeks and neck. Her gaze is dark and sultry, pinning Juliette to the bed. Luca finishes the water bottle and Juliette tosses it onto the bedside table next to a rather strange statue. "You haven't come yet," Luca whispers, "so I can't let you go running around telling the whole tour I'm an inconsiderate lover."

Juliette laughs as she drags her thumb across Luca's lower lip. Luca's tongue darts out to catch it, and Juliette lets her thumb slide into Luca's mouth. Luca sucks immediately, swirling her tongue, flexing as if this is simply a warm-up. Her eyes are dark, and her lids are heavy, wanton and heady.

"Oh," Juliette whimpers, her pulse pounding through every inch of her body. Luca reaches up and takes her wrist, eyes fluttering closed as she sucks on her finger, tongue flicking across it in a way Juliette knows would feel heavenly elsewhere.

She pulls her hand from Luca's mouth and surges forward, kissing her sloppy and messy. Luca moans into her mouth, melting into her.

Then, Luca pounces. She tackles Juliette into the pillows, straddling her hips. Luca's hands are everywhere. They caress down Juliette's sides, digging in and making Juliette's stomach clench, ripping a laugh from her.

Luca traces circles around Juliette's nipples as she leans down and kisses her jaw, her throat, dots her collarbones with hickeys. She keeps kissing down the line of her sternum to her stomach, tongue dipping into her belly button and making Juliette laugh again. She scrapes her teeth against her hips before she hooks them on the scalloped edge of Juliette's panties, and she tugs. It is one of the hottest sights Juliette has ever seen.

Luca uses her thumbs to drag Juliette's panties down, too impatient to use just her teeth. Juliette is grateful for it because her pussy is throbbing. Luca's clever tongue swipes up from her wet slit to her clit.

She doesn't stop there but sucks Juliette's clit into her mouth, tongue flicking rapidly over it.

Juliette has been wet and close, burning with heat for what feels like a lifetime. It doesn't take long for the velvet heat of Luca's mouth to be almost too much. "Close," Juliette whispers, reaching down and threading her fingers through Luca's ponytail. She holds her tight, and Luca hums.

The blinding orgasm paints Juliette's vision white. Her toes curl and every nerve shatters, only to be rapidly reforged. It's embarrassingly quick, but she can't even begin to care.

The only word she has on her lips is the same one on her wrist: *Luca.*

When she finally opens her eyes, she's panting and pliant. She turns her head and finds Luca lying next to her, shoulder to shoulder. Juliette wriggles a bit, bumping into Luca's. The heady scent of sex is in the air, sweat dewing on their bodies, and it's stifling in the bedroom.

Still, exhaustion floods over Juliette, the jet lag and long flight catching up with her now that the nerves of excitement have been flushed from her veins. She yawns and rolls onto her side, laying her head on Luca's chest and slotting their legs together. "That was fun," Juliette murmurs. She shifts her ear, and she can hear the frantic thrum of Luca's heart. "Sleep now, and then round two later?" Juliette murmurs, her eyelids too heavy to stay open. Being pressed skin-to-skin with Luca is calming, and she feels satiated in ways she never has before.

Juliette throws her arm around Luca and curls in tighter until Luca's fingers bury into her hair and scratch at her scalp. She usually isn't one for cuddling after sex, and if she does, it's only for a short time.

Still, she never wants to leave. And it isn't just the jet lag keeping her down.

She realizes, just as sleep is about to take her, that she feels content with Luca, happy to just relax in Luca's arms.

THIRTY

LUCA

It's dark when Luca jerks awake. Her heart thunders in her chest, but the nightmare is already slipping through her fingers, details too fuzzy to remember. The fear claws at her throat, and she swallows it back, pressing her knuckles against her sternum. She is sticky with dried sweat, and her limbs are heavy on the satin sheets. She hears soft snoring and panic floods through her.

Luca forces herself onto her elbows. Juliette is beside her, turned away, and Luca stares at her back. She blinks and her sleepiness falls away, her memory of their night piecing together. Juliette's breath rises steadily, her curls in a tangle across the pillow. Luca can't fill her lungs with enough air. She shoves the sheets off her legs and stumbles into the bathroom.

She stares at her reflection in the mirror, her fingers tentatively touching the hickeys fanning across her collarbones and down. "Oh, wow," she mutters. Her hands shake as she pulls out her hair tie and runs her hands through her sweaty hair, tangled from Juliette and the bed.

Luca doesn't regret what happened—quite the opposite. She never wants to stop. And even though her heart hammers at the thought, she doesn't feel the familiar tug of panic that often spirals her thoughts out of control. Maybe she's still a little sex-addled and syrupy.

She brushes her thumb along the bruise that shadows the edge of her breast. She likes that Juliette has marked her, as if Luca belongs to her. It sends a shiver down Luca's spine.

Luca shuffles back out of the bathroom, carefully tiptoeing as she pulls on the first hoodie and pair of shorts she finds. Juliette should be exhausted and dead to the world, but Luca still gently clicks the door closed. She wanders up to the roof, desperate for some fresh air. It's late, past four in the morning, and abandoned. The night is a heavy ink curtain, but there's a gentle ocean breeze.

Luca slides into one of the many loungers and curls her legs into her chest, pressing her cheek against her knees. Her stomach curdles as she tries to weave through the complicated mess of emotions boiling in her gut.

Once again, Luca knows so much of what she's feeling is informed by her worry about being hurt. But Luca can't deny that something has shifted between them. Whether they admit it or not, Juliette cares about her. From checking in on her during sex to bringing her snacks and talking about her fears, it soothes some of the nagging anxiety that Luca usually lets rule her life. Juliette is her *soulmate*. Even if Juliette doesn't value that as much as Luca does, she decides she can trust in that.

Luca lifts her head and stares at the lightening sky. Soft pinks spread out from the silhouette of Miami's skyscrapers. She uncurls her legs and heads back to her room, more clear-headed than before.

The air-conditioning chases away the heat and humidity from Luca's skin as she steps back into the lavish room. Her phone buzzes on the table, and she snatches it up. Half past six in the morning.

There are about a dozen missed calls from Vladimir.

Confusion and panic ribbon through her, and she clicks on one of the many missed call notifications without listening to the voicemails.

Vladimir answers on the second ring. "Luca?"

"What's wrong?" she asks, sinking onto one of the couches.

"Do you happen to know where Juliette is?" Vladimir asks calmly.

Luca chews on a hangnail, debating how to answer. "Yes, why?" she asks finally.

"Is she in your room?"

Luca glances at the closed door. "Yes. Why? What's going on?"

Vladimir sighs, and then in English says, "Antony Ricci called me and demanded to know where his daughter is."

Luca winces. "Yikes."

There is a bit of muffled yelling, and Vladimir sighs heavily into the phone. "I have a very angry Antony at my door because apparently, Juliette never told her family she made it to Miami. And her father accused me of sleeping with Juliette," Vladimir explains far too calmly in Croatian.

Luca chokes on her tongue. "What?"

"Anyway, once I assured him I was not having a secret love affair with his daughter, we tried to figure out where she was or if she was kidnapped."

Luca drops her head into her hands. "Oh, God."

Vladimir pauses. "You don't have to tell me, but why is Juliette in your room?"

Shame clogs her throat. "I'll get her and send her down," Luca says, her voice strangled. She doesn't want to explain.

Vladimir hums. "Okay. Let's go for breakfast down by the water. Karoline told me about an excellent place." He sounds too normal, and Luca coughs over her nearly hysterical laugh.

She slowly gets to her feet. "Sounds good." She hangs up and pushes open the bedroom door.

Juliette is sprawled like a starfish in the middle of the bed, still completely naked, and beautifully golden among the ghosts of white sheets.

Luca pauses, not wanting to disturb her, but she knows she has to. She pads over to Juliette's side and sits down, gently shaking her leg. "Jules?" She flicks on the bedside lamp.

Juliette barely stirs, lost in a deep slumber.

"Jules, you have to wake up now." Panic laces through Luca. What if Antony Ricci comes up to her room and demands to see his daughter? She would rather not confront him now. "Please, wake up." Fear digs its talons in, and she clenches her fists.

Antony Ricci is not Luca's father.

Juliette twists over and wraps an arm around Luca's waist, half dragging her down. Luca yelps, caught off-balance, and Juliette plants a sloppy kiss on her cheek. "Time for round two?" she asks into Luca's ear, her voice husky.

As much as she wants to curl into Juliette's side and pick up where they left off, her anxiety threatens to swallow her whole. "Jules, you have to go."

"What?" Juliette's playfulness morphs into confusion. "Why?"

Luca wriggles, and Juliette lets her sit up again. Her throat is tight, and she struggles to find a delicate way to tell her. "Your father is looking for you."

"He's not here?"

"Apparently he is, Jules," Luca says. "Where is your phone?"

Juliette blinks against the light blearily. She has a streak indented on her cheek from the pillow, and Luca's gut twists. She looks so soft and sleepy, and Luca wants nothing more than to cuddle her. Her brow pinches in adorable confusion. "Backpack," she whispers, finally piecing together what Luca told her.

She finds it in the front pocket and hands it to her. It's on Do Not Disturb, hiding all the missed calls. "Shit," Juliette hisses, scrolling through her phone. "I have to go." She throws the covers off.

Luca sits on the edge of the bed and shivers, cold prickling on the back of her neck as Juliette scrambles to pull her clothes on. Luca's leg bounces, and it won't stop.

"Hey, I'll come over later, yeah?" Juliette says as she swings her backpack over her shoulder. She's missing her shorts, and Luca realizes she put on Juliette's this morning. She wriggles out of them and hands them over. "Thanks." Juliette pulls them on, shoves her phone in the back pocket, and then tilts her head.

"Luca, it's okay. Antony is just worried. I mean, he'll want to kill me. But it's fine."

"I know," Luca says, chewing her lower lip with her teeth. Logically, she does know this, and yet her heart hammers as if she's run down a drop shot.

Juliette pauses. Luca wants to tell her to hurry, but then Juliette's hands are cradling Luca's face, and everything stills. For once, Luca has to look up to see Juliette.

"Hey, what's wrong?" Juliette's thumb arcs over her cheekbone, surprisingly tender.

Luca swallows again, her mouth dry. "It's complicated," she whispers, because she doesn't know if she can verbalize the feelings that are swelling inside of her, roiling like waves during a storm.

Juliette's gaze searches hers, warm and imploring, bursting with emotion. Worry, hope, concern, and maybe affection, too. It's a little unnerving to see her bare of any mask. "We can talk about it now. I don't want to run off if you're upset about something."

Her words settle a few of the jagged pieces scraping against her insides, melting them into softened goo. Luca curls her fingers around Juliette's wrists, anchoring herself. She breathes, and for once, it doesn't feel like her lungs are full of holes.

"It can wait. Go talk to your dad."

Juliette hesitates but then she dips her head and kisses Luca, thoroughly. "It's nice that I can just do that," she whispers against Luca's mouth as she pulls away.

"Do it again," Luca breathes, indulgent as all of her anxiety blurs into radio static.

Juliette chuckles and swoops in for another. Luca slides her hand up the back of Juliette's neck, reveling in the way she moans against her mouth. Exercising self-control, much to her own detriment, Luca lets go of Juliette and slumps back onto the bed.

"Leave before I tell you not to," Luca says, and she hears Juliette laugh, clear and bright.

"Don't miss me too much." Juliette squeezes her knee.

"Wouldn't dream of it, Ricci," Luca shoots back, her face too hot for her liking.

Juliette is still laughing as the door closes. Luca sighs, limbs boneless.

THIRTY-ONE

JULIETTE

Arguments with her father always follow a specific pattern that Juliette knows like the back of her hand. Unlike their argument in London, Juliette can't muster the energy to be upset this time. She is light on her feet as she makes her way down the stairs to her room.

She knows she should feel apologetic and submit to her father's intense gaze, but Juliette doesn't regret a single moment of being with Luca. She *does* feel guilty for forgetting to text, but that doesn't mean Antony had to fly to Miami to scold her.

After a significant amount of fake groveling and promising she wouldn't worry him again, Juliette wants to turn around and go right back to Luca's room. Instead, she tells her father she'll practice with him tomorrow for an extra hour and then goes to hit the gym to get rid of her excess energy. When she returns to her actual hotel room, it's still fresh and unused.

However, the couch is currently being dominated by one particularly pesky younger sister.

"Livia." Juliette groans as she traipses into the living area.

Livia taps quickly on her phone. "Hey, Jules," she says without looking up.

"What are you doing here?"

Livia sets her phone on her knee and dumps a handful of Skittles into her palm, letting them rattle around as she frowns at them. "I came with Dad," she says, as if that explains anything.

"What about Claudia? Octavia? You're supposed to be in London," Juliette says, trying not to expose her frustration.

Livia finally looks up at and acknowledges her with a blink of her big brown eyes. "You need Instagram photos." Juliette groans and slumps into the love seat opposite her. "Miami is the perfect place for new ones. We go to the boardwalk every year."

"No, you go with Claudia every year." Juliette lifts her sweaty hair off her neck and twists her curls around the hair tie. She desperately needs a shower, but with the prospect of Livia dragging her into the crowds, she's willing to procrastinate.

"Okay, well, she's in London, so that's not going to happen. I already have enough content for *her* Instagram." Livia plucks two yellow Skittles and shoves one in each cheek. "Want some?" She holds out her bag.

Juliette leans forward and watches the artificially colored candy land in her palm. "No red?" she asks, disappointed and a little suspicious at the probability.

Livia looks sheepish. "I ate them already, sorry."

"The world is so cruel to me," Juliette bemoans, tilting her head back and tossing all of the Skittles in her mouth, mostly to watch Livia's horror as she chews them all together.

"So, are you taking me to the boardwalk or not? You could bring Luca."

Juliette jerks and nearly chokes on the Skittles. Livia smirks at her.

"Why would I want to bring her?" Juliette asks, coughing to clear her throat.

Livia raises a singular brow in question. "Well, considering how you came to Miami early to spend time with her, I thought you might want to, you know, spend time with her." Her words are pointed.

"How do you know that?" Juliette demands, her stomach churning. If Livia knows, who else does?

Livia sighs, exasperated. "Keep up, Jules. I know everything."

"Everything?" Juliette asks, and Livia nods.

"Just ask her." She stands up and crumples the now-empty bag of Skittles.

Juliette clears her throat. "I don't think Luca would be comfortable with that. There are a lot of people on Miami Beach."

Livia tilts her head, her wild waves barely held back by her glasses. "That's exactly why it'll be fine. No one is looking at you in Miami Beach. It's the best place to be incognito."

Juliette can't argue with that. Livia flicks her shoulder as she passes. "Shower first. You're gross. And wear something nice."

"It's not a date, Livia," Juliette snaps, her cheeks heating.

Livia's mouth twitches, and it's clear she's holding back a laugh. "Of course not, Juliette," she drawls, clearly meaning the opposite. "This is for marketability. The stans want to see you looking gorgeous and perfect."

Juliette fake gags and rolls her eyes. But Livia, as always, is right.

Juliette wonders if she should text Luca while she diffuses her curls. The longer she waits, the less likely it'll be that Luca will say yes. Realizing it might be awkward to explain over text, Juliette finishes doing her hair and gets dressed. She knows Livia will yell at her if she wears her beaten-up sneakers with her silky white midi skirt and simple white tank, but they're comfortable, so she does anyway.

Unfortunately, she can't procrastinate picking out her jewelry because Livia sends her the exact lineup. A new diamond bracelet for a sponsorship post, gold rings, and her gold tennis racket necklace. She fluffs out her hair and pops on her cherry lip gloss before slinging her satchel over her shoulder and heading upstairs to Luca's room.

Nerves twist in her stomach as she knocks. She should've called instead. Easier to be rejected over the phone.

It doesn't take long for Luca to open the door. "Oh, hey," she says, blinking as she takes in Juliette.

"Hi," Juliette says. She feels overdressed and a little stupid. Luca is in an oversize T-shirt that hangs over the edge of her shorts— if she's even wearing any. Part of her hopes that she isn't.

"Sorry, I have the curtains open," Luca says, a sheepish smile on her lips.

Warmth spreads in Juliette's chest. "It's okay." There goes her idea of pushing Luca into her room and going down on her again. Probably for the best. Livia would kill her if she's late. "I wondered if you wanted to come to the boardwalk with me."

Luca's eyes widen. "Oh, okay. You want to be seen with me? In public?" Luca asks, tilting her head and brows furrowing.

"My sister, Livie, is coming too. It's a casual thing," Juliette says, wanting to cringe the moment she does. She hates how she can't read Luca's expression whenever her mouth slides into an impassive line. "She wants to take pictures, get food, dip her toes in the water. Anyway, it's okay if you don't want to. I know we're just . . . " Juliette trails off, unsure of what to say. Luca seems to be struggling with words too. "It's probably weird meeting my little sister and hanging out with us. It's fine if you don't want to. Really."

"I'd love to come," Luca says suddenly, and she tucks her hair behind her ear. "Livia is the only Ricci sister I haven't met, so I might as well remedy that, right?"

Relief washes the tension from Juliette's shoulders, and she smiles, a little breathless that her clumsy offer somehow worked. "Great! I'll meet you in the lobby in half an hour?"

"Yeah," Luca says, her smile widening and exposing her dimple. If they weren't in the middle of a hallway where anyone could spot them, Juliette would've stepped into Luca and kissed it.

"See you soon," Juliette says, giddier than she has any right to be. Especially because this is *not* a date.

"This is absolutely a date," Livia says as she sits at the hotel bar, one leg crossed over the other.

"Shut up," Juliette hisses.

Livia glances up at her from under her long lashes. Once again, she's dressed much cuter than Juliette is used to. It's like she raided Octavia's wardrobe, with her striped blue-and-white shorts, white crop top, and a white button-down that Juliette is almost certain was Leo's at one point.

"And who are you trying to impress?" Juliette gestures at Livia's outfit.

Livia blinks. She isn't wearing her glasses, and Juliette can see she has on mascara. "No one," she snaps, a touch too defensive.

Juliette narrows her eyes.

Livia presses her lips together. "I won't call this a date, and you won't ask questions. Deal?" She jabs a finger in her face, and Juliette smirks, but nods.

Livia hops off the stool and waves across the lobby at Luca, abandoning her cola.

Juliette rolls her eyes and tosses a couple of bills on the bar to pay for it before following after her.

"Luca Kacic! I don't believe we've met," Livia says, holding out her arms and wrapping Luca in a hug. Luca looks surprised, but she indulges Livia by returning the hug. Their height difference is comical, and Juliette stifles a laugh.

"Livia Ricci?" Luca says as she pulls back, and Livia nods.

"The one and only."

Juliette looks over Luca. She's wearing light-wash mom jeans with a white V-neck top tucked into them. Juliette is reminded of their indoor practice when the sprinklers soaked them both. Her hands are itching to slide beneath the soft white cotton and touch Luca again. Luca slips her hands into her back pockets and leans on one hip. She is long and lean and looks so tan in white. Juliette wants to eat her.

"Juliette?" Livia snaps her fingers in front of her face, and she realizes Luca is smirking at her.

"Yes, pipsqueak?" she asks to annoy her.

Livia glares and elbows her. "The Uber is here."

As they head out to the car, Luca leans in close. "I meant to tell you earlier, but you look really good."

Juliette looks up, and Luca's smile has softened. "Thank you." She knocks her elbow against Luca's, since she can't take her hand and twine their fingers in public. "You don't look half bad either." She dips her voice, flicking her eyes down Luca's body.

Luca's cheeks turn the most adorable rosy color, and it's Juliette's turn to smirk.

THIRTY-TWO

LUCA

The boardwalk is a riot of color, people, and lights. The sun hangs low, burning bright gold and streaking the sky with soft shapes of pink and purple, while the shops lining the boardwalk are illuminated with warm lights and vibrant umbrellas.

Luca trails a few paces behind Juliette and Livia, who is giving Juliette instructions and scolding her to act natural while she snaps hundreds of photos. Most are of Juliette taking photos with her vintage camera of the beach and people on the boardwalk.

Crowds weave around them, caught in their own little bubbles, and no one pays them any attention.

It's strangely euphoric. A weight lifts off her shoulders at being able to wander through the throngs of people without having to act a certain way. She doesn't need to smile, worry about where her hands are in photos, or focus on giving every kid an autograph. She does love doing those things, it's an integral part of her job as a professional athlete, but it does get exhausting.

Luca has never been to the Miami boardwalk before—too many people—and yet, nostalgia aches in her chest. It reminds her of the February Carnival in Zadar that she used to go to as a child with her mother. Colorful, bright, full of laughter and music, and the scent of fried food wafting in the air.

But the Floridians are wearing big sunglasses to ward off the sun instead of masks to ward off evil spirits.

The ocean is off to their right, crystallized aqua, and full of women in string bikinis and men in Speedos, all toasting over some occasion. Luca smiles as she looks away, just in time to catch Juliette with her camera trained on her.

"Hey," Luca admonishes even though she isn't upset, "no photos, paparazzi."

Juliette flushes. "Sorry." The wind ruffles her curls, getting a few strands caught in her lashes.

"I'm kidding, relax," Luca says, walking in step with Juliette as they weave around a bunch of teenage girls taking a group photo, arms wrapped around each other.

"You always catch me, it's hard to get a candid of you," Juliette says, fiddling with the camera. She holds it close to herself, protecting it from anyone who could carelessly throw their limbs into her path.

"I guess I always know when you're looking," Luca says, and she expects Juliette to laugh and look away, but instead her gaze stays steady with hers. The sun slants perfectly over Juliette's face, the silhouette of the palm leaves tracing her cheekbone. "Thank you for inviting me," Luca says softly. A small smile touches Juliette's lips, more shy than usual.

"I'm glad you said yes," Juliette says, and Luca's heartbeat picks up. She rubs the back of her neck and nods, suddenly too hot under Juliette's gaze.

"Jules!" Livia breaks the moment, coming out of nowhere, and Luca almost stumbles into her. "Can you get me a fruity cocktail of some sort?" she asks, batting her lashes.

"You're twenty," Juliette says.

Livia pouts. "I can legally drink in Europe! It's not fair that America has silly rules."

Juliette frowns at her, but with a heavy sigh, she slips her vintage camera back into her satchel and nods. "Fine. But only one." She looks at Luca. "You want anything?"

Luca shakes her head. She isn't one for cocktails, preferring a small glass of wine when she does indulge. "I can come—" Luca starts to say, but Livia's arm loops through hers.

"Thanks! You're the best!" Livia calls over her shoulder as she tugs Luca toward an open storefront ornamented with dream catchers and wind chimes.

A shopkeeper sits on a stool next to one of the tables covered in racks of necklaces, eyeing them as they approach. They sweep through the thin gauze that hangs as a doorway. It's much smaller inside than Luca anticipated. Most of the wares are on the tables outside, but the two rows of counters hold dozens of sparkling crystals.

Another shopkeeper sits next to the counter, watching them under hooded eyes as an elderly woman asks about getting a ring polished.

"Do you like crystals, Luca?" Livia asks.

"Crystals?"

"Yes. They're used for all sorts of things. I snuck a clear quartz into each of my sisters' tennis bags to help them reach their dreams. It's like channeling energy. Or at least that's what the internet tells me."

Luca fiddles with her fingers as Livia moves with ease through the middle aisle.

"I'm not much of a jewelry person," Luca says. Every necklace or bracelet she's ever worn, she's fiddled with until it snapped or wore away.

"What about a fidget ring?" Livia asks, spinning one of the ring stands. "You pick at your nails a lot."

Luca shoves her hands into her pockets, swallowing back a defensive retort. "I don't like wearing rings."

Livia pauses. "Interesting."

She isn't sure what Livia is aiming at.

"How about a rose quartz?" Livia says, plucking an oddly shaped pink crystal from seemingly nowhere. "How is your love life?" She says it casually, as if she's simply asking about the weather, but suddenly it all slots into place.

She's asking about Luca's relationship with Juliette.

Luca bites her lip, trying not to think about Juliette's slick fingers driving into her and pushing her over the edge. She has no idea what to say.

Livia drops the rose quartz back into a tray and cocks her head.

"Come on, Luca, you're going to have to think of an answer for Claudia and Octavia. I'm the least scary Ricci."

Luca highly doubts that, but she keeps her mouth shut. "We're friends," Luca says finally.

Livia slinks closer, her fingers trailing across the crystals. "Those hickeys tell a different story."

Luca snaps her hand up to cover them with her palm. She had tried to cover them with concealer as best she could, but the heat must've made her sweat some of it off.

Livia smirks, but it's not unkind. "Come on, I'm not trying to interrogate you. I only want to know that you're not just fucking around with my sister."

Luca swallows. "Quite the opposite," she says softly. She doesn't add that she worries that Juliette is going to ruin her heart.

"What's your opinion on soulmates?" Livia asks suddenly, her hands stilling. Her focus lands entirely on her. She and Juliette have the same warm, bright, amber-brown eyes, and Luca is vividly reminded of how Juliette seems to see right through her.

"It's complicated," Luca murmurs, and Livia frowns, unsatisfied. "I know Juliette wants a choice in who she loves, and I want to *be* loved. If she chooses me, then that's great." She looks away from Livia, unsure if she should've laid all her cards on the counter like that.

"What about you choosing her?" Livia asks softly.

Luca's throat tightens, her lungs constricting. It's suddenly too dense and humid in this tiny shop. "I can't stay away," Luca admits, saying the thought out loud is more frightening than just thinking it. Like her mother, she realizes, she has attached herself to her soulmate, for better or for worse. "We're trying to figure things out. It's new for both of us."

"Be careful with my sister, Luca, and we'll get along just fine," Livia says, patting Luca's arm as she exits the shop without getting anything.

Luca sways in place, her vision spiraling as dizziness crashes over her. She needs to breathe. She pushes out of the crystal shop, but the boardwalk is too crowded. Too many people are talking, and her head throbs with a headache. She cuts through the crowd toward the beach and the rhythmic crashing of the waves.

Luca gets to the sand and rips her shoes and socks off, jogging down closer to the water and a secluded patch of sand out of earshot of the other beachgoers.

She digs her toes in the sand.

She breathes in the salty Atlantic air.

She focuses on the frothy white foam washing up to her toes.

And slowly, as she focuses on real sensations, her panic loosens and she sinks into the sand, breathing hard.

Juliette is her soulmate. They *should* work. She plunges her hands into the sand. It's warm between her fingers and grounds her again.

She doesn't need to leap with both feet immediately. She can warm up first, get her muscles loosened, and then slowly work her way into the relationship.

The tennis metaphor washes a sense of calm over her. Tennis is what she understands. It's her safe space. Maybe they aren't playing singles against each other. Maybe they're playing doubles, and they just need to find their rhythm.

JULIETTE

Juliette hands off Livia's drink as she catches sight of Luca making a beeline for the beach.

Livia shoves her shoulder. "Go talk to her."

Juliette flips her off as she jogs along the boardwalk and down to the sand. She pauses to unlace her shoes before she continues scanning the beach for Luca. It reminds her of their first night in Naples, and she shudders. Better not to think of that.

Eventually, she spots Luca sitting alone, staring out at the ocean and the deepening twilight. The ruby sun silhouettes the Miami skyline as shadowy spikes on the sand and paints the water with a shimmering ribbon of dancing gold. She plops down next to Luca and sets her satchel and shoes next to her, not caring that she's getting sand all over her silky skirt.

"Hey," Juliette says, leaning sideways to bump their shoulders together. Luca's T-shirt is soft against her skin.

"Hey," Luca echoes, her voice barely there.

The waves lapping along the shore and the burble of the crowd create a soft atmosphere. It reminds Juliette that they're in public, and as much as she would love to wrap her arms around Luca, she can't.

"Are you okay?" Juliette asks, studying her profile.

Luca's eyes are pinned to the horizon, and her lips are twisted into a deep, worried frown. Her chest rises and falls in shallow heaves. With the topaz luminance of the flaming sunset caressing her features, she is the most beautiful person Juliette has ever seen. She would give anything to capture this image forever with her camera, but she knows if she moves, the moment will be broken.

"Was this a date?" Luca asks suddenly, turning abruptly to look at Juliette.

She startles and swallows. "Did you want it to be?"

The breeze skips off the water, and a few of Juliette's curls tumble over her face. Before she can move them, Luca reaches up and tucks them behind her ear, her thumb curving beneath her jaw.

"You tell me," Luca whispers.

Juliette swallows, butterflies tickling her stomach as Luca doesn't drop her hand and doesn't stop staring at her. Her eyes are hazel-green in most lights, but in this golden hour, they're almost gilded.

"I don't want to just be fuckbuddies, if that's what you're asking," Juliette says finally.

Luca's hand drops, and Juliette knows she's stuck her foot in her mouth again.

"I would like to date, yes," Juliette says quickly. "I want to get to know you."

Luca bites her lip and looks away. Juliette wonders what she is so afraid of, why she can barely breathe.

"I know we're rivals," Juliette begins, and Luca looks up from under her lashes, staring at her with a surprisingly vulnerable expression.

"And I'm drawn to you, and I want you like last night, of course I do. But, I also want to know you, exactly as you are." Juliette watches a blush rise on Luca's honeyed cheeks, her lip still caught in her teeth.

"You terrify me," Luca breathes.

Juliette blinks. "Really?" She realizes they're both tilting into each other. She trails her fingers across Luca's wrist, following the ridges of her veins and the blend where her tanned forearm connects to her paler skin. Luca shivers, goose bumps prickling along her skin as Juliette brushes her thumb across them. Juliette wants to throw her arms around Luca and hold on to her. The moments tick by as Luca breathes and collects herself. Juliette curves her hand over Luca's and squeezes gently.

Luca looks up again, hopeful and sad at the same time. Her eyes are wide, almost pleading, and Juliette sees her lower lip wobbling before she bites it again. "I can't promise I'll never hurt you, Luca," she murmurs, loving the way Luca's breath hitches as Juliette says her name. "I don't want to be who I was. I don't want to be jealous, spiteful, or petty. I know we're rivals, but I want us to be so much more. I want to know you in all ways and—" Juliette pauses, hating the shaky feeling in her chest, but she knows she has to put herself into this vulnerable place. "I want you to know me."

Luca closes the gap between them and kisses Juliette. It's so surprising that Juliette freezes, her lips parting, and Luca captures Juliette's gasp with her own lips.

Juliette is grateful for the falling of the light as she tilts her head and kisses Luca back. Warmth travels through her like the first brush of morning light.

Luca recoils suddenly. "Sorry, I—we're in public," she says, and Juliette laughs at the panicked look on her face. "Shut up," Luca snaps without venom, elbowing her in the ribs.

"Oh, you wound me," Juliette says dramatically, flopping back into the sand. A bubbly, giddy feeling expands in her stomach, and she keeps laughing.

Luca leans on her elbow next to Juliette, clearly fighting off a smile. "Do you think I passed your sister's test?" she asks as Juliette's laughter calms down.

"Test?"

Luca looks up, her eyes darting across the beach, scanning for Livia. "Yeah, I think she's trying to gauge if I'm right for you."

Juliette shakes her head, not caring if she's getting sand in her curls. "I'm literally your soulmate. What is there to gauge?"

Luca frowns, and Juliette reaches up to touch the edge of her mouth. Luca's worry melts into tender affection.

Juliette knows now why lovers call their feelings warm and fuzzy, because Luca's gaze makes every fear melt away.

"Come to my room tonight," Juliette whispers, rolling onto her elbow so she can be even closer to Luca. "I don't want to sleep without you."

"We have practice tomorrow," Luca murmurs, but she doesn't say no. "We can't do too much."

Juliette smirks. "Just a little bit then?"

Luca rolls her eyes but starts to smile. "Just a little bit," she echoes.

"Can't wait," Juliette whispers. She closes the narrow gap between them, indulging in kissing Luca sweetly, enjoying the tingling sparks spreading across her skin as Luca's fingers sweep against her bicep and drop to stroke across the exposed skin at her waist.

Luca breaks the kiss but doesn't go far, just brushes her lips across Juliette's cheek. "What do you think your sister would think if we had dinner by ourselves?"

Juliette laughs. "I think that was her intention." She forces herself to sit up. "I think she's going on her own date right now."

Luca sits up next to her and runs her fingers across Juliette's curls, dusting away the sand. "Who is she dating?"

Juliette shakes her head, more sand spraying over them, and Luca scrunches her nose. "No idea, but she'll tell us when she's ready." She reaches into her satchel for her phone.

PICCOLA POLPETTA

> I got all the pictures I want so you're free
> to enjoy your "not" date with Luca 😉

Juliette texts her an eyeroll emoji before shoving her phone back into her bag. "Well, shall we go?" She gets to her feet and dusts off her skirt.

Luca holds out her hand and Juliette pulls her to her feet, swaying into her and wrapping her other arm around Luca's waist.

"Jules," Luca admonishes softly, but she makes no move to step away.

"Luca," Juliette teases, tugging her shirt free from her jeans and drawing teasing circles against Luca's lower back. Luca's eyes darken, and Juliette has to bite back a smile. "You in these white shirts drives me crazy," Juliette admits, warmth pooling in her stomach. She slips her hands into Luca's back pockets and cups Luca's ass.

Luca snorts. "Says the woman in this skimpy silk thing." Her cheeks are flushed red.

Juliette jolts as Luca's hands wrap around her hips, her thumb dipping below the silk, and the warm pool of heat spikes into lightning. Luca's tongue slides, purposefully along her lower lip, as if she's remembering the taste of Juliette.

"Come on," Juliette says, "the sooner we get back to the hotel, the sooner I'll be out of this outfit."

Luca lets go, and Juliette barely holds back a whine at the loss of warm contact. Luca must notice her flicker of distress because she leans down and grabs Juliette's bag. "Let's go."

THIRTY-THREE

LUCA

They sneak through the side door so nobody sees them coming in together.

Luca loves and hates in equal measure the sudden giddiness in her chest. It feels silly, like they're trying to hide from Juliette's parents. The back of their hands keep brushing against each other as they make their way toward the rear elevator. Luca discovered earlier that it's the only one without a glass back wall overlooking Miami.

"Jules! Luca!"

Luca freezes and spins on her heel, pulse pounding in her ears.

It's only Remi Rowland.

"Hey, guys, can I steal you for a moment?" Remi says as she gets closer. She has a towel thrown over her shoulder and is in a vibrant orange bikini, rivulets of pool water coursing down her body.

Luca can't quite keep her eyes on Remi. She bounces on her toes, nervous energy radiating around her in waves, as if one touch will jolt her out of her skin. Luca has never seen her like this before, not even during a stressful match.

"Sure?" Juliette says, looking over Remi. "Are you okay?" At least Luca isn't the only one who noticed.

Remi nods so hard that her braids fling water droplets. "Yes, I'm fine. Well, I'm more than fine." She glances around the empty hallway with its odd flickering lights. "I wanted to tell you that I took your advice."

Luca glances at Juliette, confused, but Juliette's face brightens. "Really? How did it go?"

Remi takes a deep breath. Then, with a blinding smile, she says, "She agreed that we could go public with our relationship. With our family, our friends. For my birthday."

Juliette gasps and throws her arms around Remi. "That's brilliant!" Juliette screeches. Remi laughs as she hugs her back.

"It is! God, I'm *so* relieved." Remi nods again and can't seem to stop, making her look like a bobblehead. "So, we're going to have a boat party. Get it all out in one fell swoop."

"That's a great idea," Juliette says.

"Would you come?" Remi asks, a little loud, like she's forcing the words out. "And you too, of course, Luca," she adds.

Luca smiles and nods, still a little unsure of what is happening.

"Of course, Remi," Juliette says, squeezing her shoulder.

"Thank you," Remi says, sagging in relief.

"No problem. Plus, I won't lie, I'm dying to know who this mysterious soulmate is." Juliette playfully touches Remi's wrist wrap.

Remi lightly smacks Juliette's hand away. "Shut up."

Juliette cackles and reaches behind her to hit the elevator button. "Subtlety is not your strong suit, Remi."

Remi splutters, at a loss for words.

Luca enjoys, more than she should, seeing Remi struggle to find a quippy remark.

"Whatever. A couple of us are hanging out by the pool if you want to join," Remi says, throwing her shoulders back in an effort to collect her dignity.

Luca bites the inside of her lip, worried that Juliette will suddenly abandon their plans and choose to be with Remi and her crowd of friends.

"No, thanks. We've been walking around all afternoon. I've got an early practice, so I can't get too crazy," Juliette says casually, and Remi's eyes dart to Luca.

"Okay," she drawls, giving Juliette an intense and not-at-all subtle side-eye. "Well, I'll text you the details later. Have a good night!" She jogs away down the hall.

"So, who is your guess for who her soulmate is?" Juliette asks, her eyes sparkling with a mischievous light.

"Do you know?" Luca asks, and Juliette shakes her head.

"Nope. I was just winding her up." The elevator pings and the doors slide open.

Luca steps inside and leans against the back wall. "I think it's Xinya."

Juliette's eyes widen. "You think?"

Luca nods. "I think Remi was in her box at Wimbledon."

Juliette considers this, a little frown appearing between her brows at the mention of the tournament. Luca reaches out and smooths her thumb across the crease. Juliette giggles, and her brows relax. "Interesting. I guess we'll find out."

The elevator stops at their floor and Juliette hooks her fingers through the loops of Luca's jeans, tugging her out into the hallway painted in vivid sunset tones.

Luca feels giddy bubbles fizz to life in her stomach again as Juliette pulls her down the hall. Luca feels half-drunk even though she's not, and she stumbles into Juliette when she stops abruptly.

Antony Ricci leans against Juliette's door, his piercing dark eyes scanning over his daughter before lifting to Luca's face. "Just as I suspected," Antony says in his thick, rich Italian accent. His head tilts, but his gaze never wavers from Luca's face. He is unblinking as he stares into Luca's soul. "Fraternizing with the enemy?" His gaze narrows as he focuses on Juliette.

Juliette's shoulders tense and Luca steps back, but not before she catches sight of Juliette's hand reaching back for her. "Don't be dramatic," Juliette says, and Luca can practically hear her roll her eyes.

Antony says something in low, vibrating Italian.

"Must we rehash this again?" Juliette asks in English, which Luca knows is deliberate.

"I'll go," Luca says, her skin crawling under the cold, piercing stare of Antony Ricci. It reminds her too much of her own father. And while she knows this is cowardly, her hands shake and are suddenly clammy.

"Luca—" Juliette says, but Luca is already gone.

LUCA

Once back in her room, Luca rushes into the bathroom. Her mind is spinning, twisting, curving in on itself like a snake eating its tail.

She turns on the sink and splashes her face with cold water, but it doesn't make her feel any better. Her stomach slithers with something oily, a pressure building in her head as she tries not to think about Antony or Juliette.

"Fraternizing with the enemy" is distinctly dramatic, perhaps for the effect of getting Luca to back off. Which is exactly what he got. Does Antony have enough influence in Juliette's life to break them up?

What could he even break up?

They're only now beginning to unravel whatever taut and fragile feelings are between them. Adding a disapproving and overbearing father into the mix certainly won't make their relationship development any easier. Luca can't lie and say she likes Antony, but he is Juliette's father. And they could be family one day.

Luca clutches the edge of the sink as a wave of dizziness crashes over her at the thought. That is too far in the future. She stares at her reflection and draws in a deep breath, even as her own features begin to swim and rearrange oddly.

Luca sinks to the floor before she passes out, the cold touch of the tile soothing against her knees and palms. Too many thoughts, too much all at once. She leans back onto her heels and shakes her head, hoping to jar loose the thoughts that keep plaguing her.

It's an anxiety spiral. And really, it's over nothing. Of course Antony would want to look out for his daughter and keep her focused. But from all she's seen of him, he's all bark and no bite.

Slowly, she gets to her feet and washes her hands, then scrubs her damp hands through her hair. Cool droplets race down her temples and burning hot neck. "You're fine," she tells her reflection, even if her stomach is still twisted in knots. "This is fine."

A knock on the door makes Luca jump, and she hates how pale and wan she still looks.

She pinches her cheeks in an effort to bring some color back, but it only achieves a strange and unnatural splotch on the top of her cheeks. Sighing, Luca goes to the door anyway.

She isn't surprised to find Juliette standing in the hallway, cheeks flushed and her hair in a wild halo around her head, as if she's been tugging on her curls. "Is everything okay with your father?" Luca grinds out in halting syllables.

Juliette nods. "Can I come in?" she asks, her hands fluttering around her, as if she can't decide whether to reach out or clasp them together.

Luca steps back and wordlessly lets Juliette enter. Tension snaps in the air, and Luca wants to cringe away. "Sorry, the curtains are open," Luca says as she lets the door shut. She hurries to close them. It gives her some space from Juliette.

"I'm sorry about him," Juliette says in a rush, as if the words will be lost if she doesn't say them immediately. "He's melodramatic and he only wants what's best for me and my sisters."

Luca yanks the flamingo pink curtains over the vibrant nightlife of Miami and tries to steady her breathing. "It's okay, I get it." She turns slowly. Juliette's eyes are huge and shimmering, a pleading in them that Luca is thrown off by.

Juliette shakes her head, manic in her movements. "No, it's not okay. He's trying to control my life and I won't have him drive you away."

"Is that what this is about?" Luca asks, tilting her head. Juliette thinks Antony would drive Luca away, not that she might be convinced to leave Luca?

Juliette stills, looking up with warm, sweet eyes. This is the first time Luca has ever really seen her look frightened.

"I thought he was going to convince you I wasn't worth the effort,"

Luca says, and Juliette blinks, bewildered. It's oddly comforting to see all of Juliette's emotions play out across her expressive face.

"No, he's just being a control freak," Juliette says firmly. "He wants to make it clear that he thinks that you're going to distract me. As if I can't focus on multiple things at once." Juliette rolls her eyes. "Maybe I'll tell him to fuck off." She waves her hand, saying it flippantly, as if none of it matters.

"Don't ruin your relationship with him. Set boundaries, but keep him in your life."

Juliette's forehead scrunches. "What? Where is this coming from?"

Luca crosses an arm over her chest, scrubbing the knuckles of her other down her sternum as the pressure builds again. The truth is simple but harsh. "You never know how much time you'll get with him. And I don't think you should dismiss him. He is worried about your career and happiness." She hates how bitter the words taste in her mouth.

Juliette stares at her, mouth slightly parted and her eyes searching Luca's face.

Luca shakes her head before moving away from the curtains to the kitchen. She needs a cup of tea, something to soothe the ache in her throat. She busies herself with the kettle. "Ignoring the issue isn't a healthy way to deal with this."

"You don't know him like I do," Juliette says, and the springs tightening in Luca's chest snap.

"He's a better father than a lot of us get," Luca says, and she immediately regrets it. She knows the subject of fathers is a sensitive one for her, and truly, what right does she have to give advice to Juliette?

"Luca," Juliette murmurs, her voice so soft and quiet that the defensive thorns around Luca start to soften and unfurl.

"My father is dead," Luca says suddenly, popping the chamomile bag into the bottom of one of the too-small ceramic cups. She fishes her honey out of the pantry next to all of her granola bars.

Juliette's breath catches. "Oh, Luca, I'm so sorry."

Luca bites her lip and tips her spoon into the honey. "It's fine. He died a while ago. Before I went to college." Luca wishes she could force her voice to be flat, but it's raspy and trembling.

Juliette stays quiet, either thinking or waiting for Luca to fill the silence.

"He was a complicated man," Luca continues. She's unsure of where the words come from. Maybe a deep-rooted desire to make Juliette see that she shouldn't dismiss her father. "I think he loved my mother and me, but he was a product of his upbringing. He thought that caring too much was a weakness we couldn't afford." The more she speaks, the more she feels like a snake shedding its skin.

She feels rather than sees Juliette, the warmth radiating off her skin, her hand, the second before she cradles Luca's cheek, grounding her in this moment. Her thumb strokes against the fragile skin beneath her eye, and it's almost too tender.

There will always be more to say, more to try to explain. There will always be sadness and anger and shame whenever she thinks about her father. She will always resent and miss and love and hate her father, even if she tries to tell herself that he doesn't deserve the emotional space.

Luca shakes her head. Juliette's hand slips away, but then she wraps her arms around Luca's waist and rests her cheek against Luca's shoulder blade. Juliette's touch is grounding, but Luca is relieved she doesn't have to look Juliette in the eye. "There's a lot I wish I could say to him, but he'll never hear it." She sighs, and Juliette squeezes her closer. "So, if you can, or you want to, I would try to repair whatever crumbling link you still have."

The kettle bubbles and hisses, filling the quiet and dissipating the tension. It's become comfortable now. "You want tea?" she asks.

"Sure," Juliette whispers, rubbing her cheek against Luca's shoulder.

Luca grabs another cup and tosses a chamomile bag into it. "Honey?"

"Yeah," Juliette says, her voice a little croaky. Luca drops her hands to Juliette's, squeezing her wrists.

Then, Juliette peels off of Luca and moves to lean against the counter. Her cheeks are blotchy, and her eyes are a little red-rimmed. "Hey," Luca whispers, cradling Juliette's cheek gently now.

Juliette looks up, and her lips twitch into the barest hint of a smile. "Sorry," she whispers.

"For what?" Luca asks, sliding her hand along Juliette's neck to the nape, gently tugging her closer. With her free hand, she sweeps Juliette's curls back off her face.

"You bare your soul and father issues and instead of me comforting you, I'm the one crying and you're making me a cup of tea." She shakes her head a little, almost chuckling.

"Tea is my lo—" Luca cuts herself off, rephrases. "The way I take care of people." She presses a kiss to Juliette's forehead. "Sorry to trauma dump on you."

Juliette's hands splay along her waist, holding on to Luca. "No, thank you for telling me that. I needed to hear it. You're right."

Luca shrugs. "I don't mean to be right. I only want to help." She murmurs the words against Juliette's skin, and she feels her shudder.

Juliette nods, and Luca pulls away to pour the boiling water into two cups. Luca dishes a ribbon of honey into the cup, watching it swirl in the water.

"You're surprisingly sweet," Juliette says as Luca hands her the warm cup.

"Surprisingly?" Luca asks, unsure if she should be offended.

"I used to think you were cold," Juliette admits, "and when you're not focused on tennis, I thought you were aloof and snarky. I didn't think you were kind."

Luca rolls her eyes. "People contain multitudes, Jules," she says. Then, with a crooked smile, she adds, "I can go back to snarking you if you want."

Juliette sips her tea and then sets it down. Before Luca can say anything, she's wrapping her arms around Luca's neck and brushing their noses together. "I want you exactly as you are, Luca Kacic." Juliette sounds so confident, so sure of her conviction, that Luca's stomach flips.

Exactly as she is.

"Oh."

Flaws, cracks, rot, and all. It's a terrifying thought, and Luca swallows, all amusement fizzling away. Juliette doesn't look away from her, her eyes so warm they're like molten honey.

And despite Juliette's admission, it isn't anxiety that buzzes in Luca's chest. The thought of being known and loved anyway makes her breath catch, her heart hammer against her breastbone, and a deep throbbing ache bloom in her chest.

Except it isn't pain or discomfort or fear—it's longing. Luca wants this. She knew she wanted Juliette on a physical level, despite the fear that Juliette would break her heart. But today, Luca realized she wants Juliette more than just as a lover. It's a terrifying thought, one that she can't get out of her head, but now that she knows Juliette wants her too? It's almost too much to bear.

It looks and feels too much like love.

Luca draws Juliette into her for a kiss to keep from saying the words too early, but pours all her feelings into the kiss, hoping Juliette feels it anyway.

THIRTY-FOUR

JULIETTE

It is funny the things you learn about someone when intentionally staying the night.

Earlier, while Luca ordered room service, Juliette had raided Luca's suitcase and put on a pair of her sweatpants and a T-shirt. She is hiding from Livia and Antony, and she doesn't have the energy for a conversation or argument, so she stays in Luca's room.

Which, to be honest, is nicer than hers.

Juliette lounges in Luca's bed as she watches her go through her meticulous nighttime routine.

"What's that?" she asks as Luca pops a pill with a swig of water.

"Melatonin," Luca says before crawling into bed and kissing Juliette silent.

Juliette pulls back after a moment and tilts her head at Luca. "Why?"

Luca rolls her eyes. "Why do you think, Jules? I don't sleep well." She rolls onto her back, and Juliette snuggles into her shoulder. The herbal sweetness of lavender washes over her in calming waves as she breathes in Luca.

"Do you want to talk about that?"

Luca sighs, long and resigned. "Not really, no."

Juliette nods. She wants to know everything she can about Luca, but she doesn't want to push her, so she focuses on what she can do to help. She lets her fingertips skate beneath the hem of Luca's shirt, tracing nonsensical patterns onto her stomach and hips. Juliette loves the way Luca shivers under her touch. She caresses the line of Luca's sternum to her navel, up and down again, adding gentle pressure like she's seen Luca do dozens of times.

Slowly, she feels the tension unwind from Luca's body until she is boneless against the pillows. "Oh," Luca whispers.

"What?" Juliette asks, lifting her head to look at Luca's face. Pink tinges across Luca's cheeks and ears.

"Nothing," Luca says stubbornly. "I'm not going to inflate your ego."

Juliette can't help but burst out laughing. "You don't have to say it, darling, I can tell." Even if sometimes it is difficult for Juliette to see past the hard wall Luca's built around herself, her body never lies.

"I'm going to kick you out of my bed," Luca grumbles even though her lips threaten to tip upward in a traitorous smile.

"No, you won't," Juliette purrs, curling her leg around Luca's and pressing soft kisses to Luca's throat, if only to feel her pulse jump. "You know an orgasm helps you sleep, right?" She slides her hand up Luca's stomach again, curving her palm to cup Luca's breast and rolling the heel of her hand over Luca's already hard nipple.

"Yeah?" Luca is breathless. "Are you going to do something with that information?" Her chest preens upward, and Juliette kisses the corner of her mouth.

"Maybe?" She lets go of Luca's breast and drifts her hand down her chest again, dipping her fingertips beneath Luca's sleep shorts and finding she isn't wearing any underwear.

"I did just get ready for bed," Luca says softly as Juliette sweeps her fingers along the fuzz of hair on her mound.

She twists onto her elbow so she can see Luca's face. "We can just go to sleep," she says teasingly, pulling her hand free of Luca's shorts, but she lets it roam across her trembling lower stomach.

"You started this," Luca says, her fingers threading through Juliette's hair. Warm tingles shower down Juliette's spine at the scratch of Luca's nails against her scalp, and she almost loses her train of thought.

"Maybe it's not worth having to change your shorts?" Juliette asks, as if truly pondering.

"Do you want me to beg, Jules?" Luca whispers, fingers tightening in Juliette's hair, and she leans into Luca.

"You do it so prettily, Lou," Juliette says, and Luca grimaces.

"Oh no, Nicky is the only one who calls me Lou."

Juliette pauses. She likes how Luca uses her nickname, and she wants one for her. "Luce?" She suggests and Luca fake-gags. "Lux?"

Luca blinks, her brow furrowing. "Lux?"

"Because you're my light," Juliette says, and Luca laughs.

"You're so—"

Juliette pinches Luca's nipple between her fingers and twists, just enough pressure to cut off what Luca was about to say.

"What was that?" Juliette asks sweetly, letting go and slipping her hand back into Luca's shorts. Her hips tilt up, and Juliette skims two fingers on either side of her clit.

"Perfect. You're absolutely perfect," Luca breathes, her lashes fluttering closed. "Don't stop, please."

Juliette's stomach flutters at the way her voice catches on *please*. She takes her time, circling her fingers around Luca's clit, speeding up and slowing down at random. She never goes beyond the gentle touches, no matter how much Luca whines in the back of her throat.

"Don't hold back," Juliette whispers against Luca's throat. She rucks up Luca's shirt and cups her mouth around Luca's nipple, her tongue flicking, pointed, just the way Luca likes.

Luca's breath shudders through her teeth. Juliette loves watching how Luca's body locks up and then relaxes, her muscles flexing and shifting as she leans into Juliette's hand. Luca's knees spread wide, and Juliette slides her hand down, fingers slick. She circles her thumb against Luca's clit, nudging against it at different speeds and pressures. Piece by piece, Luca falls apart in her arms. Juliette's name falls like a litany from Luca's mouth as she comes.

"God, you're so gorgeous," Juliette whispers as she strokes Luca's thighs. A flood of warm affection threatens to overwhelm her.

"Shut up," Luca pants, tugging Juliette closer so she can hide her blotchy red face in her neck. Juliette laughs as Luca's hair tickles her skin and Luca nibbles kisses up the column of her throat to her jaw.

Heat crackles through her body as Luca's fingers skate down the ridges of her ribs, squeezing her hip.

Before, whenever she was around Luca, she felt tight and jittery, like all of her limbs were twisted on too tight. But now, as Luca explores her skin with curious fingers, she melts.

Her body immediately coils as Luca's fingers sweep through her slick heat before she dips two into her slit, curling against her walls and sending pleasure spiking through her body. Her fingers move shallowly, but the heel of her hand grinds against Juliette's clit. "Fuck, Lux," Juliette breathes, and Luca chuckles in her ear.

It's as if Luca has a road map to every sensitive spot on her body, and in true Juliette fashion, it does not take long for her thighs to shake and her toes to curl. Heat burns through her gut, searing every nerve with vibrant pleasure.

Luca peppers her face with kisses as she returns to her body. She opens her eyes to see Luca's face, bright with unbridled joy.

She loses track of time, twined in Luca's arms and indulging in languid, soft kisses. She wishes she could live in this moment forever, caught in the rose-soft glass of whatever is unfolding between them.

Eventually, though, they wordlessly rise and clean themselves off. They rotate around each other like twin stars, hips bumping, knuckles grazing, and stealing kisses.

Luca collapses on the bed first with a yawn while Juliette twists her curls into a bun on the top of her head. "Come here, you're too far away," Luca whispers, splaying her hand across the bed.

Juliette laughs as she slips beneath the sheets again. Luca wriggles closer and wraps her arms around Juliette, letting their bodies slot together perfectly. Usually, Juliette doesn't like being the little spoon, but as Luca interlocks their legs and Juliette tucks her forehead into the hollow of Luca's neck, she finds she doesn't mind. Actually, she loves it. Especially as she breathes in the dreamscape of Luca and lavender, as she finds warm comfort in Luca surrounding her.

"I needed this," Luca murmurs, and Juliette nearly misses it as sleep crashes over her.

"Me too," Juliette mumbles before she slides into inky dreams.

Luca is gone before Juliette's alarm rips her from sleep. She flails her arm out for Luca as her eyes adjust to the murky light slipping beneath the curtains. Her side of the bed isn't even warm anymore. Juliette swallows the knot of disappointment in her throat.

She sees a message from Luca time-stamped an hour earlier, telling her she's going out for a run with Vladimir. Beneath that are a flurry of messages from Livia.

PICCOLA POLPETTA

> Before you get rightfully pissed, I truly didn't realize you were in the background.

> And I'm not the only one who clocked it.

> It's fine Jules, trust me, it's not that bad.

> I promise

> (guess some tennis girlies were on the boardwalk last night)

Her heart drops into her stomach as she scrolls through the pictures that accompany Livia's messages. The first is of Livia, a selfie she posted with them in the background. It seems like they're only talking, but Luca's head is bent toward Juliette. Livia has done the most helpful thing and circled them in red.

The rest are from other Twitter sources, threads compiled by fans, and most are surreptitiously low-angled but close enough to make out Juliette Ricci and Luca Kacic. Several of them are of Juliette with her camera lifted, taking a picture of Luca. She can't see Luca's face in this photo, but she remembers the beginning curve of her smile. The next is closer up and of both of them. Juliette with her curls flying in the breeze, the sun burnishing the edges of them gold, and Luca squinting into the sun, her smile wide and her dimples adorable. The composition is actually really nice, which makes Juliette irrationally angry.

The final thread is the weirdest for her. It's a punch in the stomach to see herself staring at Luca like that. The smile on her mouth is wide and natural, and she looks so . . . happy. Luckily it's from when they were coming off the beach and not making out, but still. Juliette looks as lovestruck as she'd felt. They're both wrapped in their own little intimate world, and it says too much.

Heart-eyes Ricci spotted on the boardwalk with rival Kacic! Some random "news" source that is more like a stalking account writes in their post.

She scrolls through the replies, and heat crawls over her skin. Almost all of them are positive, but they're too prying, too violating.

@riccisbackhand
told y'all something was happening with them. look me in the eyes and tell me i'm wrong about them being soulmates 👀 i'll wait

@paytoninafountain
god I wish I could find my soulmate so they could look at me like ricci looks at kacic

@wta4me
they're so important to me #juluca

Juliette tosses the phone down to the end of the bed and throws her arms over her face with a groan. Maybe she has done this to herself. She's certainly stoked the flames of Twitter before, encouraging speculation about her and Luca. But it's more fun when there is nothing at stake. Now, everything feels so fragile and Juliette selfishly wishes they'd just keep their thoughts, opinions, and theories to themselves.

A current of energy and jitters course through her body, and she throws herself out of bed to hit the gym. She knows it might not be wise to wear Luca's clothing, again, but she finds a nondescript pair of shorts and a black tank top. Luca is taller but thinner, so the shirt is a bit too long and spans a little too much over the breasts, but it works for her purposes. It's less incriminating to wear that than it would be to wear Luca's pajamas down to her own room to get her sneakers and sports bra.

As she heads down the stairs to her floor, she knows she shouldn't care. This shouldn't matter. She has never let fan speculation or gossip get to her before. But this nags at the back of her throat. For once, she wants this one thing to be hers and hers alone.

Although with her meddling sisters and overbearing father, maybe that was never destined to be true. With their status as professional athletes, the fans will always crave a slice of their lives, a moment to look behind the curtain and get a peek at the intimate details. The media keeps nothing sacred. That was the first lesson Juliette learned from watching how Octavia and Claudia conduct themselves in the tennis world—Octavia keeping everyone at arm's length and letting the media demonize her as "aloof" for being private, and Claudia letting in too much spotlight to use attention as a whip, forcing the media to love and hate her in the same breath. She realized it would be no use trying to be anyone other than herself. Unfortunately, this means the media witnessed every single one of her hormone-induced breakdowns on the court and labeled her an *immature brat* before she hit her second growth spurt at nineteen. But now, after having let everyone see her, it's almost impossible to close off that tap of access, especially when she wants everyone to know she's more than her teenage self.

Juliette barges into her room and slams the door shut. She shakes off the thoughts as she changes clothes, then shoves her headphones over her ears. This will blow over. Everything always does.

It does not blow over.

At least not quickly.

Juliette doesn't see Luca for the rest of the day, which she expected. They're on different practice schedules, and she's sure her father is somehow pulling the strings so they don't end up anywhere near each other.

"Do you know where Livia is?" she asks Antony as they finish their early dinner and strategy meeting. They've been diligent in avoiding the topic of last night and Luca. Even though his glare tells her that he isn't letting it go, she practiced really well and he can't complain when she's showing how dedicated she still is.

Antony blinks, tilting his head to stare at Juliette as if she's grown three heads. "I have no idea. She's an adult."

Juliette huffs and wonders if Antony should have ever become a father. "Well, I'm going to go find her. See you tomorrow?"

Antony nods stiffly, turning back to his phone without comment. Eventually she'll have to deal with his anger, but she has bigger things to deal with right now.

Livia picks up her call after three rings, which is two more than usual. "Hey, Jules, what's up?" She sounds breathless, like she's been running.

Juliette pauses in the middle of the hotel lobby, narrowing her eyes. "Where are you?"

"In my room? Why?" She hears the snick of a door closing.

"Livia, we need to talk," Juliette says, trying to hold back the tide of frustration building in her chest.

"Uh-oh, full name. Is this about the selfie? As your PR manager—"

"You are not my—"

"I think it is a bit of an overreaction," Livia continues, bulldozing through her as she always does. "And before you ask, no, I cannot make the other people take down the photos."

Juliette pinches the bridge of her nose. She is not having this conversation in the middle of the lobby, even if she doubts anyone around her can understand rapid Italian. "We need to talk about this in person. What room are you in?"

"No!" Livia squeaks.

"What the hell is going on with you?" Juliette hisses into the phone, turning away from a family who is staring at her with open curiosity.

"Nothing! Nothing you need to worry about. I'll talk to you later tonight. It's a family cocktail night at Octavia's rental house."

Juliette wonders if it's too late to be adopted into another family. "I thought Octavia wasn't coming to Miami? And why did no one tell me this?"

Livia huffs. "You clearly do not look at our group chats. Octavia isn't playing Miami, but she's here to support you, Claudia, and Leo. Duh. Anyway, check your texts for this cabana she booked without my knowledge, and I'll see you there. Oh, and bring Luca!"

Juliette's stomach drops through the floor. "Last time I did that, I blew up the internet. And that's what—"

"Don't be so dramatic. It's only the tennis sphere. You didn't even trend. Plus, this is actually private. You know Octo."

Juliette can't argue with that. "I think this is all moving too fast." She moves toward the stairwell, the jittery energy becoming static in her ears.

She hears the sigh of a couch moving as Livia folds into it. "You're just afraid, Jules," she says.

"Of course, I'm afraid," Juliette says, and she punches open the door to her floor. "Look, I have to go." She hangs up before Livia can get in another word. Her phone buzzes again and she picks it up without looking at the screen. "Livie, I told you, I'll talk to you later." She jams the phone between her shoulder and ear, impatiently slamming her key card into the door.

"Juliette?" Luca's voice crackles through the speaker.

The phone slides from where it's scrunched against Juliette's neck and falls to the floor. She scrambles to grab it and stumbles into her room. "Sorry, Luca. I thought you were Livia." Her satchel slips off her shoulder and smacks to the floor. Fuck, she hopes her camera didn't break.

"I gathered that," Luca says dryly. Then, with more concern, she asks, "Are you okay?"

"Great, fantastic, why wouldn't I be?" Juliette is aware she's breathing too fast, and her vision is spinning. She's falling and feels like at any moment she's going to splinter into thousands of pieces on the ground.

"Jules?"

She realizes she's crouched on the ground, her hand on the floor to keep her steady. "Yeah?"

She breathes in deeply. Then she tips back and sprawls on the floor, staring up at the ceiling. She counts the speckles of black paint artfully splattered across the cream.

"You sound like you're panicking? Do you want me to come to your room? Is that where you're at?" Luca's voice threads through the phone, tiny and with a little quaver, but Juliette closes her eyes and listens to the lilt of her accent around the vowels without really comprehending what she's saying.

"My sisters are having a cocktail party tonight," she says. Her throat tightens, and when she blinks her eyes open again, her vision spirals. "Livia wants me to bring you."

"Okay," Luca says slowly.

Juliette swallows. "It'll probably be overwhelming. Much like the Connolly Cup except they'll all be grilling us about each other. I understand if you don't want to come." The words fall out in a tumbled rush, and Juliette isn't sure if they're in the right order. Is she even speaking English anymore?

"Do you want me to come?" Luca asks, and Juliette latches on to the sound of her voice again.

"I don't want you to be uncomfortable," Juliette says numbly. "And they're not as bad as my dad, but they're meddlesome and complicated."

"That isn't what I asked, Juliette," Luca says patiently. "Where are you? Why don't we talk about this in person?"

"No!" Juliette barks, and she cringes the minute it leaves her mouth. Her head aches and she wonders if she's going to be sick.

"So, you don't want me to come?" Luca asks.

Juliette hates how flat her voice is.

"No, I'm sorry," Juliette says, her eyes prickling. "It's not you. There are pictures of us from the boardwalk online. I know it shouldn't freak me out, but it does, and I can't explain it."

She covers her eyes, and that somehow makes everything worse. Her stomach twists. She doesn't know what she's doing. She listens to Luca breathe on the other side of the phone, somewhere else, and not near her. She wants Luca here, but she doesn't want Luca to see her like this over nothing.

"Juliette, what is this really about? Who cares about rumors? We're allowed to be friends in public."

"I've never had something like this, and if we let the world in, it'll be ruined," she whispers.

Luca sighs. "Juliette, it's okay. Everything will be fine. Breathe, please."

Juliette exhales sharply, her lungs burning. She hadn't even realized she was holding her breath. "I feel sick," she says.

"Jules, seriously, where are you? I think you might be having a panic attack."

Juliette laughs, but it sounds high and hysterical to her ears. "It's so fucking stupid, Luca! I shouldn't be! I'm fine, really." The walls bend inward, and she claws at her tight throat.

"Panic attacks aren't rational."

Juliette looks at her hands, and they appear alien. Crystalline spikes of agony drill into her stomach, and she wonders if she's going to throw up, right here on the phone with Luca.

Her pulse pounds, too loud, like a drum in her head. Her stomach heaves, but nothing travels up her throat. Words drift in and out, cutting through her bleary, dizzying world like radio static clearing as a car swerves in and out of reception.

"Juliette, please, breathe. What room number are you in?"

She listens to her own harsh intake of breath. It rattles around her lungs as if there are tatters in the tissue, letting air escape without her control.

"Two one three," she whispers into the phone, digging her nails into the plush carpet beneath her. She wishes her stupid heart would stop pounding so hard.

"Hey, Jules." A face blurs above her, cool fingers touching her cheek. She tries to swallow, to say something, but her throat is still too tight. "Hey, just focus on breathing. It'll be over soon. Can you sit up?"

Juliette clutches Luca's forearm and slowly manages to sit up. Her vision blurs and she gasps, but then Luca's arm slides around her shoulders and holds her up. She buries herself in Luca, throwing all of her weight into her. It's as if her bones have been replaced with lead, but with her face buried in Luca's shoulder, the strange terror in her chest begins to loosen its grip.

One of Luca's hands loops up and down her back, while the other holds the back of her head, thumb caressing the shell of her ear.

"Talk to me," Juliette whispers. The silence around them is stifling, and she's too aware of her own breathing.

"Anything specific?" Luca asks.

The rumble of her voice against Juliette is already soothing the fragmented pieces inside her chest, so she shakes her head.

Luca starts talking. Juliette understands none of the words, but slowly, in drips and whispers, her breathing evens out and her vision stops spinning. She still feels shaky, but as she finally draws back from Luca, she can see clearly. "Fuck, I wish I had one of Claudia's Xanax," she mutters as she presses her knuckles into her aching eyes.

Luca gently tugs Juliette's hands away from her face. "How do you feel now?"

Juliette blinks, focusing on Luca's concerned face, the crease between her brows, the deep frown marring the corners of her mouth. In this light, she can see flecks of emerald in her hazel eyes. Luca's thumb sweeps against her lower lip, and a warm tingle sparks across her bitten mouth. "Shaky," Juliette whispers.

Luca nods. "It'll pass. I promise."

"How often have you had panic attacks?" Juliette asks, curling her finger around a strand of Luca's silky hair. She focuses on the texture, rubbing her thumb against the bluntly cut ends.

Luca shrugs. "A lot. More when I was a teenager." Luca looks at her from under her long lashes, feathery blond and faint in the slant of sun creeping in. "Do you want to talk about it? I understand if not. We can deal with it later."

Juliette searches Luca's face, looking for some sign of what she really wants, but all she finds is tender concern.

"Not right now." Juliette shakes her head. "But I would like some tea?"

Luca's concern cracks into a smile. "Now you're speaking my language."

THIRTY-FIVE

LUCA

"What's bothering you?"

Luca's gaze snaps up to Vladimir. "Nothing. Why do you ask?" She glances sideways at the cameras being set up for Miami's press day. Players mill around the back of the main stadium, waiting patiently for their turn and hiding from the vicious sun.

Vladimir's brows raise over his sleepy, hooded eyes. His cheeks are flushed from a sunburn Luca doesn't remember being there the other day. What else has slipped her notice since her thoughts have been consumed by Juliette?

"I'm only checking in," Vladimir says evenly, patting Luca's shoulder, and a bit of the tension in her chest unwinds.

She fiddles with her wrist wrap, the humidity sticky against her skin. Even though this is literally part of her job, Luca's insides feel more scrambled than usual. There's a lingering question about whether she's fully recovered from her injury. The hard court swing is always her favorite, but there's a deepening pressure at being the number one player and being on her preferred surface. On top of all that, her mind keeps picking at the things Juliette has said, at the posts about their rivalry and whether there's more between them, at how people seem to be looking at them even more now. So many comments and tweets are about how this is normal for Juliette. She's always been a flirt who flits from person to person, having flings and two-week-long relationships. Luca had never cared to look into Juliette's past lovers, but now it's all Twitter wants to throw at her. A full thread of every person she's held hands with or had in her box. It's all piling on and threatening to snap Luca in half.

Those are the thoughts that *should* be plaguing her and eating away at her confidence. Instead, it's Juliette's sudden panic attack that has left Luca feeling woozy and off-balance the most. Dark thoughts infect the cracks she knows she should patch up, but much like a scab, it's easier to peel away the healing flesh and see what lies beneath.

She's just doing this to mess with you.

You're just one of many in a string of failed relationships.

She pinches the inside of her elbow to ground herself and focuses her gaze away from the concrete pad of cameras and lighting equipment until she spots Nicky's bright splash of red hair on the grass. "I'm going to talk to Nicky," she tells Vladimir.

Luca knows she's been withdrawn from Nicky and has not answered a single one of his texts. It isn't uncommon; she is historically bad at texting. Still, her stomach twists in anxious knots as she walks across the lawn. Nicky has always been understanding of her tendency to avoid interactions when she's too busy or stressed. And he knows she prefers to talk in person.

Luca calls out to him, but he doesn't turn his head. Magnus Akerman, Nicky's on-again, off-again partner, glances up and flicks Luca a wave. He sits next to Nicky, long legs sprawled out and his knee barely nudging Nicky's.

"Hey," Luca says, and Nicky's head turns slowly, tilting up as he squints at Luca.

"Oh, are we friends now, Kacic?" Nicky asks, an undertone of ice sending a shiver down her spine.

"What the hell are you talking about?" Luca asks, glancing at Magnus.

Magnus's brow scrunches, but as always, he says nothing. He's always been one to simply skirt in the shadows of Nicky's light, following him around like a dutiful wolf. The commentators love to call him the Swedish Servebot, but he's only just made his debut in the Top Ten last month.

Nicky's mouth twists. "What do you think?" He scrambles to his feet and brushes the grass off his shorts. "Friends usually tell friends when they're dating someone," he hisses, glaring at Luca.

"What?" Luca's stomach bottoms out.

"And the fact that I found out you've been screwing Juliette Ricci from Twitter?" Nicky rakes his hands through his hair, sending it into fiery disarray.

Luca doesn't know how to process any of the words coming out of Nicky's mouth. "They shouldn't know about that," Luca whispers because that is the thing currently digging holes in her brain.

Nicky chokes on a nearly hysterical laugh. "So it's true?"

Luca knows she needs to say something else, but the sun is too bright and her focus slips to Nicky's clenched fists.

"I don't understand," Luca whispers.

Nicky shakes his head. Magnus stands and touches Nicky's shoulder, but he brushes him off. "It's your life and I shouldn't be so upset about this, but fuck, Lou, after everything we've been through, you can't tell me what's going on with you and Ricci?"

Luca tries to take a deep breath, but it's hard with the pressure crushing her lungs. "This isn't really about Jules and me, is it?" Luca murmurs.

Nicky's facade of anger shatters into hurt. He looks away and crosses his arms over his chest, defensive in a way that Luca has never seen before. "Whatever. It doesn't matter now."

Luca follows Nicky's gaze and sees that several players and media interns are glancing at them out of the corner of their eyes. Luca's skin crawls, distinctly aware that this isn't a conversation to have in public, but her stomach aches to think that she hurt Nicky.

"It does matter," Luca starts, but a springy ponytailed woman with too much energy bounces up to them.

"Nicholas Andrews? We're ready for you," she says with a bright smile.

Luca watches as Nicky's face transforms from barely concealed hurt to a bright, cheerful smile. After years of practice, it's a smooth transition, but Luca still sees how much Nicky hides behind his eyes. Because she's known him since they were sixteen and he was the only person at tennis camp who would talk to her. Because she's seen him hide his emotions from everyone, but never from her. He always confided in her about *everything*, but now, she's pushed him so far away that he won't talk to her.

"What is happening?" She turns on Magnus as soon as Nicky is out of earshot.

Magnus's shoulders hitch up to his ears and he holds up his palms in surrender. "I have no idea."

Luca pinches the bridge of her nose. "Shouldn't you know? What's been going on with him?"

Magnus shrugs. "I've been asking him that all week. He won't talk to me." He stares after Nicky, who is clearly and shamelessly flirting with the producer lacing a microphone through his collar. "Are you going to Remi's boat party?"

Luca nods, looking away from Nicky. Her stomach churns. This is *her* fault. How is she going to fix this?

"Talk to him there, Luca." Magnus clasps her shoulder and gives her a little shake, which Luca knows is meant to make her feel better, but it intensifies her nausea.

Usually, she would've dismissed the haunting paranoia in her chest as her typical anxious thoughts, but she can't help but worry this party is going to end in sinking ships.

JULIETTE

"Drama on the Miami lawn this afternoon," Claudia says as she sashays into Octavia's room.

Juliette sits up so fast her head spins. The room is permeated with the scent of hair spray, grapefruit, and lilac.

Claudia holds out her phone. "Apparently the Licky stans think they're fighting."

"The what?" Juliette snatches the phone out of Claudia's hand and scrolls through the feed. There's a video of Luca and Nicky arguing over something, but it's cut off by him being rushed off to do his media interviews.

"Luca and Nicky? Their 'ship' name. Kinda cute, I think," Claudia says, plopping down on the bed next to Juliette.

"They have a ship name?"

Claudia groans. "Of course they do. If a man and a woman are best friends, the internet will immediately think they're secretly madly in love."

"Leo and I have one," Octavia says from the vanity. She's straightening her silky dark hair into elegant flips. "Leoctopus."

"Gross," Juliette says, and Octavia flips her off.

Juliette stares at the posts, scrolling through them without really seeing them. She clicks on the #juluca and frowns at the flood of tweets about the pictures from the other day on the boardwalk. "But wait, if people think Luca and I are in a relationship, this speculation isn't just going to go away."

@RowlandGarros
wait! jules and luca not clawing each other's throats out? we keep winning 👀 #juluca

@luckyclaycic
bitch if we dont get another juluca interaction during the hard court swing imma lose it fr #juluca

@nickyssmile
y'all are clowns for thinking #juluca has a chance. #licky is the friends-to-lovers arc we want

"What does half of this even mean?" Juliette asks, thrusting Claudia's phone back at her. "This was meant to be over." She drops her head into her hands.

"Miami is built for things not to blow over," Claudia says, patting her shoulder.

Juliette groans. "That does not help."

"Octo! Do you have a red lipstick? Mine ran out." Juliette doesn't look up as Livia's footsteps tap down the hall.

"Yep, come in," Octavia calls, and the door creaks open.

Claudia gasps, and Juliette looks up in surprise.

"What the hell are you wearing?" The words fall out of Juliette's mouth before she can stop them.

Her little sister, who is rarely seen out of her favorite sweatpants and oversize T-shirts, her hair always stuffed into a floppy and frizzy bun, is wearing a dress.

"Where did you get this? Wow, I didn't know you had curves," Octavia says, swiveling around to look at her.

Livia is in a slinky black dress, dripping from her silhouette and revealing more than Juliette ever expected to see. Her hair is slicked back into a high ponytail, her usual frizzy mess tamed into bouncy ringlets.

"What? I'm going to the party." She rubs her palms down her thighs, and Juliette blinks at the double slit that reveals her thigh on both sides.

"Not in that. No fucking way." Juliette will not have her baby sister harassed by drunken tennis players all night.

Livia's eyes narrow. "Yes, I am. Red lipstick, Octo."

Octavia stares at her.

"I am an adult. I was invited to this party, and this is what I'm wearing. If you have a problem with it, too bad," Livia says, her hand still open and expecting.

"Livie, we're looking out for you," Claudia starts.

"Don't give me that shit, Claudia. If anything, I'm the one keeping all of you in line. So, what, you get to be crazy and wild but poor little Livie can't have one night of fun?" Livia's chest heaves and color floods her cheeks. "Give me one good reason why I shouldn't look and feel good going to this party."

"Every tennis player that matters will be there, probably drunk, and I'd rather not have my baby sister sexually harassed. Is that enough of a reason?" Juliette snaps. Heat bubbles beneath her skin— anger, but more than that, fear. She can't let something happen to

Livia. She trusts Octavia and Claudia to protect themselves, but Livia is the softest of them. She is sweet and innocent.

Or so she thought.

Livia starts to reply when Octavia cuts her off quietly. "Who are you meeting there?"

Livia freezes. "No one," she snaps, too quickly.

"Livia," Claudia tries to say, but Livia shakes her head.

"No!" Her voice raises and shakes, so unlike her that Juliette is unsure whether she's about to laugh or cry. "You all get to have your secrets and I don't press you on it. I don't tell anyone, I keep us all safe and our images crystal clear. So, for once, let me have my fucking secret." Livia stamps her foot, which only makes her look even more like a petulant child.

Octavia stands, setting her straightener down. "Well, I think you look lovely."

Juliette blinks. "Octavia," she starts, but Octavia's iron glare stops her.

"Thank you," Livia says breathlessly, taking the red lipstick Octavia holds out. Then she storms from the room without another word.

Juliette blinks, frozen in betrayal.

"What the hell was that about?" Claudia demands.

Octavia meets their gazes in the mirror and shrugs. "She's right. She's an adult."

"She shouldn't be wearing that," Claudia says, running her fingers over her hair and sweeping the thick mane off her neck.

"No, probably not, but it doesn't matter now." Octavia straightens her shoulders. "We have a better chance of keeping an eye on her if we don't drive her away." She shoots them a dark look, eyebrow raised.

Then, she sweeps to the closet and pulls out a pair of crisp white sneakers and a strand of pearls. "This will match your jumpsuit," Octavia says, tossing them at Claudia. She can't catch them in time, and they clatter to the floor, effectively ending the conversation.

Juliette presses her knuckles to her sternum, hoping it brings her some comfort like it seems to do for Luca.

It does not.

Her phone lights up on her lap, and she opens her messages to find a text from Antony with practice notes. She should ignore them until tomorrow, but she opens the document and finds it's significantly longer than his usual notes. Under the first header, "To Work On," Juliette scrolls through three pages of errors she made during her practice.

> Slow on footwork.
> Racket speed through the ball significantly slower.
> Sluggish on decision-making.
> Inconsistent ball toss on serve.

As it continues, Juliette's throat closes. She knew she was distracted at practice that morning, but not this badly. She hasn't had such a scathing review of her game since she was twelve and tried to play with a sprained ankle. Now she has no excuse for practicing so horribly.

She knows why she was tired, slow, preoccupied.

At the end of the document, Juliette's heart stops.

> Without getting to a quarterfinal, you'll drop out of the Top Ten
> to number twelve.

Juliette slides her phone into her purse, but her father's words are seared into her skull. They weigh heavily in her chest, a physical manifestation of how out of control she feels and how much it has ruined her game. He knows Juliette better than anyone else, and he has always wanted what was best for her. He wants her to reach her goal of being number one. The further she falls, the harder it'll be to win tournaments and claw her way back to the top.

So maybe it is time she listens to him.

THIRTY-SIX

LUCA

Remi Rowland's boat is much like her tennis game. Sleek, graceful lines, large, and powerful, with a bit of character in the strobing lights.

Luca trails behind Juliette, their hands lightly tangled to keep from getting lost in the crowds around the other boats. Camera flashes pop, and Juliette's hand jerks away. Luca sticks her hands in her pockets and diligently ignores the stinging hurt in her chest.

Claudia leads the way, a bottle of champagne held over her head like a beacon as she boards Remi's boat with Octavia and Leo not far behind. It seems that the entire men's and women's tours have been invited, and once onboard, Luca is swept into the mushy waves of conversations in a dozen different languages.

"Hey, look who decided to finally show up!" Remi bounds over and relieves Claudia of the champagne.

"And we brought sparkly!" Claudia says.

"Bubbly, Claudia, bubbly."

Claudia blinks, dumbfounded.

"Never mind." Remi passes the champagne bottle off to a waiter flitting by. Then, she pulls Octavia and Claudia into a hug. "Thanks for coming."

Claudia kisses her cheek. "Wouldn't miss it for the world. Now, when do we get to meet the soulmate of the hour?"

"We have a bet to resolve," Leo says. His arms sling around Octavia's hips, drawing her close and hooking his chin against her shoulder. Hot jealousy at their easy intimacy flares in Luca's chest, and she is tempted to take Juliette's hand, but she's looking off into the distance.

Remi groans. "Let me get you all drinks." She has the telltale sparkle of a woman already a couple drinks deep. Luca assumes it's a necessity, since the last time she saw Remi, she was buzzing with nerves.

"What a terrible host you make, my love," a familiar voice purrs from behind Octavia.

Luca leans into Juliette. "Told you," she whispers in her ear, and Juliette flinches.

Xinya Chen swivels into their little circle with a tray of drinks. Luca grabs a vibrant blue cocktail adorned with a sparkling orange umbrella. Juliette doesn't take one, simply crossing her arms.

"Thank you, baby," Remi says as she hands off the now empty tray to someone. Xinya grips her glass with white knuckles, betraying her nerves despite her easy smirk.

"I would say I'm surprised, but I'm not," Luca says, and Remi chokes on her drink. "Come on, you were in her box at Wimbledon. Not hard to connect the dots."

Xinya surprises Luca by taking it in stride and laughing. "I tell her to keep it in her pants all the time. I'm surprised we even need . . . this."

Remi, having recovered from her coughing fit, throws her arm around Xinya's shoulders, dragging them together. Remi's fingers curve against the slope of Xinya's neck, and Xinya's arm winds around Remi's slender waist, causing their hips to bump. It is an easy and intimate move. Remi is affectionate like that to most people, but to see Xinya lean into her, tension easing out of her shoulders . . . it's telling.

"All right, go on, mingle!" Remi shoos them farther onto the boat, so they don't keep blocking the passerelle.

Luca drifts, wandering across the deck. Juliette is withdrawn, pulling away and forcing distance between them that Luca doesn't understand. Ever since a few photos of them on the boardwalk made a few more waves online than they expected, Juliette's been jumpy, but Luca can't parse why that's bothering her *now.*

Luca leans against the railing, looking over the Miami harbor and the lapping black waves frothed with skyscraper light. It's warm and humid, but nerves nip at her like an unpleasant chill.

"Lou!"

Luca turns into a hug that is more of a tackle. She gets a mouthful of ginger hair and is smothered by the scent of spice, sandalwood, and tequila. It's such a different reception from the previous afternoon that she doesn't even hug him back.

"Nicky, how much have you had to drink?" she asks, catching Nicky's forearm to keep him from falling on his ass.

"A couple of these?" Nicky hoists a drink, and it sloshes dangerously. Luca draws him closer to the railing before the cocktail ends up all over a woman's back. "I just needed it tonight, y'know. Thought if I acted like the best friend, people would treat me that way."

Luca's stomach kicks bile into her throat. She takes both of their drinks and sets them on the floor. "You don't talk to me anymore," Nicky continues, swaying against Luca, close enough to be able to count every faint gingery freckle on his face.

"I'm sorry, Nicky," she says, but Nicky pushes her away and throws himself dramatically against the edge of the railing.

"I don't want to talk about it."

Luca glances around. Dozens of eyes are on them, curious and sharp. "Come on, let's dance. You love to dance," Luca says, reaching for her best friend. This time he doesn't flinch away, and he lets Luca wrap her arm around him and guide him away from the edge of the boat to the dance floor. The music radiates through the soles of Luca's shoes and through to her very bones. It's too loud for her to think and almost too overwhelming for her to enjoy.

Nicky allows Luca to pull him into the sweep of dancers. It's like a chaotic and complicated tango, everyone's faces blurring together, and Luca wonders if this is what it feels like to drown, her breath harsh but not reaching her lungs.

It could be three seconds or three hours for all she knows. Time does not exist here. She remembers small details between the stretches of forgetting. Leo and Octavia wrapped aound each other, Octavia's fingers threaded tightly through Leo's curls to ensure he doesn't drift away from her. Then, Claudia's head thrown back as she laughs. A man Luca doesn't recognize kissing the line of Claudia's throat. Xinya and Remi are twined around each other, Xinya's face hidden in Remi's neck and Remi's hands rubbing her back soothingly. Luca spots Livia with one of the Volkov brothers, her hair obscuring her face as she dances. And then she loses everyone in the chaos.

"Love is overrated," Nicky bemoans as they find themselves in the eye of the dancing. Luca barely manages to keep Nicky upright as he sways like a dandelion in a windstorm.

"Come on, you and Magnus are good, right?" Luca asks, and Nicky shakes his head.

"No, I don't know. We fuck, but we don't figure anything out. We run in circles." Nicky drops his head into his hands, and Luca pats his shoulder.

Luca rips her gaze from Nicky. She thinks she catches a glimpse of Juliette moving through the party, but then she's gone. Luca cranes her neck up in an effort to get new air into her lungs. The ceiling above them sparkles with vibrant, neon stars. How did they even get inside?

"I don't want to be here anymore. This isn't fun," Nicky whines into her ear.

Luca looks up at him. His bright blue eyes are glassy and he's breathing hard. She links their elbows together and then fishes them out of the dancers and back onto the deck. A free lounger beckons her and she guides him over until he can slump like a broken doll against it.

"Let me get you a water, and then we'll leave. I'll be right back, okay?" She waits for Nicky to nod before she starts across the deck in search of a waiter.

"Luca!"

Luca turns, and Juliette nearly runs into her. Luca steadies her with a touch to her shoulder. Juliette's eyes are bright, her hair frizzy in the humidity. "I'm sorry, but can I talk to you?" she says, wringing her hands.

Luca's stomach twists but she nods. "Yeah, sure," she says automatically even though she knows she should get back to Nicky. She wishes she would've stayed on the dance floor, melting with everyone until she wasn't in her body anymore.

Juliette leads her to the secluded lower deck, farthest from the dance floor and bar. The music is almost muffled, as if Luca has stepped onto an entirely different boat. It's dark apart from the bright red sidelight casting ominous shadows on the lapping waves.

"So," Juliette says, looking up. Her face is framed with crimson. "We need to talk." There is a finality to her tone, different from the frantic question moments ago.

Luca shifts, her shoulders rising to her ears. "About what?"

Juliette takes a steadying breath, twisting her fingers together. "I don't think we're going to work out," she says.

"What?"

"I think we should stay away from each other. I think it'd be for the best."

Luca's throat and mind are full of cotton. She can still hear the buzz of the music in her ears. "I don't understand."

"Those photos of us online. It's been really distracting for me, and I had a panic attack over them. Clearly that isn't good for me or my game. I had a disastrous practice. I realized I can't be worried every time I'm with you." Juliete's hands lock around her wrists, clammy with sweat. "Please, I'm doing what is best for both of us."

Luca makes the mistake of meeting Juliette's wide brown eyes. Pain and hurt tighten the corners of her mouth, but there is a determination in her gaze that Luca is intimately familiar with. She wrenches out of Juliette's grasp.

"No, you aren't. You're doing what's best for *you*," Luca hisses. "You hide behind your competitiveness and charm, but I see you, Juliette. I know you're afraid of losing control. Of not having the story spun your way for one second." Juliette reaches for her again, and Luca cringes away. "You said you didn't want to be petty and jealous anymore."

"This isn't about that." Tears gleam scarlet on Juliette's cheeks and she scrubs her hands over her face. "I'm doing what is best for both of us. I want to play and win tournaments. I can't do that if I'm with you."

Luca stares at her. "Unbelievable."

"We can still be friends—"

"Was this your plan the entire time? Make me fall for you and then break my heart?" Luca demands, and Juliette recoils.

"No!"

Luca plants her hands on the boat's railing as the world spins around her. Pain lances through her chest, her heart shattered—again.

"I thought you would understand!" Juliette's voice cracks. "We're rivals, and we both want to be the best."

"We could be the best *together*," Luca snaps, her throat so tight her voice sounds thin and reedy.

"That's so easy for you to say! You always win!" Juliette throws her hands up.

"So, it is still about jealousy," Luca scoffs, pushing off the railing. "Well, I don't want anything to do with you now."

Juliette pants, her chest heaving.

"I should've known," Luca continues. "You made it clear that soulmates mean nothing to you. You told me so many times that you'd never choose me." The words are sharp and cruel like shards of glass in her mouth. "You want this? Fine." Luca curls her fingers into fists, nails digging into her palm. "We'll go back to being rivals, and I'll be damned if I ever let you win."

Luca spins and walks away from Juliette, ignoring the calls of her name. She clamps her hand over her mouth as a sob threatens to overtake her. She can't believe how stupid she was to believe that Juliette cared about anything other than herself.

Luca presses her knuckles against her chest, trying to suppress the pain rippling from her heart. She wonders, wildly, if it will be bloody when she pulls her hand back, as if Juliette has literally carved out her heart and left nothing but a gaping wound. She wishes she could turn off the tap on the riot of feelings that threaten to spill out of her like rancid oil.

The sounds of the party crash against her head as she stalks back to it. She twists her fingers together, flexing her knuckle bones and joints to a stretching point before snapping them back the other way. Luca bites her lip and wishes she'd never had a taste of Juliette.

Nicky is right where she left him, a forlorn ghost among the solid outlines of drunk tennis players. Time blurs as Luca focuses on leaving, on safely getting them into a taxi. Nicky is a slurring mess, half draped across Luca's lap. She watches the glittering lights of Miami weave by. She threads her fingers through Nicky's hair, trying to calm herself as much as him.

She brings Nicky to her room and lets him pass out on her bed. She slumps onto the couch, halfway to the kitchen in an effort to make tea, but her emotions catch up to her. She curls her legs into her chest and wraps her arms around herself in an attempt to become as small as possible.

She presses her forehead to her knees as a disgusting, raw sob rips free from her chest.

Many times, when she'd been a child, her mother had found her curled up in a similar position, hiding from her father and trying to hold back tears. And like then, she wishes someone was here to comfort her. To rub her back and gently brush the hair off her face, to pull her into the warm tenderness of a blanket and tell her it will all be okay.

It is harder to stop crying than Luca expected. It's been bubbling up for weeks, months, perhaps even decades. She's had big losses that weigh heavily on her chest, a burden all athletes can relate to. And she's cried over those before. But it's nothing like this.

This swallows her. This is full-body bawling, and she can't stop. She is certain she's never felt like this before, but it still is like horrific déjà vu, like she's lived through it already. Perhaps this is an ancestral pain, a ripple effect from generations of emotionally stunted Kacics. Perhaps it runs deeper than that. Perhaps this is the unfolding of fault lines that will eventually rend her soul in two. She wonders if a soulmate breaking your heart is fatal.

But eventually, because she is only human, the indescribable and insatiable urge to cry tapers off. Her face is a mess, sticky with snot and tears. Her eyes are swollen, and a truly skull-cleaving headache pounds away in her brain.

She needs to put the pieces back together. She doesn't need Juliette.

"Lou?"

She looks up, and Nicky is standing in front of her.

"What's wrong?" he asks urgently.

Luca fully intends to explain, but when she opens her mouth, she crumples again. A sob rips free before Nicky crushes her into a hug.

"Did she hurt you?" Nicky asks into her hair, his hand rubbing against her back and calming the spasming emotions making it hard to breathe.

"Juliette broke up with me. Said we'd be better off as friends." The words hurt to say.

Nicky nuzzles against her temple. "Oh."

"I don't know what to do," Luca says, lifting her head. Nicky cups her cheek, brushing her tears away.

"I'm not the best person to ask what to do," he says, his face blotchy and his lower lip quivering.

"I'm sorry, Nicky," Luca murmurs. "I shouldn't have ignored you."

Nicky tilts his head. "I forgive you. It's clear whatever was between you and Juliette was intense."

Luca nods. "God, this is such a mess." She mops her face with her sleeve.

Nicky laughs, a hoarse and broken thing. "We're both messes." He dips his head, pressing their foreheads together. "Maybe that's why we're best friends."

Luca takes Nicky's open hand, clasping their palms together. "What do we do now?"

"You don't have to do anything right now. I think our best course of action is to eat our weight in ice cream."

Luca almost manages to smile.

THIRTY-SEVEN

JULIETTE

If loneliness is an island, Juliette has shipwrecked herself.

She has never had her heart broken before. There have been moments she thought her heart was broken, like when the doctors told her she would have to undergo wrist surgery or when she lost the Australian Open final. But this hits different. It's raw and unlike anything she's ever felt before. It's worse.

Juliette thought she would feel better if she broke up with Luca, tried to be just friends, but Luca's words still ring in her ears. She stumbles off Remi's boat and onto the marina. Music and conversation laps in from the bobbing boats, but Juliette heads toward the end of the dock. She sits down on the damp planks and hangs her feet over the dark water.

She reaches for her phone, tucked in her purse. Her father's notes taunt her as she opens it. "This is for the best," Juliette whispers to herself, but the words taste like ash in her mouth. A lie, one she's failed to convince herself to believe. She looks at her shaking hands and remembers Luca's gentle touch as she calmed her out of the panic attack.

She taps out a message to the one person who will understand.

Juliette looks up, her breath coming unsteadily as she searches for the stars, for something to guide her. But, of course, this is the city, and the light pollution leaves the sky as simply a void of darkness smoked with orange-tinged clouds.

Footsteps clatter on the boards behind her, but she doesn't look until there is a soft grunt.

"What's wrong, Jules?" Claudia asks urgently.

Juliette opens her mouth to explain, but no words come to her lips. She has snapped her own heart into pieces. She closes her eyes. She feels washed out. Would her skin be gray if she looked? She isn't used to feeling deadened, words meaningless against her tongue.

"What happened?" Claudia asks, her eyes pleading for answers.

"I broke up with Luca," she says, simply. It is the hard and cold truth.

"What?" Claudia slumps onto the dock next to her. "Why?"

Juliette opens her phone and turns it to Claudia, shows her the notes on her practice. "Luca is too distracting. I can't handle having a relationship with her."

Claudia breathes out heavily. "Fuck," she mutters.

Juliette looks at Claudia. Rain mists down, glittering like diamonds on her gold curls. It's cool and soothing against Juliette's skin. "I know it's better this way, but it doesn't feel like it right now."

Claudia sighs. "So, you let her go because you think it's best for both of you." Her lips purse. "Like I did."

Only Juliette and her sisters know that Claudia let the love of her life go because it was the best for her. And even though it broke her heart, she knew it would be better for her lover to find her soulmate. Claudia may not have a soulmark, but she believes in the idea of them enough to not stand in the way of soulmates. "Did it feel like this when you did it?"

Claudia nods, biting her lip. It's clear she wants to say something she thinks Juliette won't want to hear.

"What? Tell me what you're thinking." Juliette swallows roughly.

"Jules, I won't try to tell you what's best for you, but I think you were beginning to know what love is. How all-consuming and intense it is, but also, how hard it is. There isn't a day that I don't regret what I did. This is . . . different. I think you're afraid, Juliette."

Juliette hates how Claudia's words hit her like a hammer. "I am afraid, Claudia! I didn't even want a soulmate. I just want to play tennis!" She drops her head to her hands.

Claudia strokes her back. "I know. And you're the only one who can decide what is more important to you. For what it's worth, I think you can fight for both."

"You think I'm an idiot," Juliette mumbles miserably.

Claudia sighs. "No, Jules, I think you're reacting to change, and that's normal. I only want you to be happy, and this decision doesn't seem like it'll make you happy."

Juliette looks up and tilts her head to the sky again, rain and tears dampening her face. "I guess I'll find out."

Claudia pulls her into a hug but says nothing else.

LUCA

Luca has four days to pull herself back together and refocus. The grind of a tournament is exactly what she needs to put thoughts of Juliette behind her, but everywhere she looks, she's reminded of what she could have had.

The scent of grapefruit that used to lull her to sleep reminds her of Juliette pressed in close, arms around her waist, nose against her throat.

The closed curtains remind her of Juliette's fear of heights.

Her favorite chamomile tea reminds her of soothing Juliette multiple times, and even lying in bed without the warmth of Juliette makes it impossible to get comfortable.

It is through absolute sheer force of will that Luca wins any matches. On the court, she forgets everything but the ball. The squeak of shoes against the hard ground, the strike of the ball against her strings, and the blister of the Miami sun—it all makes Luca forget that she is Luca Kacic. Still, it's by the barest of margins that she beats the other Bulgarian twin, Tatiana Valcheva, in a tiebreaker to make it to the semifinal.

Unfortunately, Remi Rowland is the next match waiting for her, and Remi's fresh from a first-set retirement when her opponent suffered from heat stroke.

Off the court, Luca is a mess. She knows it's stupid, but it's as if her chest has been punched through with a Juliette-size hole.

Vladimir immediately notices her lack of focus, sleeplessness, and terrible appetite.

"A good win out there today," he says as Luca sinks into the ice bath. The shock of the cold after burning in the sun makes her mind go blank.

Vladimir leans against the wall. She can vaguely hear the other players talking in the locker room on the other side of the half wall. She wonders if Juliette is there. She lost in the first round, but maybe she's supporting her sisters. Luca shakes her head, trying to jar loose any thoughts of Juliette.

"Good win today, but I need to beat Remi tomorrow to definitely keep my rank through the US Open," Luca says. Last night, when she couldn't sleep, she'd obsessively crunched the numbers. "And if I lose, I'll have to win Cincinnati."

Vladimir sighs. "It won't be the end of the world if you lose the number one ranking, Luca. You've had a tough year, and you should be proud of what you've accomplished."

"But if I lose—"

"Everyone loses, Luca. It's part of the sport. It doesn't take away from all that you have accomplished."

Vladimir's words are still circling in her head as she steps onto the Center Court to face Remi Rowland.

The crowd is immediately rowdy and roaring as they step onto the court. Remi is the obvious favorite, even though Luca played tennis for Florida in college. Nothing will make the crowd root for her over the local, feisty American kid. The media will probably say that it bothered Luca during their match, not being the crowd favorite, and that her mind was elsewhere.

It is true that her mind is somewhere else entirely. She can't stop thinking about how perfectly Remi has played since publicly announcing her relationship with Chen Xinya.

Luca gets aced on match point, and she watches Remi blow a kiss to her box and her soulmate. The hard agony of defeat rings hollow in her chest, made more disappointing after her terrible performance.

But it's the slither of jealousy in her gut that is the worst.

She only needs to work harder, be better, and focus more. It'll all unfold exactly as it needs to.

She only needs time.

THIRTY-EIGHT

JULIETTE

"Where is your head at, Juliette?" Antony asks.

They're sitting in a booth at the back of the vegan restaurant Claudia convinced them all to come to after winning the Cincinnati Open doubles' title. The Phoenician Taverna is their favorite restaurant that also serves vegan food and Claudia hadn't wanted to celebrate without her doubles partner, Xinya.

Claudia, Xinya, and Remi are currently at the bar, taking some sort of tequila and spinach shot. They'd played spectacularly, and Juliette is pleasantly sunburned from sitting in her player box for two hours.

Still, Juliette can't find the energy to enthusiastically party with her sister and friends. It's been two weeks since she broke up with Luca, and it seems that perhaps Luca feels similarly, even if she is playing better than Juliette. On court, she's even colder. She plays, wins, and leaves. There is no joy in her face, no fist pumps, no energy outside of points. Whenever the camera focuses on Luca's face, Juliette can see the dark circles beneath her eyes and the chapped skin of her lower lip. She still sweeps through her opponents without much trouble, because she's just incredibly talented. In the promotional videos the WTA makes them do, she's so charming with her smiles and jokes. Everyone's been mentioning how much Luca's come out of her shell this season.

 @julesisthesun
the edits that will come from this interview alone will be fire. get on it girlies!!

@gamesetvroom
she's taking every tournament this swing, istg she's gonna charm her opponents into defaulting.

@liviasburner
If luca kacic has millions of fans i am one of them. if luca has ten fans i am one of them. if luca has only one fan, that is me. if luca has no fans, that means i am no longer on the earth. if world against luca, i am against the world.

And even if Twitter sees this newer side to Luca, Juliette sees how she's still guarding herself. She's keeping everyone at a racket's length and Juliette longs to see her true smile, the one that makes her eyes crinkle at the corner. She wants, despite herself, to hear Luca's honking laugh. Juliette doesn't know if she's just projecting but Luca doesn't *seem happy either.* And Juliette feels ripped to shreds, left in tatters.

"Onto the next tournament," Juliette says finally, tracing water rings into the table from her glass's condensation. She lost in the first round of Miami, and then in the second round of Cincinnati to a random player. Maybe she's cursed to never play well again.

At least in Miami, Luca lost in the semifinals to Remi, setting up the strangest final in the history of tennis, between Remi and Xinya. It was the first time that confirmed soulmates had ever played against each other. And it was *fun* to watch. It was clear that they knew each other's games inside and out. Remi always plays high risk, never backing down from trying to clip the line with every stroke. Her serve almost always bailed her out with blistering speed and accurate placement. Xinya, on the other hand, relied on her athleticism, variety of shots, and never missing to win. And with both of them playing their best, it came down to a few points toward the end of each set.

Xinya won in the third set tiebreaker, falling to her knees as she did. Then the camera had flipped to Remi. If Juliette hadn't been watching the match, she would've thought Remi won. The glow of pure joy and pride on her face made Juliette's throat burn. When Remi reached Xinya, she hugged her and spun her around. In their speeches, they thanked each other for making each other better. After, they held up their interlocked hands instead of their trophies, because they mattered more to each other.

Juliette had wanted to turn the channel, but Claudia had the remote and wouldn't stop cooing over how cute they were. Her stomach clenches at the memory, and she worries she'll spew falafel and eggplant all over the table.

"Are you still going to the match tomorrow?" Antony asks, yanking Juliette out of her thoughts. The lighting is low, casting deep shadows over the crags of Antony's face, making him look even more stern as he frowns.

"It's Octavia's final. I have to," Juliette says, even though she feels nauseated at the thought.

"I know that isn't all of it," Antony says. He pauses, for dramatic effect, then adds, "Your head is still wrapped up in Kacic."

The sound of Luca's name strikes the still-raw nerves in Juliette. She can't even lie and tell her father that this isn't about Luca, because it is. Even though she broke up with her, Juliette is haunted by the decision. She may not be playing as horribly as she did the day after her panic attack, but she is far from her best. "Come on, Juliette, tell me what's going on." Antony reaches across the table and takes her hand, stopping the incessant circles.

Juliette shakes her head, the back of her throat tightening again. God, when did she get so weepy? "We were trying to make a relationship work between us." She lays her cheek against her other hand, looking out into the restaurant to avoid Antony's gaze.

"Why?" Antony asks.

Juliette barks out a humorless laugh. "Why?" She slams her hand onto the table, making her father startle. She flips her arm over, the strip of black circled tightly around Luca's name hiding it. "Take a wild fucking guess."

Antony looks chagrined, and he frowns. "There is no need to use that language," he says primly, if only to regain control of the conversation.

Juliette rolls her eyes, not even caring to restrain it. "Oh, I'm *so* sorry. I'll do better to answer your dumb questions respectfully," Juliette says, letting sarcasm drip as heavy as sap.

Antony's eyes narrow, and a muscle in his jaw flicks. "Luca Kacic has no right to your feelings. Especially if it jeopardizes your tennis."

"I know!" Juliette snaps, the embers of anger sparking into flames. "Why do you think I broke up with her?"

"That was a mature decision, Juliette," Antony says, giving her a loaded look. He pities Juliette for ever believing a relationship with Luca was worth it. "You shouldn't go to the match tomorrow regardless. It won't be good to watch Kacic. Not so close to the US Open. Not after your failure in this tournament."

It's such a slap in the face that Juliette rips her hand out of Antony's. "Don't quit your day job as my coach, okay? I don't need your judgment on my life." She slides out of the booth.

"Juliette!" Antony calls, but Juliette is already weaving through the restaurant, and she bursts out the door into the evening air. The sun slinks below the horizon, a bleached wash of soft oranges and baby pinks aglow on puffy clouds. The Ohio wind ruffles her curls and caresses her cheeks, surprisingly refreshing.

She looks up at the sky, slowly deepening to indigos and twinkling with stars. She thought the pain of pushing Luca away would fade with time, but if anything, it's worse. Juliette walks aimlessly until it's fully dark and the moon is somewhere behind the clouds, hiding her face like Juliette is hiding her own.

By the time she realizes she's hopelessly lost, she is in the middle of nowhere with only the glittering sea of stars above her, an expanse of tall, waving corn threatening to engulf her to her right, and a long empty road to her left.

She pulls out her phone and sees she has a couple of missed texts from her father about her schedule.

Typical. No apologies.

There are a few messages from Octavia about the match tomorrow.

Usually, it would be Livia, but she's been pissed since the party. She had come to Claudia and Xinya's doubles match but sat in the back row, stiff and frowning with her sunglasses on the entire time.

Livia is still the content manager for all three of them, so she's continued to do her job and book them flights and hotels, and post on their social media. All her texts have been impersonal, including the one sitting unopened about Juliette's approval of a T-shirt post.

Juliette considers launching her phone into the corn.

However, she does the mature thing and turns it off before she begins the long trek back to the hotel. It's late when she returns, swiping in with her key card. She nods at reception before her eye is caught by a lanky figure moving through the lobby.

For a moment, her heartbeat skips, and she thinks . . .

But no, it's simply a janitor with a mop on his shoulder.

She trudges to her room, feeling like a fool for hoping to see Luca. For thinking maybe she'd see the same misery she feels reflected in Luca. That Luca might storm over to her and shake her and tell her she's being stupid.

Maybe she is being stupid.

She goes through the motions of getting ready even though she wants to collapse face-first into the freshly fluffed pillows and let sleep take her away from her messy feelings.

Juliette finally opens Livia's text. A new one flashes at her. It's a recommendation to post something about Claudia's doubles' win and wish good luck to Octavia. Juliette groans and considers ignoring the suggestion, but she doesn't want to seem petty by ignoring her sisters' success when she's flopping.

She yanks her camera out of her satchel and lays back against the covers to start flipping through her photos. None of them are particularly great, so her eyes glaze over until she hits a photo she forgot she took.

She gasps, her stomach suddenly aching as she stares at Luca. In a jolt, Juliette is back on Miami Beach. She can feel the tickle of saltwater air in her nose, hear the din of a crowd in her ears. The beginnings of Luca's smile is just starting to curl at the corners of her mouth, the dimple on her left cheek starting to show, a shadowy hint of the real thing. She is squinting against the sun, but her gaze is fixed firmly on the lens. On *Juliette*.

Juliette scrolls back further, to pictures of a night she sometimes wishes she could forget, but can't. Luca at the gala, bathed in red light. Juliette's shaky hands give the photo a blurry edge. But Luca's eyes are on her . . . again. Sharply in focus, as if Juliette is the only one in the room.

With her heart heavy in her chest, pressing her into the bed like an anvil, she goes to the first photo she ever took of Luca. Her fingertips tingle with the memory of Luca's cheekbone against her skin.

She'd caught Luca midgasp, with her cheeks just starting to flush, a soft gradient of rosy pinks that Juliette knows spreads all the way down her neck and chest. The lighting is low, but Juliette had adjusted the settings to make Luca visible. Her eyes are so soft, windows to her emotions. Longing and want and *hope*.

Juliette hugs her camera against her chest, unable to look at Luca looking at her like that. Its weight presses against her collarbones, much like the swell of yearning that surges outward from her heart. She *misses* Luca. Her presence, her humor, her insight, her *love*. Even if they haven't said it yet, Juliette knows it down to the marrow of her bones.

She may be able to get her career back on track without Luca, but *fuck*, she doesn't *want* to. She doesn't care if her life spirals out of control again because Luca grounds her.

Juliette breathes out, the tightness in her chest unwinding.

She has to fix this.

THIRTY-NINE

LUCA

A storm brews on the horizon. Luca can't see it, but she can feel it as she steps out onto Center Court. If she squints, she swears she can see a crackle of electricity in the snapping heat. The sky is a marbled tapestry of charcoal and dove gray. The temperature has been cruel, rising steadily all week until Saturday, where it is reaching a crescendo, and the threat of the storm is ratcheting up. The hair on the back of her neck rises, and goose bumps bubble across her skin as the crowd roars. Luca hopes she can win quickly.

She shouldn't be worried. She has played Octavia Ricci twice before, winning both times. But she is Juliette's sister, and Luca can't afford to think about Juliette right now.

Luca readjusts the strap against her shoulder, watching Octavia's lithe silhouette walk down the sideline to the opposite bench. She closes her eyes in an effort to focus through the 1990s pop music and burble of the crowd. Her palms are already sweaty as she grabs her racket and jogs to the net for the formalities. She keeps her energy and focus in order for the first game. Her serve snaps, the court is fast, and the balls lance through the heat. Octavia is a slow starter though, Luca knows this, so she has to stay on top of the game. Pounce before Octavia sinks her teeth into the match.

Octavia struggles to guess where her serve will go. And when she does get into a rally with Luca, she has Octavia dance on a string, running her from side to side until Octavia makes an error or Luca ribbons the ball down the line for a winner.

Luca's mind is unusually clear. The match is playing out in even, clinical strokes, and she wins her first service game easily. They switch sides, and Luca straightens her strings, plucking at them as more of a habit than them actually being uneven. She glances to her left, eyes lifting, and meets the intense and intimately familiar gaze of Juliette Ricci. A shiver traces down Luca's spine as Juliette holds her stare before taking a breath and leaning back in her seat, lazily lounging with her arms crossed.

Luca knew that it was more than likely that Juliette would be at the match. She thought she was ready for it. She'd seen her around the tennis complex without issue. Sure, her pulse had sped up, but she hadn't spiraled.

She snaps out of her stupor and jogs to the baseline, heart hammering in her chest.

She hadn't thought it would affect her this much, to see Juliette. Still, her stomach clenches uncomfortably at the idea that Juliette had positioned herself front and center so Luca could see her. Regardless of whether it was intentional or not, Luca won't let it affect her.

JULIETTE

It is odd to be sitting in the opposite player's box than the one Juliette had been in less than twenty-four hours earlier. Now, instead of being flanked by her father and Octavia, she's in the center of the box next to Claudia and Leo.

She watches her sister exit the tunnel, waving at the crowd. To the untrained eye, anyone would think Octavia was the pinnacle of calm. But Juliette can distinctly see the tension shifting in her shoulders, her nerves in the way she fiddles with her watch, the way she smooths the collar of her tank top down.

Sweat trickles down Juliette's neck, and she sighs. Maybe she should have followed her father's advice and gotten on the plane to New York. She uncaps her water bottle and sips, the coolness soothing her aching throat for a moment.

At this point, it doesn't matter. She's already here, feet from the court, and it would only upset Octavia if she left.

She had thought the sight of Luca would knock her breathless, but instead, her heart rate picks up, and her skin prickles. Intense longing sweeps through her so fast it's dizzying. Luca looks focused, intense, energized. She looks more tan in her black and white kit, glowing and beautiful.

Luca and Octavia are matched in strengths and weaknesses. Octavia is fast as lightning with quick hands that neutralize Luca's heavy power. But if Luca stays aggressive on the baseline, she might be able to cut Octavia apart with short angles. Still, no matter how their styles line up, it will come down to their mental fortitude.

"Do you think Octavia can pull this off?" Claudia asks, leaning into Juliette, whispering so Leo doesn't hear her. He is sitting on the other side of Juliette, leaning forward and already dialed in to watching, intense as ever.

She shrugs. "If she stays true to her game. Moves Luca around, drags her into the net." She's watched almost all of Luca's matches this year, and she's played Octavia enough to know her game inside and out. Luca can catch fire and paint lines, but if she starts throwing in errors, Octavia will stay in the points and whittle Luca to the bone with her pinpoint accuracy and swift feet.

The first game flies by in typical Luca fashion. The heat has the ball snapping off the court, and Luca's serve, while simple in its motion, is one of the hardest on tour. As usual, she looks calm and focused, which Juliette finds incredibly irritating.

It isn't until Luca is getting ready to return that she looks sideways, and her gaze immediately finds Juliette's. It's like a lightning strike through her veins. Deep pangs of longing and desire thoroughly override her every thought.

She leans back, as if she can escape the gravity of Luca's gaze by simply extending the distance between them by a few centimeters. She crosses her arms over her chest as if she can protect herself from the searing hot focus in Luca's eyes. Luca's mouth is parted, cheeks flushed—whether from the heat or Juliette, she'll never know.

Then the moment is broken, and Luca looks away.

The second game goes similarly to the first, with Octavia serving as well as Luca.

Luca takes a deep breath as she bounces the ball beneath her racket. There is a tension to the flex of her forearm, and her serve isn't nearly as hard or well-placed as her first game.

It's the first competitive point of the match and Juliette finally finds herself able to relax and enjoy watching the spectacular tennis.

Whenever Juliette used to watch Luca, she was consumed by jealousy. Now, all she sees is the perfect balance of Luca's body as she glides fluidly across the court. She is comfortable and confident, at ease on the court like she is when she's carefully spooning the perfect amount of honey into a teacup. Coordinated and smooth, like she is when she draws Juliette into her, threading her fingers through her curls, tucking Juliette into the angles of her body and making them fit.

And yet, when Octavia's ball drops short, well inside the baseline, and the expected move is for Luca to drive the ball down the line for a winner, her steps pause and stutter. She's off-balance, and she drills the ball into the net. Octavia's point.

Luca stops, breathing heavily, and plants her hands on her hips, staring at the ball for a few seconds before spinning around and heading back to serve. Juliette watches her shake her head and spin her racket before taking four balls from the ball kid.

In the first service game, she looked calm and composed. She never reveals her emotions on the court, much like Octavia. Luca glances across the stadium to her box and Juliette follows her gaze.

There is only one person sitting in a sea of empty blue seats opposite Octavia's box. Vladimir Orlic. The former Croatian legend has one leg crossed over the other, leaning sideways in a pose of nonchalant casualness. When he sees Luca looking, he gives an encouraging clap and nod but is otherwise impassive.

The next point is an easy one-two punch from Luca, an out-wide serve, and then she's moving forward to take the popped-up short ball out of the air for a swinging volley.

Even Juliette claps politely for that one along with the crowd, who are hungry for a competitive match.

Octavia, not to be outdone, attacks Luca's next second serve, and suddenly it's an epic game of cat and mouse. Whenever one of them gains an offensive upper hand, the other battles to take it back until one of them puts the ball away.

Eventually, Octavia manages to draw an error from Luca, her forehand just missing the baseline by millimeters, and Octavia is up a break point.

And then Luca does the unthinkable, the regrettable, and the nearly impossible.

She double faults.

Her first serve lands in the net, and her second serve sprays so long it doesn't even hit inside the baseline.

Luca's racket cracks against the blue acrylic hard court. The graphite rim of the racket splinters and crunches in on itself.

Juliette flinches. In the time she's watched Luca, she's never seen her smack her racket against the ground. She is one of the only players who never lets her emotions get the best of her.

"That was unexpected," Claudia whispers.

Juliette can only watch in shock as Luca storms over to her bench and tosses her racket onto her bag.

Is she cracking under the pressure?

Guilt gnaws at her insides, and Juliette wants to jump down onto the court and hug Luca until she calms down. She grips the arms of the chair, knuckles white.

Unfortunately, she's stuck in the stands, burning with regret and guilt, and Luca is all alone.

FORTY

LUCA

The first set is slipping through her fingers like water, and Luca doesn't know how to hang on.

Her hands shake, and for the first time, being on court is not helping with the anxiety that wants to pulverize her ribs.

She wants to channel it into a more useful emotion, but it's terror that grips her. She knows Vladimir's eyes are drilling holes into her back.

Never smash a racket was the first lesson Luca learned from Vladimir and the one she has never broken.

Until now.

It was an impulsive slip of the hand. A moment of feral weakness that now makes her feel sick.

It's her mistakes that have caused the lopsided score.

She presses her knuckles against her chest, dragging them down her sternum. It doesn't help; if anything, it intensifies the feeling in her chest.

She chews on the inside of her cheek, just for something to do, a sensation to focus on.

The umpire calls time and Luca jumps off the bench, shaking out her limbs in an effort to calm the trembling in them.

Her racket is slippery in her palm.

The heat rises. The air is thick and stifling, pressing in on her.

Her emotions are sliding out of control.

Luca feels a panic attack rising like an unstoppable tide.

And Octavia is calm and focused on the other side of the net, nearly lackadaisical in her effortless serve and aggressive backhand.

And when Luca's third backhand sprays wide, she loses it again.

"What the hell do I do?" she yells at Vladimir.

Vladimir strokes his jaw but says nothing.

Anger bursts through, and she nearly hurls her racket into the crowd and quits the match. It is the sheer terror of losing that stays her hand. "What do I do?" she asks Vladimir again.

"Calm down," Vladimir mouths, holding out his hand in a motion for Luca to relax.

"Calm down?" Luca snaps. "What the fuck kind of advice is that?" She swipes her face furiously with the towel, and Vladimir doesn't respond. He never responds to such outbursts.

Not that Luca has them very often.

She loses Octavia's service game. It is 3–1 but the gap feels wider than she could ever conquer.

The crowd roars. She's giving them a spectacle, and she hates it.

Perhaps all of her luck has finally run out.

Tennis has failed her. *She* has failed. She can't even keep her emotions in check enough to play with Juliette Ricci in the stadium. It is driving her mad.

The first raindrop slithers down her neck.

Instead of being refreshing, it's irritating, and it makes her want to throw up or cry or something else equally ridiculous.

She double faults on the first point of the fourth game.

Luca curses and smacks her racket against the sole of her shoe, pins and needles shimmering through her foot at the contact.

"Audible obscenity warning, Miss Kacic."

Luca doesn't even have the energy to argue it, she just tosses her racket into the air in frustration, but it slides out of her slippery fingers and cracks on the ground.

She double faults the second point.

"What am I doing wrong?" She whirls around to Vladimir, wheezing even though she hasn't run for a point.

Vladimir heaves a sigh. "You have to breathe," he says firmly.

"Fuck off," Luca snarls.

"Audible obscenity violation, Miss Kacic. Love, forty."

Luca wonders if it is possible to burst into flames. She certainly feels like it might be possible.

She spins a first serve in to try to staunch the bleeding, but Octavia rams a forehand back at Luca so fast she can barely get her frame on it. It skyrockets into the air and into the burbling crowd, who are growing rowdy in light of Luca's behavior.

When Luca goes to get her towel, she sees Vladimir gathering his backpack and sweatshirt. She freezes. She had never considered that Vladimir would actually leave. Every word dies on her tongue as she watches Vladimir shuffle out of the player box, disappearing up the stairs and into the flood of people rushing to get into the stadium to watch the final.

Her box is an empty sea of blue. There is not a single person there for her.

She is utterly alone.

JULIETTE

This is truly a disaster.

Juliette is in actual pain being forced to watch Luca melt down. Before, she might have felt a sick satisfaction at seeing Luca break. And if Octavia was winning fair and square, by playing better, she could swallow it. She would be happy, even.

After Octavia breaks for the second time and puts herself firmly ahead, Juliette gets up. "I'll be back," she whispers to Claudia.

Claudia gives her a sympathetic grimace. They want Octavia to win, of course, but not like this.

The first few raindrops patter down as Juliette weaves her way out of the stadium. She isn't exactly anonymous in Cincinnati, but within the crowds who are eager to pile in, no one is paying attention to her as she drops into the main crowd.

She catches snippets of what people are saying about Luca.

"Meltdown."

"Unstable."

"Never seen Kacic act like this."

"Point penalty for audible obscenity? She's better than that."

It's all supremely out of character for Luca, and Juliette tries to swallow around the lump of guilt clogging her throat. This isn't precisely her fault, but she knows she's contributing to Luca's panic.

She shelters beneath the concrete overhang, watching as people stream past. Some off to the plaza of gift shops selling tennis paraphernalia, others to a smoothie bar called Maui Wowi.

Even though it's painful, Juliette opens up her Tennis Channel app and clicks into the final.

She turns down the volume; she doesn't need to know what the commentators are saying about Luca.

Octavia is about to hold to go up 5–1. The camera pans to Luca as she wipes her face with the hem of her shirt. She looks pale and shaky, all the color drained from her face and her breath coming in uneven pants. It is glaringly obvious when they switch over to Octavia that the player's box behind her, the one for Luca, is completely empty.

Even Vladimir has left Luca.

Her gut wrenches. And a few seconds before the TV feed catches up, the sky opens, and rain pours from the heavens.

Delay. Luca will have time to regroup.

She must be lucky after all.

As a player, even one knocked out of the tournament, it doesn't take much for her to sneak into the locker room. She can't imagine Luca hanging out in the players' lounge or gym considering what was happening out on court.

Juliette takes a deep breath before slipping through the door. It's eerily quiet, the only sound the dripping of a showerhead that isn't fully turned off. The walls are painted a soothing blue color, soft like the Ohio sky. Juliette pokes her head around each of the rows of lockers until she spots a lonesome figure hunched on the bench.

Juliette hesitates.

The last time they spoke, Juliette broke both of their hearts. Now, she's here to ask forgiveness and fix what she tore apart. She knows Luca is more than likely to reject her. She's in control here, and Juliette almost can't breathe through the fear.

But she can't imagine her life without Luca in it, so she steps out from the shadow of the lockers. Her shoes scuff against the floor, and Luca's head snaps up.

She blinks as if struggling to process what she's seeing.

"Hey," Juliette says, clearing her throat.

"Here to revel in my misery?" Luca asks, her voice a thin, fragile chord. Her eyes are wide and glossy, and her hair is greasy and wet from the rain and dried sweat, the braid unraveling. She curls in on herself, as if she can flatten herself and disappear.

Juliette drops down onto the bench next to her. "I'm here to see if you're okay." She touches Luca's knee. She doesn't flinch away, and Juliette takes it as a small victory.

Luca squeaks out a breathless chuckle. "No, I'm not."

Juliette squeezes gently, her thumb brushing circles against Luca's kneecap.

"Why are you here?" Luca's voice shakes.

"I'm here to apologize," Juliette says, and Luca looks up, her eyes glassy. "I fucked up. I let my need to be in control take hold of me. I didn't think we could work if we were together. I was afraid of how much I cared for you and how that would affect me and my life. I didn't want anything to change, but I was already changed. I realized today how much I care about you. How much you mean to me. I finally realized how wrong I was. So, Luca, I am so sorry for hurting you and pushing you away and being so selfish."

Her vulnerability hangs like a knife between them, and Juliette can't breathe. Luca can either set it down or cut Juliette straight to the bone.

"You want to be together?" Luca asks softly.

Juliette nods. "I don't just want to be together. I want to know everything, from your favorite color to your darkest nightmare. I want to make love to you and kiss every inch of your skin. I want every moment with you. I want your snark and your anxiety and your brilliance and your sweetness and everything in between. I even want the hurts we'll inevitably cause each other. I want us to break each other's hearts and stay together anyway. I want us to be there for each other, through every soaring high and every soul-crushing low." She takes a deep breath. "I want it all, Luca Kacic. I want you. I want us."

Luca's breathing is sharp and rapid between them, and somewhere in the midst of Juliette's speech, she's started crying. Juliette cradles Luca's face, warmth spreading through her as Luca tips into the touch, her eyes tender and gleaming, every emotion in them. Juliette strokes her cheekbones, and curves her thumb down to where she knows Luca's dimple would appear should she smile. The tears are warm against the pads of Juliette's fingers.

They come together like magnets, drawn together by a cosmic hand. Luca presses her face into the crook of Juliette's neck, her arms wrapping around her. Juliette cradles the back of Luca's head, keeping her close and hiding her from the world around them, while her other arm wraps around Luca's waist. She tilts her head against Luca's temple, their edges melding together in warmth. And time becomes meaningless, as it usually does with Luca in her arms.

Luca pulls back, slowly, her breathing a little more under control. "Next time you feel overwhelmed and out of control, *talk* to me." Juliette's vision blurs as tears finally spill free. She swipes them off her cheek, nodding.

"If anyone can understand that, it's me," Luca adds. "We understand each other. Not just because we're soulmates, but because we're both tennis players."

"I finally realized that being with you doesn't mean being out of control. You make me feel content," Juliette admits, and Luca starts to smile, that dimple curving against the edge of her mouth.

"I forgive you, Jules," Luca says, pressing their foreheads together.

Relief crashes like a wave over Juliette. "Thank you," she breathes, the dizzying feeling of falling and spiraling out of control finally subsiding.

FORTY-ONE

JULIETTE

The rain does not let up through the evening. It continues steadily, drumming heavy fingers through the night.

Unfortunately, Cincinnati does not have a roof over any of its courts, so the final is moved to the next day if the deluge lets up.

Juliette's original flight to New York City leaves in three hours, but instead, she knocks on Luca's door with a healthy dinner from Phoenician Taverna in her hands. Even though Juliette wants to scarf down as much unhealthy food as she can, since it will be her last opportunity for three weeks, she knows Luca needs to be strong and steady for the remainder of the final tomorrow.

She smothers down her pinch of guilt. Octavia can still win the match, and she doesn't need Juliette to actively sabotage Luca to do that.

Luca opens the door, once again in a comfortable white hoodie and black cotton shorts that look too good on her, even if they're baggy.

"Well, hello there," Luca says. She smiles as Juliette steps inside. As the door closes, Juliette wraps her arm around Luca's neck and kisses her. It's quick but it still sends a shimmer of excitement through Juliette's stomach.

"I come bearing gifts." Juliette holds up the takeout bag.

"As requested," Luca says with a roll of her eyes, and Juliette kisses her quiet, thoroughly addicted to the way Luca sinks into her.

Luca swipes the bags from Juliette's hands and heads into the kitchenette. They fall into an easy rhythm of unpacking the food.

Still, Juliette feels like she has been without Luca for too long and she encircles her fingers around Luca's wrist and tugs gently. Luca moves willingly into Juliette's space, pressing their hips together and Juliette's back into the counter. Her hands land on either side of Juliette's waist.

All Juliette does is gaze at Luca. She reaches up and traces Luca's cheekbone, the soft point of her nose, the dimple that's popped out with her smile, her always animated brows, her temples, and into her silky hair, loose and dry.

"What are you doing?" Luca asks.

Juliette looks back into her eyes and smiles. "Memorizing the shape of you," she says.

Luca blinks and she turns her head slightly, away from the heat of Juliette's gaze. Her cheeks tint pink, and Juliette cups her palm over her cheek to feel the heat. She runs her fingers through Luca's hair, pressing her palm flat between her shoulder blades to draw them into a single long line, the space between them nonexistent, even though it makes the counter dig uncomfortably into her back.

Luca tips her forehead against Juliette's and closes her eyes. She draws a shaky breath, and Juliette recognizes the insecurity trying to lay claim to Luca's thoughts. So Juliette lifts her chin and kisses Luca. It is as easy as breathing, and it only takes a second for Luca to relax, all hesitation flowing from her as she melts into Juliette.

It's slow and syrupy, an exchange of tender sweetness and languid moves. Luca's hands skim across Juliette's body, ushering blooms of heat across her skin. She arches into Luca, moaning softly.

Luca dips her head and buries her face in Juliette's neck, lips pressed to her throat. "You're going to be the death of me," Luca whispers.

Juliette tugs on Luca's hair so she can see her face. She loves how unguarded Luca looks, her lips kiss-swollen and red, her cheeks blotchy with heat, and her pupils blown black. "Maybe."

Luca's fingers slide underneath Juliette's sweatshirt. She leans back to look down at Juliette. Her hands smooth up Juliette's stomach, spanning across to cradle her ribs and rest there, her thumb sweeping temptingly beneath her breasts.

Juliette shivers. The heat of Luca's palms combined with the rough scratch of the calluses from years of tennis create the perfect combination of sensation. Then, before Juliette can register what she's about to do, Luca claws her fingers and rakes them down her sides.

Juliette crumples into Luca, knees weak, as laughter is punched out of her against her will. She grabs onto Luca's elbows and presses her forehead against her collarbones as Luca laughs at her. "Now you're going to kill me," she says, breathlessly.

"I like hearing you laugh," Luca says, but mercifully lets go of Juliette's ribs, giving her the chance to breathe properly. "Come on, I'm starving," Luca says, once Juliette is able to stand upright again.

They gather the boxes and plastic forks, already arguing over which movie to watch until they settle on a dorky romantic comedy that they lean into making fun of while they polish off the food and relax into the squishy couch cushions.

Juliette hauls Luca's legs into her lap and, in between quips about how overbearing the parents are about the bakery they own, she massages Luca's calves.

Luca gasps, and her head tilts back. Juliette resists the urge to lean over and nip at Luca's exposed throat. "Achy?" she asks, digging her thumbs into Luca's ankle.

Luca nods as her eyes roll back with pleasure and her whole body falls slack. Juliette isn't even paying attention to the movie anymore, instead focusing on unwinding the tension from Luca's body.

"How did you learn to do that?" Luca gasps out.

"My father would do it for us whenever we had a particularly rough day. Although, I almost always kicked him in the face by accident."

Luca's toes curl as Juliette prods at a knot in the sole of her foot. "Wow, that feels so good," she moans.

Juliette laughs. "You seem to like this better than when I eat you out."

Luca blushes. "No," she squeaks. "I can like both equally well."

Juliette laughs but continues the deep massage. The credits are rolling by the time Juliette is satisfied that every knot is worked out of Luca's muscle fibers. It looks like she's about to pass out, so blissfully relaxed.

"I still have to go to New York tomorrow," Juliette blurts out.

Luca's eyes flutter open, and she looks at Juliette. For a moment, the only sound is the gentle tap of slowing rain on the windows. The curtains are open, but there is little light in the tiny town of Mason, Ohio. A faint flicker from a nearby streetlamp baths them in amber, little speckles of shadow cast by rain droplets.

"Of course," Luca says softly. She struggles to hide her disappointment. Juliette can see it.

Juliette draws shapes across Luca's skin, warmth building beneath her fingertips. "When are you coming?"

Luca sighs, her toes flexing against Juliette's thigh. "I don't know. I'll need to talk to Vladimir, and I think I've messed it up with him."

"Surely he'll forgive you. He's been your coach for, what, ten years?"

"Fourteen," Luca mutters.

"Exactly. He'll understand, right?" Juliette knows her relationship isn't the best with her father, but she knows he would forgive her if she had a breakdown on court like Luca.

"I still need to call him," Luca says. "I'm worried though. I've never lost it on court like that before."

Juliette hums and Luca tosses her head back, throwing her arms over her eyes. "I'm just so angry at myself."

"Come on, a lot of shit has happened in the last few weeks." Juliette tries to ignore the tight ball of guilt in her throat. "Was it a panic attack?" she asks after a beat.

Luca sighs. "Something like that. I was overwhelmed, and for the first time ever, the tennis court wasn't a safe and calm place."

Juliette's heart wrenches, and she squeezes Luca's knee. "Tell him that, then. He'll understand."

"I know," Luca whispers, dropping her arms and looking at Juliette with a soft, unguarded look. "It's always hard to talk about."

"I think you need to talk to someone about your anxiety," Juliette says. Luca frowns and shifts, clearly uncomfortable with the topic. "A professional. It will help you with your private life and your tennis," Juliette adds, taking Luca's hand and twining their fingers together.

"I'm fine," Luca says, halfheartedly tugging on Juliette's hand. Juliette tightens her grip.

"You've been coping. But everyone needs help. It will be uncomfortable, but it'll help you in the long run." Juliette pauses, but Luca is still guarded, defensive. "And I'll help you find a good fit. You won't be alone. Not anymore."

Luca finally meets her gaze. Juliette can see her debating it and she holds her breath, waiting for Luca to settle on a decision.

"You're right." The tension drains out of her, and Juliette exhales slowly. Her lashes flutter closed, but her thumb sweeps down to caress Juliette's wristbone, the strap still hiding her name beneath.

"I usually am," Juliette teases.

Luca opens her eyes to roll them at her. After a pause, she tilts her head. "Can I suggest something for you too? I think you should consider getting a new coach."

Juliette freezes, her instinct to immediately tell Luca an emphatic *no*.

"I've seen the way he talks to you during matches and practices," Luca continues. "It's . . . intense."

"I want that," Juliette protests. "He helps me stay focused that way."

Luca frowns. "Okay, but it doesn't seem to be doing any favors for your relationship. You said before that he is too controlling of your life. Maybe finding a new coach would be a good first boundary to set," Luca says softly, as if not to spook Juliette.

Juliette opens her mouth, but no argument falls from her lips. Luca does have a point.

She sighs. "All right, I'll think about it."

Luca nods. "That's all I ask."

But she'd rather think about something else right now.

"Would you want to come to New York a week early and stay with me . . . ?" Juliette trails off.

"Stay with you?" Luca prods.

Juliette bites her lip to keep from smiling. "I have a friend with a fun artist's studio apartment she lets me rent in the city. It's private, and it has the best golden hour sunlight."

Luca squeezes her hand gently. "Yeah? I think I'd like that."

"Good," Juliette says, a little breathless. "Win tomorrow, okay? And we'll celebrate when you get to New York."

LUCA

Luca blinks, surprised. "I would've thought you'd want your sister to win."

Juliette shrugs coyly. "I mean, I love Octavia, but she's not my soulmate."

Luca tilts her head. "She's dating Leo Mantovani, right?"

Juliette nods. "They're soulmates."

"They seem like they fit," Luca says, remembering how easily it seemed that they twined together.

"They do, but they're still . . . complicated," Juliette says with a wince. "Love is complicated, I guess."

It's an impulse, but Luca tugs the wristband free of Juliette's wrist. Her gaze burns the side of Luca's face. "Does it have to be?" Luca asks softly. Luca turns their linked hands and gently traces the familiar curve of her name. A shudder cascades through Juliette. "I don't think it's the love that's complicated. I think it's us. Humans."

Juliette's smile gleams like the crescent moon. "Are you getting philosophical now, Lux?"

Luca is grateful for the darkness as her cheeks heat. "Maybe," she murmurs. She shuffles and heaves herself into a sitting position but keeps her legs draped over Juliette. She wraps her free arm around Juliette's shoulders, anchoring herself upright. Slowly, she lifts Juliette's arm and presses a barely there kiss to her own name.

Juliette's breath rattles as she exhales, shaky, across Luca's face. "I've always—" Luca starts, but she breaks off. Juliette's stare brightens.

"What?" Juliette's voice is husky but urgent, nearly desperate. "You've always what?"

Luca bites her lip and swallows. "Isn't it obvious?" she asks, digging her fingers into the soft curls she's always been fond of. "I've always liked you, Jules," she admits finally, into the silence. Her heart throbs against her breastbone, and an ache she's carried forever balloons outward. "I'm drawn to you. Sometimes the tug is so strong that it hurts."

Juliette sighs, and for a heartbeat, Luca fears that Juliette is about to tell her this was all a mistake, that Luca's feelings are too intense. She shovels the fear into a hole and forces herself to stay relaxed, but the longer Juliette stays quiet, the more her throat tightens.

"Shit, Luca," Juliette whispers, "you make it so hard."

Luca tenses, the words raking down her spine like hot coals. Her hand goes limp, but Juliette's grip tightens. "Excuse me?"

"No, no, no," Juliette says quickly, desperate again. "Fuck, sorry, I'm not saying this right. I don't want to freak you out."

"Little late for that," Luca wheezes, hating how shrill her voice has gone. Every nerve in her body lights up with anxiety.

"I love you," Juliette says, the words rushed out in a whoosh. "I love you, I love you, I love you," she repeats, like a prayer.

Luca is too stunned to respond, even though every bone in her body screams at her to say it back.

"I know it's too early, but I love you. And I can't tell you how many times I've thought it and almost said it. It won't fix our problems, and it won't magically make us work, but—I love you." Juliette's head drops, as if holding on to the three little words had kept her upright and functioning and now saying them has cut all the little strings.

All Luca can conjure up to say is "You've got to be kidding me."

Juliette blinks, but before she can question it, Luca hauls her into a kiss because it's the only logical thing she can do. The kiss is sloppy, and bruising, but it's necessary. Luca's body is soaked in flame, heat budding across her skin like blisters.

Luca rips her mouth off Juliette's and shakes her head. "I was going to say it first."

"Oh," Juliette gasps, and then she's laughing. "Should we start over then?" she asks through giggles.

Luca groans and lets go of Juliette, flopping back onto the pillows.

Juliette is still laughing as she shifts Luca's legs. And then her knees are planted on either side of her hips and she's leaning over her, fingers wrapping around Luca's wrists and peeling her hands away from her face. Juliette grins down at her, curls framing her face, and slowly, she lifts Luca's hands over her head, pressing her wrists into the pillows.

Heat pulses through Luca, and she squeezes her thighs together, suddenly desperate for Juliette to touch her somewhere else. Juliette is still laughing, her sunlike smile crinkling the corners of her eyes.

"Come here, you idiot," Luca says, tilting her chin up.

Juliette giggles against her mouth as she swoops down to kiss her. It's messy and exploratory, deepening as Juliette sinks into kissing her breathless.

Luca whimpers, intoxicated by the luxurious grapefruit and sandalwood scent overwhelming her. She's dizzy when Juliette finally pulls back, letting go of her wrists to brush Luca's hair off her face. Luca cups Juliette's cheeks, and she thrills when Juliette tilts into the touch, her face softening. "I love you," she says, and the words are finally free from the cage inside her heart. "I love you."

She loves Juliette's goofy, broad smile. She loves how Juliette's fingers trace her cheek, her dimple, the curve of her cupid's bow. "We're going to be insufferable, aren't we?" Juliette asks with a huffed laugh.

Luca rolls her eyes, but the feeling of absolute, inescapable, incandescent love swallows her whole, and she doesn't mind at all. "We're already insufferable," she counters, and she can't stop smiling, even as Juliette leans in to kiss her again.

FORTY-TWO

JULIETTE

Juliette has never been a morning person, but she doesn't mind waking up next to Luca. Even so, her alarm blares too loud, and she smacks the bedside table to snooze it, sending it spiraling off the edge. She flops back, too sleep-addled to rescue it.

Instead, she turns onto her side and reaches for Luca. Her fingers graze sleep-warmed skin, and she wraps herself around any bit of Luca she can find.

Luca stirs, mumbling something unintelligible. Juliette buries her face into the space between Luca's shoulder blades and slots their legs together.

Nine minutes later, as Juliette drifts pleasantly in the soft dozing stage of waking up, her phone blares again. She sighs and considers letting it scream on the floor until it eventually stops.

Luca smacks her hip, twisting in her arms. "Turn that off," she whines.

Juliette huffs. "Fine, fine," she mutters, nearly rolling off the bed to grab her phone and cancel the alarm. She considers going back to sleep, but she needs another flight to New York. Her father is surely going to want to maim her, but that is far away and unimportant at the moment.

What is important to Juliette is draping herself over Luca and peppering her face with kisses. She tries not to laugh as Luca's nose scrunches in an adorably affronted way.

"It's weird to watch someone sleep," Luca grumbles.

"What were you dreaming about?" Juliette asks, resting her chin on Luca's shoulder.

Luca sighs. "You."

"Aw."

"Letting me sleep in peace," Luca adds, and Juliette gasps.

"How dare you," she says, rolling off Luca and crossing her arms over her chest.

"No, I was joking, come back here, you're warm." Luca follows her and throws herself over Juliette.

Juliette considers playing hard to get but a loud banging on the door jolts them both out of their playful sleepiness.

"Who is that?" Luca asks, her eyes going wide.

"JULIETTE RICCI. OPEN UP, I KNOW YOU'RE IN THERE."

Juliette's heart stops, and she claws her fingers into the sheets.

Livia.

"THIS IS IMPORTANT." The banging intensifies.

Juliette swings out of the bed, still shocked by Livia pounding on the door at the crack of dawn. She throws the door open and Livia bursts in, slamming the door shut behind her. She's absolutely manic, panting and flushed as if she's run a mile in three minutes.

"Livia, what's going on?" Juliette asks. "And how did you figure out which room was Luca's?" She glances back toward the bedroom.

"Doesn't matter," Livia says, grabbing her wrists. "Why aren't you in New York?" she demands, her eyes wild and huge.

"Luca, obviously." Livia squeezes, hard, and she winces. "Ouch, Livie."

"Fucking *fuck*, Jules." She shakes her head.

"Livie, calm down. Tell me what's wrong?"

Livia shakes her wrists. "There was a random pop-up drug test for you this morning," she gasps out.

"What?" Juliette isn't sure she heard her right. "There was a what?"

"There was a drug test for you this morning, Jules. Except I had put down that you were going to be in New York because I thought you were, but then Dad calls me and he's panicking, and he couldn't get a hold of you and now you've missed it." Livia lets go of her and laces her fingers behind her head. "This is so bad, so bad."

"Jules?"

Juliette spins around. Luca stares at them with open confusion, her head tilted, a crease formed between her brows. "One second." She turns back to Livia, who has begun pacing.

"Livie, it'll be okay. We get three misses, right?" She takes Livia by the shoulders and gently guides her into the living room. She slumps onto the couch, her head falling into her hands.

"Yes, I know, but it isn't a good look."

Juliette glances up at Luca, lingering in the doorway. "Can you make her a cup of tea?" Luca nods, vanishing around the corner to the kitchenette.

Juliette sits next to Livia and rubs her back. "Livie, why are you so stressed about this? I'll deal with him." Her stomach clenches at the thought, but she has to soothe Livia. She's on the verge of hysterics.

"Because it's my fault!" Her lower lip trembles. "If I weren't such a petty bitch, I would have checked in with you once I thought you landed in New York and then you would have told me you were staying here, and then I could have changed your location."

"Livia, this isn't your fault. This was very last-minute, and it isn't up to you to make sure everything is perfect," Juliette says. "Even if I had told you I was staying here, would you have remembered to change the location anyway? For a random drug test?"

Livia swallows. "Probably not."

"Exactly. This is why they give you three missed chances before it becomes an actual issue." Juliette knows it isn't that simple, but she wants to keep Livia from spiraling further.

Luca returns with a cup of tea. "I didn't know if you liked honey, but it is soothing," Luca says as Livia takes the cup, cradling it between her palms.

"Thank you," she whispers.

Luca lingers, awkwardly caught in the middle of the living room. "Can you give us a moment?" Juliette asks, and Luca sighs in relief, nodding as she leaves again. Not that it really matters, since Luca can't speak Italian. "Look, Livie, I know this situation isn't great, but there isn't anything either of us can do about it now. All we can do now is move forward."

Livia swallows. "Dad is pissed. He's flying here now to chew you out."

Juliette sighs. "That seems like a waste. I'll be in New York later tonight."

"He's convinced you need to be reeled in. He thinks you don't care about tennis anymore," Livia says, sipping her tea.

Juliette rolls her eyes. "Just because I have someone in my life that I care about doesn't mean I've suddenly stopped caring about tennis. It's my job and it's a lot of my life, but there are other things I love."

"Love?" Livia's eyes narrow, and Juliette smiles sheepishly. Livia's eyes flick to the empty hallway where Luca vanished, and one brow raises in question.

"Yes, Livie. Love." Saying it out loud, telling her sister makes it feel as though feathers are brushing her insides. It's oddly pleasant, but also a little uncomfortable. "And . . . I need to apologize for the party."

Livia's face softens, but she looks away.

"I understand that you're an adult, and I stepped out of line reacting like that." Juliette thinks about how their father is already flying back to Cincinnati, as if Juliette is an unruly child and not a fully formed adult. "I should have understood it sooner. All of us should have, considering who our father is."

Livia snorts. "Damn right."

"And I'm sorry for not seeing you as an adult and for not supporting you. I've taken you for granted, and for that I'm sorry. I've missed you." Juliette touches her hand, and Livia awards her with a faint smile.

"You just miss my impeccable planning skills," she teases.

Juliette laughs. "I missed my little sister. You're the backbone of this family, and I love you."

"Love you too," Livia whispers, tilting sideways to bump their shoulders together. "I know I wasn't acting the best, but for the first time, I had someone who was only mine. It was fun sneaking around with him and keeping it a secret. I felt like my own person." Her head drops onto her shoulder.

"Well, none of us are going to push you about it. But if you ever need someone to talk to, we've got you too, Livie." Juliette squeezes her hand.

"I know. Thank you." Livia is quiet for a while as she gulps down her tea. "The funny thing is, I was going to tell you all that night."

"Oh."

"He'll be at the US Open, so we'll try again there," Livia says.

Juliette sighs dramatically. "I guess I can wait until then."

Livia chuckles, lifting her head. "Are you gonna talk to me about Luca?"

"Are you going to tell me how you knew which room was hers?" Juliette counters, and Livia hesitates.

"Erm, I would, but it was rather illegal."

"Livia!"

She, at least, has the grace to look chagrined. "Look, I needed to find you and you weren't in your room. So, I might have hacked the hotel guest list to figure out which room they gave to Luca."

"Livia!" Juliette drops her head into her hands. Of course her little sister hacked the hotel system. At this point, she probably should have guessed. Or maybe learned to stop asking.

Livia shrugs. "It was important."

Juliette can only groan.

FORTY-THREE

JULIETTE

Juliette meets her father in the lobby of the hotel.

"Good to see you haven't been kidnapped," Antony says as he brushes past Juliette to the elevators.

Juliette follows her father up to the new room Livia booked herself when the final was moved to the next day. Her sister is nowhere to be found, probably with her new boyfriend or editing a slew of posts to ensure as much damage control as possible should news of her missed drug test leak.

When they enter the freshly cleaned room, Antony surprises Juliette by not exploding the moment the door clicks closed. He drops his bag by the couch and sits in the desk chair, hands folded in front of him, as if they're simply discussing the latest football scores.

"I would like you to explain yourself," he says.

Juliette has been preparing for this for hours. Making calls and turning her speech over and over in her head. She takes her time sitting in the love seat opposite Antony, curling her legs beneath her to get comfortable.

"I am in love with Luca Kacic," she says, because that is truly the only explanation she can offer.

Antony's calm facade breaks apart. "You are in love with Luca Kacic," he repeats, each word slower than the last, as if he can't believe he's saying them.

"Yes," Juliette says, "and I decided that staying here and making amends with her was more important than going to New York last night. I always intended to catch a flight in the morning and get there before our afternoon practice."

Antony huffs. "And that is an acceptable excuse for missing a drug test?"

Juliette considers the question. It feels like a trap, and maybe it is. Antony has always been adept at weaving Juliette into a spiderweb of words. "No. But it was a random one. Of course, it is my fault that I didn't change the time slot I was available, or the location I was in, and I recognize that."

"Oh, so you recognize that you've jeopardized your entire career for some girl?" Antony's voice raises, and Juliette can almost see the lecture forming behind his eyes. "There is time for love later. *After* you are a Grand Slam champion."

"Luca isn't *some girl*. She is my soulmate. And I know you don't understand that." Antony recoils as if Juliette has slapped him. "I'm happy you and Mom worked out despite not being soulmates. My whole life, I wanted to be like you guys and choose who I loved. I didn't want to be tied to someone without any choice."

Antony opens his mouth, but Juliette holds up her hand.

"But I have chosen Luca. I do love her, and her well-being matters to me. I would choose her even if she weren't my soulmate."

"But your career—"

"Will never be as important as loving and being loved," Juliette says calmly. She watches her father take this in and try to process it.

"After everything I've done for you, you want to throw it away?" A vein throbs at Antony's temple. "I only want what is best for you, Juliette."

Even if Antony believes that, Juliette knows it isn't actually true. That mistake led to weeks of misery. "No, you want what is best for our careers. Why do you think Octavia fired you?" Antony flinches. Juliette knows it is a low blow, but she continues on. "You are trying to control every aspect of my life and I will not let you come in between me and my happiness. Not anymore."

Antony stands suddenly. His eyes widen, shock and fear scrawled across his face. "Anymore?"

Juliette takes a deep breath. Then she stands and crosses the short living room to her father. "I know it's hard to hear, but I need balance. I love tennis. And I will always be grateful for everything you've sacrificed for me, but I get to make my own choices. I have to be okay with making those choices and embracing this change."

"And you choose to skip your drug test?" Antony's brows rise. "That 'change' would mean throwing away a year of your tennis career, maybe more, facing backlash from the media. Not to mention the cut to your lifestyle."

Juliette sighs. "As I said, I don't want to do that, but there is nothing I can do about the missed drug test now. I don't regret not going to New York, but I know to be more diligent with my life. I can take care of scheduling and changing time slots and following the rules. But I can't live in fear of what people will say about me."

"But, Juliette, you have so much of your life to fall in love. Your tennis career isn't guarenteed."

"Tennis and love aren't mutually exclusive. Luca has helped me begin to grow, and my career will be more sustainable if I'm *happy*."

Antony stares at her as if he's seeing her clearly for the first time. Then he deflates, as if there is nothing more he can say. He shakes his head. "Fine. Do as you will. I suppose you're an adult."

Juliette wants to laugh. *Suppose?* "Thank you for understanding," she says instead.

Antony's eyes narrow as he tries to parse if Juliette is being sarcastic or not.

Juliette sucks in a deep breath. "Speaking of understanding . . . I'd like you to just be my dad."

"What?" Antony recoils, stumbling back to sit on the couch.

"I don't want you to be my coach anymore," Juliette says, twisting her fingers together. "I want to have a proper father-daughter relationship going forward. I still want you to be in my box and be there for all the big moments in my career, but as my dad, not as a coach."

For a beat, there is only silence. But Antony doesn't appear angry. A sadness blooms over his face. "I thought we did have a proper father-daughter relationship?" he asks softly. "It's always been easier with you, we're so similar. I thought I learned from my mistakes with Octavia and changed. My goal has always been for you, for all of you girls, to achieve your dreams."

Juliette winces. "It's become too tangled. And I've been feeling resentful of you. I don't want to continue down this path and realize in a few years that we hate each other. You've done so much for my career and I *have* achieved my dreams. And I think I need someone else to help me reach the next level so I can keep moving forward. So, I've spoken to Karoline Kitzinger, and she's agreed to be my coach at the beginning of next season."

"You've already moved forward with her?" Antony inhales sharply.

"I'm taking control of my life and my career." Juliette tries to swallow through her tight throat. Antony stares at her, face impassive, and she braces herself for his anger. She should be used to it by now, but her stomach still twists with nausea. "And I want you to be happy for me. Happy that I've found a love like you and Mom have. I don't want you to see Luca as my rival, but rather as someone who is making me, as a person, better."

Antony's gaze falls to the floor. "You really love her like that?" he asks.

Juliette breathes out heavily. "Yes." Sometimes that love swells within her so much she thinks she'll fly away and somehow that thought doesn't scare her at all.

"Then, I am happy for you, Juliette." He looks up, dark eyes glossy. "I never realized that was something you would want. It's been difficult to hear, but thank you for telling me anyway. I guess I've been so busy focusing on your career that I haven't seen you. You really have grown up."

She smiles hesitantly. "Will you still coach me until the end of the year?" Juliette asks, biting her lip. The last possible hiccup.

Antony smiles and nods. "Yes. And if Kitzinger doesn't work out, I'll always be ready to coach you again."

She laughs as relief washes over her. She grabs her tennis bag off the floor. "So, shall we catch the next flight to New York?"

Antony stands with a nod. Then he surprises her by looping his arm over her shoulders. "I love you, Jules."

Juliette's eyes burn and she bites back tears. "Love you too, Dad."

As they taxi to the airport, Juliette's chest feels lighter than it has in months. Everything she's wanted to say is off her chest. Even so, there is a responsibility lying on her shoulders. She has control over her life and her choices. Still, the weight is welcome. She loves to embrace a challenge.

LUCA

Luca meets Vladimir in one of the secluded booths in the breakfast bar of the hotel. She has her hood up in an effort to stay incognito, but she lowers it as she slides in across from him.

"Good morning, Luca," Vladimir says coolly. He doesn't look up from the muffin he's buttering.

"Hi, Vladimir," Luca murmurs, twisting her fingers together. "I'm so sorry," she blurts out, unable to hold on to the words any longer.

Vladimir pauses and looks up. "I know," he says. Slowly, he sets down the butter knife and muffin. He looks tired, as if he didn't get much sleep either. "Tell me what happened out there. I've never seen you like that."

Luca bites her lip, unsure of how to explain. So, she simply lays it all out on the table. She tells Vladimir about Juliette and their relationship and how Juliette broke up with her. How seeing her made her focus slip and she spiraled.

"It's no excuse for my behavior, and I'm sorry. I shouldn't have acted like that."

Vladimir shrugs. "No, you shouldn't have, but no use dwelling on it now. Did Juliette apologize? Are you two okay?"

Luca nods, biting down her smile.

"Good. Being happy is important, Luca," Vladimir says, reaching across the table and curling his fingers around Luca's wrist, over her wrap. "And I only want you to be happy. You are not alone. I apologize for leaving yesterday. I knew you weren't okay, and I shouldn't have left you alone."

Luca blinks. "It's okay."

"It's not, Luca. We're basically family, and someone doesn't just leave their family because they're having a bad day. I know you. I have for years. I let my own feelings get in the way and I made a mistake." Vladimir squeezes her wrist, and Luca tries to swallow past the lump in her throat.

"Okay," Luca says, unsure of what else she can say without bursting into tears. "We're okay."

Vladimir smiles and lets go of Luca's wrist. "Are you all right to play the rest of the final? You have a lot of work to do," he says, and the tension eases out of Luca. Vladimir has always known how much he means to Luca, not only as a coach but also as a friend and father figure. And he knows when to change the subject because some things can be left unsaid.

"I know," Luca says, but she does feel ready. For the first time in weeks, her hands are steady as she pulls out her phone and opens the spreadsheet she made on all of the players she's ever played.

Vladimir peels the wrapper off his muffin. "Let's go through your strategy again."

Luca steals one of Vladimir's strawberries and launches into her plan of attack.

As Luca walks back on court for the final's restart, she looks at her box. Vladimir is front and center, as usual. But her gaze drops to the empty seat next to him. One day, Juliette might sit there. Her heart skips and she can't help but start to smile at the image.

Even though Luca is down 5–1 in the first set, she feels renewed, like the match just started. And while Octavia wins the first set, Luca doesn't see the next two sets as a burden. As she stands on the baseline, ready to serve in the first game of the second set, she feels as light as a feather. Even if she loses, Juliette still loves her. And that is worth more than a trophy.

Luca wins 2–6, 6–3, 6–4, and while Juliette isn't in Ohio anymore, she knows she's watching—hopefully with pride and only a little bit of annoyance that Luca beat her sister—as Luca lifts the Cincinnati trophy.

FORTY-FOUR

LUCA

It takes a lot of Luca's mental energy not to appear shocked by the artist's apartment that Juliette opens up for her.

"It's awesome, isn't it?" Juliette turns in a slow circle with her arms out, as if to properly display it. Her eyes are bright and excited, giddiness written on every line of her body.

Luca tries to look at the apartment with fresh eyes. It's certainly . . . artistic. Although the first word that springs to mind is *kitschy*.

It is bright, though. A lovely summer breeze drifts in from the open kitchen window, ceiling fans stirring the late August wind. The creaking shelves to her left are laden with artfully stacked books, an antique desk to her right. Photos and oil portraits line the walls, some crooked and others asymmetrically organized together.

"It's interesting," Luca says, spying checkerboard tiles in the dining room area that leads into a kitchen.

Juliette wheels Luca's suitcase deeper into the apartment to where Luca assumes the bedroom is. She takes one last glance around the mismatched living room before following. The bedroom isn't large, but Juliette's artist friend didn't compromise with a tiny bed. It's fluffy and piled high with blankets they probably won't need, since a wheezy air conditioner in the window is threatening to kick the bucket.

"No tub, but the shower is big enough for both of us," Juliette says with a suggestive waggle of her brows.

Luca laughs, too loud, and she pinches her palm in an effort to calm the storm of nerves threatening to drench Juliette's happiness.

"Is everything all right?" Juliette asks.

Luca tries to smile, but she can't help picking at the skin around her thumb again.

Juliette frowns, unconvinced. The afternoon sunlight catches her just right, illuminating her hair to vibrant gold and bronze, honeying her skin, and shooting amber ribbons through her brown eyes.

Luca licks her lips and fumbles for the right words. Her tongue is mush in her mouth, her insides twisting into elaborate knots. "Sorry, uh—" she starts, shaking her head. "It's stupid," she blurts.

Juliette steps forward and out of the light. She gently tugs Luca's hands into hers, lacing their fingers together. A bit of the tightness in Luca's throat loosens with her touch. "Tell me? Please?"

Luca is powerless to say no. "It's really nothing. I feel anxious in new places, that's all. It'll go away." It's already ebbing away as Juliette holds her hands.

"Will walking around help? We can go to the store and get food." Juliette tilts her head, and Luca nods.

"It would, actually, let's go."

The city is warm and sticky, but the fresh air and Juliette's voice sweep the rest of her unreasonable anxiety away. Now, she only feels the giddy nervous energy that comes with holding a secret close to the chest.

She manages to keep herself together as they gather groceries, get a quick lunch, buy bottles of wine, and head back to the apartment. They lapse into easy conversation on the subway, each sway of the car tipping them back and forth, almost into each other and then farther away like they're two rogue stars spinning off balance but still locked together by unseen gravity.

By the time they return, the apartment is bathed in beautiful golden sunrays. It's hot in a pleasant, summer nostalgia-type of way. It sinks into Luca's skin, calms the fizzy feeling in her stomach, and makes the chilled wine taste even sweeter.

In the tiny kitchen, she's almost overwhelmed by the woody and earthy scent of Juliette's perfume mixed with the citrus curl cream she uses and the fresh lavender on the windowsill. It's distinct and heady and makes her head swim.

Luca doesn't resist flicking on the old radio. She holds out her hand to Juliette.

"Really?" Juliette asks, aglow in the linen-softened sunlight.

"Dance with me," Luca says, completely serious.

Juliette laughs, taking her hand. Her eyes gleam like the wine-dark sea and she beams like she's swallowed the sun. Together they sway in circles, wrapped in each other's arms and trading kisses. Perhaps it's only fitting that now they dance together, after so long dancing around each other. They've found a groove and a harmony that weaves effortlessly. Luca knows they're objectively terrible dancers, but that isn't the point. They may bump together, uncoordinated, but there's never anger, only sweet joy.

Juliette tugs Luca into the living room and pushes her onto the couch. "Stay there. Don't move."

Luca holds up her hands as Juliette vanishes into the bedroom. Luca doesn't know what to expect, and her heart thunders in her chest. She grabs her glass of wine from the table and takes a swig, the ice clinking unpleasantly against her teeth. She shudders and puts it down.

When Juliette returns, she is braless in a gray tank top and shorts slung low on her hips. "Hi," she says, standing in the doorway.

"Hey, yourself," Luca says, leaning her elbows onto her knees.

"I want you," Juliette says.

Luca's breath hitches, fervent heat growing in her stomach. "Come here, then."

Juliette comes closer and kneels in front of Luca. "If you ever want to stop—"

"I'll say Margaret Court, don't worry," Luca says with a laugh. Juliette bursts out laughing too, lowering her head to Luca's knee.

"Glad you remembered that," Juliette says wryly.

"How could I forget?"

Juliette's laughter fades as she takes Luca's arm. "May I?" she asks, fingers brushing the wrap keeping her soulmark obscured.

Luca nods, the laughter catching in her throat. Juliette pulls the wrist strap free and sets it on the coffee table behind her. She lifts

Luca's wrist and presses a kiss to her palm, to the tips of her fingers, to the wristbones that jut beneath her skin, and finally to her own name.

"This is the first time I've seen it," Juliette says softly, hovering her hand over Luca's forearm and aligning their marks in the air.

Luca shivers despite the heat, and she swears it's like the first time again, at the net when their palms connected. Radiant heat, incandescent, shimmers through her veins, and from the look on Juliette's face, she's experiencing the same vivid sensation.

It isn't an emotion or feeling, but instead like every particle, every molecule, every atom has stilled. It is undeniably . . . peace.

Luca curls her fingers around Juliette's forearm to connect their marks together, skin-to-skin, ink-to-ink for the first time.

"Wow," Luca breathes, and Juliette looks up at her with big, round eyes.

"This is incredible," Juliette murmurs. Then, slowly, she loosens her fingers and Luca reluctantly lets go, their skin's connection breaking.

"I guess I know what to do if I ever have another panic attack," Luca says as her fluttering nerves return slowly, more from excitement than actual anxiety.

Juliette nods and blinks, looking a little dazed. "Yeah, wow, that felt so good. It was like all of the discord fell into perfect harmony."

Luca smiles. Of course Juliette would come up with the perfect philosophical simile to describe the indescribable. "Come on." She stands and pulls Juliette to her feet, leading her to the bedroom.

Luca sits on the edge of the bed. The lighting has shifted to be lower, more burnished gold than bright white.

She feels the bed dip and turns her head as Juliette drops her chin to Luca's shoulder. "Ready?" she asks, her voice a low, sultry murmur.

Luca draws in a deep, fortifying breath and nods.

FORTY-FIVE

JULIETTE

Juliette kneels back on the bed, memorizing the line of Luca's back, the sharp edge of her bony shoulders, the curve of her waist to the flare of her hips. Juliette pushes the edge of her T-shirt up and sees those delicious back dimples. She is so undeniably and wildly sexy that she drives Juliette feral.

"God, you're perfect," Juliette murmurs as Luca turns to face her.

The sun slants over her face at the perfect angle as she looks up at Juliette. Her left eye has more flecks of green, while her right one is more gilded gold. Juliette wonders how she never noticed before.

Luca's mouth parts, and her lashes flutter as Juliette touches her jaw. She skims her fingers down the column of her throat as Luca's gaze softens with a reverent and gentle trust.

Juliette's throat threatens to close, and she blinks rapidly as Luca sinks into the touch, a shudder shaking Luca's shoulders. "Can I undress you?" Juliette asks.

"I don't know," Luca says, a cheeky smile tugging at her mouth. "Can you?"

Juliette walked right into that one. She drops her hand from Luca's throat and shakes her head. "My dearest Lux, my most majestic partner and glorious girlfriend, *may* I undress you?" Juliette asks, laying the teasing on extra thick, if only to get Luca to roll her eyes again.

Luca grins, her eyes crinkling. "I want nothing more."

Juliette touches Luca's shoulder. "Up on the pillows then."

Luca scrambles to the middle of the bed.

Juliette crawls onto the bed from the bottom, and Luca laces her hands behind her head. She cups Luca's hips, brushing her thumbs beneath the cut of them before dipping beneath the waistband of her sweatpants. "Lift your hips, babe," Juliette murmurs. The term of endearment slips out easily, and she loves how it makes Luca's eyes darken.

Her hips arch up, languidly. Juliette shimmies the sweatpants down her hips and, with a sharp tug, pulls them down to her knees. She slowly works the pants down over her calves and ankles until they finally fall free.

Juliette tosses them to the wayside, forgotten and unneeded. She lavishes soft, barely there kisses on Luca's bony ankle, up to her calf, the inside of her knee again, the tender inside of her thigh. Luca's breath hitches, but Juliette doesn't kiss her where she wants. Instead, Juliette moves to the opposite thigh, kissing a trail down her right leg.

When she finally looks up at Luca, her fists are clenched into the comforter, her eyes dark and mouth ajar. Juliette wants to lurch up and kiss her, but she restrains herself. "I told you I wanted to"—she pauses, spider walking her fingers from Luca's knee to her thigh—"know"—her thumb dips down to brush against her inner thigh—"every"—she sweeps her fingertips across the laced edge of her panties—"inch"—she slides her fingers beneath the band of them— "of you"—she finishes, peeling the panties from Luca's hips slowly.

Even though Juliette has seen every inch of Luca's body before, in the luminous sunlight, the pale skin the sun never touches is new and exciting.

Luca's breath catches, and Juliette lowers her lips to kiss both of Luca's hips as she gently tugs her underwear down and off.

Luca lowers her hips and lets out a breathy laugh. "You're going to break me," she mutters, eyes squeezing shut.

"I'll always put you back together," Juliette promises. This time, she is not going to push Luca away. Luca's eyes are a little unfocused around the edges. Juliette smiles and leans over her to indulge in a kiss.

Luca latches on to her immediately, fingers lacing through her hair and tugging her closer. She makes a soft whimpering sound as Juliette licks into her panting mouth. Before, when they'd been hungry and desperate, this clash hurt, but now Juliette is careful and thorough.

And when she finally pulls back, her heart is throbbing in her chest, and she's breathless. Luca tucks her curls behind her ear and smiles. "Now who's a little flushed?" she teases.

Juliette shrugs. "Let me tell you a secret," she murmurs, letting her eyes drift over Luca's mouth. She brushes her fingertips over her wet lower lip. "I don't have any problem telling you that you're an incredible kisser and it's hard to keep my mouth off you."

"Is that right?" Luca asks, trying for confidence, but she's out of breath.

Juliette nods, pecking her mouth again. "I wanted to kiss you about a thousand different times today."

Luca draws Juliette down for another tender kiss. "Maybe you should've," Luca says when she releases Juliette again. "I wouldn't have complained."

Juliette chuckles. She shifts back, sliding Luca's T-shirt up. "Put your hands up," Juliette says, "let me admire you."

Luca rips her shirt off and keeps her arms above her head, one hand holding her wrist and showing off the stark black ink of Juliette's name. Fiery red and gold streaks of sun play across Luca's skin. Her thighs are moon-blanched, pale like she normally is, similar to her stomach and chest.

Juliette's hands flutter uselessly, unsure of where to touch first. Luca lets one arm rest on the top of her head, soulmark still revealed, but her other hand trails down her neck, languid and light. Then, she cups her breast and plucks at her nipple, making her lashes flutter.

Juliette's mouth waters as Luca's legs tip open, displaying her flushed center. Her hands shake. She is consumed with the desperate need to touch. "I want to make love to you," she says suddenly, her heart hammering.

Luca blinks. "Oh."

"This isn't just sex," Juliette says. She's never been more sure of anything in her life. "I want to be able to see your face," Juliette adds.

Luca scrambles to sit up and drags Juliette into an all-consuming and desperate and sloppy kiss. "Need you, Jules," Luca pants against her mouth.

"Get comfortable," Juliette says. Luca works a pillow underneath her back, so her hips are tilted up at an angle. Juliette pushes Luca's knees wider so she can see all of her. She gently slides one finger into Luca's slick folds. She takes her time before adding a second, and it isn't until Luca is squirming that she uses her other hand to rub against her clit.

Luca's body pulls taut like a bowstring, and a guttural groan is punched out of her. The sound ripples through Juliette, and the heat boils in her.

"Come on," Luca whines, bucking her hips.

Juliette steadies her with a hand on her hip. She pulls out her fingers, much to Luca's displeasure. "What's the rush?" she asks as she uses her other hand to press a finger into herself.

"I want to feel you," Luca gasps out. "Please, don't make me wait."

Juliette drops her head to pepper kisses on the inside of Luca's thigh. "Let me take care of you," Juliette murmurs.

"Jules," Luca whines.

"I love you," she whispers, unable to stop herself.

"I'd love you more if we fucked," Luca gasps out, her hips flinching.

Juliette clicks her tongue and decides they're both sufficiently wet. She moves, her whole body trembling as she straddles Luca's thighs and slides until their bodies meet. Luca's hips roll up and their clits nudge together.

Juliette pauses, panting and afraid to move and get away from the hot wetness of Luca. She wonders, delirious and trembling, if it's possible to melt during sex. The sweet, delicious heat of Luca's pussy meeting hers might make her.

Juliette reaches for Luca's hand, twining their fingers together, and their soulmarks bump. It's a searing blaze of gorgeous energy, and

Juliette swears she can see the fabric of the universe twisting together, aligning in a spectacular wash of color that saturates them both.

Luca grinds her hips up, and pleasure spikes through Juliette. She drops to her elbows to kiss Luca. She's sure if they aren't touching, skin-to-skin, from forehead to toes, she'll combust into thousands of sparks, and they'll start a wildfire in the middle of New York City.

"Jules," Luca breathes against her mouth as they barely even kiss. "Please."

Juliette's wrist lifts off Luca, and clarity rips through her. Despite how much she wants to drag this out, she's desperate. She thrusts her hips into Luca and Luca meets her, the slick heat grinding together making it hard to keep an even pace. Luca clings to her, fingernails raking down her shoulders and threading in her hair.

The simmer of her orgasm winks on the horizon. Juliette blinks the sweat out of her eyes so she can see Luca properly. Cotton fills her throat, emotion washing over her in powerful waves, consuming her in love that burns through all the hatred and jealousy she's ever harbored. How could she ever consider a negative feeling toward Luca when all she knows now is ultimate, unequivocal, and ardent love?

Luca is splayed out below her, vulnerable and trusting, panting and sobbing, falling to pieces, and hanging on to Juliette as she does.

"Jules," Luca whispers, and then Juliette feels Luca's fingers press against her, curling inside of her and pumping in and out. Flames of pleasure consume her and leave nothing but glorious ash behind. "Come for me," she whispers.

Juliette does, shuddering and trembling and she rocks her hips down. Luca shudders, and Juliette can feel her throbbing through her own orgasm, the pulsations a feedback loop that seems to elongate Juliette's orgasm.

"I love you, I love you, I love you," Juliette says, over and over again because it's all her body is capable of knowing.

Love is all she is. Love is all she can be.

It's so intense that Juliette has no idea how long it takes her to come back to reality.

She has collapsed on top of Luca, exhausted and burning hot like she's run a marathon with a fever. She turns her head, forehead pressed into the juncture of Luca's neck and shoulder. A hand runs over her curls, over and over again.

"Hi," Juliette breathes against Luca's skin, delighting in the way she shivers and turns her head, chin knocking against Juliette's head.

"Hi," Luca breathes back.

Juliette twists onto her back. "Wow," she says, staring up at the ceiling. Light flutters across the room, thoroughly golden as the hour burns its brightest for a few moments more.

"Yeah," Luca whispers back.

Juliette forces herself up onto one elbow and surveys Luca.

She is a glorious and gorgeous mess. A blush spreads from the top of her cheekbones down to her chest and nipples. She is breathing heavily, and her legs are shaking. Sweat dews across her skin, soaking into the sheets beneath her. Her lashes flutter as she struggles to keep them open.

A flush of pride washes over Juliette. Luca turns her head slightly and catches sight of Juliette's face. She gives her a crooked half-smile, dimple popping out as a small shadow in the glaze of sunlight.

Juliette drops her head to Luca's shoulder, kissing her overheated skin. She feels like a lunatic, loving the taste of Luca against her lips. She is overcome by the simple fact that this woman is hers, and she is Luca's.

"We need to clean up," Juliette whispers, knowing her thighs are sticky. She would much rather stay in this moment forever.

"I hope you don't expect me to," Luca says with a raise of her brow. She gestures to herself, lax and boneless. "I don't know if I'll ever walk again."

"That good?" Juliette asks, half-teasing.

Luca doesn't shy away from it and nods. "The best."

Juliette kisses her before she heaves herself into a sitting position and swings her legs over the side of the bed. She hooks her backpack strap around her ankle and drags it closer. She digs her wipes out of the side pocket and wipes herself clean. Then she takes care with several more wipes to clean Luca.

"Come here," Luca says as Juliette tosses the wipes in the garbage and smacks the air conditioner to get it rattling to life again.

Juliette crawls back onto the bed and collapses on her stomach. Wordlessly, they weave together, legs twining and foreheads touching, a pleasant warmth blooming wherever their skin touches. Luca's eyes close and Juliette presses kisses to her lids.

"I love you," Luca whispers, her voice hoarse and raspy.

Juliette bites her lip as once more, emotion surges to the surface. She closes her eyes against the prickling onslaught of tears.

The warm, familiar brush of Luca's fingers against her cheek makes her eyes open. She stares at her, eyes wide and full of unabashed and unashamed love. Juliette shivers, but Luca presses in closer, arms wrapping around Juliette and drawing her even closer. In the brilliance of the sunlight, there are no secrets, no hidden emotions, no unseen vulnerability.

And as Juliette breathes through the overwhelming surge of emotions too big for her body, she relaxes into the safety of Luca's arms.

FORTY-SIX

LUCA

Luca is certain she has never slept better in her life. In the blissful oblivion of nothingness, there are no nightmares that plague her. Eventually, she's jostled awake by Juliette as she sits up and untangles their bodies. Or perhaps they'd already drifted apart while asleep, overheated and too sweaty to be pressed skin-to-skin forever.

The thought doesn't disturb her like she thought it would. She knows that when she opens her eyes, Juliette will be within reach. And so, when she does open her eyes, she indulges in reaching out and running her knuckles down the length of Juliette's spine.

Juliette slides her hands through her curls, sweeping them off her neck. "Hey," she says, "I got some water." She turns and hands Luca a bottle before curling into the pillows.

It soothes her aching throat. "Thank you," she murmurs. It's gotten dark fast, the sun gone. All that remains of their sunny day is the heat that's settled into her bones. A lamp on the table across from them casts a tawny light onto Juliette's face.

"We should do that again," Luca says, and Juliette laughs, her smile bringing the soft fluttering in Luca's stomach to life again.

"A lot more," Juliette agrees.

"I needed that. And I don't just mean getting laid. Which I did, but I also needed you." Luca wants to cover her face, wants to hide from the vulnerable truth. Juliette gazes up at her, eyes liquid soft. "I needed the physical connection, and it transcended what I thought it would be. I've never felt like this before."

Juliette traces her fingers along the curve of Luca's hip. "Like what?"

Luca swallows. "Whole." She touches her sternum. She usually has a flutter of anxiety coiled into a tight ball behind her ribs, but it's silenced. Perhaps not gone, but at ease. All the puzzle pieces have been slotted together, and she knows she'll be okay.

Juliette's smile widens, so big it's like she can't contain it. "Me too." She turns, getting onto her stomach and lying next to Luca, propped on her elbows. "I wish we would've worked this out sooner," she murmurs, taking Luca's hand and playing with her fingers.

"I know," Luca says.

"I'm sorry. It's my fault. I haven't been a good person." Juliette swallows thickly, and when she looks up, her eyes are glossy.

"Hey, it's okay," Luca soothes, pulling her fingers free to cradle Juliette's face. "Don't think like that. We can only look to the future."

Juliette sniffs and cants her cheek into Luca's palm. "Still hate that I was a jealous bitch. That I hurt you."

Luca knows Juliette will let this guilt fester. Luca's pain has already transmuted into a scar, scabbed over and healing. They have each other now. "Want to know how you can fix it?" Luca asks, keeping her voice light and teasing.

"How?"

"Order us food. I'm starving."

Juliette bursts into laughter, and her head drops into her folded arms.

Luca weaves her fingers through Juliette's curls, brushing her thumb across the different strands of bronze and caramel and gold.

"Of course, Your Majesty. What would you like?" Juliette asks, slipping out of Luca's loose grasp to grab her phone.

Luca licks her lips at the beautiful cut of Juliette's naked body, bronze even in the low light. "You," she says honestly.

Juliette smirks over her shoulder, coy and sultry at the same time.

LUCA

By the time the food arrives, Luca is beyond satiated. Juliette had taken her time breaking Luca apart again with her sensational mouth. Then, while Luca was showering, Juliette had slipped in, and they made love again, lazy and slow, with Luca pressed against the cool tile of the shower and Juliette wrapped around her from behind, water tracing warm fingers across them.

After, they'd dried each other off with care, kissing languidly until the pizza guy rang the doorbell. Now they're arranged in their usual position on the couch in pajamas, the pizza having been demolished within the first ten minutes of whatever stupid movie Juliette chose.

"Hey, Luca?" Juliette pauses the movie, her free hand resting on Luca's ankle and tracing aimless patterns on her skin. "You know how you said you would've been okay with me kissing you a thousand different times today?"

Luca tilts her head. "Yeah?"

Juliette breathes in deep, tipping her head back against the couch. "Did you really mean that? What if we were public? Like Remi and Xinya? I know I panicked about the media having pictures of us hanging out together, but I think if we controlled how we revealed our relationship, I'd be okay with it."

Luca considers Juliette's words, chewing on the inside of her cheek. "I don't know. Genuinely. I don't need to be public. I want you to be comfortable with this first." Luca takes Juliette's hand, twisting their fingers together.

Juliette breathes out a sigh of relief. "And you know I don't want to hide it because I'm ashamed or anything, right?" Juliette asks, a little desperation in her voice.

Luca nods. "Relax, Jules," she says soothingly. "As long as we're together, it doesn't really matter to me what the media knows."

"I don't want to hide it for years like Remi and Xinya did. I know the public will find out eventually," Juliette says with a smirk. "I can't keep my hands off you." Her hand slides up Luca's calf and knee until she can splay her fingers against Luca's thigh.

"I don't want you to," Luca says, tilting her hips to try to encourage Juliette's hand to slip a little farther into her shorts where she wants it.

Juliette brushes her thumb back and forth against a patch of skin that Luca missed when shaving, so featherlight it almost tickles. "I want you to understand that I don't want to lose you, and I'm worried some outside force is going to try to rip us apart."

Luca swallows. That is a concern. But she curls her fingers around Juliette's wrist, her fingertips brushing her soulmark. It makes Juliette shiver and calm drip into Luca's mind. "I understand."

Juliette relaxes against the couch. "Okay," she says, a yawn eclipsing the word.

Luca snuggles back into the couch and pillows. It's comfortable now that the air conditioner is rattling away, driving out the excess August heat.

"You pick the weirdest movies," she says, changing the topic as Juliette unpauses whatever rom-com she's picked. It's snowing on-screen.

"*Love Actually* is a god-tier choice after sex," Juliette says haughtily, and Luca rolls her eyes.

"Jules, it's August."

Juliette glowers at her. "It is always the season for Christmas cheer. Plus, look at how hot Keira Knightley is!" She gestures to the screen, and Luca huffs, conceding that point.

And even if she wants to complain, in the blissful afterglow of sex and pizza, Luca has truly never been happier.

FORTY-SEVEN

LUCA

It is ninety-five degrees on court, and Luca feels like she's standing in a pool of magma. No matter how much she dries her face, sweat drips into her eyes. Summer has come back for a cruel last day, the autumn equinox only two days away.

Regardless of how the heat threatens to drag her into an exhausted slumber, Luca feels excellent. It's always nice to play on hard courts, even if heat shimmers off them like a mirage. Despite the rising temperature, the atmosphere in New York is electric, and it buzzes in her blood.

Karoline Kitzinger stands before her, looking cool and collected in her light linen suit. Luca wonders how they managed to convince her to be the on-court interviewer, but she's surprisingly charming when she's not heatedly trying to encourage them to win.

"Luca, congratulations. We all know how immensely talented you are, and after that incredible comeback in Cincinnati, I can't help but feel you're hitting your stride. What is it about this New York atmosphere that invigorates you to play your best tennis?" Karoline asks.

A dozen different replies rise to her lips, but she chooses the most neutral. "Well, I am most at home on the hard courts, and I have really found a love and appreciation for New York. This city has treated me well."

The crowd roars, and Luca allows herself to smile, even as bubbles of anxiety simmer below the surface.

"You, Zoe Almasi, and Remi Rowland are locked in a war for the number one ranking. You have to win the title to lock in your ranking for the next few weeks. What are your preparations to ensure your success?" Karoline asks.

"I haven't really been thinking about the rankings, if I'm being honest. Not for a few weeks. I'm trying to live in the moment, and every match is difficult, as you know," Luca says, and Karoline nods. "But I try not to put too much pressure on achieving a certain ranking and instead focus on enjoying the game and hoping that I can play my best. I'm excited to play more matches and see where I can get to."

"One final question," Karoline says with a lightning quick smile. It knocks Luca off-balance. "I know players don't like to speculate on who you're playing next, but you're either playing Ingrid Karlsen or Juliette Ricci in the semifinal on Friday. What are your thoughts on those two?"

Luca knew this question would come up eventually. "Well, I don't know Karlsen that well. I've played her only once, but I know Ricci really well." Luca scratches her thigh, where a love bite from Juliette is still healing.

Karoline's fair brows jump into her hairline. "Really well? In a keep-your-enemies-closer sort of way?" There is a sharpness to her eyes, and Luca realizes her mistake. "Because Ricci is your rival?"

Luca shrugs. "That's what people say, but we have a lot of respect for each other. I got to know her during the Connolly Cup." She hopes everyone watching will attribute the flush flaming across her face to the hot sun and court.

"Would you consider her your rival?" Karoline asks.

Luca shrugs. "You'd have to ask her that." She holds up her hands, her smile placating. "Regardless, I'm going to try to be as ready as possible for either of them, because they're both super different players with distinct styles. They've both had an amazing season, and they're both playing really well." Luca pauses and then adds, "I just hope it's a long, excellent match for all the fans to enjoy, and whoever I play is a little tired on Friday." Luca snickers, winning a ruckus of laughs from the crowd.

"Well, excellent work today, Luca, you've played incredible tennis in this blistering heat. Get your well-deserved rest, and we'll see you in the semis."

Luca steps back from the microphone with a gracious *thank you* and waves to the crowd, squinting away from the sun.

JULIETTE

Juliette's match gets pushed deep into the night because of a men's quarterfinal going five sets. And even though Luca should be sleeping, she can't miss the match. During the tournament, their schedules rarely aligned, but at the end of the night, they would collapse into their bed and wake entangled in a mess of limbs, hair, and sheets.

After three grueling sets, Juliette finally crushes Karlsen in the deciding tiebreaker. Despite how Luca's eyes burn, she keeps herself upright as she watches Juliette's postmatch interview.

She looks tired, dripping with sweat and hair lank against her shoulders, a red line ribboned across her forehead from her tight headband. But there's a brightness to her eyes that Luca knows intimately well.

Payton Calimeris is conducting the interview. "Congratulations, Juliette," she says. "That was an amazing performance against Ingrid, who has had such an incredible run and been on court for half the amount of time you have."

The camera focuses on Juliette's face, and the edge of her mouth lifts into a barely-there smile. Juliette talks through her strategy and the emotions of the match, stumbling through some of the words, which betrays how tired she is. It's strange to watch her now, with her media mask in place and her guard up. Before, Luca thought this version of Juliette was the only one that existed—the carefully crafted persona of a charming athlete that oozed with saccharine charm and silver-tongued sharpness.

But Luca knows the deeper parts of Juliette now. The ways she's quietly sensitive and vulnerable, but still willing to be brave and goofy. Her profoundly caring and kind personality that isn't without its wicked edges, insecurities, and jealousies. People are patchwork mosaics of not only their experience and genetics, but also of everyone they've ever known, and Luca yearns to know every quilted block of Juliette.

"So, you'll be facing your rival, Lucky Luca Kacic, on Friday. How are you preparing for that match?" Payton asks.

The mask melts away as Juliette laughs. "Rival, huh?" Chuckles scatter through the crowd.

"Would you say you're not rivals? She did say to ask you about it," Payton says with a cheeky grin.

Juliette tosses her head back and huffs out a laugh. "Of course she did," she murmurs, a touch too fond. Luca wonders how tennis fans will analyze that. "I think we've come a long way since January and the Australian Open."

"Understatement of the century," Luca says out loud, even though she's alone.

"Of course, for the drama of it all, we're rivals," Juliette continues. "We're both vying for the same titles, the same accolades, the same acclaim. But at the end of the day, we're both just human beings, and I think over the last couple months since the Connolly Cup I've come to understand Luca more and more. Our relationship has certainly changed." There is an undercurrent to Juliette's words that makes the hair on the back of Luca's neck stand up.

Anyone could read between the lines, read deeper into what Juliette has said and the familiarity in which she uses Luca's first name. If someone is looking really closely, like Luca is, they could plainly see the love on Juliette's face.

"So, will it be easier or harder to play Kacic since you're, shall we say, tentative friends?" Payton asks delicately.

Luca snorts. Tentative friends. Right.

Juliette scratches her arm, adjusts her wrist wrap, and smiles to herself. "I think we both know how to do our jobs and be professionals. I think it'll be a really good match because we're both competitive. I don't think it'll be harder to play her, because it's always difficult.

She's an unbelievable tennis player, and even if I haven't always given the most glowing praise about the way she plays, her tenacity and fortitude have to be admired. She won't make it easy, I know that, but I don't think it'll affect us outside of the court."

Payton nods. "Well, thank you so much, Juliette, and congratulations on this spectacular win. Go get some rest, you certainly deserve it, and we'll see you on Friday!"

Juliette nods and waves to the crowd before stepping away. Luca watches, barely listening to the commentary as Juliette signs a can of tennis balls and hits them into the crowd with a smile as bright as the sun.

Eventually, the coverage flips back to the booth, where a couple of former players are giving their analysis. Luca leaves it on as white noise while she brushes her teeth, sprays her lavender sleep mist, and takes her melatonin.

She's exhausted, heat-beat, and aching, but she can't find sleep yet. She stares at the wall and mulls on Juliette's interview. They haven't talked about what it will be like to play each other in any match, let alone the semifinals of a Grand Slam. Maybe they should talk to Remi and Xinya?

"We'll figure it out," Luca says to herself, as if speaking it aloud will make it manifest into existence and prevent it from festering in her brain. And eventually, despite her spinning thoughts, sleep rises like a tide and sweeps her into blissful black.

FORTY-EIGHT

JULIETTE

The night before the semifinal, Remi convinces the four semifinalists to dine together. It wasn't difficult, considering Juliette is dating Luca and Claudia is her sister. Half of the Connolly Cup is represented, and it's almost normal around the table.

Claudia and Remi try to press Juliette on how she feels playing Luca, and vice versa, but they adeptly swerve around Remi's questions. Eventually, Claudia gets the hint and maneuvers the conversation into other topics, and from there, the evening passes smoothly.

"I never thought I would become actual friends with Remi," Luca says as they walk back to the apartment. A chill nips the air, a reminder that winter and the off-season is around the corner.

"She's really not that bad once you peel back the layers," Juliette says. "She's an onion."

Luca wrinkles her nose and curls her lip. "That's rude and a terrible metaphor."

Juliette gapes at her. "Have you never seen *Shrek*?"

"No?"

"We will have to rectify that immediately. As soon as this tournament is over," Juliette says, appalled by Luca's lack of movie taste.

Luca shakes her head, but she's smiling as Juliette unlocks the door. "Speaking of after the tournament, we should talk about tomorrow."

Juliette chews the inside of her cheek. "Yeah."

"I heard what you said in your on-court interview last night," Luca says as she strips out of her jeans and T-shirt.

"I meant every word of it," Juliette says as she pulls her hair back into a high bun and heads into the bathroom.

Luca leans against the doorjamb in her sweatpants and one of Juliette's oversize graphic tees. Juliette bites back the urge to abandon this conversation and wrap herself entirely around Luca until their bodies melt together again.

She looks in the mirror and almost laughs at herself for how love-struck she looks.

"This is our job. We knew it would happen eventually," Luca says quietly.

"How do you feel about it?" Juliette asks as she loads her toothbrush up with toothpaste and starts brushing.

"I don't want this match to change anything between us, and I'm worried it will." Luca's voice is low, as if she's afraid to even utter the words.

Juliette's stomach drops. "Because of my jealousy?" she asks around her toothbrush.

Luca sighs and steps into sight of the mirror. Her arms slide around Juliette's stomach, and she rests her chin on Juliette's shoulder. "Yes," she admits. Juliette winces, the word stinging. Luca's arms tighten around her. "In a perfect world, we'd both play our best tennis, and we wouldn't have to deal with the complicated emotions that come with losing."

Juliette nods and finishes brushing. Luca releases her enough to let her rinse her mouth, and then Juliette twists around and wraps her arms around Luca's neck, keeping her close. She cards her fingers through her silky straight hair, gently pulling a knot loose and brushing it back from Luca's face.

"I love you," Juliette says, and Luca nods, her jaw still tight. "And I love tennis. And tomorrow we get to do the thing we love so much. I'm excited, actually." Luca blinks rapidly, surprised, making Juliette smile. "It's just a match, and no matter the outcome, my feelings won't change about you or tennis."

Tension flows out of Luca, and she tilts to press her forehead to Juliette's. "We'll be all right?" she asks quietly.

"We'll be all right," Juliette echoes, leaning up on her tiptoes to kiss her. It holds a promise, and Luca's mouth moves against hers in reply. She draws back a fraction and smirks. "Maybe this time I'll beat you."

Luca snorts. "Good luck, darling."

Juliette kisses her again, fleeting and soft. "So, are we ruling out distracting each other to win points?" she asks teasingly.

Luca's hand cups Juliette's left breast, thumb drawing over her nipple. Juliette shivers, even though she still has her bra and shirt on. "I don't think it'd be appropriate to get your tits out on live television," Luca says dryly.

Juliette laughs and tilts her head back, giving Luca a chance to kiss her neck. "Thanks for the idea. I might pull it out for match point."

Luca smirks against her throat and lifts her head to stare at Juliette fondly. "You're ridiculous."

"So are you for being in love with me, my strange noodle."

Luca rolls her eyes, but her cheeks flush pink. "Come on, let's not wait for match point for you to distract me," she says, her other hand sliding down to grab Juliette's ass, drawing their hips together.

"Brush your teeth first," Juliette says, letting her arms fall. "I can't believe you ate garlic when you knew we were sleeping together. Or was that a plot to disturb my sleep?"

Luca lets go and moves around Juliette to the counter. "I did offer you a bite."

Juliette crinkles her nose. "You know I hate shrimp."

Luca gets a strange expression on her face for a moment before she turns thoughtful. "I didn't, actually."

"Still so much to learn," Juliette says, stealing another garlicky kiss. "Luckily, I am an excellent teacher," she says as she steps back and smacks Luca's ass, just because she can. She loves how Luca jolts as if shocked, and her pupils expand.

"None of that tomorrow either," Luca says, sounding breathless and slightly strangled. She grabs her toothbrush and shoves it in her mouth.

"Damn. Plans foiled," Juliette says in a singsong as she exits the bathroom.

She sprays their bed with the lavender mist Luca loves so much and wriggles under the sheets.

"Hey," Juliette says as Luca leaves the bathroom and heads to her side of the bed.

"What's up?" Luca asks as she pops open her melatonin bottle.

"I think we should do it."

Luca raises her eyebrows. "Jules, we've been doing it for weeks."

Juliette groans. "No, I have an idea."

"Tell me."

So Juliette does.

"Once that can of worms is open, it can't be undone," Luca says as she flicks the lamp light off and slides into bed.

"Why not make a statement?"

Luca laughs and twists over on her side to kiss Juliette. "You're crazy and I love you," she whispers against Juliette's mouth.

"So, is that a yes?" Juliette asks, and Luca nods.

"Yes."

FORTY-NINE

JULIETTE

Juliette has never been more grateful to be playing the first semifinal on Friday. Her nerves have been eating her alive for the whole day, and she knows she couldn't have sat through Remi and Claudia's semifinal without bouncing out of her skin.

The last time she played Luca, she felt a strange cocktail of smugness and excitement to crush Luca to bits. But now, as she stands in the tunnel and shifts from foot to foot, she's almost unable to contain her smile. These nerves are from excitement. She's ready to have *fun*. To play the game she loves the most, with the person she loves the most.

She sneaks a look back at Luca, who bites her lip to hide her smile. It's fun to hold on to a secret that no one knows and yet they all speculate about.

Her name is announced, and Juliette walks onto the court. New York's cooled rapidly, the late afternoon air carrying the scent of crisp autumn. The warmth lingers, the kind of afternoon that bleeds into a perfectly cool night. It's the fall equinox, the sun's rays equally balanced, not unlike the way Juliette and Luca have balanced out.

Juliette takes a deep breath and waves to the crowd as she heads to her bench. She slips easily into her usual routine—setting up her water bottles, tapping her strings to check the tension, unfolding her towel, and putting her watch away.

Juliette blinks and she's at the coin toss. The lights glitter above them, the sun dipped below the edge of Arthur Ashe Stadium. It's filled to the brim with screaming tennis fans who want them to rip each other's throats out. A thrill of exhilaration courses beneath Juliette's skin, and she bounces on her toes.

Juliette wins the coin toss and elects to serve first. She catches Luca's eye before they warm up, and despite her steely exterior, she can see that Luca's excited and ready.

Their combined nervous energy leads to a very chaotic beginning. The first four games are breaks, unlike their match in Australia, when they held throughout the first set. Juliette's backhand goes wildly out every time she doesn't slice, and Luca has an unprecedented nine double faults by the end of her second service game.

It's a slow grind to get into the groove, but Juliette finds hers first and finally manages to hold. It becomes easier and easier to melt into the logistics and strategy of the match. It's unbelievably fun to fight against Luca, and the crowd is so into it. They scream and yell, thoroughly enjoying this chaotic and wild match. Juliette hangs on by the skin of her teeth to hold and stay in the set.

Much like their first match, their first set goes to a tiebreaker. It swings wildly in Juliette's way in one point and then rapidly back to Luca.

And it's a final stab volley from Juliette that gives her the tiebreaker and the set, 7–4.

The court is rendered in stark clarity. The absolute focus she's exerting is sure to give her a headache later, but she's never felt more in control of herself.

The second set is a fresh opportunity, and Luca is never one to back down. It's one of the many things she loves about her. They wear each other out with long points, and the set drags into another tiebreaker. But this time, Luca's serve paints the lines so fast that Juliette is surprised there aren't scorch marks on the ball.

She overcooks a forehand down the line to gift Luca the second set.

The third set is no less spectacular and demanding. The odds of who will win must be swinging rapidly between them.

Juliette tries to keep her focus, tries to keep her intensity, but mistakes slip through the cracks, and Luca pounces on each of them. She is fearless, she is ruthless, and this time, Juliette isn't frustrated by it. She is playing well, but Luca is simply better today.

When Luca breaks to go up 5–3, Juliette knows she won't stop fighting, but she also recognizes her chances have become slimmer than a sidewalk crack. Her muscles are burning, the cruelty of the last match finally taking its toll.

Luca catches her eye on the changeover before she serves for the match, and Juliette smiles. Whereas before she might have been sick with jealousy and anger, she feels light. They've played an incredible match, and this is the most fun she's had in years. Even more fun than the Australian Open.

Luca's shoulders relax from her ears, and she tips her head in acknowledgment, in understanding.

Juliette knows the crowd would love to see more of an emotional spectacle from both of them, but they're past that now.

Luca serves two lightning strikes. Two aces, and she's up 30–0.

Juliette steps in to crack Luca's next first serve down the line because she has absolutely nothing to lose.

Luca claps her palm against her strings, and Juliette smiles.

Luca spins a serve out wide, and Juliette barely gets it back, launching them into a 30–shot rally that ends with Luca trying to slice a backhand that sinks into the net.

Juliette's lungs burn, and she wipes her face with her towel for a second of respite from the overstimulation of the moment.

Luca silences Juliette's hope with a one-two punch, a serve down the T, and an inside-out forehand that Juliette barely tips with the end of her racket.

Match point.

Juliette watches Luca take her time getting to the baseline. She breathes in deeply, bouncing on her toes, and the nerves on her face smooth into complete calm.

There is no way Juliette could've ever dreamed of touching Luca's final ace. It is perfect.

As it goes past Juliette, she waits for the shatter of her heart as she loses, but there is none. Disappointment curls in her stomach, but that is overwhelmed by a swell of pride for Luca. She slides her headband off, and despite her loss, she's smiling.

She meets her soulmate at the net, but this time is different. She knows Luca is hers. This time as their hands touch and gold sizzles through her veins, Juliette can't imagine feeling happier. Juliette pulls on Luca's hand, dragging her in for a hug. She tilts her head and whispers, "I love you so much, and I am so proud of you. Congratulations, you played incredibly." She doesn't care that the microphones will pick up on her words. It won't matter in a moment. She needs Luca to know that Juliette is burning with love and pride and everything in between.

I love you, Luca mouths, their foreheads pressed together. "Do you want to do this?"

"More than anything," Juliette says, dropping her racket to wrap her arm around Luca and kiss her in the center of the largest tennis stadium in the world.

Everything vanishes apart from Luca. All Juliette focuses on is the familiar contour of Luca's lips against hers. Her racket bumps against Juliette's back as her arm wraps around her, and the only space between them is the net. Luca is sweaty and burning hot against her, tasting like salt and bananas, but Juliette loves it.

It lasts both a heartbeat and an eternity.

The world rushes back as they finally pull away from each other. Luca grins, and Juliette laughs because it is pure insanity but there is no other way she would have done it. Arthur Ashe Stadium is going absolutely wild. She looks to the camera in front of them and pulls her wrist wrap free, showing off Luca's name.

"Celebrate later, yeah?" Juliette asks as they finally head to the chair umpire.

"Yeah," Luca says, breathless. Juliette can barely hear her over the chanting and the cheers and wild stomping of the crowd.

She shakes the umpire's hand and heads to her bench to pack up her bags. She doesn't think she's ever smiled this much after a match before. Juliette waves to the crowd and then turns around and waves to Luca until she is swallowed by the cool darkness of the tunnel.

As soon as she's in the locker room, she is tackled into hugs by Remi and Claudia. Her adrenaline is seeping away and she's exhausted, but she clings to her sister and best friend to make sure they don't all topple over.

"YOU'RE ABSOLUTELY INSANE!" Remi screams, shaking Juliette's shoulders.

"I can't believe you did that on ARTHUR FUCKING ASHE. You two are mad as hell but I love it!" Claudia says, kissing her cheeks.

Juliette laughs, a bit dizzy from the way they're bouncing around her. "Sorry to outdo your boat party and Miami win," Juliette says, and Remi tugs her into another hug.

"All right, I want to see her interview," Juliette says to get Remi to release her.

Claudia bounces around in a circle with Remi while Juliette heads into the players' lounge. Luca is standing at the microphone with Payton Calimeris, but the crowd is still going wild.

"Well, Luca, it might not be your first wild match against Juliette Ricci, but you two have certainly made sports history tonight," Payton says. She looks so surprised but is beaming with pride.

Luca laughs, still smiling. "It was something," she says, scratching the back of her neck.

Juliette gasps as she sees Luca's wrap is gone, showing off her name on the pale skin of Luca's inner wrist.

"I know we should talk about the match, but we're all wondering. Did you two plan that?"

Luca shrugs. "We did. Figured we might as well take advantage of being on the biggest stage in the tennis world."

"You have the crowd in a frenzy. First, the amazing tennis from the both of you, and then the kiss." Payton shakes her head with a laugh.

"I guess you all have your answer to the rivalry question," Luca says, radiating pure joy and happiness.

Giddy laughter bubbles up from Juliette's stomach, and she can't contain it. It is too insane to fathom that this is real. She loves

er rival, and she doesn't have to be shy about it. She wants to keep
aying it. She wants to shout into the summer air that she loves
Luca Kacic.

Love burns golden in her veins with every beat of Juliette's
heart.

EPILOGUE

LUCA

Luca wins the US Open in straight sets against Remi Rowland. It is not an easy win, despite what the scoreboard says, but it is a win, and Luca breathes a sigh of relief at the end of it. Two Grand Slams in a single year. Not a one-Slam wonder after all.

Not even the recent commotion of her semifinal match against Juliette is able to break her focus. It didn't take long for articles about their complicated relationship to start popping up. The press conferences, their Australian Open Final, the collision during the Connolly Cup, and every other tidbit they can find. It all culminates in a mashed-up version of the truth with a lot of romanticization thrown in for the hell of it. Many even draw parallels between Karoline Kitzinger and Payton Calimeris's rivalry to theirs.

When she hits a final ace to clinch the title, Luca looks up at her box. There is more than one person sitting there. It was always something people commented on or sneered about if they disliked her. But now, sitting next to Vladimir, is her rival.

And the love of her life.

Juliette Ricci.

And, of course, the slew of Ricci sisters, Leo Mantovani, and her best friend, Nicky. And even though Luca once thought that her friends and family would bring unnecessary pressure to her shoulders, her whole body is as light as a feather as she goes to shake Remi's hand and pull her in for a hug.

And as she holds the trophy in her hands, standing as a Grand

Slam champion again, she only has eyes for her soulmate. Juliette
smile is so bright, it's as if she's swallowed the sun.

At the trophy ceremony at the Australian Open, Luca had felt an
intense draw to Juliette that she had to fight. Now, there is no tugging sensation, nothing threatening to drag them together, nothing
intensifying when they part. The line pulled taut between them has
slackened, at ease with the fact that they have finally accepted the love
destined for them.

Now that their love has been lifted to the surface, shimmering and
radiant in the daylight, it is hard to imagine they ever hated each other.
Luca doubts they ever did.

Love is a tricky mistress, often looking like hate when twisted in
a certain direction. They believed that it was the ugliness of hate and
jealousy and obsession and anger tangling them in cruel knots. And, of
course, there will always be struggles, snags. They've torn each other
apart, but they've sewn each other back together, mixing in ways that
truly make them halves of a whole.

Their love is one of imperfections. Of hope. Of forgiveness. Of
understanding.

And no matter what anyone says or writes or speculates, that fact
will always be true to Luca. To Juliette.

So, unlike most things that start vile and cruel, their ending is
sweet and satisfying.

Even though Luca doesn't say *I love you* at the end of her US Open
speech, she knows Juliette hears it loud and clear in every word.

And that night, Luca draws Juliette into her with ease. It is nearly
autumn in New York, and the end of their cruel summer is sealed with
a kiss.

ACKNOWLEDGMENTS

Thank you, first and foremost, to Miranda. You were the first person to tell me that this story was meant for so much more. Thank you for your endless support, your hope, your optimism, your creative genius. Thank you for always being down to talk tennis, for titling this book, and for being my best friend. I would not be here, writing these words, without you. (I'm not at all sorry I dragged you so firmly into the world of tennis.)

My endless thanks and gratitude to my spectacular agent, Trinica Sampson-Vera. Thank you for seeing the potential in this book and encouraging me to embrace this sapphic love story. I am so grateful that you understand me and my work. You understood and loved Luca and Jules from the beginning, and you helped them flourish on the page. You have championed and encouraged and advocated for me tirelessly. Here's to many more books and acknowledgments!

Thank you to the entire New Leaf team. I couldn't have dreamed of a better team to support me and my career!

Thank you to Melanie Iglesias Pérez, my wonderful and passionate editor. Your enthusiasm and love for this book has changed my life. Your editorial notes really made this novel shine, and they always made me so excited to dive back in. Thank you for giving me the chance to give this joyful story to the world and thank you for making it sparkle.

Thank you to Elizabeth Hitti, Megan Rudloff, Zakiya Jamal, Shelly Perron, Davina Mock-Maniscalco and the entire Atria team! Your endless support for me and my book has been a dream come true.

Thanks to Kelli McAdams and James Iacobelli for the beautiful cover design and Liza Rusalskaya for the perfect illustration of Juliette and Luca. Every detail is so thoughtfully and beautifully crafted. I'm so honored to have my story be bound within this incredible design.

To my entire family, thank you for always encouraging me to chase my dreams. For believing in my talent, my dreams, and my words. This book fundamentally wouldn't exist without you because you gave me my love of tennis. Thank you for taking me to tournaments, for watching endless amounts of tennis on TV, and letting me take off school to watch the French Open semifinals every year. Thank you, Dad, for teaching me how to play tennis and being the best coach in the whole wide world. Thank you to Michael, for being the best brother and always playing tennis with me. Thank you, Mom, for always being there in the bleachers cheering me on and bringing that extra pair of shoes I needed. (And an extra special thanks, Mom, for reading this book with a keen eye and making sure I didn't accidentally mess up a score!)

Thank you to Stig Dyrdal, Wallis Kinney, and Davaisha. There are not enough words in any language to describe how much I love and cherish our friendship. I would not be the writer, let alone person, I am today without your love, support, creativity, humor, grace, and compassion. I am so grateful to get to share life with you and write books with you by my side.

My eternal gratitude to Lexie Krauss, an extraordinary friend, bookseller, and soon-to-be agent! Your encouragement and confidence in me gave me the strength to keep pursuing my dream of being a published author in the darkest of days. You have always been in my corner; answering all my inane questions and believing in me. Thank you for your support.

More and more thanks go to Kelly Hudson and Jessica Delaney, and all in our incredible writing community, the Trouble Troop. Thank you everyone for being on this writing journey with me and I cannot wait to be on yours.

Thank you to the fanfiction community and to every writer who has written a soulmate!au fanfiction. I am forever indebted to you, because your stories and imaginations have inspired me to play in this beautiful playground and create such joyous art.

And thank you, finally, to my dear readers. Thank you to all the readers who found this story early and loved it deeply and fiercely. And a special thanks, in this regard, to Kay. Thank you to whoever has finished this book, I hope you found the escapism and queer joy in these pages you needed. You are loved. You are worth it. Thank you.

ABOUT THE AUTHOR

Katie Chandler is a romance author who loves adding in a speculative twist to her kissing books. She is passionate about writing joyful queer love stories full of tenderness, angst, and spice. You can usually find Katie writing with a fully caffeinated iced beverage, a Taylor Swift album blasting, and her yellow lab, Blue, who makes sure her feet are toasty and that she takes regular breaks to give him treats. When not writing, Katie spends her time watching tennis with her snuggly black lab, Bunny, chasing her thieving chocolate lab, Bear, who thinks her socks are his chew toys, and wondering where her glasses are. (They're nestled in her hair.)

Atria Books, an imprint of Simon & Schuster, fosters an open environment where ideas flourish, bestselling authors soar to new heights, and tomorrow's finest voices are discovered and nurtured. Since its launch in 2002, Atria has published hundreds of bestsellers and extraordinary books, which would not have been possible without the invaluable support and expertise of its team and publishing partners. Thank you to the Atria Books colleagues who collaborated on *Backhanded Compliments*, as well as to the hundreds of professionals in the Simon & Schuster advertising, audio, communications, design, ebook, finance, human resources, legal, marketing, operations, production, sales, supply chain, subsidiary rights, and warehouse departments who help Atria bring great books to light.

Editorial
Melanie Iglesias Pérez
Elizabeth Hitti

Jacket Design
Kelli McAdams
James Iacobelli
Liza Rusalskaya

Marketing
Zakiya Jamal
Morgan Pager

Managing Editorial
Paige Lytle
Shelby Pumphrey
Lacee Burr
Sofia Echeverry

Production
Laura Wise
Chloe Gray
Shelly Perron
Davina Mock-Maniscalco

Publicity
Megan Rudloff

Publishing Office
Suzanne Donahue
Abby Velasco

Subsidiary Rights
Nicole Bond
Sara Bowne
Rebecca Justiniano